PLAYING

CRYSTAL KASWELL

Copyright

PLAYING

Written by Crystal Kaswell.
Cover by RBA Designs
Photo by Wander Augiar
Model Jacob Cooley

Also by Crystal Kaswell

Dangerous Noise

Dangerous Kiss - Ethan

Dangerous Crush – Kit

Dangerous Rock – Joel

Dangerous Fling – Mal

Dangerous Encore - series sequel

Sinful Serenade

Sing Your Heart Out - Miles

Strum Your Heart Out - Drew

Rock Your Heart Out - Tom

Play Your Heart Out - Pete

Sinful Ever After – series sequel

Inked Hearts

Tempting - Brendon

Playing - Walker

Pretending - Ryan - Coming March 2018

Chapter One

WALKER

"Thanks for letting me know." My stomach drops like a stone. This is inevitable. Obvious. But it feels like a surprise.

"I'm sorry, Mr. Williams."

"Don't worry about it." My fingers curl into a fist. I press my cell to my cheek. There's nothing else to say. Nothing that will change this. Still, I'm not going to shoot the messenger. "Thanks for your help." I end the call and slide my phone into my front pocket.

The cool air gets hot.

The sounds of the party flow into my ears. Laughter. Conversation. Booming bass.

Bullshit.

It's all bullshit.

This isn't fun.

It's toxic.

The loud music fails to fill my head.

To drown out the thought running through my mind.

Again?

She pulled this shit again.

I'm surprised again.

My heart is a lead weight again.

I'm not taking this anymore.

She's on her own.

She wants to destroy herself. Fine.

I'm done being collateral damage.

I take a deep breath and let out a heavy exhale. Peel my shoulders from my ears. Perfect my poker face.

I step through the open door. Back into Sandy's living room.

She's over the moon. Dancing with her boyfriend, amber beer bottle pressed to her bright pink lips.

We're here to celebrate their new place, them moving in together. I'm happy for them. Really.

Love is great for other people.

I'm not interested.

Don't get me wrong. I love women. I love planting between a woman's legs, throwing her on my bed, getting her screaming my name.

But that's where my relationships stop and end.

Sandy's eyes catch mine. She pulls the bottle from her lips. Mouths *you okay?*

I nod *of course*. I will be. As soon as I find someone to get me out of my head.

I grab a plastic cup from the bar and fill it with room temperature whiskey. It's not good shit. It burns my throat.

Someone is behind me. Pressing her chest against me. "Are you okay, Walker?"

I turn to face a pretty woman with a red pout. One of Bree's friends. An old one. Her name escapes me.

"Fine, yeah." I take another swig. Let the drink sand off the rough edges. I'm a hypocrite, yeah, but it's necessary.

"How is Bree? I haven't seen her in forever."

"She's Bree." And this conversation is over. I nod a goodbye and move through the makeshift dance floor. The song flows into the next one. I think. I can't tell this music apart.

Friends chat on the couch.

A couple is sitting in the arm chair, making out.

A woman is leaning against the wall, her fingers wrapped around her plastic cup, her lips curled into a frown.

She looks as miserable as I feel.

And as desperate to be somewhere else.

Perfect.

I move closer. She's curvy. Pretty. Dark hair in one of those asymmetrical cuts. Like Leighton's, but shorter. Blue eyes. Soft lips.

She looks smart. Serious. Like a suit.

But there's something else about her. The tight jeans, the leather jacket, the purple gem hanging between her tits.

Fuck, she has nice tits.

There goes my train of thought.

Good riddance.

I move next to her. Copy her stance.

She looks to me. Gives me a long once-over. It's slow. Deliberate.

I bring my glass to my lips. "Let me in on your secret. This *is* where the cool kids hang."

"What makes you think I'm a cool kid?" She taps her glass with her purple fingernail.

"I don't."

"You don't?"

"Not yet. Just want to make sure I'm in the right place."

She laughs. "Because you're cool?"

"You think otherwise?" I run a hand through my wavy hair. This is easy mode shit, but I'm not in the mood for a challenge tonight.

"I spend most of my time with PhD candidates. My cool scale is skewed."

"What are you studying?"

She stares back into my eyes, assessing something. She nods like she's sure. "Psychology. If you want a fighting chance don't make a dumb comment about it."

"A fighting chance?"

"At taking me home."

I laugh. "You have me figured out?"

She takes a long sip of her drink. "Just that."

"You don't like people making comments about you studying psychology but you guess their motivations."

"Are you suggesting there's a correlation?"

"It's possible."

Her lips curl into a smile. Her eyes fix on my chest. My forearms. My eyes. "And you..."

"And I..."

"What do you do?"

"Does it matter?"

She laughs. "No."

"How do you know Sandy?"

"I live next door."

"You want to get out of here?"

She finishes her glass. Her eyes fix on mine. She nods. "Yeah."

I take her hand and lead her to the door.

Chapter Two

IRIS

The cool air is a welcome reprieve from the heat of the party.

My heels click against the walkway. What am I doing in these things? They're job interview heels. They're comfortable, yeah, but they're something Mom would wear. I'm pretty sure Mom has this exact pair in her closet.

It's only a few dozen steps to my apartment.

Thankfully, it's quiet.

I pull my key from my purse and slide it into the door. I don't want to be at that party. Going home is the right call.

But inviting a stranger with me?

I press my lips together.

I turn back to... him. "I never asked your name."

"Walker." He offers his hand to shake.

"Iris." My palm presses against his. It does something to me. Makes the air feel hot again.

His dark eyes fix on mine. They light up with desire. Anticipation.

He seems like a good time.

And he's hot.

Obscenely hot.

Tall. Broad shoulders. Strong arms covered in ink. And I mean *covered* in ink. I've never found it appealing before—Lily and I used to argue about that all the time, back when she spoke to me—but it looks good on him. It makes him seem even more carefree. Even more like a perfect distraction.

God knows I don't want to listen to the thoughts racing around my head.

I turn the key and press the door open. "Come in." I suck a breath between my teeth. It's been a long time since I've slept with anyone. And that was Ross. I've never slept with a stranger.

Am I out of my mind?

"Thanks." He steps inside and presses the door closed behind him. His eyes move over my apartment slowly, like he's assessing every detail. His gaze stops on the bookshelf. His lips curl into a smile.

"What?"

"You read extended universe books."

My cheeks flush. I've been trying to re-connect with all the things I used to love. It's not going well. "*Star Wars* is mainstream now."

"You're embarrassed by it?"

"No." Maybe. Definitely.

He laughs as he pushes his t-shirt up his arm. He taps his shoulder with his finger.

Oh.

Right there, on his shoulder, that's a *Star Wars* tattoo. It's part of a sleeve of movie and pop-culture themed tattoos.

It's cool too. Well, as far as nerdy tattoos go.

Okay, who am I kidding?

The framed scene of Luke on Tattooine, looking out at

the setting suns, is the coolest ink I've seen in forever. And I've been staring at ink nonstop for the last few months.

"You're a nerd?" I ask.

"And you are too."

"Maybe." I pull my cell out. "Hold on." Walker seems like a normal, non-ax-murderer, but safety first.

I text Sandy.

Iris: I invited your friend Walker over.

Shit. How does this go? I'm telling her where to find me. And him. That's it. I think.

Sandy: OMG! Girl, get some. He's fine. If I wasn't with John, I'd be first in line.

Iris: He's safe?

Sandy: He's a good guy. I've known him forever. But he is a slut. Make sure he wraps it up ;) Have fun xoxo.

I set my cell on the dining slash coffee slash studying table.

My apartment is a decent size for Brentwood, but that isn't exactly huge. The main room is cozy.

He raises a brow. "Someone you want to talk to?"

"Checking in with Sandy."

"Did she tell you to sleep with me?"

"Yeah. How did you know?"

"It's not the first time."

I can't help but laugh. "You're that irresistible?"

"You did invite me here."

He is. And he knows it.

Usually, that annoys me.

But I kind of like it on him.

Walker.

The tattooed, slutty sci-fi fan.

He's intriguing.

Too intriguing. I'm not opening myself up to heartbreak again.

I know I shouldn't stereotype, but the tattoos and the man-whoring don't suggest stable, supportive boyfriend material.

Then again, clean-cut guys haven't exactly been good to me.

I move to the kitchen—it's on the other side of the coffee table—and grab a glass. "You want water?"

"Sure."

I pour two glasses and hand one to him.

He's smiling.

"What?"

"Women don't usually offer water."

"That's bad strategy."

"Yeah?"

"You need to stay hydrated if you want peak performance."

He chuckles. "True."

"You keep laughing."

"With you."

"With me?"

"I promise. I like you, Iris." He takes a long sip and sets his glass on the table. He moves toward me. Closer. Closer.

There.

He peels my fingers from my glass and sets it on the counter.

His hands go to my hips.

He leans in close.

My eyelids flutter together.

I rise to my tiptoes and press my lips to his.

He tastes good. Like whiskey. Fuck, it's been too long since I've really savored a sip.

Or a kiss.

He slides one hand under my blouse and presses his palm against my lower back.

He pulls me closer.

Sucks on my bottom lip. Softly. Then harder.

I bring my hand to his hair. Part my lips to make way for his tongue.

Lust pushes aside every other desire. I don't want good whiskey. Or understanding. Or dinner.

I only want this tall, handsome stranger's body pressed against mine. Erasing every thought in my head.

I slide my hand under his t-shirt. He's hard. Strong.

My hand explores the lines of his torso.

The other knots in his hair.

Desire spreads through my body as his tongue dances with mine.

As he peels off my leather jacket and tosses it on the coffee table.

He cups my breasts with his palm. Slides his thumb into my bra to play with my nipple.

Fuck.

This is intense. It's different like this. Good different. But scary different too.

Slowly, he backs me into the wall.

He pins me with his hips. His tongue plays with mine. His thumb toys with my nipples, one then the other.

I don't know his last name.

And I don't care.

Some free, uninhibited Iris is taking over. No, I know that Iris. It's just she usually only comes out after four or five shots.

He pulls back.

I stare into his eyes. "Bedroom."

He nods. Steps backward to release me.

I move through the living room.

My bedroom is small, but it's nice. I flip the switch for the string lights. The soft glow of the white paper lanterns bounces off my plain grey bedspread and sheets. Off my Ikea vanity and dresser.

They make the room feel homey.

Comfortable.

Like a place for old lovers.

Walker shuts the bedroom door and leans against it. His dark eyes pass over me. He drinks me in.

His eyes find mine. "Take off your jeans."

"What?"

"Your jeans. Lose them."

"No." I press my lips together. Where the hell is this objection coming from? This guy is hot as hell and he's already setting me on fire. I very much want to lose my jeans.

"No?"

"I don't do that."

"You have sex with your pants on?"

"No. I don't do the whole guy barking orders thing." That was Ross's thing. It was always weird. Awkward.

His voice gets light. "Barking?"

"Yeah." I can't help but laugh. Okay, he isn't exactly *barking*, but the point stands. I copy his posture.

It doesn't work standing.

I sit on the bed and spread my legs in that *blow me* position guys love.

"Take off your jeans," I demand.

His eyes brighten. "Not sure I need to for that."

"Yeah?"

"Yeah." He takes another step toward me. Drops to his knees between my legs.

"You... you're not one of those guys who doesn't—"

"Fuck no." He presses his palms against my thighs and pushes my legs apart. "You're gonna have to pull me away."

"Yeah?" My tongue slides over my lips. My limbs get light.

It's been a long, long time since I've come from someone's mouth.

Longer since I've enjoyed it.

He undoes the button of my jeans. His eyes meet mine. "I don't bark orders."

"Then what was—"

"A request." He looks up at me. "Lift your hips."

"And that's a request?"

"I can't do this with your jeans on."

"True." I lift my hips.

He unzips my jeans and rolls them to my knees. My ankles.

His fingertips skim my skin as he drags his hands up my calves, my knees, my thighs.

His fingers curl into the straps of my thong.

Genius decision. Thank you, past Iris. For once, we're on the same page.

"You're not into dirty talk?" he asks.

"I am. Just not—"

"Ruff. Ruff."

What? I stare back at him.

"That's barking."

I laugh. "You know what I mean."

"I do." He nips at my inner thigh. "Would you like to come on my face?"

"You're teasing me, aren't you?"

He laughs. "Yeah. You're fun to tease." His voice drops. "I'll have to see how fun."

He tugs at the straps of my thong then slides the garment to my ankles.

"I mean it, Iris." He brings his hands to my hips and pulls me to the edge of the bed. "You're gonna have to drag me away."

I try to find a response, but I don't have anything. I want it. Him. Everything.

He plants a kiss on the inside of my knee.

I pull my blouse over my head and toss it aside.

Then the bra.

My breath hitches as he drags his lips up my thigh.

Fuck. I'm already buzzing with anticipation.

"Lie back," he mumbles into my thigh. It's softer, but it's still demanding. Needy.

Like he really is desperate to dive between my legs.

I fall onto my back.

Slowly, he brings his mouth to me.

My hand goes to his dark, wavy hair. It's the perfect length for grabbing.

He pins my legs to the bed as he licks me from bottom to top then top to bottom.

He's takes his time.

Like he's savoring it.

Like he—

Fuck.

He flicks his tongue against my clit.

My legs fight his hands.

He pins me harder. He pries my thighs apart. Keeps them pressed against the edge of the bed.

It's strange, feeling this vulnerable with some guy I barely know.

Good.

But strange.

Every flick of his tongue pushes away my concerns. My nerves fade. I forget that I barely know him. I forget the last few months. And the three years before that. I forget everything but his soft, wet mouth against me.

Mmm.

I tug at his hair.

Buck my hips against his mouth.

He holds me in place. Groans against me. Licks me hard. Soft. Fast. Slow. Up. Down. Left. There.

"Fuck." My thighs fight his hands.

He scrapes his nails against my skin. He has me pinned. He's in control. I shouldn't like it—I never like that kind of thing—but I do.

"Walker." I buck against his mouth.

He stays on just the spot. Licks me with long, soft strokes. Then harder. Harder.

There.

"Don't stop," I breathe.

He doesn't.

He keeps that same rhythm. That same speed.

Tension pools in my sex.

It's intense. Different. Good different.

He takes me higher. Winds me tighter. I tug at his hair, holding his mouth against me.

Almost.

There.

The next flick of his tongue pushes me over the edge.

I groan his name as I come.

My sex pulses. Everything goes white, this beautiful, bright, blinding shade of pleasure. It's the only thing in my world. The only thing in the universe.

He's still going.

Licking me with those hard, steady strokes.

It's intense. Too intense.

I tug at his hair. "Fuck me. Now."

He pulls away. Nips at my thigh. Pushes himself to his feet.

I watch as he tosses his t-shirt over his head.

Pulls a condom from his back pocket.

Unzips his jeans and slides them—and his boxers—to his feet.

Fuck.

He's big.

And it's been a long time.

He stares down at me as he tears the wrapper and slides the condom over his cock. "Turn over."

I stare back at him.

"Please." His voice is heavy. Needy. Like he's not sure if he wants to tease me or *tease* me.

I push myself up.

He brings his hands to my legs. Helps me flip over. Onto my hands and knees.

I plant my feet on the floor. Arch my back to bring my ass into the air.

"Fuck, Iris." He drags his fingertips over my sex. "You always get this wet?"

My response is a groan.

God, that's hot. How can five words be that hot?

He teases me with one finger.

Then two.

I clutch at the sheets to stay upright.

That feels good.

Too good.

I need him inside me. His fingers. His cock. His everything.

I need it too much. The way I used to need—

"You like it rough?" He slides one finger inside me. Then two.

Fuck.

My eyelids flutter together.

I rock my hips. Rise onto my tiptoes.

How do I like it?

I don't even know.

I always went along with whatever Ross wanted.

He pushes his fingers inside me. It's slow. Deep. Intense.

"Slow at first." I swallow hard. How does he talk about this stuff so casually?

I mean, I appreciate his excellent communication skills.

And how much his dirty talk sets me on fire.

But I can't return it. Not with that kind of confidence.

"Then harder." I rock my hips.

He murmurs a yes as he drives his fingers inside me.

It feels good. But I need more.

"Fuck me," I breathe.

"This first." He drives his fingers into me. Again. Again. Again.

It pushes me toward the edge.

Fills me with this strange mix of satisfaction and need.

It's good.

But I need *him* inside me.

"Walker. Please." I arch my hips. Heel—toe my feet to spread my legs. "I need you inside me."

He lets out a low heavy groan and brings his hands to my hips. He holds me steady as he brings his body onto mine.

His tip strains against me.

Desire floods my senses. Yes. More. Everything.

He pulls back and does it again.

Again.

Again.

I dig my fingers into the sheets. I rise onto my tiptoes. I get dizzy from anticipation.

"More." I push aside my inhibitions. "Harder."

His fingers dig into my hips.

He thrusts into me full force.

Fuck. He's big. It's intense. But good intense.

He holds me in place as he pulls back and drives into me again.

Again.

He fills me with deep, steady thrusts.

Each winds me up. Each sends bliss to my fingers and toes.

He slides one hand around my hip and plants it between my legs.

He rubs my clit with his thumb as he drives into me.

Damn. That's intense.

He's good at this.

Way too good at this.

It defies explanation.

But then logic isn't all that interesting at the moment.

I...

He...

His thumb finds just the right spot.

"There," I breathe.

His groans fill the room as he drives into me. As he rubs me right where I need him.

He's bringing me all this pleasure. And it's making him groan. And he...

Fuck.

His name rolls off my lips.

It makes his groan lower. Louder.

The tension in my sex builds with every thrust and brush of his thumb.

It winds tighter and tighter.

"Harder," I breathe.

He digs his nails into my thigh as he drives into me. Harder. Faster. Deeper.

Mmm.

A few more thrusts and I'm there.

All that tension winds tighter than I can take. Then everything releases.

A wave of pleasure rocks through me.

My sex pulses. It pulls him closer. Makes him groan.

I moan his name as I come.

My grip on the sheets releases. My arms go slack.

"On your back." He pushes me flat on the bed.

I spread my arms. My legs. Arch my back.

He places his body on top of mine. One hand on my hip. The other on my shoulder.

With one quick motion, he drives inside me.

The weight of him pushes me into the bed.

It feels good. Safe. Comforting.

It's just physical. Just sex. It doesn't mean anything. You're never going to see him again.

I can't push the thoughts away.

This is too intimate. Too good.

I rock my hips to meet him.

He drives into me.

His movements get faster.

He loses control of his breath. Pulls me closer. Groans into my neck.

He's almost there.

And I need him there.

"Come for me." The words fall off my lips. A wave of nerves follow, but they disappear with his next thrust.

I can dirty talk.

At least when it's someone I'll never see again.

It makes him groan.

And go harder.

And pull me closer.

A few more thrusts and he's there. He shakes and shudders and groans my name as he comes.

He pulses inside me.

It's satisfying in a way it never has been.

Slowly, Walker peels his body off mine. "You have a trash can?"

"Yeah." I motion to the one next to my bed. "There's tissues—"

"I see them."

He takes care of the condom then plants on the bed next to me.

I roll onto my elbow and look up at him.

His dark eyes are so pretty.

His everything is so pretty. Not that he's really *pretty*. He's more handsome. Exactly handsome. Exactly halfway between rugged and pretty.

He brushes my hair behind my ear. "You want to go for round two?"

"You can?"

His laugh is soft. "I need ten minutes."

I nod. Yes. Round two is a good idea. And maybe three.

But that's it.

Tonight.

Only tonight.

Chapter Three

IRIS

There are arms around me.

Warm, strong arms.

My eyes blink open.

Bright light flows through the blinds.

The arms turn me over.

That's him. Walker. He pushes himself up. Stretches said arms over his head as he yawns.

He looks even more irresistible with the late morning light falling over his chiseled torso.

His dark eyes fix on mine. "Sleep. It's early."

I nod to the window. "How early?"

"For a Sunday." He grabs his jeans from the floor and pulls them on. "I have to go. Work." He pulls his t-shirt over his head, covering that perfect torso.

I want to trace all the lines of his ink. Again.

I want...

I want to get up. To make him coffee. And breakfast. Which is ridiculous. I can't cook to save my life.

Does pouring milk into cereal count as making someone breakfast?

Does a guy this cut even eat carbs?

I swallow hard. What the hell do I say here? "It was fun." Amazing. The best sex I've had in forever. Or maybe ever. Definitely ever.

"Yeah. It was." He leans over the bed and presses his lips to my forehead. "Sleep tight, Iris."

I nod. "The front door locks automatically." Look at me, one-night stand expert. I make a mental note to high-five someone, but there isn't anyone I want to share this with. Only Lily.

My eyelids flutter together.

The door opens and closes.

I have that appointment.

I have to get up soon.

But not yet.

I pull the covers over my head.

And I let my head fill with memories of his body against mine.

THE APARTMENT SMELLS LIKE COFFEE. GOOD COFFEE.

I push myself up. Slowly, I peel off the covers, step onto the hardwood, and move into the main room.

Sure enough, there's coffee warming on the counter.

And there's a note next to it. Pen on a piece of paper.

Call me if you want to go again.

- Walker

And there's his number.

It's not exactly a profession of undying love.

It's an open invitation to booty call.

I want to sleep with him again.

God how I want to sleep with him again.

But that's far too dangerous.

I like him.

I don't want to like him.

I don't want to give anyone the chance to hurt me again.

I tear the note in half and drop it in the trash under the sink.

Chapter Four

WALKER

"You smell like pussy." Dean smiles wide. It's his usual *I'm going to turn everyone's life upside down* smile.

The guy's been my closest friend for ten years now, and I'm still not sure when he's serious and when he's fucking with me.

"And?" I move to the hand sink in the back and turn it on.

Dean follows. "And you've been finished for two minutes without offering details."

"Guess I'm not as depraved as you." I run the water warm and pump soap into my hands.

"You'll get there."

I rinse. Towel dry. Turn off the faucet. "We all need goals." Not that I have any at the moment. I have everything I want. I'm a co-owner. The shop is kicking ass. I spend my days putting ink to people's skin and my nights *enjoying* the women of the greater Los Angeles area.

Life is good.

Except for shit with Bree.

But that's staying in the corner of my mind.

I'm done picking up the pieces.

I'm done hoping she'll give a fuck about getting better.

I'm done, period.

"So..." He leans against the wall and shoots me a look. *Spill it.*

"It was amazing." There's something about Iris. Not just the way her body responds to mine. Or her lush thighs against my cheeks. Or her soft tits.

Fuck, I'm getting distracted.

Dean taps his toe against the floor. "That's it? It was amazing?"

"Yeah."

"You like her or something?"

"I'm twenty-four."

"And?"

"Don't you think we're getting old for this shit?"

"Are you hearing this, Leigh?" He turns to the front desk. Shoots Leighton an *isn't this the worst thing ever* look.

"I don't know. Who's Leigh?" She folds her arms.

"It's cute," Dean insists.

"What if I call you D?" she asks.

"Don't. He'll like it," I say.

He's already smiling. "That's how you think of me, as D?"

"As a dick, yeah." She shakes her head, sending her short hair in every direction. It's a purple-grey color now. It's nearly the same cut as Iris's, but it looks different on her.

Don't get me wrong. Leighton is a babe and she dresses to kill. But I don't see her as a potential fuck. I know her too well.

"You're both perverts." She brushes her hair behind her ear.

"And that's a bad thing?" Dean feigns offense.

"Don't you have an appointment?" she asks.

"He's late." Dean turns to me. "What was she like?"

"Responsive."

"That's it?" Dean shakes his head. "You're going soft on me."

Leighton laughs. "Had that problem before?"

"Have you?" He shoots her an accusatory look.

"Yeah. All women have. And most men too. Your fucking dicks are prima donnas." She folds her arms. "With how much you drink..."

He flips her off.

She laughs. "Hmm. Seems personal, *D*. Something you want to confess?"

"I know my limits," he says.

"That means you've tested them," she teases.

"I know my dick better than you do, honey. Now, if you want to get to know it—"

"I know enough. You never stop talking about it. If I have to hear about how mind-blowing you think your Prince Albert is one more fucking time—"

"Sounds like you want to try it out."

She ignores him. Turns to me. "You were wearing that yesterday."

"We already established that he smells like pussy." Dean shakes his head. "I can't believe this shit. No details."

Leighton rolls your eyes. "You're like a child."

"You love it," he says.

She shakes her head. Turns to me. "A little detail? Please, Walker. You know I'm on a self-imposed dry spell."

Yeah. Something about how she's tired of making the wrong choices with men.

She looks at me with puppy dog eyes.

Her eye makeup is the same as Iris's was. That long line. Only hers is purple.

"I was at a party. She didn't want to be there. We went back to her place," I say.

Leighton nods *go on*.

"She sat on the bed. I rolled her jeans to her ankles. She was wearing this lace thong that curved over her soft hips. She made this hot as fuck gasping noise when I tugged her panties to her ankles."

"TOO MUCH DETAIL!" Leighton bites her lip. Desire spreads over her expression.

She asked.

I'm not about to skimp.

"She was so fucking eager. She started arching her back and letting out these needy sighs as I dragged my lips up her thigh. When I pinned her legs to the bed—fuck. She tasted good. And she was so fucking responsive. Like it had been ages since anyone licked her properly."

"Ugh." She bites her lip. "You're such a guy."

"Please, Leigh. Fifty bucks says your panties are drenched," Dean says.

"Yeah. But... Uh..." Her blush spreads to her chest. "How do you know she wasn't coming on some other guy's face the night before?"

"I know." All right, maybe she was with someone recently. But not someone who fucked her properly. Not with the way she groaned my name.

"You jelly 'cause you want my boy's tongue on your cunt?" Dean asks.

"Ew. You guys are like brothers. That's just... no." She shakes her head.

"You know Dean and I will take you out. Play wingman," I say.

She scoffs. "Yeah, that's gonna work. Two built, tattooed bodyguards scaring off every guy in a hundred-foot radius."

"You don't mean that." Dean feigns humility.

She cocks her hip. "You always start with your mouth?"

"Not usually." Fuck, I *am* stuck in a routine. The last dozen women, it's been the same thing.

How the fuck is it possible I'm bored of one-night stands?

She sighs. "Why do I do this to myself?"

"I'm sure Brendon has something that can take the edge off," Dean says.

"I'm not taking Brendon's used sex toys. Especially knowing he uses them on Kay." She sticks her tongue out. Shakes her head with disgust. "I have my own... you know what. Never mind. It's none of your business."

He turns to me. "Come on, Casanova. Keep going. It was just getting good."

"I'm not a porn site. If I was, I'd charge a fortune," I say.

"I don't want some porn site. That's fake shit. I need the real dirt," he says. "What was she like?"

"Different," I say.

"You like her."

"Of course I like her. I wouldn't fuck her if I didn't."

"No. You *like* her."

"I don't like anyone."

"I thought so. But I guess I'm the only soulless one here." He shakes his head. "Damn, Walker. First Brendon. Now you. Another one bites the dust."

"You can't trick me into offering more details."

He smiles wide. "You sure?"

No. He can. I usually love replaying my conquests. But it feels different with Iris. Like I shouldn't.

Fuck.

Maybe he's right.

Maybe I do *like* her.

But it's not like that means I'm going to fall for her.

Dean's wrong. Well, not about him being more soulless. But about me being at all open to anything beyond a fuck.

I like Iris.

I want to fuck her again.

But that's it.

It isn't going to mean more than that.

The bell rings.

That must be my eleven o'clock.

I shoot Dean a *cut it out* look and I turn to the door.

That's her. *@FruedianSlip*.

Iris.

Chapter Five

IRIS

I slide my hands into my front pockets.

Of course Walker is a tattoo artist.

Of course, he's the one Sandy recommended.

Of course, she neglected to mention that last night.

I take a deep breath and exhale slowly. How does this go?

He's staring at me with those dark eyes. Expecting... something. I don't know.

The girl at the counter is staring too. But that's probably because we have the same haircut. This long bangs on one side, short on the other side pixie slash bob is trendy. After everything, I needed to see a different person in the mirror.

I know, I know. A dramatic haircut to signify a life change is a bit obvious, but it works.

I don't see Iris the fuck up in the tattoo parlor's mirrors.

I see Iris the PhD candidate who has her shit together.

Who's reminding herself she's not destined to past fuck ups.

Apparently, Walker is the William I've been emailing about said tattoo reminder.

Maybe tattoo artists have pen names. Maybe that's a normal thing.

A guy about Walker's height, with wavy dark hair and blue eyes, steps forward. "I'm Dean." He offers his hand. "You looking for someone?"

I shake. "Yeah. I have an eleven o'clock. With William."

He chuckles. "That's Williams." He nods to Walker. "Guy's got his names mixed up. Walker Williams. Should go the other way, huh?"

I try to laugh, but I can't quite manage it. This is weird. Twelve hours ago, he was naked in my bed. I was climbing on top of him.

And now I'm here.

And we're both dressed.

And his friends slash coworkers are watching.

"I, uh..." I move forward. I'm an adult. I can handle this like an adult. Really. I can. "I'm sorry I'm late. I, uh—"

"Needed your sleep?" Walker smiles.

I laugh. "That's a good way of putting it." There's something about his smile. It disarms me. Puts me at ease. That describes him perfectly. He's easy to talk to. He's just... easy.

Not slutty. Not un-slutty (last night is certainly a check in the manwhore column), but not necessarily slutty.

More... carefree.

Or is that how he wants to look?

He seemed pretty upset last night when he came over to me.

And he's at work. He has to be friendly.

Stop shrinking him, Iris. You're not even going to be that kind of shrink.

I clear my throat. "Yeah. I, um. I'm going to need coffee after this."

"It's a small piece. You'll be done in half an hour." Walker motions to a half-room to his right. It has high walls and an open doorway. It's some privacy. Enough for this.

Far too little for a second round, but enough for this.

"You ready?" he asks.

"Yeah. Thanks." I slide my backpack off my shoulders.

Walker looks to his friends. Dean, I guess. He shoots the guy a curt look. Then he shoots a softer one to the girl with the purple-grey hair.

God, she's cool. Between the three of them and their tattoos and ripped jeans, I'm hopelessly outclassed in the cool department.

He motions to the teal chair. It's set up like one of those seats at the gym, one for chest flies. It's at a forty-five-degree angle.

I sit.

He pulls out a tray.

"Why do I feel like I'm at the dentist?" I hug my arms over my chest.

His taps my wrist with his pointer finger. "You can call this off. I'll wave the cancellation fee."

"Generous."

He nods.

"Won't your manager get upset?"

"I'm my manager."

"Oh."

"I co-own the shop." He peels my arms from my chest. He brings my left arm to the tray and wipes my forearm with rubbing alcohol. "You won't hurt my feelings if you leave."

"You're still the guy who did all the work on your Instagram?"

"Yeah."

"Then I'm sticking around."

He moves the temporary tattoo onto my forearm, right

under the crook of my elbow. "I shouldn't tell you this, but anyone could do this."

"Yeah?"

"Yeah. It's a simple stencil. I'm happy to take the shop minimum for it, but if you don't want to work with me—"

"No. It's fine." I force myself to smile. It is fine. Or it's going to be fine. If I go to another artist or another shop, then last night meant something. And it can't mean anything. "Really. I'm good."

"You still want it here?"

"Yeah."

"Exactly?"

"Can I see it first?"

"Nah, I'm gonna strap you down and do it freehand."

I stare back at him.

His dark eyes get bright. "Kidding."

"Oh."

"Sorry." He peels the plastic off the temporary tattoo, presses it to my skin, and wets it. "I know better than to *tease* when you're in the chair."

I make an uh-uh noise as my gaze fixes on the tattoo gun behind him.

The needle doesn't scare me. But the ink?

It's terrifying. There are no do overs or blank slates or quick fixes. Once the ink is on my skin, it's there forever.

"Are you a virgin?"

"You should know."

He laughs as he pulls on plastic gloves. "Is this your first tattoo?"

"Oh. Yeah."

"You don't like needles?"

"It's more the permanence."

He nods *I get that*, peels off the temporary tattoo's paper, grabs a mirror and hands it to me. "What do you think?"

That's it, right where I need it.

You are not your mistakes.

I hand the mirror back and stare into his dark eyes.

He cocks his head to one side. "You sure you're up for this?"

"Yeah. I just need coffee."

"Didn't like what I made?"

"No. It was good. I just..."

"Need more?"

"Yeah." Something like that.

He motions to the chair. "Is this how you want it?"

I stare at the temporary tattoo. It's exactly what I need. It's everything. It's perfect. "It's perfect."

"You can tell me if it's not. I know you're not shy about your preferences."

My cheeks flush. "Was that a problem?"

"Fuck no." He grabs the rubbing alcohol, wets a cotton swab, cleans the temporary tattoo off my skin. "I like you bossy."

"Barking orders?"

He chuckles. "Yeah." He presses a stencil to my skin and tapes one side. "Now stop distracting me or I'll fuck this up."

"Oh. Sure." I watch him tape the stencil to my skin.

He grabs the tattoo gun. "You ready for this?"

"Will you distract me?"

"Sure." He turns the gun on for a second. "This is what it sounds like."

"Okay."

"You didn't bring anyone to hold your hand."

"Is this where you ask women if they have boyfriends?"

He brings the gun to my skin. "I don't usually date clients."

"You date?"

He laughs. "I don't usually fuck clients." He looks up at

me. "On three. I'll do one mark. So you can see how it feels."

I nod.

"One. Two. Three." He turns the gun on.

The needle hits my skin. It hurts. More than other needles have. And without the promise of bliss.

But it's nothing compared to... well, to everything.

I make my voice confident. Strong. "I can take it."

"You can take a lot."

My cheeks flush.

"Shit. You're distracting me again."

"That was all you."

He shakes his head. "Be good, Iris. I know you want to get my clothes off again. But you have to wait until I'm done with this."

I can't help but smile. "I'll keep that in mind."

He looks up at me. Raises a brow. *You ready?*

I nod. I am.

He turns the gun on and brings it to my skin.

Fuck. That hurts.

My fingers curl into fists.

My teeth sink into my lips.

It's a steady pain. The same stab of the needle over and over.

"You're getting a PhD, right?" he asks.

"Right."

"Where?"

"UCLA."

"Good school."

"Yeah. Great psychology department." I take a deep breath and exhale slowly. It does nothing to distract me from the needle stabbing my arm several times a second. It's uncomfortable. But tolerable.

"How far into it are you?"

"Just started."

"So, what, four or five years to go?"

"It's a six-year program." And I took a leave of absence winter quarter. I'm already behind schedule.

"Damn." He moves the gun to the next level. "That's a commitment."

"More than ink on your skin forever?"

"Not when you put it that way."

I press my lips together. That's two letters down. Three. Almost there.

"Are you going to be a shrink?"

"No. Most people who are counselors get a Doctorate of Psychology. A PhD is more focused on research and teaching."

"Which appeals to you?"

"Research."

"You are a nerd."

"Who suggested otherwise?"

"You." He finishes the first line and moves to the second. "It's cute that you hide it."

"You always torment women when you're tattooing them?"

"Of course. They have to listen. It's perfect."

I laugh.

He holds my arm steady. "Don't move."

"Don't make me laugh."

"Sounds fair, but I don't like it." He holds my arm as he traces the last word.

I stare at the beige wall. At the framed tattoo art. At the heart string lights lining the roof. "This shop is kinda girly."

"You're teasing me now?"

"Just saying."

"Co-owner's girlfriend helped decorate it."

"Oh. Is he here?"

"Not right now. I'm sure he's *with* her."

"You don't approve?"

"Nah. They're happy. It's good for them. Just—"

"Not for you?"

"Something like that." He curves the gun over the last letter then turns it off. His eyes meet mine as he moves backward. "There. Done."

There. Done.

I watch him pull off the stencil.

He takes me to the mirror. Marvels at my ink with me.

It's perfect.

You are not your mistakes.

"Come on." His fingers curl around my wrist. "I have to clean you up."

I'm buzzing. From the adrenaline and from his touch.

I follow him to the chair.

Watch him rub some ointment over the ink then wrap it in plastic.

We move to the counter. I pay with my credit card. Sign for a generous tip.

Stare at the new ink.

This is really on my skin.

It's really happening.

And he's there, next to me, offering me something. A tube of that same ointment.

"I'm guessing you did your research, but in case you didn't, wash it well tonight. Then use this. Same thing for a few days. Don't wrap it or bandage it. And no swimming for two weeks." He hands over the tube.

I nod. "Thanks."

"You still want that coffee?"

I press my lips together. Pull my backpack from the floor. "Yeah."

"I have an hour until my next appointment." His eyes meet mine. "You want some company?"

Chapter Six

IRIS

It's a simple question, but it feels profound.

You want some company?

I have no idea.

Thankfully, the question isn't *some*.

It's not a date with *someone*.

It's Walker.

I want to get coffee with Walker.

I want to get lunch and ice cream and dinner and post-dinner coffee with him.

And I really, really want to lead him back to my apartment so he can fuck me senseless.

I want it too much.

It's dangerous.

I press my lips together. I try to find a polite no. *Thanks, but I need to get to work.*

Thanks, but I think it's best if we never see each other again.

Thanks, but how about we skip the coffee and go straight to the backroom slash office instead?

I stare into his eyes.

I don't want to say no.

I want to say yes.

It's just company.

Just coffee.

I nod. "Only if you promise it will be great coffee."

"I know just the spot."

THE AIR IS WARM. THE BREEZE IS SOFT. THE SUN IS HIGH IN the bright blue sky.

It's a beautiful day.

But then, it's always a beautiful day on the Westside.

Venice is a lot like the gated community in the valley where I grew up. It's more crowded and less sauna like in the summer. And it's harder to find parking. And it's a million times more hip.

But it's the same lemon sun and bright sky.

That particular cliché about California is true.

The breeze rustles the palm trees lining the street.

It's picture perfect.

A sunny spring day by the beach.

A walk with a gorgeous, tattooed man.

"I hope you don't mind hipsters," Walker says.

"My haircut doesn't give me away?"

He laughs. Tugs on my backpack straps. He's wearing it. Holding it for me. Like in high school. "And now you have ink. You're on your way."

"Mom would be so proud." She already is. My parents suffocate me with praise. It's sweet. But it's too much. *You're so strong, Iris. You've already made it a month. You'll get through this. And Lily will come around. You'll be best friends again. We'll be one big, happy family again.*

"Is she?"

"Yeah." I run my fingers through my hair. I'm still

buzzing. I can still hear the tattoo gun's hum. I can still feel the needles on my skin. "Do you usually ask women about their moms on dates?"

"I told you. I don't date."

"Then what is this?"

"Coffee." The back of his hand brushes mine. "And conversation."

"It's been a while since I've been on the market, but I'm pretty sure that's called a date."

"Ah."

"What do you mean *ah*?"

"Explains a lot."

"What?" My rubber sole hits the pavement. My canvas shoes are comfortable. But ordinary. At least they're purple. That gives them personality. And it's something I know. I love the color purple. It's not much, but it's a start. "If you tell me I was rusty, I'm going to—"

"Hit me?"

I shake my head. "Dig my water bottle from my backpack and pour it on your head."

"Viscous."

"I try." I let the back of my hand brush his wrist.

He leans into the touch. Brushes his fingertips against my palm.

"What did it explain?"

"I'm not sure I can answer honestly with such a brutal threat hanging over my head."

"Are you chicken?"

His laugh floats into the air.

It makes me warm. Fills me someplace I'm normally empty. There's a distinct lack of laughter in my life. I want more of it. More of him.

"Well, some of us have balls." I drag my fingertips over his palm. "And I'm not afraid to say it. Coffee and conversation the day after sex is a date."

"You want it to be a date?" He nods to the street to our left. *This way*.

I follow him onto the slanted street. It's familiar. Somehow. "I'm not looking for a relationship."

"A fling?"

"Depends on the definition."

"Hmm."

"You're doing it again."

He laughs. "Maybe."

We stop at a red light. I turn to him. Stare into his dark eyes. I can't quite figure them out.

This *is* a date. A date he invited me on. But he's insisting it's not.

Maybe he's as terrified of commitment as I am.

His eyes are inviting. Dark. Deep. Beautiful.

Ahem.

"You are not your mistakes." The light turns green. He takes my hand and leads me onto the street. "You messaged me about it a while ago."

"I was working up my nerve."

"It takes a lot of people a while."

"And you?"

He laughs. "Not anymore."

"Now it's more like *I have an hour to kill, let's find some free skin?*"

"Close. But not quite. That no swimming shit is serious."

"And you're a swimmer?"

"It's not obvious?"

No, it is. He's carefree. Tan. Toned. Broad-shouldered. "You're a surfer?"

"I know." He flips his wavy hair. "Not a blond. I defy stereotypes."

"Are you from Southern California?"

"You won't believe me."

"I'm from the Valley. Try me."

"Ah."

"This again?"

He nods to the coffee shop on our left. It's all white with a blue sign and curvy letters. I recognize the chain. It's from San Francisco and each iced coffee is tiny, expensive, and to die for.

"I'm going to have to call off this non-date."

"You like it." He moves into line behind a guy with hipster glasses. "Besides, I'm buying your coffee."

"But it's not a date?"

"Call it what you want."

The guy in front of us finishes his order. We move forward. Walker orders the fancy black iced coffee. I order the fancy sweetened one.

Mmm. Sugar and caffeine. Truly, the source of all happiness in the world. Especially when other vices are off limits.

My tongue slides over my lips. My thoughts get sharper. More focused. It's the same as it was. I know. It sounds ridiculous, but it's the same to my brain.

Mmm. Fix. Almost. Here. Need. It. Now.

My toes tap together.

My fingers tap the counter.

Now.

I. Need. It. Now.

I force my fingers to steady.

I can handle waiting for coffee.

Really.

I press my hands into my sides as we move to the pick-up counter. This is a small shop. Hardwood floors. White walls. Three shiny white tables with uncomfortable looking trendy chairs.

And coffee.

All the sweet, sweet caffeine and sugar I need.

I force myself to look at Walker. Conversation is a good distraction. And this *is* a date. I need to carry my half of it. "Where are you from?"

"Beverly Hills."

I don't believe him. I stare into those eyes, trying to figure him out. He's telling the truth. I think.

"Told you."

"But you're..."

"You're stereotyping me?"

"No. Then I'd be saying you must really have issues with your parents to rebel from your life of privilege."

"Ah."

"You seriously have to stop with the ah."

"Are you going to escalate the threat to coffee on my head?"

"That's a waste of coffee."

"That gives me leeway." His eyes light up as he smiles.

It really is a nice smile.

I admit it. I stare. I stare until the barista is calling my order. Then I pounce on my sweet, sweet caffeine.

Mmm. Sugar. Coffee. Happiness.

"Shit, Iris. You're making me jealous." Walker presses his palm into my lower back as he leads me toward a table.

"Am I moaning that much?" I am. But I can't help it. It's so good.

He nods as he takes a seat. "I like it." He looks up at me with a wicked smile. "This is familiar."

My cheeks flush. Thoughts of last night fill my head. His fingers curling into my thighs. His lips on my skin. His cock driving into me.

Ahem.

I sit.

Cross my legs.

Take a long sip.

Stare at my new ink instead of at him.

"Is that one mistake, or a few?" He sucks his coffee through his straw.

"A few." Hundred. Or thousand. Or maybe hundred thousand.

"Something in particular?"

"Yeah."

He doesn't ask for an explanation. He just leans back and drinks his coffee.

I copy his cool posture. His *oh, look how relaxed I am*, but I can't nail it. My limbs feel awkward. My back is straining. My arm just won't hang over the side of my chair.

He laughs. "Am I that obnoxious?"

"Not quite."

"I usually ask people about their ink. What it means. Most people want to talk about it."

"I already paid you."

"And fucked me."

"True." I take a long sip of my coffee. "But you don't strike me as the kind of guy who has to convince women to fuck him."

"I don't know. Tried pretty hard last night."

"Yeah. *You want to get out of here?* That's an entire sentence."

"Usually I pin 'em to the wall right there."

"Really?"

He raises a brow. "What do you think?"

"I don't know. You're different than most of the guys I know."

"The grad students?"

"Yeah." And the guys from my old job answering phones. And from my old life. Every part of it.

"Your ex have a name?"

"Ross."

"When did you breakup?"

"A few months ago." Right before I went to rehab. He's still in love with old Iris. He still wants her back. He texts every so often. Sometimes, I give into my loneliness and text him back.

I miss him. He wasn't a great boyfriend. He certainly wasn't a good influence.

But he...

He was fun. For that Iris.

"Who did the dumping?" Walker sets his drink down. He leans close, intrigued.

"Hard to say exactly."

"Oh?" He raises a brow.

"You really don't date."

"I told you."

"You're asking all the wrong questions."

"You mean girls don't get wet talking about their exes?"

"Not usually."

"Shit. I better make a note." He pulls a marker from his pocket, uncaps it, and scribbles on his arm. *Don't ask babes about their exes.*

"Or their moms."

He adds *or their moms*. "I appreciate the tips."

"Uh-huh."

He caps the marker. His eyes find mine. They're bright. Joyful. "Really."

He's a fun guy.

More fun than Ross.

Certainly better in bed.

Certainly more interesting.

"Was he your mistake?" He takes another sip.

I follow suit. I'm already halfway done with this coffee. I

can order more. The price is a crime, but I have plenty saved, and I have my stipend, and my parents are more than willing to offer money anytime I need it. Even after everything.

"Is that a no?"

"I don't know. That's a hard question. The person I was then was happy with him."

"And who was she?"

"Someone else."

"When did you breakup?"

"On Christmas."

"Shit. I'm gonna have to buy you another coffee."

"You really are digging yourself into a deeper and deeper hole." I take a long sip. Mmm. Usually, I wouldn't let him buy me another coffee. But I'm tempted to take him up on his offer. Not just for the caffeine. But for everything.

"You have anyone you call?"

"Hmm?"

"For sex."

"Oh." I fight my blush. Wet my dry throat. "Not at the moment." Or ever. But he doesn't need to know that.

"Me either."

"Oh."

"I like you, Iris. I had fun last night. More than I've had in a long time."

"Really?"

"I know. I seem like a slut. I am." His brow scrunches. He's thinking something. He must figure it out, because understanding spreads over his expression. "But I'm tired of one and done. I want something steady. With someone I like." His eyes meet mine. "With you."

"What exactly do you want with me?"

"I want you to be my fuck buddy."

Chapter Seven

WALKER

Iris blinks twice.

Her blue eyes fill with surprise.

A blush spreads over her cheeks.

She wraps her fingers around her cup, brings it to her lips, sucks coffee from the straw until she's slurping ice.

"You want another?" I take my last sip.

"I have to study."

"I have a one o'clock. I'm not gonna take up your afternoon." I push my empty cup aside. "I don't bullshit. Or play games. If you're not interested, say no. It won't hurt my feelings."

"Not at all?" Her lips curl into a smile. "That doesn't make me feel special."

"I'll be devastated. Spend the entire week wondering if I'm a lousy fuck."

"You're not."

"Yeah?" I lean back.

"Yeah." She copies my posture, leaning back, spreading her legs.

"I know you're mocking me, but you're gonna make me hard if you keep copying poses from last night."

She presses her knees together. "Okay. I'll take another coffee. The same one. Thanks." Her gaze goes to her new ink. She's transfixed.

You are not your mistakes.

I've done a lot of tattoos the last five years. Thousands. Plenty of them were similar sentiments.

But I've never wanted to pry one apart before.

I've never been hungry for the story behind the words.

I don't dig into this kind of shit.

I don't do late-night conversations or heartfelt promises or teary confessions.

I don't let anyone that close.

Anyone but Bree.

And Bree's the only person who hurts me.

Math has never been my strong suit, but it doesn't take a genius to add that up.

I move to the counter. Order another round of coffees. The guy at the register gives me a look. *Really, more already?*

I hand him a ten and stuff the change in the tip jar. He's an asshole yeah, but I know working shit jobs. I moved out of my parents' house the second I could and I refused to take a dime. Pride or self-reliance, I don't know. Or care.

It was what I wanted.

So I did it.

I waited a lot of fucking tables while I was apprenticing.

I never skimp on the tip.

Or associate with anyone who does.

Iris is looking at her cell. Whatever she's staring at must be important. Her brow is furrowing. Her blue eyes are focused.

I meant what I said.

I'm not going to hog her afternoon.

Dean is right. I like her. But I don't want her carving out space for me.

I want easy.

Casual.

There. I grab our coffees, move back to the table, hand hers over, take my seat.

"You like making me wait." She slides her cell into her backpack.

I let my voice drop. "Yeah. I do."

She takes her straw between her lips. Looks me in the eyes as she sucks coffee into her mouth. "I'll get you back for that."

"Good."

She moans as she takes another sip.

Fuck, I want that moan again.

She drops her cup on the table. Looks me in the eyes. Raises her brows. "Something you want to say?"

"You moan like that again and I'm gonna be late for my one o'clock."

Her teeth sink into her lip. "Here?"

I nod to the bathroom in the back corner.

"Really? A bathroom?"

"You've never wanted it that badly?"

"Well..." She pulls her arm—the now tattooed one—over her chest. Wraps her fingers around her other arm. "For a guy who doesn't play games you're taking your time explaining this."

I take another sip. "I've never done the fuck buddy thing before."

She cocks her head to one side. "Really?"

"Is it that surprising?"

She holds up her thumb and forefinger in the *a little* gesture. "Okay. Well. I do like you, Walker. I already know you're... skilled."

My smile spreads to my ears. "That's it?"

"Not that you brag?"

"Never."

"That was..." She takes a long sip. "It was the best sex I've had in a long time. I'd like to do it again."

"That's it. We meet up. Do it again."

"Then?"

"Whatever we want."

"But is it this—" She motions to the table and the coffee. "Or is it—" She puts her hand in the shape of a phone and brings it to her ear. "*Hey, Iris, babe, want to come over? I've got an appointment at three, but I can squeeze in a few orgasms.* We do our thing, then I go home, and I call you the next time I'm in need of satisfaction?"

"Like this."

"Sounds like dating."

I shake my head.

"Okay. We can make that a rule. No dates."

"A rule?"

"Rules are good. They help you outline your boundaries."

I can't help but smile.

"What?"

"Nothing."

"I sound like a shrink, don't I?"

"It suits you."

She sticks her tongue out *no thanks*. "Fine. We won't call them rules. We'll call them—"

"Call it what it is."

"Okay. It's a rule." She stirs her drink with her straw. "No one else."

I nod. "Of course."

"And we... we can hang out as friends. But no dates. No roses or moonlit walks on the beach. No romance."

"I don't do romance."

She must believe me, because she nods. "We can call it off whenever. No questions asked. No explanation required."

"Sounds fair."

"Okay. I, um. I'm not sure how you seal this kind of agreement."

I nod to the bathroom.

She laughs. "Let's stick with this." She offers her hand.

I shake.

Her eyes go to the clock on the wall. "You're gonna be late."

"I know." I pull my cell from my pocket and slide it to her.

She picks it up, punches in her number, sends a text to herself.

Her phone buzzes in her backpack.

She hands my cell back to me.

Walker: Hey, babe, this is Walker, your booty call. I want some of that sugar, but first I need to brag about how great I was the other night.

Her lips curl into a smile. "I think I nailed you."

"I'm flattered."

She pushes herself to her feet and slings her backpack over her shoulder. "I'll see you soon, Walker Williams."

"And I'll see you soon, Iris—"

"Iris Avery."

My last appointment takes forever. We go for broke, finish the back piece. When I'm done, I'm tired and achy and ready to crash.

But it's chest and triceps day.

I head to the gym down the street with Dean. It's our thing. We're on the same routine. I spot his chest presses.

Then he spots mine. Then we devolve into bragging about who has the bigger biceps.

Amongst other things.

It's as fun as working out gets.

And it feels good. Like I'm accomplishing something. Getting bigger. Better. Stronger.

We spend the hour teasing each other.

I drive home. Park in the underground lot. Get lost in the familiarity of moving along the walkway, unlocking the door, tossing my keys on the table.

"Hey." A woman's voice grabs my attention.

Not *a* woman.

My sister.

She's on the couch in all black. Her palms are pressed into her thighs. Her expression is soft. Apologetic. "Is this okay?"

"What the fuck, Bree?"

She looks at me with tired eyes. "I need a place to crash tonight."

"I took your key."

Her expression gets sheepish. "I had an extra." She turns toward me. "Please, Walker."

"Beverly Hills too far for your Uber driver?" Our parents keep threatening to cut her off and failing to pull the trigger. But, hey, they'll use those purse strings to convince her to check into rehab stint six. And she'll guilt them into paying her rent when she bails on that one too.

"Just for one night. I promise."

"Why aren't you staying with Mom and Dad?"

"You know how they are."

They're a lot more understanding than I am.

"Walker." She folds and unfolds her legs. "It's been a while, huh?"

No. I dragged her to rehab two fucking weeks ago.

"I know you're pissed I checked out early. But I couldn't

take any more group therapy. Those people have problems. I just..."

"Show me your arms."

She pushes her sleeve up her left arm. Then the right.

She has bad scars on her left arm, right in her elbow crook. From injecting at the same place over and over again.

But her arms are clean.

No track marks.

"I stopped shooting up a long time ago." She says it like it's an accomplishment.

Is it?

I don't have a fucking compass when it comes to my sister. Sabrina. Bree. I never know what to call her. Bree was my nickname for her as a kid. It feels too much like she's someone I can trust. But calling her Sabrina... that's too much the other way.

She's been putting me through the ringer forever. She started using in high school. It was bad for a few years. Then our parents threatened to kick her out and cut her off.

She went through her first rehab stint. She tried to stay clean for a while.

She slipped.

I get that. Life is hard. Temptation is everywhere.

But when she bailed on her second rehab stint?

Got back with her lowlife dealer ex?

Refused to go to her weekly therapy sessions?

Got in the driver's seat wasted and landed a DUI?

Addiction is one thing.

Telling everyone offering you help to go fuck themselves is another.

"Walker." Her voice gets soft. That same tone she used when we were kids. To reassure me when Mom and Dad were fighting.

She's my big sister.

She's supposed to protect me from this shit.

Not show up at my place with more excuses.

I run my hand through my hair. "You can stay."

Her eyes light up. She claps her hands together. "Thank you. I love you. I'll make dinner. You don't have anything in your fridge. But you're close to that market. Is it a Safeway or something else?"

"You can stay *if* you tell me why you checked yourself out."

"Do you have any idea what it's like being locked away from the world?"

No.

"Not having your cell? Or email? Or any way to talk to the people you care about?"

"Who do you care about?"

"You." Her expression is earnest. Soft.

But is it bullshit?

I don't know.

"I do, Walker. I love you. You're my best friend. I hate that I'm disappointing you. But I couldn't take it. I couldn't spend any more time wandering around the grass, listening to everyone talk about how beautiful the ocean is from the hill. I couldn't take any more hippie counselors telling me how lucky I am to be alive."

"You are lucky to be alive."

"Yeah. But..."

But landing in the ER from an OD wasn't enough of a wakeup call the first time.

Or the second.

Is anything going to get through to her?

Her voice stays soft. "The group therapy counselor asked me what I was grateful for and I had nothing. He gave me all this shit. I snapped. I had to leave."

"You can go back."

She shakes her head. "Being there makes me want to drink."

I believe that, but it's not like drinking is her problem. One of them, maybe, but not the one that's landed her in the ER twice. "And being here doesn't?"

"No." She looks at me with puppy dog eyes. "You always make me feel like we're kids again. Like the only thing I'll ever want to abuse is sugar."

"Are you sober?"

"It's been twenty-four hours."

"The question stands."

"Yeah. Of course."

It's far from an *of course*. "You can stay. For one night. That's it. I have someone coming over tomorrow." Well, I plan to.

"Oh." Her voice perks. "You're seeing someone? Tell me all about her."

"It's not like that."

"What's it like?"

"We're friends."

"Oh. Well, that's good. Friends help." Loneliness creeps into her voice. All her friends are other addicts. If she really is trying to stay sober, she doesn't have anyone but me.

And I'm being an asshole.

I force my voice to soften. "Yeah. She's cool. Iris. You'd like her." Before everything, Bree was the picture of friendly. She liked everyone. "Emma crashes here sometimes. When she's pissed at Brendon."

"Emma." She smiles as she recalls my friend slash coworkers' spitfire little sister. "She's probably pissed at him a lot, huh?"

"Yeah." Resenting your sibling is something I understand well. "Less now that she's accepted Brendon and Kaylee."

She nods with understanding. A million years ago, she dated Brendon. Slept with him. Whatever.

I doubt she remembers his sister's best friend. Even if she remembers Emma well.

Fuck. That really was a mess.

At least it's out in the open now.

"She doesn't stay with the other guys?" she asks.

"I don't think so." Dean's older brother, Ryan, is the fourth and final shop co-owner. They don't exactly get along, but they do love each other. And they manage to work together. They don't get this level of frustration.

Not that I discuss it.

"Hmm." She moves into the kitchen and pulls the fridge open. "You think maybe Emma has a thing for you?"

"Emma would tell me."

"Maybe."

"I'm gonna shower. I'll order in dinner. What do you want?"

"I don't mind cooking."

"No. You're staying here until you leave in the morning." Safeway sells every kind of booze. I don't trust Bree to—the sentence ends there. I don't trust Bree. "Pick out a movie. We'll watch something."

"Anything in particular?"

"Anything." I move into my bedroom and drop my cell on my desk, next to my sketchbook.

I'm not artsy, really. I got into tattooing more for the thrill of holding a gun than the thrill of my art on someone's body.

But I take pride in my shit.

I work hard to hone my skills. Figure drawing classes. Sketches. Jumping on trends Ryan abhors. He's still scoffing at watercolor tattoos.

I flip my sketchbook open to the latest page. Pick up my

pen. Draw *Am I A Sucker or Am I Doing the Right Thing?* in big bold letters.

It's right next to my mockup for Iris's tattoo.

She wanted simple text, but I wanted to try adorning it. There's one with hearts. One with flowers. One dripping blood.

She loved them all.

But, still, she wanted simple text.

She thought she was breaking my heart rejecting my mock-ups.

But I don't let my ego get wrapped up in this shit.

There's only one thing that breaks my heart.

And I really am fucking done.

I move into the shower. Strip. Run the faucet hot.

The water washes away the day.

But that voice is still echoing around my head.

Fuck, I'm never getting close to an addict again.

To anyone.

Chapter Eight

IRIS

Streaming a yoga video washes away the stress of studying psychological statistics, but it does nothing to distract me from my problems.

It's a recovery focused yoga series.

It's supposed to help.

And it does.

But it forces me to confront all the ugly parts of my past. The nearly three years of lying to my coworkers and friends, of running away from my problems, of escaping every intense feeling for a calm, easy opiate high.

I've been clean almost three months now.

It's good. Better. But it's scary being a blank slate. I'm tired of being *Iris, the recovering addict*. There's more to me. I know there is.

Which is why I'm reading this horrifyingly cheesy pop-psychology self-help checklist.

Finding Yourself After Falling: An Addicts Guide to Life After Recovery.

I know. It's ridiculous.

But I don't have much else to go on beyond purple and

coffee and *you are not your mistakes*.

I fix a frozen dinner, bring it to the couch, scoop soggy green beans to my mouth. They're more palatable than this chapter.

A Ten Step Checklist to Finding Yourself After Addiction.

One. Eat Well.

I stare at my Lean Cuisine. This is well. Ish. I never paid much attention to what I ate when I was using. It was whatever was around. A bagel from the break room. A takeout sandwich at the place near the office, whatever Ross was eating.

I guess I can work on this one.

Two. Exercise.

In progress. I'm doing this yoga recovery program. And sometimes, I do weights at the gym. But I don't really enjoy it. Or focus on my body. I tune out with pop-culture podcasts that don't quite hit the spot.

Three. Make amends for past mistakes.

Uh... Next.

Four. Find sober friends.

Not going that well. I force myself to go to Narcotics Anonymous (NA) meetings, but everyone is so... positive and encouraging and it feels weird. Wrong. Fake. I don't click with those people.

I can talk to my classmates and my adviser and my supervising psychologist about research. But it never gets deeper than that. I tried telling a friend about rehab. Alice was as interested in addiction research as I am. She was open-minded. Hell, she was madly in love with some celebrity who had just publicly admitted to his history of drug addiction.

But as soon as I told her about rehab, she stopped returning my texts. She started avoiding me in class. She acted like I didn't exist.

If an informed PhD candidate can't accept my past, who

the hell can?

Five. Get enough rest.

Coffee makes this difficult. As does staying up all night, poring over past mistakes.

Six. Figure out your goals.

This one is done. My next five and a half years are devoted to my goal—becoming a research psychologist.

Seven. Keep a journal.

Eight. Read.

Nine. Find new hobbies and passions.

Ten. Accept yourself.

I toss the book on the couch and focus on scooping my TV dinner. The green beans are still mushy. The steak is overcooked. The potatoes are far from crispy.

It's food.

It satisfies my hunger.

But it's not enough. Not really. I want something good. Something better.

Maybe I can learn to cook.

That's a hobby. A passion even.

That—number nine—is where I need the most help.

I have no idea what I love. Or what I want out of life besides finishing school.

I'm going to figure it out. By the end of the quarter. That's my deadline for picking a summer internship. If I don't know what I want to do here, in Los Angeles, I'm taking an internship in New York.

I can't be here unless I know *why* I want to stay sober. Not over the summer. There are too many bad memories. Too many opportunities to fall back into old habits.

With school, it's easy. I'm distracted. Focused. Enthralled. The long periods of nothing and grunt work that come with internships...

I can't handle that.

I finish the TV dinner, clean the tray, toss it in the recycling. It's late. Almost midnight.

But I'm wide awake.

I grab my current book from the shelf, set up on the couch, and try to lose myself in the words. It's not exactly literature, but it's an interesting story. It feels like something I should love.

But I don't.

I like it.

It passes the time.

But it doesn't grab my heart and refuse to let go.

That's a lot to ask from one book. Not every book can be amazing. But what if none of them are? What if all those years of drug use killed my ability to feel passionately about anything besides school?

I get through three chapters.

Then my phone buzzes.

My lips curl into a smile as I read the text.

Walker: Hey babe, it's your booty call. What are you up to? Ready for some epic bragging?

Iris: Reading.

Walker: One of those Star Wars books?

Iris: Maybe.

Walker: It's cute that it embarrasses you.

Iris: What are you up to?

Walker: Texting you.

Iris: Before that.

Walker: Watching a movie.

Iris: Anything good?

Walker: No. Can't even remember the name. I couldn't concentrate.

Iris: Is this where you say you were too busy thinking of me?

Walker: I have some game.

Iris: You sure about that?

Walker: Shit. Where's my marker? I need to make another note. Remind babes you're thinking of them.

Iris: Were you?

Walker: Yeah. I was thinking about how good my name sounds on your lips.

Iris: It does.

Walker: About pinning your thighs to my bed and licking you until you're screaming it again.

Iris: I didn't scream.

Walker: I didn't bark.

Iris: Point taken.

Walker: How was studying?

Iris: Hard. Statistics aren't my strong suit. I need to really understand them to do research.

Walker: Makes sense.

Iris: It's late.

Walker: Is that a "I'm heading to bed" or "this is a booty call, isn't it?"

Iris: Isn't it?

Walker: No. I have family staying at my place. And I'm not that tacky.

Iris: No?

Walker: What about me is tacky?

Iris: What about me being fresh out of a relationship is "ah"?

Walker: You seemed like you wanted to be out of your head.

Iris: I did. Nothing about you is tacky. Assuming you're not about to send a dick pic.

Walker: Only if you ask nicely.

Iris: Would you really?

Walker: Don't know. I never have. I don't really think about shit that way. I take things as they come.

Iris: Maybe later.

Walker: Iris, you have to stop toying with my ego.

Iris: Do I?

Walker: Yeah.

Iris: Or?

Walker: Or you'll hurt my feelings.

Iris: That's it?

Walker: What's worse?

Iris: You don't seem like the type who bruises easily.

Walker: Hmm.

Iris: I'm doing it again, aren't I?

Walker: If the... what the hell defines a shrink?

Iris: A "Hmmm, interesting, tell me more," a couch, and a box of tissues?

Walker: That's quite the stereotype.

Iris: That's what you're looking for.

Walker: You go to therapy?

Iris: You really don't have game.

Walker: Shit? I'm not supposed to ask babes about therapy either?

Iris: I'm pretty sure that's a hard no.

Walker: Damn. You're blowing my mind.

Iris: Am I?

Walker: No. But you... well, I have enough game to know babes don't like the words "blow job."

Iris: We don't.

Walker: Why is that?

Iris: It isn't sexy.

Walker: You prefer "suck me off"?

I swallow hard.

Walker: If it's not a barked order?

Iris: I'm not sure.

Walker: What if it is?

Uh...

Heat pools between my legs. I don't get it. I don't like being ordered around.

Or maybe...

Maybe I just didn't like it with Ross.

Maybe with Walker, it's different.

We've only been together once, and I already know *everything* is different with Walker.

Walker: I'll have to try it out.

Yes. He should try it out. We should skip all this talking.

I should invite him over.

But he's already said he has family visiting.

He's unavailable for banging.

And this... talking to him... it's nice.

Iris: You should.

Walker: What else should I do?

Iris: Throw me on the bed and take me from behind.

Walker: Next time.

Now.

Damn. It's like the coffee. I want my fix. Not the release of an orgasm. But everything that comes with sex. The smell of him, the taste of his lips, the warmth of his body against mine.

I've never wanted someone like this.

In this visceral way.

Is it sobriety?

Or is it him?

Walker: Are you panting yet?

Iris: Yes.

Walker: I'll have mercy. Change the subject.

Iris: You're kind.

Walker: No. I'm hard. And I'm not gonna fuck myself with my sister in the next room.

Iris: Oh.

I let my eyelids flutter together. I let my head fill with thoughts of him stripping out of his clothes, wrapping his hands around his cock, and—

Buzz.

Walker: Isn't going to therapy part of training?

Iris: In my program, it's strongly encouraged. I see someone every week.

Because it's supposed to help me figure out how to stay clean. How to want to stay clean.

Not because it's required.

But this is the truth.

And it's really none of Walker's business.

We're fuck buddies. Not lovers. He doesn't get the key that unlocks my heart. That's the whole point of casual.

Iris: For someone who doesn't date or do relationships, you ask a lot of personal questions.

Walker: This is why I need you. To teach me the ways of wooing women.

Iris: You have problems with that?

Walker: Well...

I can see him smiling. Hear his laugh. Feel the warmth in my gut.

Walker: No. I don't. But what if I get into an accident that mars my perfect face? Then I'll have to rely on my personality.

Iris: You think it's perfect?

Walker: You don't?

Iris: No comment.

Walker: That's a yes.

It is. He's out of this world hot. And way out of my league too. All those years of not caring what I eat coupled with the post rehab sugar addiction means I'm not exactly in tip-top shape.

I'm getting there.

I'm going to complete all these stupid steps. Including the exercise one. And the eating one. And the sleeping one...

Well, I'll save that for last. Or second to last. Before making amends. There are too many people on that list. I'm not ready for it.

Iris: You'll still have your perfect body.

Walker: Thanks for noticing.

Iris: Can I ask you something?

Walker: I asked you if you're in therapy. Seems fair.

Iris: How much do you work out to look like that?

Walker: Enough.

Iris: Not an answer.

Walker: A lot. My friend and I train together. It's like a dick measuring contest. We're always competing to see who's stronger and bigger.

Iris: Bigger?

Walker: Not that.

Iris: Never?

Walker: No, we've never whipped it out, started stroking, then grabbed the measuring tape.

Iris: Your friend who was at the shop? Dean?

Walker: Yeah. How'd you know? Never mind. It's obvious from three seconds in his presence. He's not the most grown up.

Iris: But a good friend?

Walker: Yeah.

Iris: Who may or may not be more well-endowed.

Walker: Iris, that hurts.

Iris: I don't believe you.

Walker: Okay. It doesn't hurt. I'm not exactly lacking.

Iris: I don't think you're supposed to brag about that.

Walker: You've already tested the equipment. You know how it functions.

Iris: You're different than anyone I know.

Walker: You too.

Iris: Really? How?

Walker: I can't explain it. You know what you want. But then you don't. But you know you want to know.

That's actually really accurate.

Iris: It's the barking comment, isn't it?

Walker: Yeah. Or maybe I just like smart chicks with edgy hair-

cuts and fantastic tits.

I swallow hard.

Walker: I'm still thinking about them in my hands.

Iris: And?

Walker: Uh-uh. You're not gonna tempt me to unzip.

Iris: You sure?

Walker: You're welcome to try.

I kind of want to.

I want to pull off my t-shirt and send him a picture of my bra.

Then to lose the bra and send him that pic.

I...

I can't believe how much I want him thinking of me.

Touching himself to thoughts of me.

I barely know him.

Iris: You're going to turn me into a sex maniac.

Walker: That's the goal.

Iris: Why's your sister crashing?

Walker: Fuck. Boner killer. Maybe I should give you a few tips about game.

Iris: Probably. It's been a while.

Walker: She's between places. She'll stay with my parents after this.

Iris: They still in Beverly Hills?

Walker: In a five-bedroom, three-bathroom with a pool.

Iris: You walked away from a pool?

Walker: My complex has a pool.

Iris: Whew. You have some sense.

Walker: No swimming for two weeks.

Iris: I won't. I promise.

Walker: After the two weeks, I'm going to take you surfing.

Iris: You are?

Walker: Yeah. I want to teach you.

Iris: Why?

Walker: Can't a guy have intentions besides seeing a babe in a clingy wetsuit?

Iris: Can he?

Walker: You ever surf?

Iris: No.

Walker: Then let me teach you.

Iris: Why?

Walker: 'Cause I want to. I don't have complicated motivations. I want something. I do it.

Iris: Okay. In two weeks. I'm supposed to try new things.

Walkers: Supposed to?

Iris: It's gonna sound stupid.

And I can't tell him.

Walker: I have a much higher bar for stupid than you do. I promise.

Iris: I'm doing this ten step program.

For life after addiction.

But I need to spin it some other way. I'm not letting another person look at me the way Alice did. I'm not letting anyone else hurt me like that.

I'm not telling anyone until I'm sure they're worth trusting. Until I'm sure I want to trust him. Until I'm sure I want more than easy.

Iris: For life after a breakup. And that's one of them. Trying new things. Finding new hobbies.

Walker: Ah.

Iris: Ah?

Walker: Sleeping with tattooed manwhores is a new thing.

Iris: True.

Walker: What have you tried so far?

Iris: Barre classes.

Walker: Verdict?

Iris: You ever done one?

Walker: Really?

Iris: I've never seen a guy at one, but you might live to defy stereotypes.

Walker: Not that one.

Iris: I wasn't into it. Too much stuff that isn't scientifically accurate.

Walker: Yeah?

Iris: Yeah. There's no such thing as toning. And you can't make muscles longer. I don't like those classes that focus on how you look.

Walker: You look fucking amazing.

Iris: Yeah?

Walker: Yeah. Your ass is perfect.

Iris: I always thought it was a little big.

Walker: That's not a bad thing. And your tits. Fuck. You're trying to get me to unzip, aren't you?

Iris: You did this to yourself.

Walker: No. I never get this hard by myself.

Oh. My cheeks flame. Then my chest. How is he so casual with that information?

I want to be a dirty talking sex god too.

Does that count as a hobby?

Iris: Thanks. I guess I've also tried tattooed manwhores.

Walker: How was that?

Iris: Good.

Walker: Only good?

Iris: Great.

Walker: You busy Friday?

Iris: Not in the evening.

Walker: I get off work at four. Come to my place. At six. I'll fuck you senseless. And I'll... it's a surprise.

Iris: I don't have your address.

He sends it.

Walker: Just do me one favor, Iris.

Iris: Yeah?

Walker: Skip the panties.

Chapter Nine

IRIS

Friday, I wear my best *casual but sexy, I totally get that we're friends with benefits* dress.

At least, I think this black skater dress says *I'm fun, and also hot, and I'm not going to put strings on you, and you better not put strings on me*.

It's a lot to ask from a dress. I admit that.

I wait until I'm parked in front of Walker's building to slide my panties to my feet.

I press my knees together. Following his dirty demand makes me hot.

I guess, when it's Walker, I don't mind being bossed around. At least not like this.

I slide my panties into my purse, step out of my car, click the electronic lock. We're in that northern part of Santa Monica. Close to the beach but far enough away from the action of Third Street Promenade that there's parking.

This is such a normal apartment building.

But it feels like I'm stepping into some other universe. One where I demand what I want. Where I know what I want. Where I get what I want.

I cross the street, move to Walker's apartment, knock lightly.

Footsteps move toward the door. "Hey."

"Hey."

He pulls the door open. Gives me a long, slow once over. His eyes light up. With excitement. Passion. Desire. "Come in."

I step inside.

He closes the door behind me. Clicks the lock.

The living room/den/kitchen is a nice size for an apartment this close to the beach. And there's a closed bedroom door in the back corner of the room.

He motions to the kitchen. There are bags and bowls and measuring spoons laid out on the counter.

I shoot him a curious look.

"You have any idea how to bake a cake from scratch?" he asks.

I shake my head.

"Good. It's a new thing."

"You're going to teach me to bake a cake?"

"Fuck no." He laughs. "I've never done it." He presses his palm against my lower back and leads me toward the kitchen. "We're gonna learn together."

That... actually, that sounds really fun. And delicious.

He unpacks the paper bag. Sets flour, sugar, baking soda, baking powder, cocoa powder on the counter. "You sucked down those sugary coffees like you couldn't get enough."

"True."

"I'm not gonna say something stupid about you like sucking shit."

"Good. That would be stupid."

He slides his hand to my hip. Pushes me against the counter. His dark eyes meet mine. They're on fire. "I am gonna get you so wet you're begging me for it."

I... Uh... "Oh." I swallow hard. How did he transition to dirty so seamlessly? "Now?"

His smile gets devious. "Now. And later." His fingers skim the edge of my dress. "This first." His voice switches right back to normal. Like his hand isn't inches from my ass. He taps a paper sitting on the counter. A printed recipe. "Had to use the shop printer."

"Really?"

"Dean gave me hell."

"He seems like the type."

"Leighton—the girl with your haircut—"

"I noticed that."

"I like it better on you."

"Yeah?"

"Yeah." He brushes my hair behind my ear. "She thinks it's sweet."

"It's different."

"I still have no game?"

I laugh. "You could stand to work on your smoothness. Some lines like *baby, this isn't sweet compared to you*."

"Sounds like romance."

"Only if you mean my personality." My cheeks flush. Did I just say that? Did I really suggest he talk about how I taste?

His lips curl into a smile. "Dirty girl."

I feel like one. Like he's already turning me into a sex freak. "You like it."

"Fuck yeah." He turns so he's facing the counter. Reaches for the cocoa powder. "You like chocolate?"

"Who doesn't?"

"I hear rumors." He motions to the coffee maker on the other side of the counter. "We're doing chocolate with mocha frosting."

"Ambitious."

"There's no point in doing shit if you're gonna half-ass it."

"Can I put that on a poster somewhere?"

"Sure. As long as you credit it to *Walker, the guy who makes me come until I can't stand it*."

Mmm. Yes. Now. Please.

Who needs cake when sex is on the table?

Even delicious, sugary cake with coffee flavored icing.

He leans closer. Slides one hand over my ass. Brings his lips to my ear. "You're adorable on the edge."

"Adorable?"

"Hot as fuck." He drags his hand over my hip as he pulls it back to his side. Then, like he isn't teasing me, he picks up the recipe. "We're supposed to start with flour."

We should start with fucking.

He looks to me and cocks a brow. "You okay?"

"We're really doing this?"

"I told you, Iris. I like making you wait."

Okay. I can live with that. Actually, it's really hot.

God, how is he so hot? The confidence in his dark eyes sets me on fire.

Need to focus on anything else. Now.

I pick up the bag of flour. "You have scissors?"

"Yeah." He turns, grabs them from a drawer, hands them to me handle first. "Do the honors."

I snip the bag open.

He grabs a measuring cup. "What the hell does it mean sift?"

It sounds familiar. Mom was never the type to make baked goods from scratch, but I went to a few slumber parties where eating raw cookie dough was the highlight of the night. "I think you scoop it with a fork."

He pulls a fork from the drawer and hands it over.

I spoon, well, fork flour into the measuring cup. It takes forever to fill it. Or maybe it feels like forever with Walker's body next to mine.

And all that warm air against my tender flesh.

He slides his hand over the sides of my hip. Over my ass. Then the other hip.

He brings his lips to my ear. "You followed orders."

"I thought it was a favor."

"Either way."

I nod. Force my gaze to the printed recipe. Sugar. I pick up the scissors and snip the bag open.

He plays with the hem of my dress. Pulls it up my thighs. Higher and higher and higher. Until it's right at the bottom of my ass.

"I... Uh..." My breath hitches in my throat. I don't want to bake a cake. I want to bend over and demand he fuck me.

He moves behind me. Pulls my ass against his crotch.

He's hard.

Fuck, I want that. I want him. I want it more than I've wanted anything in a long, long time.

"It's driving me fucking crazy too." He releases my dress and takes a half step backward.

I nod. Yes. Crazy is a good way to put it. I mean, really, we shouldn't use the word crazy casually. Mental illness is no laughing matter...

But he is driving me fucking crazy.

"You're good at this." I force my attention to the sugar as I scoop and pour it into the mixing bowl.

"Thanks."

I want to be good at it. At this master level of teasing.

I focus on our task. Pretend I'm here to bake and not to come in his bed.

"You want to do the honors?" I point to the baking soda and the teaspoon. "Since we're learning together?"

"Teamwork. I like it." He scoops the proper amount of baking soda into the mixing bowl. Then the cocoa powder.

I measure oil.

He measures vanilla.

I crack three eggs.

He adds the coffee.

"That's everything." I stir.

"We need to taste it."

Yes. I need to taste him. His lips, his neck, his chest, his cock. I need him in my mouth. I need to drive him fucking crazy too.

He reaches for the bowl. Picks up the spoon and brings it to my lips.

I stare into his eyes as I lick off the batter.

He pulls it away. Brings it to his lips. Does the same.

But he does it better. There's something fierce in his eyes. Something that promises he's going to lick me a hell of a lot more thoroughly.

He drops the spoon in the bowl.

Brings his thumb to my lip. Wipes a drop of batter from my lips and brings it to his mouth.

I... Uh...

"We should get this in the oven." So it's no longer a distraction. So there's no reason why I can't tear his clothes off. So I can give up on this whole *focus on baking* thing.

He nods. Opens a high cabinet and pulls a baking tray from it. "I didn't know I had this until today."

"You don't cook?"

"I do. Just not with this."

"Would you teach me?"

He chuckles. "Teach you what, sweetness?"

Sweetness. I like it. I shouldn't like it—who the hell does he think he is giving me a pet name—but I do. "Everything."

"Yeah."

I clear my throat. "I mean cooking. I never learned."

"Sure." He slides his hand over my hip. "Tonight?"

I shake my head. Not tonight. Absolutely not tonight.

His smile spreads over his cheeks as he sets the tray on the counter.

I pick up the bowl, tilt it to pour the batter into the tray.

He takes the tray and slides it into the oven.

Sets a timer for forty-five minutes.

His eyes fix on mine. "Not sure that's enough time." He brings his hands to my hips.

He lifts me into his arms like I'm weightless. I'm on the short side, but I'm definitely not weightless.

Walker carries me to the couch and lays me on my back.

I stare up at him as I sink into the leather.

He pushes my dress up my thighs. Places his body between my legs. Leans down to bring his lips to mine.

My hand goes to his hair.

I hold his head against mine.

I kiss him hard.

I want more of him. I want too much of him.

He drags his fingertips up my thigh. "I want you groaning my name when you come."

I nod. Yes. I want that too. I really, really want that.

He leans in.

This kiss is harder. Hungrier. Like he's as needy as I am.

His fingertips brush my inner thigh.

The other.

Higher.

Closer.

Almost.

There.

He brings his thumb to my clit.

Fuck, it's intense. I'm already wound tight. I'm already desperate to unravel.

I pull him closer.

Kiss him harder.

He groans against my mouth as he rubs me.

I wrap my legs around his hips.

His hand stays slow. Steady.

Fuck exercise.

This is how I want to be in my body.

His touch gets harder.

I nip at his lip. Tug at his hair.

"Fuck. Walker." I press my lips to his neck. Wrap both arms around his shoulders. I'm lying on my back, but, still, I feel like I'm about to fall over.

"Say it again," he murmurs into my neck.

"Walker."

He sucks on my tender skin.

Rubs me with his thumb.

Then he's teasing my sex with one finger.

Two.

"Fuck." I pull him closer. Shift my hips. Groan into his neck. "Deeper."

"I like you bossy, sweetness."

"Now."

"Not yet." He teases me. Again. Again.

Again.

I reach for his hair.

I dig my nails into his back, pressing his t-shirt into his skin. There's too much fabric in the way. I need his body against mine.

I need all these layers gone.

I need to be naked with someone. Physically, at least. 'Cause I'm sure as hell not about to do it emotionally.

I push his t-shirt to his shoulders.

He tosses it over his head.

I pull back enough to stare into his eyes. "Take off my dress."

He slides my dress up my thighs. "Lift your hips."

I do.

He pulls my dress over my ass, up my torso, over my head. It lands on the hardwood floor. "Take off the bra."

I reach around my back, unhook it, slide it off my shoulders.

He lets out a low, heavy groan. "Fuck. You have amazing tits." He presses his lips to mine. Soft. Then harder.

His tongue slides into my mouth. Swirls around mine.

He breaks our kiss to drag his lips down my neck. My collarbone. My chest.

He looks up at me as he takes my nipple into his mouth.

The flick of his tongue sends desire racing to my limbs. My sex clenches. My thighs shake.

I need more.

He moves to my other nipple and toys with it. He flicks his tongue against it. Sucks soft. Then hard. Then he's scraping his teeth against my tender bud.

Mmm. My hands knot in his hair.

I let my head fall back.

Let my eyelids flutter together.

He brings his fingers to my sex.

Teases again.

One finger.

Two.

Three.

Again.

Again.

"Please." I spread my legs. "I need you inside me."

"Fuck." His groan is heavy.

In one swift motion, he slides his fingers inside me.

It's intense. Like it's been months and not days. Like it's been an eternity.

It's different than last time.

I know him now. At least, I'm starting to.

I want more of *him*. Not of the sexy stranger who sets my body on fire. But the guy behind the dark eyes and the cocky smile.

I...

"Fuck." I shift my hips, pushing him deeper.

He moves his hand with a steady rhythm.

He rubs slow circles over my clit as he fucks me with his fingers.

As he sucks on my nipples.

Pressure pools inside me. Every thrust of his hand winds me tighter. Every brush of his thumb pushes me closer to the edge.

It feels so good.

But it's not enough.

I need *him* inside me.

I tug at his hair, bring his head to mine.

He leans onto his free arm.

Kisses me.

I groan against his mouth. I rock my hips to drive him deeper.

His next thrust pushes me over the edge.

All the tension inside me unravels. Pleasure spills through my torso, my thighs, my chest. It spills all the way to my fingers and toes.

I groan his name against his neck as I come.

It's so much better than my hand—and I fucked myself thinking of him every night this week.

I blink my eyes open. Look up at him.

He brushes my hair behind my ear. It's sweet. Too sweet. I can't handle that kind of intimacy. Not right now.

I reach for his jeans. Undo his button. His zipper. Cup him over his boxers.

I stare into his dark eyes. "Fuck me."

He lets out a low groan. "Spread your legs, sweetness."

I do.

He reaches into his back pocket. Pulls out something. A condom.

He presses it into my palm. Stands to push his jeans off his hips.

Then his boxers.

Fuck. He really is huge. Bigger than I remembered.

I motion *come here*.

He nudges my thighs apart so one is pressed against the back of the couch.

Then he plants between my legs.

I tear the wrapper and slide the condom over his cock.

He groans as my fingers brush his skin. "Legs around me."

I nod and wrap my legs around his waist.

He lowers his body onto mine. His lips brush my neck. His chest presses against my breasts. His cock nudges my sex.

One inch at a time, he slides inside me.

Mmm.

He groans into my neck.

I dig my nails into his skin. Pull him closer. Deeper.

It feels so good, his body pressed against mine, him inside me.

Better than anything has felt in a long, long time.

It's sharper. Clearer. Nothing is dulling the experience. Not booze or opiates or nerves.

I feel *everything*.

And fuck—this is a hell of a case for sobriety.

That's not going to fly at NA, but I don't care.

It's what I want.

Every second of anticipation. Every burst of pleasure. Every ounce of satisfaction.

"Fuck. You feel so good." He nips at my neck as he drives into me. It's hard. Steady.

I rock my hips to meet his movements.

It pushes him deeper.

It makes him groan.

"Fuck. Iris." He wraps his arms around me.

Moves harder.

Faster.

"Walker." I squeeze his waist with my hips. Press my fingers into his back. I need to hold on somehow. To keep my body locked with his.

He drives into me.

I rock against him.

Our groans bounce around the room.

My breath gets heavy.

His too.

Every thrust fills me with deep, pure pleasure. I have to close my eyes. To dig my nails into his skin. To soak in every ounce of it.

I pull him closer.

He drives harder.

Deeper.

Groans my name into my neck.

I do the same with his.

Walker. It sounds good on my lips. And the way it makes his breath hitch—

Fuck.

With his next thrust, I go over the edge. Pleasure spills through my torso. I groan his name as I come.

It makes him hungrier. Needier.

He moves harder. Faster.

His groans get low.

His thighs shake.

"Fuck. Iris." With his next thrust, he comes.

He pulses inside me as he thrusts through his orgasm.

Once he's spilled every drop, he pries his body from mine.

He goes to take care of the condom.
I sit up on the couch.
I may not know a lot about what I want.
But I know I want this.
A lot more of this.

Chapter Ten

WALKER

Iris doesn't invite herself to join me in the shower.

She makes a point of waiting until I'm done to move into the bathroom.

It's perfectly reasonable given our arrangement.

Hell—I usually fucking hate it when women step into the shower with me.

But with her, it feels weird. Like I'm being rude. Or she's being evasive. I don't know. I don't get relationship stuff.

I push it aside. It doesn't matter. We're having fun. Stressing about this shit is why I don't date.

Too much agony. Too much baggage. Too much everything.

I dress and move back into the kitchen. The cake is nearly done. The printed recipe is smudged with cocoa powder and sugar.

Like Iris's lips.

Uh-uh.

Not thinking that shit.

Not getting invested.

I'm making frosting.

Thinking about round two.

That's it.

I get out everything I need—coconut oil, powdered sugar, coffee, cocoa powder—and start measuring.

The shower turns off.

I add the last ingredient.

Iris moves into the main room, towel wrapped around her curvy body, wet hair sticking to her forehead.

I want it in my hands.

I want to rip that towel off her and pin her to the wall.

She presses her lips together. "It seems my clothes are on the floor."

"How'd that happen?"

"Curious."

Dry and wet fold together as I stir. I keep one eye on Iris.

She's shy about dropping her towel, donning her bra, stepping into her dress. Then her panties. "I'm not going out without these."

"I can't convince you?"

"You can try."

I want to. But I'm not sure *I* can stand how badly I'll want to fuck her if I know she's commando.

She brings the towel to her head to dry her hair. "Is the cake done?"

"Five minutes."

"Was that really forty minutes?"

"Did it feel like less?"

Her laugh lights up her blue eyes. They're gorgeous eyes. But even with her smiling, there's a sadness in them.

I hate it.

I want to destroy it.

I hate that I want to destroy it.

I offer her the spoon "You want the first taste?"

"Okay." She moves into the kitchen. Her fingers brush

mine as she takes the spoon. She brings it to her lips and licks a drop. "Mmm. Mocha icing is too good. It's criminal." Pleasure spills over her expression. Her eyes flutter closed. Her lips part with a sigh. Her brow softens.

It's like before.

Well, not quite.

But it's still fucking inviting.

She blinks her eyes open as she hands the spoon back. "I'm doing it again, aren't I?"

"You get off on caffeine."

She laughs. "Yeah. Kinda."

"Does tea inspire the same reaction?"

"It's not nearly as intense."

"Good to know." I lick icing from the spoon. It's too sweet for me, but it's still fucking good.

"Aren't you supposed to say something about how we already had dessert?"

"You giving me tips on my game again?"

"As long as you still need them."

"Turns out you're not supposed to frost a cake until it's cool."

"Ah."

"Which means you'll have to come back here after dinner."

Her lips curl into a smile. "You had a master plan?"

"If making you come again counts as a master plan, yeah."

IRIS SMOOTHS HER SKIRT AS SHE LOOKS AROUND THE restaurant's courtyard. "Hmm."

"Hmm?"

"Candles. Flowers." She nods to the vase with a single rose on the side of the table. "Outdoor atmosphere."

"Yeah?"

"Romantic."

I shake my head. "All the places around here are like this."

"Perfect for a date?"

"Homey."

Her eyes meet mine. "I was going to ask about that."

I arch a brow.

"This neighborhood is all families."

"And?"

"And you're not exactly that type of guy."

"You're stereotyping me again."

She laughs. "Yeah. A little." She picks up her menu and runs her fingers over its edges. "But still. You could live in Venice Beach. Closer to the shop."

"It's more expensive there."

"Is that it?"

"Mostly." I like being this close to the beach. And far away from everyone else. And, hell, I like the quiet. There's enough noise at the shop all day.

She turns her gaze to her menu. Presses her lips together. "You think it has something to do with growing up in Beverly Hills?"

Probably. I'm used to this kind of suburban paradise in the city, families and expensive cars everywhere. But I'm not *that* far into Santa Monica. My building is all young professionals and artists. Well, artists who can afford the obscene rent.

"Shit." She bites her lip. "I'm doing it again."

"Iris the shrink."

"At least I caught it." She closes her menu, sets it on the table, and looks to me. "No more. I promise."

"I don't believe you."

"You shouldn't. I will. I'm awful."

"You are." I lean a little closer. The moonlight brings out her blue eyes. "But I like it."

She draws circles on the menu with her pointer finger. "I'll tone it down. I swear."

I lean back. "We'll see."

"Yeah." She copies my posture. Hangs her arm over her chair. Adopts a disaffected expression.

My laugh feels fuller than usual. "You really nail me."

"It's the other way around."

"That's cheesy."

"Still."

The server stops at our table. We order dinner and hand over our menus.

She doesn't get a drink.

I follow her lead.

It's not unusual. Especially at a place without a full bar. Not everyone is into wine—fuck knows I'm not.

But still.

It seems intentional.

I straighten my back. Move closer. "How are your steps going?"

Her cheeks flush. "Okay, I guess. I feel embarrassed even thinking about it."

"Then why do it?"

"What else am I gonna do?"

"Live your life."

"Yeah..." She pulls her arm across her chest. Runs her fingers over the ink on her forearm.

You are not your mistakes.

I still don't know what it means.

What she's trying to escape.

But I want to.

"What are the other steps?" I bring my glass to my lips. Take a long sip. Fuck, I'm thirsty. She wore me out.

"It's boring."

"Not to me."

She wraps her fingers around her glass. Stares at the water like it holds all the secrets to the universe. "A lot of basic stuff. Eat right. Sleep right. Exercise."

"Sounds reasonable."

"Yeah. I guess. It all takes so much time and energy though. Don't you think?" Her eyes go to my chest. My shoulders. My forearms. "No, I guess you wouldn't."

I chuckle. "I didn't realize I was derailing your life plan with that cake."

"It was sweet. Different." She brings her glass to her lips and takes a long sip. Another. She swallows hard. Wipes her lips with her thumb. "There's other stuff."

"I imagine."

Her eyes go to the table. Her voice gets nervous. "Get in touch with old friends. Make new ones."

"How's that going?"

Her lips curl into a half smile. "I'm here."

Yeah. But she's not quite here. She's thinking something.

I'm not used to it.

I don't like it.

I want all her attention. "And Sandy?"

She laughs. "Yeah. And Sandy."

"You don't like her?"

"No. I do. Just she..."

"Can't stop gushing about her boyfriend?"

"Exactly." Iris laughs. "I thought I was the only person who found it obnoxious."

I shake my head. "I figured it was a girl thing. That he had some amazing trait I couldn't see."

"No. He's nice. And... nice." She pulls the paper off her straw and slides it in her glass. "How did you meet?"

"I did her sleeve."

She nods. "It's good."

"Thanks."

"Really. You're a talented guy."

"I know." I lean back. Press my palm into my thighs. Truth be told, I don't know what to do with praise. I'm not used to it. Not from someone I trust.

She stares back into my eyes. "I'm working on that one."

"The guys at the shop, we do a lot of shit. You're welcome to join."

"Oh baby, you're seducing me with that invitation."

I laugh. Okay. That wasn't smooth. But I'm not sure how to handle this. Usually, I'm trying to draw a hard line between my life and a woman's. "It's fun. Leighton usually comes. And Emma and Kaylee tag along too."

"Who?"

"Brendon's little sister and his girlfriend."

"Doesn't help." Her lips curl into a smile. "But thanks. I'll consider that."

"What else is on the list?"

"Figuring out your goals and going after them. I'm good on that one. School." Her posture relaxes. Like she's sinking into the conversation.

"You have anything else?"

"Not right now." Her eyes meet mine. "What about you?"

Just keeping Sabrina out of my life. And making sure she doesn't OD in some shady motel.

Yeah, they're contradictory goals.

But that's life.

"It's something." She leans in. "Something you don't want to tell me."

"It's nothing."

She cocks her head to one side, deciding if she believes me. "I know you're easy, breezy surfer boy, but you must have something."

"No. My life is exactly how I want it." Except for shit with my sister, it's perfect.

"Exactly? You wouldn't change a single thing?"

"I'd take more money, yeah. But otherwise, no. I'm happy." In theory. In reality, everything feels stale. I need different. Fresh. Her.

"Wow."

"Wow?"

She leans back. Presses her lips together. "That's... impressive. Or bullshit. I'm not sure."

My shrug doesn't come as easily as it usually does.

The server interrupts my train of thought.

She drops off our dishes. Salmon and sautéed vegetables for Iris. Steak and greens for me.

"See." She picks up her fork. "Eating right."

"I have enough game to know not to comment on that."

"You sure?" She stabs a square of yellow squash and brings it to her lips.

"I am." I pick up my fork and knife. "Anything else on the list?"

"Reading."

"When did you start this?"

"Officially?"

"Yeah." I bring a slice of steak to my mouth. It's good. Rare. Salty. But it doesn't satisfy. I don't want food. I want to have her again.

"I guess I haven't. Not officially."

"Are you going to?"

"I don't know. That's even more cheesy."

"It suits you."

"Hey." She laughs as she flips me off.

My lips curl into a smile. She has a cute laugh. And a cute *don't fuck with me* look. "What else?"

"Journaling. Trying new things. Why are you so interested?"

"I've never met someone so methodical about getting over a breakup."

Her lips press together. Her eyes turn down. "How else are you supposed to get over anything?"

"Feel it out."

She shakes her head. "Then how do you know when you're there? "

"How you feel."

"I'd rather have metrics. It's easier to know if I'm making progress. Like the way you lift weights."

"You have no idea how I lift weights."

"Okay. How some people lift weights. You have numbers. How many pounds you can lift or how many pull-ups you can do or whatever. That's how you keep track of progress."

"And by how strong I feel."

She sticks her tongue out. "Numbers are a better measurement."

"According to who?"

"Me."

"Not everything fits into numbers."

"Yeah. But most things do." She scoops veggies into her mouth. "You were right. This place is good. Romantic. But good."

"Orgasms per fuck?"

Her cheeks flush. "Yeah. But you have to define what a fuck is."

"How do you?"

"Um. Well. One session. Where you stay in the same place. Start to finish."

"How am I doing?"

"Excellent marks."

"I feel judged."

"Then why'd you ask?"

I stare back into her eyes. I don't know what to make of her. This whole methodical attempt at self-improvement is the opposite of the way I approach my life.

I know better than to write off shit.

If it works, it works.

But why does her life need this much fixing?

"How do you feel?" I cut a slice of steak. "You never said."

She presses her lips together. Her eyes go to the table. "Listen, Walker, I like you and I really do want to be friends. But this is kinda personal."

"I get that." If there's anything I understand, it's keeping shit that bothers me locked up somewhere safe.

"This... um... this breakup." She fumbles over the word. "It's been hard. All my old friends are on his side. And um, everything is just different. You know? I feel different. And I spend my time differently. And I'm trying to do all the things I used to love, but they feel different. I don't love them as much as I used to and I don't know why or how to change it and... And it's just a lot. Okay?"

"Yeah."

"So, can we talk about something else?"

"A breakup did all this?"

Her brow furrows. Like she's thinking of an explanation. Or maybe a lie. "It doesn't matter. I want my life to change. So I'm changing it."

"That's admirable."

"Thanks." Her eyes go to her tattoo. *You are not your mistakes*. "What, um, what do you do for fun? When you aren't doing this? Or surfing?"

"I read a lot. Watch a lot of movies. Go out with Dean. Or with the other guys. Work out. Go hiking."

She nods. "Nature. I think that's one of them."

"We're going on a hike next weekend. You want to join?"

"Oh. Maybe. I don't want to impose."

"Nah. You're welcome."

"You and..."

"And Dean. We're both working until early afternoon. We're all working all the time. It's a whole thing. We're supposed to hire another artist, but Ryan hates everyone."

"Is that his thing?"

"Yeah. He hates everything. He was never a jolly guy, but he's been especially miserable since his ex walked out on him. You two could commiserate on that front." If the breakup thing isn't bullshit.

Tension spreads through my upper back.

I don't like her lying to me.

But I shouldn't care.

This is casual. There's nothing about full disclosure in our agreement. I don't have any rights to her secrets.

So why the fuck do I want them this badly?

"You're really into this whole ten step thing," she says.

"Told you. It's different. Interesting."

"I get that. But I don't need anyone walking me through it. I'm a grown-up. I can find my own new things to do and make my own friends."

"Iris, you have me all wrong."

"Do I?"

"My motives are far less pure."

She raises a brow.

"It's not about helping you find yourself."

"It's not?"

"No. It's about checking out your ass in yoga pants."

"What if I hike in sweat pants?"

"Fuck. Didn't consider that possibility."

She laughs. "This is why methodical works. Besides, you can check out my ass naked anytime."

"Yeah. Or I could do both."

"Hmm. Persuasive."

"You don't want to go, say so. It won't hurt my feelings."

"Not at all?"

My smile spreads over my cheeks. "You like thinking of me wounded."

"Maybe." She scoops a piece of salmon into her mouth, chews, swallows. "You swear your motives are all located south of your waist?"

"On my right hand."

She shakes her head.

"That isn't enough?"

"Nope."

"I work with my hands."

"You have a left hand. You'll learn to make do."

I can't help but laugh. This girl does something to me. I like it. Even though I shouldn't. "You want me to swear on my cock?"

"It is the source of your motives. Supposedly."

"I swear on my cock. I'm inviting you hiking because I want to spend the afternoon staring at your ass then stripping you out of your sweaty clothes and fucking you."

Her cheeks flush.

"I'll skip the shirt."

She holds out her hand. "Sold."

We shake.

Chapter Eleven

WALKER

My cell buzzes in my jeans.

My head fills with thoughts of Iris.

Lying on my couch.

Pulling her dress to her waist.

Flipping over, arching her back, and begging me to take her.

But she isn't the one calling me.

Incoming Call from Sabrina Williams.

No fucking way.

I stare at my cell until the call goes to voicemail.

A moment later, a new message notification pops up on my cell.

Then a fucking text.

Sabrina: Can we talk? Mom and Dad are driving me crazy. I miss my baby brother.

Walker: I have plans today. I'll call next weekend.

Or never.

Never is good.

I run my hand through my hair. I need to talk to my parents. No, that isn't enough.

I need to convince them to actually make due on their threats. The gentle approach isn't doing shit to get my sister clean, but they never manage to muster up the balls for tough love.

I slide my cell into my jeans.

Iris is going to be here soon. We're going to drive up to Malibu and take in a beautiful, blue day. And then I'm going to drive her home and fuck her senseless.

Today is a good day.

Bree isn't ruining that.

I grab a stool and take a seat at the counter next to Kaylee. She's writing something on her laptop. Every few minutes, she looks up to ogle Brendon. She gets off on watching him work. And on his dark eyes, dark hair, dark tattoos—she gets off on pretty much every single thing about him.

She's like a cartoon character with hearts in her eyes.

He is too.

It's sickening. Even if I'm happy for them.

"Hey." She looks up from her laptop. Offers me a smile. Then her green eyes are on her boyfriend.

"Dreamy, isn't he?"

She laughs. "I know you're making fun of me, but I'm going to agree anyway." She sighs with pleasure. "He's just so... focused. And tall. And beautiful."

"He is tall."

"He's everything." She sets her elbow on the counter, tilts her head, rests her hand on her palm.

It's cute how gaga she is. I'm pretty sure Kaylee has been in love with Brendon for eight or nine years now. She's been his little sister's Emma's best friend forever and she's pretty much always had a crush on him.

At some point last year, he started wanting her too.

It was fucked-up shit, because she wasn't eighteen yet.

She's only barely eighteen now.

But I do get it. Not for me, but for him. The two of them giggle like crazy around each other, share a million inside jokes, have complimentary tastes in fuck.

Back then, she was innocent the way he likes. Now... not as much.

He finishes a line, wipes his brow, turns back to her. Shoots her *fuck me* eyes.

She lets out a wistful sigh.

I laugh. "You've got it bad."

"I'm madly in love with my boyfriend, yes. You should try it."

"No thanks."

"Have you ever been in love?"

"No." But I've loved someone and that was plenty to teach me not to do it again.

"Then how can you know you're not interested?"

"Have you ever tied your boyfriend up?"

"No." Her nose screws with distaste. "Of course not."

"Then how do you know you don't like it?"

"That's a stupid question."

"It's the same question."

She shakes her head *your loss.*

I flip through my sketchbook, find my next mockup, bring it to the scanner, and get to work on making a temporary tattoo.

The printer hums.

I grab the paper and scissors. Bring them back to the counter.

Dean is on the opposite side of the counter. He plants his hands on the plastic and leans closer. "Kinky Kay. You working on something good?"

"Maybe." She presses her lips together.

"You are." He laughs. "You ever gonna show off this dirty book of yours?"

"When's the last time you read a book?" I ask.

He turns to me. "It happened once."

Kaylee laughs. "Back in high school?"

"Were they out of SparkNotes?" I tease.

"And CliffsNotes. That was bullshit." He shakes his head with mock offense. Turns to Kay. "I'll make an exception for your masterpiece."

"Uh-huh." She presses her laptop shut.

He mimes being stabbed in the gut. Stumbles backward. Falls onto the floor and stretches out like a star fish.

"He's demo-ing his favorite sex position," I say.

"Huh?" Kaylee raises a brow.

"You've never heard of starfish?" I ask.

She folds her arms. "Really?"

"Yeah. It's when the person on the bottom just lays there. No moaning, no panting, no thrusting, no touching. The pinnacle of a bad lay," I say.

"Yeah. There's a reason why Walker is so familiar." Dean jumps—actually jumps—to his feet. "It's his signature. Only he does it on top. Why do you think he never does repeats?"

"I've never seen you with the same woman twice," she says.

"Have you ever seen me with a woman?" he asks.

"Well, no... but I haven't seen Walker with one either. You never invite me out," she says.

"You're not twenty-one," I say.

"Uh-huh." She shakes her head, not buying it.

"Tell me, Kay." Dean leans in close enough to stage whisper. "Brendon ever starfish?"

Her cheeks flush. But she doesn't look embarrassed. More turned on. "No."

"He into you doing it?" Dean asks.

She shakes her head.

He looks to me. "She's barely fazed by this now."

"You have to up your game," I say.

"Seriously. How could Brendon do this to me? How could he corrupt you like that? Doesn't he know it's easier to torture you if you're a blushing virgin?" Dean asks.

"That must be painful for you," I say.

"Thank you for appreciating that." He's teasing, yeah, but there's sincerity in his voice. "You have all your shit for this afternoon or you need to stop at your place?"

"I have it." My eyes go to the clock. Ten minutes to go. "I invited Iris."

"Oh." Dean blinks twice. He runs a hand though his shaggy hair. "You're still hanging out with her?"

"We have an arrangement," I say.

"Like a girlfriend?" Concern fills his blue eyes.

It's weird. Unlike him.

"No. More like fuck buddies." And why the fuck does that bother him?

"I thought that was code for someone you only call when you want some." Brendon moves forward. He motions for us to clear the desk. "I have to check out. If you're done being idiots."

"You know we'll never be done with that." Dean's voice lifts back to bouncy.

Kaylee shoots him a look. He shoots it back. I have no idea what it means, but they seem to understand each other.

I move out from behind the desk. "You two want to join?"

"No, I have work in two hours." Kaylee runs her fingers along the edge of her laptop. "You're really seeing someone, Walker?"

"I see her naked in my bed, yeah." What the hell could bother *her* about me dating someone? She's the poster child for love being great. "Is that a problem with anyone else?"

"No. It's great. Fucking fantastic." Dean steps backward. "I'm gonna change."

"Into a tolerable human being?" I ask.

Kaylee laughs. "That's cheesy." She looks to me. "How does that work?"

"Fuck buddies? Really, K.K.?" It stands for Kinky Kaylee. That started as a joke with Dean a million years ago. "You're not that naïve. Not after six months fucking Brendon."

He shoots me a *grow up* look.

I can't argue with that. Brendon has his shit together as much as anyone could. When his parents died, he stepped up to take care of his little sister. He's basically her dad. Which makes it even more fucked that he's sleeping with her best friend.

But, hey, who am I to judge?

It's not like I always make good life choices.

"Like Brendon said, it means something different to everyone." Kaylee slides off her stool. "What does it mean to you?"

"I don't define things like that." I run a hand through my hair. Since when does anyone care about my sex?

The bell rings as the door swings open. Ryan steps inside the shop. He's wearing all black—his jeans, his t-shirt, his expression. It's the same as always, *the world is a piece of shit, and you're a piece of shit, and I'm not interested in your shit.*

He looks to the three of us. "You ever get tired of gossip?"

"No," I say. "You want to go on a hike?"

"You think I'm here for my health?" He drops his back-pack in his suite. Shakes his head *kids today*.

Brendon nods *yeah, he's right*.

They're only a few years older than Dean and I are—we're all in our twenties—but they act like they're old sages.

I look to him. "You coming or not?"

"You should," Kaylee jumps in. "I'll be fine."

He arches a brow. "You sure?"

"Yeah." She smooths her pink dress. Adjusts her blue glasses. "I have to change for work soon. Just lock this for me?" She taps her laptop.

He nods.

Dean shakes his head as he returns to the main room—now clad in basketball shorts and a muscle tank. "Mr. Brooding is joining us?"

"Yeah." What the fuck is Dean's problem? Brendon joins us on hikes all the time. Ryan too. Hell, Leighton, Emma, and Kaylee join last minute all the time. He's never had a problem before.

"Leave for your shit or get to work," Ryan calls.

He has a point. I pack up my shit.

Dean does the same.

Brendon finishes with his customer then whispers something to his girlfriend.

The bell rings.

Iris steps through the door, tight black shorts clinging to her hips, loose blue tank hanging off her shoulders.

All the bullshit at the shop fades away.

I want her against the wall.

My hands under that tank top.

Those shorts at her knees.

The rest of the world gone.

No worrying about my best friend's attitude. Or my sister destroying herself. Or how the fuck I'll get my parents to help when they're textbook enablers.

Dean steps out of his suite. "Iris, right?"

"Yeah." She offers her hand.

He shakes. "I guess you're coming with us."

"Walker invited me. Is that okay?" She bites her lip. "He promised I wasn't imposing. If I am—"

"Nah. The more the merrier. Brendon's coming too." Dean smiles wide. He sells it. To her.

I know better.

I know his bullshit too well.

I grab my backpack and move to the door. "You ready to go?" I look to Dean. "You and Brendon can meet us there."

"I didn't drive." He fights the irritation seeping into his voice.

"It's only five blocks to my place." Brendon steps forward. "We'll grab my car there."

"Awesome." Dean folds his arms.

Worry spreads over Iris's expression.

I don't know what the hell Dean doesn't like about her, but I don't care.

I like her.

I want her in my life.

That's how it's going to be.

Chapter Twelve

WALKER

I wipe my brow as I step out of the car. Even in the shade, it's hot.

Iris presses her door closed. She slings her backpack over her shoulders and lets out a soft sigh. Her lips press together. Her eyes meet mine. "You're still wearing the shirt."

"I am."

"We have a deal."

I pull my t-shirt over my head and toss it in the car. This is also going to get on Dean's nerves, but he can kiss my ass. I put up with a truckload of his attitude and he can't tolerate me inviting someone on a hike?

Iris moves around the front of the car.

She slides her backpack off one shoulder and pulls out a tube of sunscreen. She's slow about popping the cap and squeezing it onto her fingers.

She was quiet the entire drive. She turned the radio on to the local rock station and stared out the window. Because of Dean's bullshit or because of something else?

"You okay?" I turn so she can get my back.

"Yeah. A little tired."

"Not enough coffee?"

"Never enough coffee." Her fingers glide over my right shoulder. She takes her time smoothing out the lotion and rubbing it in.

It's more sweet than sexual.

More domestic than carnal.

I shouldn't like it.

But I do.

She squeezes sunscreen on my other shoulder. Takes her time rubbing it in. "He's your friend. I'm sure you know him better. But I read people pretty well."

"Iris the shrink?"

"Yeah. And he doesn't want me here."

She's right. He doesn't. But I don't know why. "We invite people to join all the time. He's probably in a mood."

"Okay." She drags her fingers down my back. "You feel good against my hands."

I let my voice drop an octave. "Yeah?"

"That too. Later." She presses her palm against my lower back. "Turn around. I'll get your chest."

I do. "I'll return the favor."

Her lips press into a smile. "I'm already covered."

"Cruel."

She laughs as she spreads sunscreen over my pecs. "I do what I can." Her eyes stay on her work. She's thorough. Methodical. She finishes one area and checks it over before moving on to the next.

Her brow furrows. Her lips turn down.

She's still upset.

It can't all be Dean.

But what the hell is it?

She looks up at me. "Done."

"I'll have to make it up to you somehow."

Her blush is slight. "You will." She moves closer.

I slide my arm around her waist. Press my palm into her lower back. "Come here."

She rises to her tiptoes and presses her lips to mine.

My other hand goes to her hair. I hold her head against mine as I slide my tongue into her mouth.

Her fingers curl into my skin.

She jumps backward as a honking horn cuts through the air.

That's Brendon's car parked on the other side of the street. He's standing in front of the driver's seat shaking his head. Dean's leaning over the center console, his hand on the steering wheel, his eyes on me and Iris.

Fucking asshole.

Usually, I don't mind Dean's antics. They're pretty entertaining. But right now, I don't have energy for this shit. I'm spending all of it keeping Sabrina out of my thoughts.

Iris pulls her arms over her chest. Taps the sunscreen against her hip.

Brendon shoots me a *what's wrong with him* look.

I shrug. Hell if I know.

Dean steps out of the car. "Didn't realize we were heading to the gun show." He pulls his t-shirt over his head and tosses it on the passenger seat.

"Your sweat isn't stinking up my car," Brendon says.

"There's no sweat. I just put it on." He motions to the garment. "Smell it."

"No thanks." Brendon moves around the car to push the passenger door closed. He clicks the electronic lock. "You two ready?"

"Yeah." I slide my arm around Iris's waist. Fuck, I'm being an obnoxious caveman about protecting my woman and she isn't even mine.

She leans in a little closer. "You look good, Dean." She

unpeels her arms from her chest and offers him her sunscreen. "You need some of this?"

"Yeah. Sure. Toss it over," he says.

She does. It lands three feet to his left.

Iris laughs. "Sorry. No hand-eye coordination."

"It's cool." He bends to pick it up. Undoes the cap. Squeezes it into his hand. "Fuck knows there's shit I'm not good at."

"A long list," Brendon agrees.

Dean moves onto the trail, spreading sunscreen as he walks. He's making a show of it. It's the kind of thing he does when women are around. *Look at my bod.*

But he knows Iris and I have an arrangement.

It must be a habit.

It better be a habit.

"It's fucking hot." Dean tosses the sunscreen back to Iris.

I step forward to catch it.

"Thanks." She slides it into her backpack. "Is it always this hot in the spring?"

"You're not from SoCal?" he asks.

"The valley. You pretty much always feel like you're standing under a heat lamp." She moves closer. "Who was the girl in the cardigan?"

"Brendon's girlfriend," Dean says. "She had to work. Too bad. We're all one big, happy family."

"Right." Brendon shakes his head *what the hell is wrong with you?*

I ignore it. Take Iris's hand. Focus on the scenery.

It's always beautiful here. Lemon sun. Bright blue sky. Sandy beige path surrounded by dusty green brush. The hills go forever.

Brendon moves ahead of us. He's not interested in our bullshit.

He never is.

Dean follows his lead. Picks up the pace.

I hang back with Iris. There's only a dozen feet between us, but it's intentional. It's a *fuck you.*

"He has to give Brendon shit about Kay." Okay, he's being an asshole. But that's not her problem.

"Hmm."

I rub her hand with my thumb. "It was a whole fucked-up thing."

"Yeah?" Her voice perks.

"You like gossip?"

"Who doesn't?"

I lean in to whisper and I explain the whole sordid story.

She nods and uh-huhs through every detail.

When I'm done, we're a hundred feet behind. Brendon and Dean are standing at the top of a hill. Brendon is looking out at the view. Dean is shaking his head *too slow, huh?*

"I guess we can't walk and whisper." She tugs at my arm as she moves faster.

I keep pace with her. This is a slow hike. More of a stroll. Usually, that annoys me. Usually, Dean and I get competitive about who can finish faster.

Right now, I like it.

I want to stop and smell the roses. Well, the ocean breeze and the brush.

Iris squeezes my hand as we catch up to the guys.

"Trading secrets?" Dean asks.

"Nothing big." Iris forces her lips into a smile.

"Uh-huh," Dean says.

"She, um, your girlfriend. She seemed nice." She turns to Brendon. "Does she work at the shop too?"

He shakes his head. "She hangs out sometimes." He motions to the trail *shall we?*

I nod and we resume the hike at an easy pace.

"Do you guys ever bring girls to the shop?" Iris asks.

"No." Brendon chuckles. "They stick to their bedrooms."

"Jealous?" Dean raises a brow.

"Yeah. I'd much rather fuck some woman I'm not gonna remember than one I love," Brendon says. "I'm seething."

"A lot of guys feel that way." Iris pulls her hand to her side. Moves forward. "Dean, you must."

"That an invitation?" He turns back to her to arch a brow. "Sorry, but I don't do threesomes anymore."

"Oh. You did once?" She tilts her head to one side, assessing his words.

"Had a phase." Dean turns back. "It's pretty simple. It's more fun to play the field. Easier."

She nods. "Yeah. I like it better too."

"Oh." His voice relaxes. "You and Walker aren't—"

"We're just having fun." She looks to me and arches a brow. *Right?*

I nod. Yeah. Of course. Fun. No getting hung up on the sadness behind her gorgeous blue eyes. Or what the hell she's really trying to get over. Or what her tattoo means.

She catches up to Dean. Walks in time with him. "Do you have a type?"

Brendon chuckles. "Anything with spread legs."

"Hey." He feigns offense. "Any *woman* with spread legs." He points to me. "Your boy isn't much more discriminating."

Iris makes eye contact. *Really?*

I shrug. "I enjoy women. That a crime?"

"Pretty sure a heartbeat is all either of them need," Brendon says.

"We can't all need a perfect little sub." Dean flips him off.

Brendon rolls his eyes.

"Oh." Iris presses her lips together. "You and... you're into BDSM?"

"It's not bondage or bust, but yeah. I enjoy ordering my girl around and tying her to my bed from time to time." He shoots Dean a cutting look then shoots me the same one. "Don't enjoy the commentary."

"So, you also have regular sex?" Iris asks.

The look he shoots her is more curious.

Interested even. "Yeah. All the time."

"Starfish?" Dean asks.

Brendon rolls his eyes.

Iris laughs. "Is that still a thing?"

"You know a guy? Or do it yourself? You can tell me." Dean mimes zipping his lips. "I can keep a secret."

She looks back to me. "Can he?"

I shake my head. Not even a little.

"My ex... sometimes. Not usually, just when he... just sometimes." Her gaze goes to the view. "God. This is beautiful."

"He say that too?" Dean asks.

She laughs. "No. He was light with the compliments."

"And my boy Williams?" Dean asks.

"My lips are sealed." She laughs.

Dean is teasing her.

Now he's okay with her?

What the fuck happened in the last ten minutes?

Iris stops in a patch of shade. She bends over to set her backpack on the ground and pulls out a water bottle. "Is he always this..."

"Annoying?" I offer.

"Hot and cold," she says.

Brendon stops in the shade next to her. He looks to me and raises a brow. "You really don't get why he's pissed?"

I shrug.

"Fuck, you're like a teenager." Brendon shakes his head.

"That mean you want to fuck me?" I ask.

He doesn't take the bait. "You're not my type."

"It's obvious. He feels threatened." Iris looks up at me.

"Like you're gonna stop hanging out with him now that you have a girlfriend."

"But we're not—"

"I know. But maybe he doesn't believe that." She sprinkles water over her forehead. It drips off her chin and onto her chest.

"He gets the same way whenever Sabrina shows up," Brendon says.

Iris turns to him. "Who?"

He shoots me a *really?* look.

Really. It's my baggage. I can keep it close.

She turns to me. "Who's Sabrina?"

"My sister." I run my hand through my hair. Suddenly, the sun feels too hot. My feet are tired. My back is aching. My stance is awkward.

"Did she and Dean date or something?" She cocks her head to one side, trying to understand.

"No. It's nothing like that." I offer her my hand.

She takes it.

Brendon shoots me a look then moves forward. "I'll stop him at the next hill."

"Yeah." I turn to Iris.

She's looking up at me with those beautiful blue eyes. "Why does your friend not like your sister showing up?"

"He just doesn't."

She presses her lips together. "That's it? He just doesn't."

"Yeah."

"Really?"

"Yeah. We've all been friends forever. They've always hated each other." That's bullshit, but it's the story I'm selling.

Iris nods like she believes me.

But I can tell she doesn't.

~

SHE'S QUIET FOR THE REST OF THE HIKE.

Dean's more friendly and more obnoxious. But normal obnoxious, not I don't like you having a girl-space-friend obnoxious.

He carries the conversation—Brendon's never been much of a talker.

I try to focus on the strain in my legs, the sun on my skin, the crystal blue ocean spreading over the horizon.

But I don't.

The ocean makes me think of Iris's eyes.

It's not nearly as brilliant or deep. Not nearly as inviting.

My attention stays on her. The way her lips turn down or up. The way her hips sway as she walks. Where her gaze shifts—sometimes the sky, sometimes the ocean, sometimes Dean or Brendon or my chest or waist or ass, but never my eyes.

It's the same the way back.

It's the same when we get into the car. She clicks her seatbelt, flips the radio on, leans back, and looks out the window.

"You okay?" I turn the car on. Hit my blinker.

"Yeah. Tired. It felt good moving my body. I'm sure that's obvious to you, but it's been a long time since I've really exercised. I used to sit a lot. At work. And I do now. I mostly sit and study. So it's kind of a revelation that moving feels good. Or that hiking feels good. But it really is amazing, the fresh air and the view. And everything."

"It is." I turn. "We can do it again sometime."

"Yeah. We should. But, um, later. I'm wiped. It was a lot." She leans down to pull her water bottle from her backpack. "Not for you, I guess?"

"The heat always drains me."

"Yeah." She plays with the cap of her water bottle. "Me too." She takes a long sip. "I'm good. Really."

She's not.

But then neither am I.

~

I PULL ONTO MY STREET.

Iris leans forward to turn the music down. The sounds of pop-rock fall to a murmur—where do they get off continuing to call this station K *Rock* and playing this stuff?

"I, um." She pulls her arms over her chest. "I think I should head home. It's late."

It's not. The sun is just starting to set.

"I took the bus to the shop." She pulls her backpack onto her lap. "Do you think you can drop me off in Brentwood? It's Saturday, so there shouldn't be too much traffic."

"Yeah, sure." I pull into my parking space. "But I gotta piss first."

"Oh. Sure."

"You can stay in the car or come in."

"I'll use the bathroom too." She shakes her empty water bottle. "And refill this."

I turn the car off, undo my seatbelt, pull the door open, press it shut.

Is this it?

The second shit gets complicated, we walk?

Am I that unable to discuss Sabrina with someone?

To share the one fucking thing I can't figure out with someone?

Iris slides her backpack onto one shoulder and presses the door closed. Her eyes meet mine for a second then they're on the concrete.

I motion *after you*.

She moves up the steps and to the door.

I slide my key into the lock and turn the handle. "You can go first."

"Okay." She moves through the living room and goes straight to the bathroom.

I press the door closed and lean against it.

This is bullshit.

I'm better than this. Stronger than this.

A few moments later, Iris steps out of the bathroom. She moves into the kitchen with careful steps. Focuses all her attention on filling her water bottle.

I head to the bathroom, piss, wash my hands.

When I step into the main room, she's sitting on the counter, tapping her feet together, sucking on her water bottle.

"If you want to know something, you can ask," I say.

She shakes her head. "I tried that. You fed me a line."

I don't have a comeback.

"It's fine, Walker. This is supposed to be easy. Casual. Whatever it is that's going on with your friend or your sister is none of my business."

"But you want to know?"

"It doesn't matter." She looks at her blue and grey sneakers. "It's none of my business."

"You can want to know."

"Okay. I do. There's a story there. And I don't like you pretending there isn't."

"And that shit about your breakup?"

Her blue eyes bore into mine. "That isn't shit. I left Ross last December. Or maybe it was mutual. It's hard to say."

"How?"

"I made a choice. He couldn't live with it."

"What choice?"

"To change my life."

"That's bullshit."

"No, it's true."

I move toward her. "Yeah, it's true. I believe that." I stare back into those blue eyes as I place myself between her legs. "But it's half the story. And your breakup isn't why you're doing all this self-help bullshit."

"Don't call it bullshit."

"You did first."

"Even so." She presses her knees against my hips. "We should head out."

"If that's what you want." I slide one hand around her waist. "Is it?"

She swallows hard. "I don't know."

"I don't believe that either."

"I don't like being questioned."

"I don't like being lied to."

"It's not a lie!"

"Misled. I don't believe you're doing this shit because you left Ross. The way you say his name—he doesn't mean anything to you."

She tugs at my t-shirt. "What the hell do you know about relationships?"

"Enough."

"How?"

"I've seen them."

She shakes her head. "It's not the same." But it's there in her eyes. She doesn't believe the story she's selling. We both know we're both full of shit.

"Did you love him?"

Her eyes turn down. "I don't know. I thought so, at the time, but now... I don't think I was in the headspace to really love someone."

"How do you know the difference?"

"You have to trust someone to fall in love with them. To

trust them to catch you. And we didn't have that. I've never had that."

"Even when you were a kid?"

"Yeah. You've been in love?"

I shake my head. "Infatuated. But never love."

"Recently?"

"No."

"Are you..." She presses her lips together. "Your sister... is there more to that story?"

I nod. "And you changing your life?"

"Yeah. But I don't want to talk about it."

"We don't have to talk."

"Oh." She slides her legs around my waist.

I run my fingers over her inner thigh. She wants to be out of her head. I want to be out of my head. I really, really fucking want to dive between her legs.

This is perfect.

I just need to ease her into it.

I bring my lips to her ears. "I can drive you home. Or we can stay here and not talk. It's up to you."

Chapter Thirteen

WALKER

Her hand slides under my t-shirt.

Her eyes fix on mine. "Let's not talk."

I nod as I pull her closer.

I lean down and press my lips to hers.

She kisses back as she digs her fingers into my sides.

Her thighs squeeze my hips.

Fuck. She tastes good. Like salt and sunscreen and Iris.

I pull her tank top to her shoulders. She breaks our kiss so I can pull it over her head.

Then she's tugging at my shirt.

It's messy.

Hungry.

"Bed. Now." I slide my hands to her ass. "I've got you."

She nods as she wraps her arms around me.

I lift her from the counter.

She clutches at my t-shirt as I carry her across the living room. "Are you really doing this?"

"Yeah." I kick the bedroom door open then lean down to lay her on the bed.

She looks up at me. "Show off."

"You love it."

She shakes her head, but she's smiling.

All the fucked-up shit from today is already gone.

And the fucked-up shit from every other day is slipping away, bit by bit.

I press her knees apart. "Take off your bra."

"Take off your shorts." She stares back into my eyes. "You first."

I step out of my shoes. Peel off my socks.

She laughs. "Smooth."

"Thanks." I push my basketball shorts off my hips.

The teasing look falls right off Iris's face.

Her teeth sink into her lip. Her blue eyes fill with desire.

She arches her back as she unhooks her bra and tosses it aside.

Fuck, this view puts the Malibu hills to shame.

She's splayed out on the bed for me in nothing but a pair of tiny shorts. And she's staring up at me like she needs me more than she's ever needed anything.

"Boxers." Her voice gets heavy. Needy. She brings her feet together. Kicks off one shoe. Then the other. Then the socks.

It's smooth.

But there's no room for comebacks in my head.

There isn't room for anything but *I need to hear her groan my name.*

It's fucking perfect.

I stare into her eyes as I slide my boxers to my feet.

She lets out a low, deep sigh.

"Take off your shorts." My voice isn't a request. It's a demand. It's a fucking order.

But it doesn't turn her off.

It makes her groan.

Slowly, she brings her hands to her hips and slides her shorts to her thighs.

I lean down to pull them to her feet.

My fingers brush her big toe. Slowly, I trace a line up the inside of her foot, her calf, her inner thigh.

Over her panties then down the other leg.

Her eyelids press together. She turns her head to one side. "Walker."

I drag my fingertips up her calf. The inside of her knee. Her thigh.

I rub her over her panties.

She tugs at the sheets as she groans.

I plant my hands around her hips and move onto the bed.

My lips find her inner thigh. She's soft. And the way she shakes against my lips—

I need more.

I need too fucking much.

But I'm not going to think about what that means.

I'm not going to think, period.

I drag my lips up her inner thigh and over her panties.

She brings her hand to my hair. Presses her legs against my ears.

Her voice gets needy. Desperate. "Please."

Fuck yeah.

My fingers curl into her hips. I peel her panties to her thighs, her knees, her calves, her toes.

They fall off her feet.

She looks up at me, her blue eyes filled with a plea. The same one that's going through my head.

Erase every thought in my head.

Give me this.

Give me everything.

I plant a kiss on her calf then I work my way up her leg. Every brush of my lips makes her shudder.

She gets louder as I get closer.

She's already wound up.

Already desperate for me.

Still, I tease her. I brush my lips against her clit then move down her other leg as slowly as I can.

I work my way up her calf, her thigh.

She tugs at my hair. "Please." Her breath hitches in her throat.

She slings one leg over my shoulder.

I bring my palm to her thigh and pin it to the bed.

She rocks her hips as she groans. "Walker. Please." Her voice drips with need.

She needs me.

And this—this is something I understand.

Something I'm good at.

Something that makes perfect fucking sense.

"Say it again, sweetness." I pry her legs apart.

"Please."

I dig my fingers into her thigh.

"Walker. Please. Please." Her voice rises to a whine.

"Please what?"

"Make me come." She tugs at my hair. "Now. Please."

Fuck yeah.

I bring my mouth to her.

She claws at my shoulder as I lick her from top to bottom.

Fuck, she tastes good.

I do it again.

Again.

I do it until her thighs are shaking against my hands, then I flick my tongue against her clit.

"Fuck." Her breath gets heavy.

I do it again.

Again.

Her hand knots in my hair.

I look up at her. Watch her eyelids press together. Watch her brow soften. Her shoulders relax.

Fuck, she looks beautiful wracked with pleasure.

Mine.

I push the thought out of my head. That isn't part of our agreement. That is a quick trip to heartbreak.

That isn't happening.

This is simple. Seamless.

I lick her a little harder. A little faster. Higher. Lower. Right. Left. Up and down. Back and forth. With zigzags. With circles.

Her breath catches in her throat.

There.

That's it.

I lick her with steady strokes.

She groans as she bucks against my mouth. As she presses her thighs against my hands.

I dig my nails into her skin, pinning her in place.

And I flick my tongue against her.

"Fuck." She runs her nails over my shoulder. "Walker. Fuck."

I do it again. Again. Again.

A few more flicks and she's shaking.

Her groans get louder. Needier.

I lick her again. Again.

There.

With the next flick of my tongue, she comes. She gets sweeter. Wetter.

My name falls off her lips.

She rocks against my mouth.

"Fuck me. Now." She tugs at my hair.

I plant a kiss on her pelvis then drag my lips up her stomach. Over her breasts. I take her nipple into my mouth and suck hard.

"Walker." It's half *fuck me now*, half *don't stop exactly what you're doing.*

I toy with her nipple until she's shaking, then I move to her other nipple and do it again.

Fuck, she's responsive.

I need this—her reacting to me, her filling with pleasure, her *everything.*

She slides her hand down my stomach. Her fingers brush my cock. She rubs her thumb against my tip.

Fuck.

I reach for the bedside drawer. Grab a condom. Bring it to my teeth to rip the wrapper.

She stares up at me as she wraps her hand around me.

I kiss her as she pumps me.

Her hand feels too fucking good.

"Lie back." She pushes herself onto her elbow. "I want to ride you."

She doesn't have to ask twice.

I lie on my back. Roll the condom over my cock.

She presses herself up. Slings her leg over my hip to straddle me.

I bring my hands to her hips to guide her body over mine.

My tip strains against her.

Then it's one delicious inch at a time.

My fingers dig into her skin.

Her teeth sink into her bottom lip. She stares back at me as she pushes herself up then brings herself down on me again.

She does it again.

Again.

I cup her tits. Rub her nipples with my thumbs.

Her head turns to one side.

A heavy sigh falls off her lips.

This is exactly how she likes it.

And fuck, she feels good around me. In my hands. On top of me.

I toy with her nipples as she drives her body over mine again and again.

My eyes stay fixed on her. I watch pleasure spill over her expression. I watch her tits shake. I watch my cock fill her again and again.

Her nails scrape my stomach.

She's almost there.

No teasing. Not now. I need to watch her come. Fuck, I need it more than I need to come.

I bring my thumb to her clit and I rub her with steady strokes.

She plants her hands on my chest and rocks against my thumb.

My balls tighten.

Her cunt pulses.

She groans my name as she comes.

Fuck, that feels good.

I rub her through her orgasm.

Then I bring my hands to her hips and I guide her body over mine.

She stares back at me as I thrust into her.

I go deeper.

Harder.

There.

Fuck.

My nails sink into her skin as I come. Pleasure spreads through my torso. My arms and legs and fingers and toes.

My cock pulses. My hips rock.

I spill every fucking drop.

She leans down and presses her lips to mine.

I bring my hand to her head, hold her against me as I kiss her harder. Deeper.

We untangle slowly.
My lips stay pressed to hers.
My thoughts stay on her.
I need her.
Too much of her.
But I'm still not ready to think about that shit.

Chapter Fourteen

IRIS

The shower turns off.

I cinch my towel a little tighter. It's strange how shy I feel. Twenty minutes ago, I was spread out on the bed, savoring the need in Walker's eyes.

Now, I'm scared we'll have nothing to say to each other.

Not that I want to talk.

We could *not talk* again.

Well... I'm not sure I can handle *not talking* again.

My thighs are spent. From the hike and from being wrapped around him.

Hell, my entire body is spent.

It feels good. Painful, but good. There's something about losing myself in movement, something I need more of.

Not just sex. Hiking, yoga, swimming, even these surf lessons Walker keeps promising.

That's something I love. Something I know I want.

I'm Iris Avery and I'm more than a recovering addict. I'm a PhD candidate in psychology and I love purple, coffee, and exercise.

I move into the kitchen, grab a glass, fill it with water, and drink it the way I used to drink cheap vodka—like I need all of it, right now.

Booze was never my thing, but it did the trick when I was lacking alternatives.

Walker steps into the main room in black boxers—only black boxers.

He's yummy as all hell.

But this is still weird.

I don't know what to say to him. Or why things only make sense when we're naked. Or why I'm so desperate to learn the real reason why he's cagey about his sister.

The same one who was staying over the other night?

There's a story there.

I shouldn't want it.

But I do.

I want to know the guy behind the carefree smile. I want to know why his dark eyes turn down. Why he frowns when he thinks I'm not looking.

I'm not willing to share my secrets. I can't ask for his.

I shouldn't even want his.

"Here." He moves into his bedroom. A few moments later, he returns with a pair of boxers and a Metallica t-shirt.

I shake my head.

"You don't like metal?"

"No. But I don't see the relevance."

He smiles. "Fuck off."

My chest gets warm. His smile does things to me. It does too much.

Chill out, Iris. It's the oxytocin flooding your brain. That's what happens after sex. Especially after mind-blowing, orgasmic sex.

It's a chemical reaction.

That's all.

Like heroin induced bliss.

But then love is a chemical reaction.

Really, everything you feel is a chemical reaction.

"You want something more hardcore?" he asks.

"Of course. Only the purest, least sell out bands."

"And who's that?"

"Uh..." I don't think I know a single metal band from the last ten years. Not my thing. Too loud. And my thoughts already scream at me.

"What do you listen to?"

"Electronic stuff." As long as it's mellow.

"Like..."

"Electro-pop. Depeche Mode. Soft Cell. That kind of thing."

"Anything from the last thirty years?"

I name a dozen relevant bands.

He motions to the laptop sitting on the dining table. "You can put something on."

"While we..."

"I'm not gonna work up your appetite then send you home hungry."

My smile spreads over my cheeks. "Your game is improving."

"Must be your help." He motions to the computer. "Put on your favorite album."

"You won't like it."

"Because I own a Metallica shirt?"

"Well... yeah."

"You continue to stereotype me."

"Maybe." I let my eyes roam his body. Narrow waist, defined torso, broad shoulders, strong arms and ink everywhere. "You're yet to find me a shirt."

"Wonder why."

"My clothes are a sweaty mess."

"You don't need to wear clothes."

"It's too cold for that."

"Music. Then I'll grab you a shirt."

Okay, fine. It's a compromise of sorts. After all, those are his clothes. I don't have any right to them. Even if it's normal post-fuck behavior.

He has his own boundaries.

Or he's teasing me.

It's probably the latter.

I move to the dining table anyway. All this talk of electro-pop is giving me a serious Tegan and Sara craving.

I take a seat and open the laptop.

A lock screen pops up.

"This is password protected." Which is smart. But certainly another point in the *he's teasing me column.*

"Is it?" he calls from the bedroom.

"I'll wait for you."

"It's *I Like Big Butts and I Cannot Lie*."

"It is not." I check anyway.

He laughs as he moves into the main room. "I bet you tried it."

"I plead the fifth."

He tosses me a grey and pink The Last Ones to Know t-shirt and a pair of blue boxers.

I shoot him a curious look.

He arches a brow.

"You like metal and emo music?"

He laughs. "I have eclectic tastes."

"Uh-huh."

"Look me in the eyes and tell me you never pined after some broken lyricist."

"I plead the fifth." I pull the top over my head. The boxers under my towel. Then I lose said towel.

"You can strip in front of me." He slides into the chair next to mine.

"I know."

He slides the computer over, taps his password, pulls up a music streaming app. "Anything you want."

I go to my favorite Tegan and Sara album and hit play.

Acoustic guitar flows from the speakers.

He cocks a brow. "This is electric?"

"I changed my mind."

"You like this coffee house rock stuff?"

"Yeah. It's relaxing. Introspective. It makes me feel calm. And a lot of bands write great lyrics."

"Lyrics?" He tilts his head to one side, playing dumb. "Kidding. I have to know them for karaoke."

"You do karaoke?"

"Sometimes. It's a shop tradition."

"Oh."

"You're welcome to come next time."

"I'll think about it." I hang the towel on the back of my chair. "Do you need to talk to your friend?"

"No. He needs to get over himself."

"It's kinda sweet... if he is worried he's going to lose you."

"Yeah. It is. In a Dean kinda way."

"You guys are close?"

"We hang all the time. Have for ten years now."

"That's nice." Really, it is. Even if I don't appreciate Dean's whole hot and cold *what do you think you're doing intruding on guy time* thing. I don't have any old friends. Three years of drug use was more than enough time to burn those bridges. And all the people I hung with while I was torching my past life are still using.

For the most part, I'm okay with it.

But I really, really miss my sister Lily.

"He can be an asshole, but he always has my back." Walker runs his hand through his wet hair. "Usually. Not today."

"Everyone fights."

"We did."

"I guess you can call it that." I press my lips together. "You promised not talking."

"You want to go again?" He motions to the bedroom. "I can be ready in ten minutes."

"Really?"

"I didn't convince you last time?"

He did. Mmm. It's tempting. But—"I'm starving."

His smile spreads over his cheeks. It really is a nice smile. Beautiful. Radiant. Everything.

Uh-huh. No feelings. It's just oxytocin. It doesn't mean anything.

Think about hot musicians.

Or maybe about how Walker is more appealing than a hundred millionaire rock stars.

He stands, moves into the kitchen, pulls the fridge open. "Shit." He presses the door closed then opens the freezer. "Not much."

"You like to cook?"

"Yeah."

"But you don't have any food?"

He shrugs. "I order in."

"Mmm."

He laughs. "I know that *mmm*."

Shit. He's right. It's total therapist *mmm*. "Why don't you cook more?"

"It's a lot of work when it's just me."

"But you... you don't have any fat."

He pats his stomach. "And?"

"Tell me you eat nothing but chicken and broccoli."

"I eat a lot of chicken and broccoli. Have plenty in the freezer. But I'm not gonna feed you that."

"No?"

"Unless you find it appetizing."

I stand. Move into the kitchen. "If you don't like it, why do you eat it?"

"It's easy."

"Do you also eat a lot of egg whites and protein shakes?"

He laughs. "Eggs."

"With yolks and everything?"

"And cheese."

"You have any?"

He pulls the fridge open. "Yeah." He looks to me with a curious expression. "You want eggs for dinner?"

"Whatever is fine."

"We can order something." He closes the fridge door. Points to the menus hanging from magnets. "Plenty of options."

A picture of chicken tandoori grabs my attention. I tap the flyer. "This place."

He picks up a *San Diego* magnet, grabs the menu, hands it to me.

"You like San Diego?"

"Who doesn't?"

"We used to go there every summer. When I was a kid. We'd stay on the bay. I'd swim all afternoon. My parents would sit in the sun and read. And then we'd watch movies all night. My dad is a big film buff. You guys probably like a lot of the same stuff."

"Shit. You're comparing me to your dad? Is that a kinky *daddy* thing?"

I laugh. "No. It's just the movies. He's incredibly clean-cut."

"It was just you?"

"And my sister."

"Are you close?"

"No. Not anymore." She shut me out. I understand why she did it. Hell, I agree with her decision. But I miss her. I hate that I have to stalk her on Instagram to get updates on her life.

"Older or younger?"

"Older."

"Mine is older too."

"You just have one?"

"Yeah."

"Sabrina?"

His eyes turn down.

I back up. "Lily."

"Lily?"

"Yeah. My parents had a theme. She tells everyone they got the name from *Harry Potter* even though the books came out when she was nine."

"No one calls her on it?"

"Not usually."

"What's she do?"

"She's a programmer." Her office is in Santa Monica. It's a fifteen-minute walk from here. Sure, it's Saturday, but there's a chance she's there. She works a lot.

Or she used to.

I don't really know what she's been doing the last two years beyond the snippets I get on social media.

I turn my attention to the menu. Everything sounds good.

My stomach rumbles. It's still weird, craving food. Wanting a flavor. Really *feeling* hunger.

I used to love Indian food.

But that was a long, long time ago.

"Vegetable curry. Medium." I hand the menu back to him.

"You eat meat?"

"Oh. Yeah. I just like vegetable curry." I brush my wet hair behind my ear. "Is that wrong?"

He arches a brow.

Okay. I'm lacking confidence when it comes to my preferences. But I'm getting there. "You got a problem with that?"

"No. As long as you aren't gonna steal my chicken curry."

"Maybe a little."

His smile is cocky. "I'll get an extra order. Eat it tomorrow if we have leftovers. You want rice or naan?"

"Rice please."

He nods. Grabs his cell phone from the counter, dials, and orders dinner.

I take in the apartment. It's nice for a small space. Not pretty the way mine is, but still intentionally decorated.

Framed sci-fi posters hang on the walls. DVD cases, paperbacks, and CDs spill from the bookshelf in the corner.

There's a lot of good stuff here. Films I've meant to see forever. And two entire rows of *Star Wars* extended universe novels.

"It'll be half an hour." Walker moves closer. He slides his arms around my waist. Rests his head on my shoulder.

It's intimate. Too intimate.

But there isn't a single part of me that wants to tell him to stop.

He plants a kiss on my neck. "How's the *Star Wars* book going?"

"It was good. I finished the next one."

"But?"

"But nothing."

"There's a tone to your voice."

"I liked it." But that was it. Like. I used to eat, sleep, drink those books. Yeah, I'm older. My tastes are more refined. But I loved those books during my snobby phase in college. They were my one guilty pleasure. Ah, simple times.

"Hard to care now that the extended universe is irrelevant."

"Yeah." It was a slight when Disney made the call to

throw out a fascinating storyline that I'd been reading for ten years—especially for a less interesting story—but that never offended me. Nothing ever offended me. Or excited me. When I was using all the time, everything was easy. Even. Good.

He kicks a book on the bottom shelf. "You ever read this one?"

"No."

He releases me. Bends to pull the book from its shelf and hands it to me. "You can borrow it."

"I'm not sure I can. That's a lot of pressure. What if I wreck it?"

"Then I'll buy another copy."

Saga. It's a classic graphic novel. I always meant to read it. Now is as good a time as any. And I'm supposed to read.

But what if it feels average too?

I can't keep living without passion. It's dull. Awful.

"You don't like graphic novels?" he asks.

"No. I do." Well, I've only read a few, but I did like them. "Thanks. I'll check it out tomorrow." I turn my attention back to the shelf. "You have a serious collection."

"I do okay."

"What's your favorite?"

"You're holding it."

"Uh-uh. I can't borrow this. That's way too much pressure."

"You'd be doing me a favor if you ruined it. I'd have an excuse to upgrade to a signed copy."

"Why haven't you?"

"Just haven't."

I hold the book to my chest. This *is* a lot of pressure. What if I lose his favorite book? What if I hate it? What if I fail to find the appeal? But I want to try. I want to love things.

And hate them. I want to feel everything again, even when it hurts. I swallow hard. "You have a lot of CDs too."

He laughs. "My high school music taste on display."

I recognize some of the more popular metal and grunge bands. "I've seen worse."

"And I need help with my game?"

I nod. Though he doesn't. At all.

He tugs at my t-shirt. "You want to watch something?"

"Yeah." I scan the rows of sci-fi. There are too many options. "You're really into this stuff."

"Told you."

"You didn't say *hi, I'm a sci-fi geek.*"

"Close enough." His voice is bright. Playful. "You in the mood for anything in particular?"

Too much. I swallow hard. "Something new."

Like this.

Liking him.

Wanting to hang out with my clothes on.

Wanting to learn his secrets.

Wanting to peel back the easy, breezy surfer boy mask and figure out exactly what makes him tick.

Chapter Fifteen

IRIS

It feels way, way too good cuddling up on Walker's couch with a plateful of spicy curry and a classic science fiction film.

He teases me about stealing his chicken curry. I tease him about his messy eating. And lick chutney off his lips. And collapse into his arms for the rest of the movie.

I want to sleep here. In his bed. With my body pressed against his.

And that's a no go.

A hard pass.

An obvious trip to feelings-ville.

I ask him to take me home, and he obliges, but I still fall asleep wishing his arms were around me.

I still wake up lonely.

I TAKE A LONG SIP AND LET OUT A SOFT MOAN.

Almost perfect.

Just a little more simple syrup.

There.

Ahh.

That's exactly it.

I press my lips together to stifle my moan. It's Sunday. In Brentwood, that means families everywhere. As in no moaning like you're trying out for a phone sex hotline.

Oh, baby, yes, just like that...

It's disturbing how well my thoughts of sugary cold brew line up with dirty talk. Maybe that's my new part-time job. Sipping coffee and moaning is already a huge part of my routine...

Okay. That's true. But the thought of strangers filling me in on their fantasies? Not so appealing. Not unless they're Walker.

Only he isn't a stranger anymore.

He's a...

A something.

I nearly skip back to my seat. The magic powers of caffeine and sugar combine to bring me to life. My thoughts get sharp. My attention fixes on the task at hand: tackling this chapter on making sense of outliers.

Data. Stats. Studies. I can do this shit.

After a round of highlights, I go through the chapter again. This time, I make my own study guide. A bullet point for every important piece of information. A short summary for every section. A little bit of extra flavor for the chapter summary.

I go to suck iced coffee from my straw, but my drink is empty.

It's already late afternoon. More caffeine is a bad idea.

I get in line anyway. The guy in front of me is tall. Tan. Broad. He looks up from his cell phone and smiles at me.

He's just like Ross. Clean cut. Business casual outfit. *Work hard, play hard.* The type who uses to get through his meetings then to unwind after them.

I smile back. He's cute, but he doesn't make my heartbeat pickup or my stomach flutter. He's just so... plain. Uninteresting. Not like Walker with his dark eyes, and his strong shoulders, and the tattoos that snake down his arm.

Ahem.

Business guy steps forward to order his nonfat latte. He turns back to me and winks.

I smile back. That seems like the proper protocol. Or something.

"A refill, please." I place my cup on the counter and fish two dollars from my wallet. I use one to pay and stuff the other in the tip jar.

The barista smiles back at me. "I love your hair." She picks up my glass. "I've been thinking about that cut."

"Thanks."

"Is it high-maintenance?"

"It looks messy if I don't trim it every six weeks, but otherwise, it's as easy as it gets."

She nods. "It looks great on you."

"Thanks."

Business guy watches from his seat at a side table. He nods to himself *oh, I get it. She doesn't like me because she's into girls.*

Okay. I'm jumping to conclusions.

I do have a problem.

She refills my cold brew. I bring it to the bar, pour in a little two percent and a lot of simple syrup. Mmm. Perfection.

I return to my seat, tackle another chapter, write up another set of notes.

One to go.

Then a bunch of reading from the other textbook in my

backpack. I thought I'd be jumping into research right away, but the first year of this program is all foundation.

It's good. Important stuff to know.

But I want to dive into a massive research project now.

I suck coffee through my straw. Open up my email. There's a bunch of stuff about my internship offers. I've been ignoring it for too long.

New York isn't as appealing as it was a month ago.

It's so far away. That was the draw, when I applied. But now that there's someone I want to see in LA...

No. That's silly. Walker and I are casual. We won't be anything come July. I need to take whichever of these is the best opportunity.

Which means I need to figure out which of these is the best opportunity.

Eventually.

I lean back and take another sip. Make a mental note to decide by the end of the month. Turn back to my computer.

My fingers move of their own accord.

Straight to Lily's Instagram. I created a new account just to stalk my sister. It's awful, I know. But she blocked me on every platform. And I have to know she's okay. Asking my parents always leads to offers to help us make up.

I want that.

But not until she's ready.

If she's ever ready.

There's a picture from this morning. She's standing with all her equally fit girlfriends, sipping a green smoothie in her spin gear.

Her last week is all cute business casual outfits and fierce eye shadow. She always looks good. She taught me how to do my makeup. And hair. And how to style my outfits. And everything, really.

Mom was involved too, but her style was—still is—trapped in the 80s.

Lily is trendy. Pretty. Fun.

My backpack buzzes.

My cell.

Walker: What are you doing?

I should work. I have a lot to do.

But I have all night. A little break can't hurt.

Iris: Thinking about you naked.

Walker: Ditto.

Iris: About me or yourself?

Walker: Myself. I'm too fine. It hurts.

Iris: It's true. Looking at you is like looking at the sun. If you do it directly, you'll burn your corneas.

Walker: It's my curse.

Iris: Is this a booty call?

Walker: At four in the afternoon?

Iris: It's happened before.

Walker: To you?

Iris: My lips are sealed.

Walker: What are you really doing?

Iris: Trying to decide on my summer internships.

Walker: What are your options?

Iris: There's a great one in New York.

Walker: Manhattan?

Iris: Yeah. And a few here. Well, driving distance. One in San Diego. Did I tell you I went to USCD?

Walker: Take that one.

Iris: Won't you miss me?

Walker: I'll be at your place every day off.

Iris: Surfing every morning?

Walker: Of course.

Iris: You do seem like the San Diego type.

Walker: What's that mean?

Iris: You know exactly what it means.

Walker: Do I?

Iris: Yeah.

Walker: You wearing panties?

My cheeks flush.

Iris: That was an abrupt subject change.

Walker: Are you?

Iris: Yes.

Walker: What do they look like?

Uh... I glance around the crowded coffee shop. Can I really have this conversation here?

Iris: Purple. There's cotton with lace trim.

Walker: Fuck, you're gonna make me hard.

Iris: You started it.

Walker: Still.

Iris: I'm completely innocent. Just trying to study.

Walker: I'm just getting ready for the gym.

Iris: Wearing...?

Walker: You want a pic?

My tongue slides over my lips.

Iris: Yes, please.

A minute later my cell flashes with a picture message. Walker from his nose to his thighs. He's wearing boxers. Only boxers.

But it's too much.

I want those gone.

I want my thoughts gone.

I want him in my bed, between my legs, groaning my name.

Iris: You're going to kill me.

Walker: Good.

Iris: How are you going to the gym? I can't fathom that. My thighs are murder.

Walker: I get any credit for that?

Iris: Maybe.

Walker: Iris, you wound me.

Iris: You get some credit.

Most of the credit.

Walker: Is it good sore or bad sore?

Iris: There's a good sore?

Walker: Yeah. You feel like you worked hard. Like a badass.

Iris: I do feel like I worked hard. And like everything hurts.

Walker: You need someone to kiss it better?

Iris: I knew this was a booty call.

Walker: It could be. But you know it's the twenty-first century. Women can make the first move.

Iris: Uh-huh.

Walker: You can booty call me.

Iris: I'll consider that.

Walker: Me too. In explicit detail.

Iris: You're dirty.

Walker: You love it.

I do.

Walker: Don't worry. It'll rub off on you.

It already is. I get the double entendre right away. Rub off. Like rub one out. Like he's going to come on me.

Usually, that kind of thing squicks me out.

But the thought of Walker coming on my ass, my back, my stomach, my chest...

Fuck. It's hot in here.

I suck cold brew through my straw. It's mostly ice. It's not enough to cool me down.

Must change topic.

Iris: Did you talk to your friend?

Walker: A little.

Iris: And?

Walker: He's acting like everything is normal.

Iris: Hmm.

Walker: You're doing it again.

Iris: I've been doing it all afternoon. I have a problem.

Walker: You aren't at home?

Iris: At a coffee shop.

Walker: Ah.

Iris: What do you mean ah?

Walker: Explains your good mood.

Iris: You don't want to take credit for that?

Walker: Post-orgasm glow only lasts twelve hours.

Iris: I didn't realize.

Walker: I'm sure you could do more extensive testing. That's a ballpark.

Iris: I think I have to.

Walker: You're a slave to science.

Iris: Thanks for noticing.

Walker: You have school Wednesday?

Iris: In the morning. But I should study.

Walker: You could study. Or you could come on my hand at Griffith Park.

Iris: Oh.

Walker: Have you ever been?

Iris: Of course. I'm from the valley, remember?

Walker: And you decided you like hiking. And I like watching you come. It sounds like a perfect mash-up.

Iris: It does.

Walker: I'll pick you up at three, buy you dinner, have you home in time for your Thursday morning class.

Iris: Have you heard of asking?

Walker: I'll see you at three, Iris.

Chapter Sixteen

IRIS

I slide my hoodie off my shoulders and tie it around my waist. It's way, way too warm for a spring afternoon. Especially in the shade of the trees.

God, there are trees everywhere. I can't remember the last time I felt this surrounded my nature.

It's calm. Peaceful. Beautiful.

Walker chuckles as he gives me a long once over.

I clear my throat. "Yes?"

"I dig the look."

Okay, it's dorky as hell wearing my hoodie like this. But it's hot. "You're jealous."

"I am." He slides *his* hoodie off his shoulders and ties it around his waist. He turns and strikes a model-worthy pose. "How do I look?"

Ridiculous. But—"Still hot."

"It's my curse."

"How do you deal?"

"Some days, it's hard."

"Only some?"

He laughs as he slides his arms around my waist. His lips

brush my neck. My cheek. He cups my ass over my shorts. "You wear this to drive me crazy, sweetness?"

"Maybe."

He presses his lips to mine. "You'll regret that."

I shake my head. I regret a lot of things. Too many. But not whatever I did to fill his dark eyes with all that desire.

He nips at my ear. "You drive me out of my fucking mind. You know that?"

My nod is heavy.

"Fuck. You're distracting me. Already forgot why we're here."

"Something about my love of hiking and your love of watching me come."

"Not helping." He chuckles. "You did that on purpose."

Definitely. I nod.

"Bad girl." He drags his fingertips over my ass and hips. "Are you wearing panties?"

"If I'm not, will that make you crazier?"

"Yeah." His voice drops an octave. "But you're coming on my hand either way."

"Now?" Now is good. Now is great.

He traces the outline of my panties, over my shorts. "No. Not until you're so desperate you're begging for it."

Mmm. He's way too good at this.

Walker takes a half step backward. He intertwines his fingers with mine and leads me up the path.

This is more of a stroll than a hike. Not that I'm complaining. The speed is just right. My blood is pumping. My body is buzzing with endorphins. With that *yes, this is what I should be doing* feeling.

With desire.

God, he has a nice ass. Strong legs. Broad shoulders. He's like a magazine model. He's so fine it hurts.

Lily would be so jealous. And so happy for me.

If she was willing to talk to me.

Nope. Not going there. I'm not here to dwell on past mistakes. I'm here to enjoy the fresh air and the view. "You come here a lot."

"No. Haven't been in forever."

"You don't bring women here for a picnic and a fuck?"

His lips curl into a smile. "I don't usually leave the apartment."

"Ah."

"Ah?" He arches a brow. Copies my tone. "How does that make you feel, Ms. Avery?"

"That was not a shrink *ah*."

He nods.

"Maybe a little."

He holds his hands close together then pulls them apart in the *a lot* gesture.

"When's the last time you went on an actual date?"

"Depends on the definition."

"Like this."

"We don't do dates."

We don't. That's a rule. But we're here. And this is clearly a date. Or... Well... "You're going to make me come. That makes this a hookup."

He smiles and shakes his head *whatever you want to tell yourself*. "It's been a while."

"Just swiping right?"

"You know dating apps?"

"I know of them."

"You dumped your ex at Christmas?"

"Yeah."

"So, it's been four months."

"About that." Have I really been sober for almost four months? And single for longer? It's hard to believe. The last three years are one blur of shitty jobs, bad friends, and Ross, all dulled by the magic of opiates and booze.

"You squeeze in a lot of rebound sex?"

The bounciness in his voice pulls me back to the moment.

"Iris?"

"Oh. No. You... um... you were the first."

"Shit, really?"

I nod. "I was never the type to sleep around."

He laughs. "Ever?" He squeezes my hand.

"Nope." I squeeze back. "Have you ever wanted something serious?"

"A long time ago. When I was a kid. I wanted the love I saw in the movies."

"Really?"

"Yeah. My sister and I used to watch eighties movies. Every weekend. We'd take turns. She'd always pick romances. I'd always pick action. Or sci-fi."

"*Star Wars*?"

"Of course. *Empire Strikes Back* is a masterpiece. And she wouldn't complain, because she was gaga for Han and Leia."

"Who isn't?" That's another thing I know. Han and Leia are forever.

He helps me up the steep part of the path. "Was bullshit what happened to them in *The Force Awakens*."

"Yeah. Fuck that. They're the best part of the movies and then there's one little line about how they're divorced. The movie barely acknowledges their relationship."

He looks me in the eyes. "You fucking with me?"

"No. They're the end game couple. They're the heart of the series. They're everything."

"You—" He slides his arms around my waist and pulls my body into his—"I'm gonna fall in love with you if you say shit like that?"

"Really?"

"It's pretty hot."

I laugh. "Being into *Star Wars?*"

"Are you really asking me that?" He nods to the path. Leads me under a cropping of trees. "Have you seen my apartment?"

It is heavily decked in *Star Wars*. "But you have all kinds of Sci-Fi."

"Yeah. And *Star Wars* is the gateway. You're gonna be debating Kirk vs. Piccard in no time flat."

No. But I... I really do care about Han and Leia. I have that feeling in my chest, the one I used to have all the time.

It matters to me.

Something besides school matters to me.

Fuck. I'm going to be the one falling in love with him if he keeps doing this to me.

That can't happen. He's might as well have *heart breaker* written on his forehead.

The path veers to the left. Walker heads right. Motions *follow me*.

We move through a cluster of trees. Then out the other side.

The city comes into view. All of it. Downtown, the Hollywood sign, the cluster of buildings in Century City, the Ferris wheel at the Santa Monica Pier, the ocean.

My lips part with a sigh. "It's so..."

"Weird to think of LA as beautiful, huh?"

"Yeah. But it is." It's like a post card. Bright blue sky, big yellow sun, rows of buildings bleeding into the coast. "The world is beautiful." I swallow hard. "Sorry. I sound like a poster."

"It suits you."

I flip him off.

He slides his arms around my waist.

"You do this kinda thing a lot?"

"Depends what you mean by *this kinda thing*."

"Explore the city?"

"I try to."

"Will you take me?" I press my lips together. I'm asking for too much. I want too much. He's not going to be mine. I can't have him showing me the world. But I want it.

"Yeah." He plants a kiss on my neck. "But I can't be held responsible for my actions if you keep wearing those tight shorts."

I laugh. "How old are you?"

"Twenty-four."

"You're old enough to control yourself."

"Not around you."

My cheeks flush. It's dirty talk, yeah, but there's an earnestness in his voice. He means it.

But does he mean his body?

Or his heart too?

I sink into his touch as I take in the view.

It's gorgeous.

For the first time in forever, my world isn't a bundle of regrets. It's beauty. It's possibility. It's hunger. "It's weird. I never really think of this place as Hollywood. All the stuff in the movies is bullshit."

"And then some."

"But I'm close to it. My dad owns a visual effects company. He loves movies. We used to go every weekend. And then we'd still watch something after dinner."

"What type of thing?"

"Everything. Classics. Foreign films. Popcorn films. I can't tell you how many times he explained that *Jaws* launched the summer blockbuster."

"It did."

I hold my hands over my ears *I can't hear you*.

His smile spreads over his cheeks. "Did you like it?"

"*Jaws*? No. It scarred me for life. I get freaked out in three feet of ocean."

"Really?"

"Shut up. It's embarrassing. Especially when you're all cool, chill surfer boy."

"You can be cool, chill surfer girl. I'll teach you. This weekend."

"Maybe."

"I promise you won't get eaten by sharks."

"Can you really promise that?"

"Yeah. They'll eat me. I'll be the one in the water."

"So I'll have to watch you die?"

"Worst case scenario."

I stare back at him, trying to figure out if he's joking.

He presses his palm to my cheek. "Shit. You're really freaking."

I nod.

His voice gets soft. "There hasn't been a shark attack here in forever. It's safe. But if you're scared—"

"No. I want to." I'm tired of being scared. I'm tired of the comfortable numb. I need to actually live my life instead of trying to get through every day for the sake of adding another twenty-four hours of sobriety to my calendar.

"What about movies without sharks?"

"I used to love them."

"And now?"

"Not as much."

"You get old. Lose the magic."

"Maybe."

"You want it back?"

I arch a brow. "Does this involve coming in a movie theater."

"Fuck, that's a good idea." He presses his forehead to mine. "But no."

"Really?"

He nods. "*Blade Runner* is playing at the Nuart at midnight Friday. Come with me."

"*Blade Runner?*"

"Don't tell me you haven't heard of it. Iris, it's a classic."

"No." I have. A lot. "I was just thinking that my dad would like you."

"You sure?" He motions to his full sleeve.

"Even so."

"That a good thing?"

"I don't know. He liked Ross. But Ross was an asshole. Just the kind of asshole parents like."

"Nice suit, good job?"

"Exactly."

"Why'd you stay with him so long?"

"Good body."

He laughs. "Really?"

"It didn't hurt." My gaze fixes on the cluster of buildings downtown. "He was charming. And a good time. And it was easy." He got me into drugs, but it's not like it was his fault. I made those decisions. I knew what I was doing. "But, he had a stronger presence. I lost what I liked. What I wanted. That's why I'm doing this self-help thing." Okay, it's only half of the why. But it is true.

"What do you want?"

I motion to the trees behind us. "I want to come on your hand. Like you promised."

His smile gets devious. "Oh no, sweetness. You aren't even close to desperate enough yet."

~

HE'S EVIL.

Really, he is.

He spends the entire afternoon leading me around the massive park, teasing me, winding me up.

The sun sinks into the horizon, streaking the sky red.

He drags me to a hidden thicket of trees, rolls my shorts and panties to my knees, and slides his hand between my legs.

I come twice.

Then two more times at his place.

I wake up in his bed, smile plastered on my face.

I like him.

I really, really like him.

And I don't even care that it's going to end in heartbreak.

Only that I get him now.

Chapter Seventeen

IRIS

Walker motions to the silver sign like it's a precious gem.

I tilt my head to one side. "And..."

"You didn't like the restaurant?"

"It was amazing." Really. I had no idea ramen was supposed to taste like *that* and not like ten cents a pack sodium overdose.

"Trust me." He pulls the glass door open and motions *after you*.

I step into the tiny, crowded store. We're the oldest people here by quite a few years. It's mostly teenagers and just barely not teenagers.

The illuminated menu on the wall promises small, medium, or large teas filled with fruit and sugar. All with or without boba.

I've lived in Southern California for long enough to know that boba means fat tapioca balls soaked in sugar syrup. Boba tea slash bubble tea is sweet, vaguely fruit flavored tea with said tapioca balls.

Back in high school, Lily and I walked forever to get to

the nearest boba place. (It was not nearly so trendy back then). She went through a phase where she adored grapefruit green tea. I copied her. I always did.

I take my place in line.

Walker places his body behind mine. Wraps his arms around my waist and brings his mouth to my ear. "We can skip it if you're dead set on coffee."

He's close. It's not *I want to tear your clothes off*. It's *I want to hold you all night. I want to kiss your pain away. I want to give you everything.*

But, right now, it doesn't scare me.

I want more of it. All of it.

I lean closer. "No. I'm in."

"Trying a new thing?"

"Please, Beverly Hills Boy. My sophomore year of high school, I devoured a grapefruit green tea nearly every day."

"And here I am thinking I'm rocking your world."

"You are. Just not with this."

His laugh is soft. He pulls me closer. Leans in to whisper. "You have it recently?"

"Not since high school."

"This place is the best. Uses fresh fruit."

"Thank you for the infomercial." There are oranges, limes, and grapefruits all over the store. It does suggest the use of actual fruit. "When are you drinking sugary tea?"

"When I feel like it."

"I don't buy it."

"Buy it." He brushes my hair behind my ear. "I only do shit I feel like."

"Always?"

"Yeah."

"Doesn't that get in the way of work and paying your bills and getting an oil change?"

"No."

"You never wake up and think *no fucking way am I moving today?*"

"Of course."

"Explain the discrepancy."

"Yeah. I'm not always psyched for leg days. But I know I want to get bigger, stronger. So, I go to the gym. It's for me."

"And the oil change?"

"I take care of my car."

"Cleaning your apartment?"

"Same thing. I want it clean. That's how I want to live. Yeah, there's shitty stuff about being an adult, but, mostly, I love it. I'm in charge of my days. I want bubble tea, I get it. I want to invite a hot grad student to watch a sci-fi classic, I do it."

"What about work?"

"I have days I can't deal with the bullshit, but mostly, I love the shop. And the guys there. Even if they're idiots."

A teenage girl with blond pigtails clears the register.

I move forward, dragging him with me. "How did you get into doing tattoos? Were you one of those kids who had a sleeve planned by middle school?"

"Kinda. I always wanted ink. Maybe it was adolescent rebellion. Maybe it was vanity. Maybe it was the thrill of marking my body. I'm not sure."

"What is it now?"

"I like it."

"That's it?"

"Yeah."

"But it's so... simple."

"Why make shit complicated?"

Because life is complicated. Things are complicated. Making them simple—that's the hard part.

The line moves. Only two customers to go. I have to make up my mind. The smell of citrus brings me back to a hundred afternoons in a similar shop, giggling about boys and complaining about homework with Lily.

Walker presses his palm into my stomach. "You okay?"

"Yeah." I move forward to break his touch. "You still haven't said how you got into tattoos."

"Dean."

"Yeah?"

"Yeah. We were friends back in high school."

"You went to the same school?"

"Different ones. But we were in the same scene."

"Scene? Really?"

"People say scene."

"Name one other person."

He pulls me closer. "You like mocking me."

"Yeah. You like mocking me."

He nods. "You're cute when you're flustered. Or needy."

I swallow hard. Sex is appealing. Very appealing. It makes sense. And with Walker, it feels...

It feels like *everything*.

But I want to have this conversation too. I want to know more about him. "Okay, you were part of the same *scene*."

He shakes his head *kids these days*. "We bounced around all the parties... everywhere." He moves closer. "How old are you?"

"No game." I shake my head.

"All right, when did you graduate high school?"

"A long time ago. And that's the same question. You thought you could trick me?"

He laughs. "You're in grad school, so you're at least twenty-two."

Twenty-five. But close enough.

He smiles. "Older."

"Oh my God!"

"Let's say you're twenty-two."

"No. Twenty-two was a horrible year. Let's say... let's just not say."

He laughs. "You gonna be one of those women getting Botox the day she turns thirty?"

"Maybe. What's it to you?"

He laughs. "You're so fucking cute flustered." He leans in to brush his lips against my neck.

Mmm. It's sweet. Soft. Caring.

My heart melts.

My stomach flutters.

I clear my throat. "You have a point."

"You're distracting me."

"You should take responsibility."

"You too." He slides his hand over my ass, pressing my dress into my skin. "What do you call this?"

"A cute outfit."

"And this?" He traces the outline of my thong over my dress.

"Being prepared."

He laughs. "All right. My point. Fuck, what are we even talking about?"

"Your scene."

He nods. "We probably hit the same party once or twice. We'd go out to the valley if we heard the girls were hot."

I shake my head. "I went to three parties all of high school."

"Still."

It's a strange thought, high school Iris and high school Walker meeting. I wouldn't have paid him any attention back then. Even if he was ink free. I didn't go through a bad boy phase. I always liked nice guys. Clean-cut, Captain America types.

On the surface, we'd be a classic good girl bad boy pairing.

But he's a responsible business owner.

And I...

Well, I'm not that old Iris anymore.

The last customer finishes his order and moves aside. I step forward. Turn my back on my true love coffee to order my old favorite. Grapefruit green tea. Half sweet.

Walker orders a lemon black tea. With only twenty-five percent sweetness.

That explains a lot—there's no way he mainlines sugar looking the way he does.

Though twenty-five percent of the sugar in a bubble tea is still a fuckton of sugar.

He leads me to a metal table outside.

I sit in the clear plastic chair. It's that same chair in every single trendy coffee or tea shop. Only it's clear instead of white.

He leans in close. His eyes find mine. They promise to blow my mind.

And to make my stomach flutter.

And to make me feel safe and warm and—

"Fuck." Walker leans back. Pulls his cell from his jeans. "I have to take this."

I shake my head. "No game." But my voice doesn't quite come across as teasing. Frustration is spreading over his expression.

"I know." His voice doesn't hit teasing either.

I motion to the counter. "I'll get the drinks."

He nods. Moves around the corner.

This particular strip mall—the micro-neighborhood Little Osaka is basically three strip malls and a short row of stores —is dead quiet. There are a bunch of empty offices and the restaurant taking up most of the space is an *all the drama happens inside* place.

I move into the store. The conversations are a quiet buzz. Two teenagers grab beige drinks from the counter.

Milk teas. A guy grabs a light pink drink. Something strawberry, I guess.

The barista, tearista, bobarista? sets two massive teas at the counter. He calls my name.

I grab the drinks and straws. Go back to the table. Stab the plastic covering of my beverage with a giant straw and take a long sip.

It brings me back immediately. The way Lily smiled as she gushed over my homecoming dress. The frown when she didn't get into NYU. Her consoling me when I tried to dye my hair blond and ended up with bright orange locks.

She was my best friend all through college. And through the first year or so of everything. Until she realized how bad it was.

She gave me a choice. She confronted me. But I refused to get help. To choose her.

"Hey." Walker slides into his seat. He forces his lips into a smile, but frustration is still written all over his face.

"Everything okay?"

"Okay enough."

I push his drink toward him. "You were right. This place is good."

"You don't look happy."

"You either." I take a long sip. It tastes like love. Like a love I'm desperate to deserve again.

"Yeah." He stabs the plastic with his straw. Brings the drink to his lips. Takes a long sip.

This is getting to be an alarming trend.

What's wrong?

Nothing. Frown. Grunt.

I'm doing the same thing.

I'm going to be a psychologist and I can't talk about my feelings.

It's sad. Really, it is.

I want to be able to do this.

And I want to know him. The parts that hurt. The guy behind the breezy smile.

I play with my straw. "Your sister?"

"Yeah." His eyes go to the shiny silver table.

"What's the situation there?"

He looks to me and raises a brow. "The situation?"

"I don't need details." In theory. "You... you look upset. There's something there."

"Yeah." He leans back. Runs his hand through his hair. "I don't usually talk about it."

"You don't have to. But I... is there anything I can do?"

"I doubt it."

"My sister and I... we stopped talking a few years ago. We didn't really grow apart. We were close. Until we weren't."

"You got into a fight?"

"Yeah. A huge one. She asked me to make a choice, and I didn't make the one she wanted."

He tilts his head to one side. "That's vague."

"And the details about your sister being a thorn in your side?"

"Fair enough."

"That was almost two years ago, that Lily stopped talking to me. It was sudden. She was always that type of person. She did what she wanted. How she wanted. When she wanted it."

"What did she want from you?"

"To..." How do I explain this without explaining it? I have to tell someone about my past eventually. Maybe even Walker. But not yet. I'm not ready to cross that bridge. "To change my life."

"Convert to Scientology?"

"No. She was right. Trust me." I bring my drink to my lips and take another long sip. It still tastes like love, but the sweetness is gone. It's over-steeped, astringent, bitter.

"You ever reach out to her?"

"Not yet. I'm trying to give her space. I stalk her on Instagram, but otherwise I'm not around."

"You stalk your sister?"

"I don't follow her around. Though I could. She's way too free with her location."

"Who isn't these days?"

"You."

"You still follow me?"

"I told you. I love your work." Really, his tattoos are amazing. "You still haven't told me how you got into it."

"Ryan. You saw him. Looks a lot like Dean only with a permanent scowl?"

I nod. That sounds vaguely familiar.

"He was already working at a shop. He got Brendon a job there. Dean got jealous. He wanted to do ink too. When I saw his first piece—everyone starts by doing a tattoo on themselves."

"What did he do?"

"A spade."

"What did you do?"

"A star." He stands, places his foot on his chair, and pulls up his jeans. There's a tiny star under his ankle.

I laugh. "It's so cute."

"I know." He shakes his head. "It's awful. I need to fix it."

"You can't. It's sweet. It's perfect."

"Yeah. It feels like a part of my history. Like a scar almost. Sure, it's ugly—"

"Take it back."

He shakes his head. "It's terrible."

It's lopsided and blurry. But the imperfection only makes me love it more.

"It's ugly and it doesn't suit me anymore, but if I changed it..."

"It would be like erasing the past."

"Exactly." He picks up his drink and takes a long sip. His posture softens as he sits. He's relaxing. Letting his guard down. "My sister... I love her. But she doesn't have her shit together. She's always looking for me to bail her out of trouble."

"Like?"

"Some loser ditching her at a bar. Whatever. Anything. I want to help. But she's at the point..." He shakes his head. "I try to put my foot down, but she always slinks back to our parents, and they let her get away with murder."

"Mine are the same way with me."

"What have you ever done bad enough to deserve that?"

"A lot."

"I don't believe you."

"Well... I have." I'm not going to tell him. But I've done plenty of shitty things. Most of them are a blur, yeah, but a few are fresh enough to sting. "My parents are proud of me for everything. They act like I've never made a mistake. Like this fight between me and Lily will blow over any day now, even though it's been two years that she hasn't spoken to me."

"That must hurt."

"It does. But I deserved it."

"And now?"

"I don't know. I'd understand if she couldn't forgive me."

"For?"

"Lying to her." That's close enough to the truth.

He leans back. Taps the chair with his hand. "It was that bad?"

"Worse."

He raises a brow. "Not sure if I believe you."

"It doesn't matter. It's true. I was miserable after college. I hated my job. I was desperate to go to grad school, but I kept bombing the GRE. I started looking for other things to blame. Or ways to feel better. I lashed out at Lily a lot." When she was trying to help me get sober, but, hey, it's still true. "Said things you can't take back."

"Still. That's your sister."

"You've never considered cutting off your sister?"

His eyes turn down.

"I don't know what she's done. Or any of the details. But whenever you mention her—it's like your whole body goes tense."

"Am I that obvious?"

I nod. "If she makes you that miserable..."

"Yeah." He presses his lips together. "I've considered it." He pushes himself to his feet. "We should go if we want to make the movie."

I nod. "Okay. You know, I'm not trying—"

"I know."

"I just... I do like talking to you. And you can talk to me. If you ever want to talk to someone about things. We are friends."

He nods. "Same goes for you." He offers his hand. "You'll be the first person I discuss this with. I promise."

I believe him.

I'm not sure what he means by *this* but I believe him.

Chapter Eighteen

WALKER

My phone keeps buzzing.

I give up on ignoring it halfway through *Blade Runner* and check my messages in the bathroom. They're all from Bree. All drunken apologies and pleas for help. Not the kind of help she needs.

The kind of help easily solved by a rideshare app.

Half a dozen voicemail messages in the last two hours. It's late on a Friday. She's probably at some shitty bar with some asshole.

I'm not rescuing her again.

It isn't happening.

I press my back against the beige wall. The bathroom is empty. The two silver stalls are unlocked. The wide sink is clean. Dry. The shiny mirror reflects my inability to cut Bree off back at me.

It's going to be like this until she ODs and doesn't get help fast enough.

Are you going to run to her side until the day you get there and she's a fucking corpse?

Shit. I don't want to do this. But I have to.

I call my parents. First Mom. Her cell goes to voicemail. I try Dad. His message greets me.

Hello, you've reached Robert Williams. Please leave a message and I'll get back to you.

It's all business. Like him.

"Dad, call me. We need to talk about Bree." I hang up.

It's late, nearly two a.m. They're sleeping. This isn't the time for this conversation.

But then it never is.

I shoot my sister a text.

Walker: You want to make it up to me? Take an Uber home.

I plant one hand on the counter and stare back at my reflection.

It continues mocking me.

This could be it. I can tell her to get lost right now. I can tell her she's out of my life forever, block her number, and never hear from her again.

It would mean ceasing most communication with my parents.

And all her old friends.

And more or less sentencing her to die with a syringe in her hand.

But it's been a fucking eternity and I haven't been able to do much about that.

It takes a few minutes for her to text back.

Sabrina: You're mad.

No shit, I'm mad.

She's like a child.

Walker: It's nearly two, Bree. Go home. Sleep it off. Call me when you're sober.

That's all I can take tonight.

I turn my cell off, slide it into my pocket, and make my way back to Iris.

Her blue eyes are glued to the screen. She leans back in

her seat as she breaks a square from a fancy chocolate bar—this place actually sells good chocolate, though it's still at ridiculous movie theater prices.

She looks to me and offers me the square.

I take it. Nod *thank you*.

She tilts her head, assessing me, looking for cracks.

Finding them.

She leans in to whisper. "Your sister?"

"Yeah."

I press my palm into my quad. Fuck, it feels weird admitting that. I'm itchy all over. Desperate to get the fuck out of this chair and be somewhere, anywhere, else.

"You want to talk about it?" she whispers.

I shake my head.

"You want more chocolate?"

I laugh. "Yeah."

The guy behind us lets out a loud *shush*.

It's an obnoxious move. But he's right. Talking during *Blade Runner* is fucked up.

She breaks off another square and hands it to me.

I nod a thank you and lean back in my seat.

Iris follows suit.

I let my hand find hers. It feels good the way it did in middle school, when holding hands was a big fucking deal. When a kiss was everything. When I actually thought I might love a woman one day.

I try to focus on the futuristic Los Angeles flashing on the screen, but I can't.

This situation with Bree is fucked up.

Usually, I jump straight to denial. Even with the guys at the shop. Even though they all know Bree's an addict.

A long time ago, Brendon, Dean, and I used to party together. Sometimes with Bree. We all drank too much and occasionally dabbled in narcotics.

We grew out of it. Got bored.

She didn't.

It's my fault she's like this.

I should have stopped her then.

Even if she was—is—my older sister.

Even if she was into it first.

I don't want to carry the weight of this myself anymore.

I want to tell someone.

No, I want to tell Iris.

I want to actually know her.

IRIS SAUNTERS INTO MY APARTMENT LIKE SHE OWNS THE place.

She tosses her purse on the couch, spins on her heel, turns to me, motions *come here*.

My lips curl into a smile. She's cute tired.

She puts a hand on her hip. "Do I have to get started myself?"

"Fuck yeah." My tongue slides over my lips. "Can I watch?"

"You want to watch me touch myself?"

"You're really asking me that question?"

"Yeah."

"Of course."

"Oh." Her cheeks flush. "I just... I never thought anyone... I've never done that."

"You want to?"

Her nod is slow. Needy.

"You awake enough?"

"Haha. Very funny." She takes a step backward. "I'll have you know I'm running on an exquisite blend of caffeine and sugar."

"And that never leads to a crash."

"Ever."

"You're an addict."

All that joy falls off her face. She shakes it off. Forces a smile. "We all have our vices." She plays with her skirt as she takes another step backward. "I *am* going to start without you."

"Good."

She spins on her heel and skips into my bedroom. She leaves the door open a crack. So I can see her strip out of her dress. Toss her bra aside. Push her panties to her knees.

Fuck, I do want to watch this.

In one minute.

I move to the bathroom, piss, wash my hands, return to the main room.

My cell sits in my jeans like a rock. It taunts me. *What if Bree didn't get home okay? What if she's walking the streets somewhere? What if you're responsible for your sister's death?*

I try to shake it off, but it won't go.

Fuck. What the hell is wrong with me? My girl—well, whatever I should call Iris—is teasing me with touching herself and my head isn't in the game.

This isn't me.

I move into the bedroom. I need to ease myself into it. To—

Iris is naked in my bed. It's a beautiful fucking sight.

But she isn't touching herself.

She's curled up on her side, fast asleep.

I leave my phone on the dresser, strip to my boxers, and get in bed behind her.

I only mean to hold her for a minute.

But as soon as my eyelids press together, the world drifts away.

THE APARTMENT SMELLS LIKE COFFEE.

The other side of the bed is warm. Iris just got up. We slept together without *sleeping together*.

I'm not stupid.

I know that means something.

And wanting to share all this shit with her...

I stretch my arms over my head as I rise. My cell is still sitting on my dresser. Still off. Still mocking me.

There's a sound in the kitchen. Humming. Iris is humming one of those mellow acoustic songs.

I listen as I boot up my cell. A dozen excuses from Sabrina pop up in text message form. Bullshit about how she is sober. About how she's going to stay sober. And a voicemail from my dad. I hit play on the message and hold the phone to my ear.

"Walker, come to dinner tonight and we'll talk. Your sister is doing well, but she misses you. She needs your support. I know you work weekends. If you're busy tonight, call me and we'll make other arrangements. We eat at seven sharp, the same as always." His voice softens. "I love you."

The line clicks.

He thinks she's doing well.

How the fuck can someone so smart be this clueless?

I leave my phone on the counter, head to the bathroom to go through my routine, move into the kitchen.

Iris is leaning against the counter, her fingers wrapped around an oversized white mug, her lips pressed into a smile. Her expression gets sheepish as her eyes find mine. "You win that round."

Fuck, her smile does things to me. Pushes aside all the shit bouncing around my head.

I don't run away from things.

But right now...

"No." I move closer. Wrap my arms around her waist. She's wearing clothes. An Inked Hearts t-shirt Ryan designed and a pair of my boxers. "We both lost."

Her smile spreads over her cheeks. "Is everything good? Last night..."

I can't think about it right now. I need to clear my head. I need to be someplace that makes sense. "We'll talk about it later."

She nods, accepting it.

It's true. I am going to tell her. And figure out how the fuck this can be casual if I'm confessing all the ugly shit in my head.

"I'll make you breakfast." I slide my hand under her t-shirt. Press my palm into her stomach. I want to fuck her senseless, yeah, but I want my arms wrapped around her more.

It's weird.

She looks up at me with a soft smile. Shakes her head. "I'll cook."

"Set my kitchen on fire?"

"I'm not *that* hopeless."

I arch a brow.

She steps back to fold her arms. Cocks her hips. Dons that adorable *don't mess with me* look. "I'll prove it."

I motion to the stove. "Go ahead."

"Maybe... just, well, I am going to look up a recipe."

"And follow it to a T?"

"Of course. That's how you learn. Or you... you don't use recipes?"

"They're boring."

"Then I'm boring."

"You're not."

Her cheeks flush. "Thanks." She moves to the fridge, pulls the door open, assess the offerings. "Eggs. And bacon."

"I can walk you through it."

She looks to me and cocks a brow. "I suppose a hands-on lesson is better than a recipe." Her gaze trails over my chest, stomach, crotch. "And later..."

"You want to get hands on?"

She laughs. "Okay. I'm not a dirty talk expert yet."

"You'll get there."

Her flush spreads over her chest. She makes a show of bending over to reach for something in the fridge.

Fuck, she has a nice ass.

That's a perfect way to turn off my thoughts.

I bring my hand to her ass. Tug the boxers up her thigh. Run my fingers over her skin. "After."

"Oh." She slides the eggs back onto the shelf. Rises to her feet. Presses the door closed.

I bring both hands to her hips and pin her to the refrigerator door.

Her breath gets heavy. "You have a thing for the kitchen."

"I have a thing for your body against mine." I can't exactly deny the pattern. I slide her shorts down her ass. I'm moving too fast. Using her.

Usually, that doesn't bother me. Yeah, I'm an asshole. Whatever. It's not like I'm lying to anyone. I make it clear it's just sex. So what if I'm using a woman to get out of my head?

She's doing the same.

But Iris...

She arches her back, pressing her ass against my hard-on. "Walker..."

"You want me to stop?"

"No."

I push the boxers to her feet.

Her fingers dig into the fridge. Her breath gets heavy as I pull her t-shirt over her head and toss it on the floor.

I bring one hand to her chest and brush my thumb against her nipples.

She groans as she rocks against me.

I toy with her again and again.

I wait until she's panting to drag my fingertips up her thigh.

"Walker." Her voice is heavy. Needy.

This makes sense.

Everything else—fuck everything else.

I pull her closer. Hold her tighter. Bring my lips to her neck to suck on her skin.

She reaches back for me. Tugs at my boxers with one hand. Scratches my thigh with the other.

She wants me inside her.

But I need her at the edge.

I need her desperate and panting.

I drag my fingertips up her inner thigh. Her breath hitches as they get closer and closer.

There.

I brush my fingers against her clit.

She groans. Her fingers dig into my skin. "Please."

"Please what?"

"Make me come." She rubs her flesh against me.

Fuck. That feels good. Too good. I want to be inside her. I want her to be my entire fucking universe.

But this first.

Always this first.

I hold her body against mine as I tease her with light brushes of my fingers.

She squirms against me, groaning and panting and tugging at my boxers.

I wait until *I* can't take it anymore to make my touch harder.

"Fuck." Her thighs shake against my hand. Her nails dig into my skin. "More."

I rub her a little harder.

She groans.

A little higher.

She pants.

There.

"Don't stop," she breathes.

Like hell.

This is where the world makes sense.

This is one thing I always get right.

This is fucking everything.

She tortures me with that lush ass. Her soft flesh is divine against my hard-on. I want to bend her over and claim every inch of her.

"Oh God." She presses her palm against the refrigerator door, knocking off a magnet. Another. Another.

Paper menus and post cards tumble to the floor.

They don't matter.

Nothing matters but Iris coming on my hand.

I rock my hips against her. Fucking boxers are in the way. I hate these damn things, but they're necessary. Otherwise, I'd already be inside her.

The room fills with her groans.

My breath.

Her nails scrape my skin.

My lips brush her neck.

"Walker. Fuck." She tilts her head to give me access.

I suck on her tender skin.

"Bite me," she breathes.

I sink my teeth into her skin. Soft. Then a little harder. Harder.

She groans. "Fuck."

I get lost in the sounds of her pleasure. The way she claws at my skin and rubs against me.

A few more flicks of my hand and she's there.

She moans my name as she comes.

I don't stop until she pulls my hand away.

She turns and presses her lips to mine. Her kiss is hard. Hungry. As desperate as I feel.

No more thinking.

She drags her fingertips over my chest. My stomach. She pushes my boxers off one hip. Then the other.

I kick them off.

Her lips go to my neck. My shoulder. She motions to the wall behind me. "Against that."

My nod is heavy.

I need those pretty pink lips around me. I need to claim her mouth. Mark it as mine.

That isn't what we're doing. Not even close.

But I can't get the thought out of my head.

I move to the wall. Press my back against it.

She plants one more long, deep kiss on my lips then she works her way down my neck, shoulders, chest, stomach.

She lowers herself onto her knees. Looks up at me as she brushes her lips against my cock.

Fuck is this a nice view.

I bring one hand to the back of her head and nudge her forward.

She brushes her lips against me again. It's soft. A merciless tease.

She does it again. Again. Again.

My hand knots in her hair.

Slowly, she takes me into her mouth.

Fuck, she feels good. Soft. Wet. Warm.

I press my back against the wall as I watch her work me.

She teases me with soft flicks of her tongue. Then hard ones. Then she's swirling it around me.

"Iris." I press my hand against the back of her head.

She groans against me as she takes me deeper. Deeper.

Fuck.

She wraps her hand around my cock and she works me up and down.

I keep my hand on the back of her head, guiding her over me. I slide the other over her shoulders, down her chest.

There. I toy with her nipple.

She sucks harder.

I rub her harder.

It's a beautiful fucking cycle.

I let my eyelids press together as pleasure floods my body. She's fucking good at this.

"I'm coming in that pretty mouth," I growl.

She groans against me. Takes me deeper. Works me harder.

I hold her head in place as I rock my hips, thrusting into her mouth.

She looks up at me with a fierce expression. Like she's daring me.

I bring my other hand to her head and rock harder. Faster.

Fuck.

My cock pulses.

I tug at her hair. Groan her name as I come.

She waits until I've spilled every drop and swallows hard.

I offer her my hand.

She takes it and I pull her to her feet. And press my lips against her. And kiss her like it's the only way I can forget the world.

Because it is.

Chapter Nineteen

IRIS

We spend the entire day together. Walker leads me through cooking bacon and eggs. It's easy. Easy enough I promise to make lunch.

He talks me into a *Star Wars* marathon. One including the prequels. But it's actually fun mocking their bad dialogue and ridiculous excess of world building. It feels like it used to—like *Star Wars* is something I love. Like movies and books and TV are capable of capturing every bit of my attention.

Like there are all sorts of things in the world capable of capturing my attention.

I set off the fire alarm when I attempt to pan fry chicken while sautéing frozen broccoli. Multi-tasking in the kitchen is still beyond my skill set.

We dress, get lunch, spend the day walking around Santa Monica and drinking ridiculous amounts of coffee. It's a beautiful blue day. Warm. Sunny. Bright.

The entire world feels bright.

It's like that all week.

Studying is easier. Classes are more interesting. My research project falls together. I look forward to my yoga sessions. And my attempt at healthier meals. And texting Walker all night.

When he invites me to a party at the shop—and promises to make me come after—I say yes instantly.

Even when he insists he's teaching me to surf the next day at eight a.m.

Eight a.m. on a Sunday.

Ridiculous.

But worth it.

He might actually be worth it.

THE SHOPS BELL RINGS.

Someone yells, "Surprise."

Then everyone is yelling it together. I'm yelling it. Even though I think surprise parties are a truly terrible idea.

All the lights flick on at once.

Ryan holds his arm over his eyes like he's a vampire protecting himself from the rays of the sun.

Dean laughs. "Happy twenty-seventh." He hands Ryan a black balloon. There are black balloons and lilies everywhere.

It's funny. But ridiculous and premature. Since when is twenty-seven old?

Walker slides his arms around my waist. He pulls my body into his. Brushes his lips against my neck.

My thoughts dissolve.

"Happy Birthday." The cute blond in a pastel cardigan hands Ryan a small present wrapped in blue paper with a turquoise bow. "I hope you like it."

"Thanks, Kay." He takes the present. Looks at her like he's not sure if he should hug her or shake hands or nod. He offers his hand.

They shake.

Relief spreads over his face as he pulls his arm to his side. This guy is not into affection.

Dean nods to a massive present sitting on the counter behind us.

Ryan nods *thanks.*

Dean shakes his head *you aren't getting away that easy*. He pulls his brother into a hug.

Distaste spreads over Ryan's face. He steps back with a sigh. "We have drinks?"

"Please." Dean motions to said counter. There's a row of top shelf stuff next to the present.

Ryan moves toward sweet, sweet intoxication, but Brendon cuts him off.

He's merciful. He doesn't hug Ryan. He simply shakes his head and hands over a present.

The girl with the purple-grey hair takes her turn. She does hug Ryan, but he actually seems okay with it.

Then a girl with dark hair that fades into crimson ends bounces forward. She throws her arms around Ryan. "Happy birthday." She pulls back with a smile.

"That's Emma." Walker motions to Brendon. "His sister." Then he motions to the cute blond. "Kaylee's best friend."

I try to shove the names into the *important things* section of my brain. I know he's told me some of this before. But Walker has this way of making me forget everything.

Like being at a party with a fresh bottle of Belvedere.

My tongue slides over my lips.

My nerves pick up. The same as my coffee fix, but duller. Need. Drink. Now. Need. Thoughts. Gone.

Walker brings his lips to my ear. "You want a drink?"

Yes. A double. Triple. Hell, bring the bottle. A few shots and I'll be dancing on the counter. I'll be happy. Free. Void of any concerns except *fun*.

"No, thank you." The words feel like a lie. But they aren't.

A part of me still wants that drink, but most of me is thinking about waking up in Ross's bed with memories of the last night a blur. Combining drinking with opiates... bad idea. Good way to OD. I knew better.

I know better.

My first few weeks out of rehab were tough, but since I found my footing, I haven't *really* been tempted. I'll have a passing urge here and there. But I never want a buzz or a high enough to actually consider using. The bad memories outweigh the bliss.

He releases his grip on my waist. "You don't drink?"

"I don't like the person I am when I drink."

He nods. "I'll skip it."

"You don't have to."

"I don't mind." He slides his hand over my ass. "You're more intoxicating."

"That's cheesy."

"What if I drag you to the back room and fuck you against the wall."

Yes. Great idea. My breath catches in my throat. "You should."

"You think I won't?" His eyes fill with determination. "Say the word, sweetness."

I shake my head. He will do it. And part of me wants him to. But the rest of me is too shy to even consider it.

"Too bad. Would have been fun." He takes my hand and leads me around the room, re-introducing me to everyone.

Ryan forces a smile.

Brendon is nothing like he was on the hike. There isn't a single sign of annoyance on his face. He has his arms around Kaylee and he's happy as a clam.

She is too.

They're like a poster for a teen drama. *The cute innocent*

blond and the tattooed bad boy. How will it play out? Tune in tomorrow at ten.

They're clearly the endgame couple.

Leighton—the girl with the purple-grey hair—smiles like she can't believe how relieved she is to see me. "It's always such a sausage fest here. Nice to have another face."

Dean steps in. He shakes his head, sending his wavy hair in every direction. His blue eyes fix on hers. "Please. You love being surrounded by dick."

"Not like this." She winks at him. "Stop reading my journal."

"It's too hot. I can't," he teases back.

"Uh-huh." She shakes her head *isn't he ridiculous?*

I nod. He's a lot of things. Ridiculous is pretty high up the list.

I turn back to Walker. "Go. Talk to your friend. I'm fine."

He arches a brow. "You sure?"

"Yeah. It's his birthday. Tease him about getting old. And —what did you get him?" I ask.

Walker's smile spreads over his cheeks. "Dean and I went in on that together."

"What is it?" I ask.

Dean laughs.

Walker too.

They share a look—the kind of look I used to share with Lily. That best friends *we're the only people who get each other thing*.

"Oh please." Leighton shakes her head. "You were talking about it forever." She moves closer to me. Leans in to whisper. "They got him a blow-up doll."

I look to my definitely not a boyfriend. "Why?"

"Hey, if he's not gonna move on to a woman, why not try this substitute?" Dean offers.

"It's cheaper than you'd think," Walker says.

"And my boy tested the equipment." Dean winks at me. "Hope you aren't jealous."

"You... you didn't, right?" I'm pretty sure he's teasing. Because giving someone a used blow up doll... and Walker wouldn't. Right?

"Yeah. Of course." Walker laughs.

Ryan joins us. He takes a long swig from his red solo cup, gives the group a long once-over, shakes his head. "Can't believe I fell for this *we need to have a meeting Saturday night because it's always dead* shit."

"It wasn't our finest work," Walker admits.

"Speak for yourself," Dean says.

"Yeah. Dean's proud when he can tie his shoes," Leighton says.

Dean shows off his checkered Vans. "Too difficult. I made the switch back in middle school."

Ryan takes another swig from his drink. "This is good shit."

"Only the best for my big brother." Dean blows him a kiss. It's sarcastic. And it's not. There's affection in his blue eyes.

"Yeah. Right." Ryan shakes his head. He turns to Leighton. "How'd they rope you into this?"

"I wanted to celebrate your birthday." She folds her arms. Hurt creeps into her voice. "Is that really implausible?"

"You're too smart to think I'd enjoy a surprise party," he says.

Her eyes fix on Ryan. "You do. You just don't show it."

He shakes his head *no way*.

"Is that the only gesture you know?" Dean teases.

Ryan flips him off.

Everyone laughs.

"I just got out of a relationship too. Well, a few months ago. Walker mentioned that you, and, uh..." This is awkward.

He's just staring back at me, all intense and glum. "It sucks, huh?"

"Yeah." He nods.

"You never want to love again," I say.

Again, he nods.

"You, um, was it a long relationship?" I bite my lip. Why am I asking him so many personal questions when he clearly isn't into sharing or affection?

"Forgive Iris. She's gonna be a shrink," Walker says.

"Oh. Yeah?" Ryan raises a brow *interesting*. "What's that like?"

"Actually, I'm going to be a research psychologist. I'm not studying clinical psychology. You know, therapy?"

He nods. He knows. "I tried that once."

Dean's eyes go wide. "You did?"

"Yeah. Thought it might help. With forgetting Penny." He takes another sip. "But it was bullshit. Didn't go back. No offense."

"It's not for everyone." I press my lips together. "Sometimes, it takes a while to find the right person. Or get comfortable. Especially if you aren't used to sharing. Not that you're—"

"No. He is. He gets it." Dean laughs. "Good thing for you Walker has a babe on his arm. You could get free help."

"You could kiss my ass," Ryan says.

Dean laughs. "A hundred bucks says you won't drop your pants."

"You're disgusting," Leighton says.

"Like you don't want to see Ryan naked." Dean shakes his head.

Her cheeks flush. "I... shut up." The blush spreads down her chest.

And she keeps looking at Ryan.

She likes him.

Maybe. I think. I'm not great at seeing the line between *I like you as a friend* and *I want your body* and *I want you to be mine forever*.

Dean pulls his t-shirt up his stomach. Pats his perfect six-pack. "You can look as much as you want, baby."

"Which is zero." She shakes her head. "What's with your aversion to clothes?"

"They hide my beauty." He shrugs, effortlessly coy.

Ryan looks to me. "That's a good thing you're doing. More important than this shit." He motions to the shop.

"Tattoos are therapeutic in their own way." My fingers go to the words on my forearm. "You're also doing a good thing."

"Nah, mostly he does himself as he cries into pictures of Penny," Dean teases.

Ryan shakes his head *stupid kids*. "Good luck with shit." He nods a round of goodbyes then turns and leaves.

I wait until he's out of earshot. "Is he always like that?"

"No." Leighton presses her plum lips together. "He's usually a lot less friendly."

"Yeah. He's practically beaming." Walker leans in to press his lips to my neck. "I'm gonna talk to him."

"Go." I lean into his touch.

He wraps his arms around me. Pulls me into a tight hug.

His lips brush mine. Soft to start. Then harder. Then he's sucking on my bottom lip, groaning into my mouth.

Every thought in my head dissolves. My eyelids flutter together. My world goes white. It's only Walker. His lips, his hands, his smile.

I really, really like him.

Want him to be my boyfriend like him.

Want him to be my boyfriend for a long, long time and maybe forever like him.

It's... Uh...

I pull back with a sigh.

His lips press into that perfect smile. He shoots Dean a playful look. "Don't entertain her too much."

"I can't help it."

Walker laughs. "Uh-huh." He turns and heads over to Ryan. He's sitting on a bench in front with Emma, Brendon, and Kaylee.

Look at me, learning names.

Woohoo.

"You like him, huh?" Dean asks.

"Oh my God. Leave her alone." Leighton presses her palms against the counter. She plops onto it and taps her heeled ankle boots together.

God, she really is cool. Like a punk rock goddess. She's wearing smooth black skinny jeans and a reconstructed Ramones t-shirt cut up and sewn together with hot pink ribbon.

"It's an innocent question." He leans against the counter next to her. Brings his cup to his lips. "You should be proud of me. I didn't demand Never Have I Ever."

"Uh-huh." She shakes her head *you're ridiculous.*

"Or truth or dare," he says.

She looks to me. "See what I deal with every day?"

I laugh. "It must be rough."

She does too. "It really is. But I love it here. Serious eye candy."

Dean motions *aww, you shouldn't have* with mock humility.

It's clear she isn't trying to pay Dean a compliment, but he is super, duper, amazingly hot. Tall. Broad. With shaggy brown hair, piercing blue eyes, and a million-dollar smile.

He looks like trouble. Like the kind of guy who will get wasted with you, fuck you senseless, then leave you with nothing but memories.

"Brendon, Ryan, and Walker are super hot, yes." She ignores him. "But the clients. All the surfer boys and the local musicians get their work done here. And I don't mean local, playing at a dive bar in Burbank. I mean fucking rock stars who live in Venice." She fans herself. "Why am I not having sex again?"

"You make bad choices," Dean says.

"That hurts coming from you." She smiles. "It's true. Turns out tattoos and muscles don't always equate to boyfriend material."

"In my experience, a short haircut and a nice suit don't either," I say.

"Tattooed manwhores aren't your type?" Dean asks.

"Not usually." I press my hands into my sides. It feels weird not holding a drink. "Excuse me." I move to the bar. Grab a cup. Fill it with grapefruit juice.

God, that Belvedere looks so good.

And it isn't opened.

It would be so, so easy to chug a few shots, let my inhibitions down, bring out fun, party girl Iris.

But the chain reaction that starts...

It isn't worth it.

I move back to Dean and Leighton. They're hate-flirting over something.

And Walker is laughing with his friends. Well, Ryan isn't exactly laughing. But he looks slightly less miserable.

"You're really into him, huh?" Dean asks.

"Seriously, Dean?" Leighton shoots him a *really* look.

"I don't sleep with people I don't like," I say.

She laughs. "Foreign concept. You'll have to explain it to him."

"Nah. It's more than that level of like." Dean's eyes meet mine. "You're looking at him the way Brendon looks at Kay."

"Like she wants to drag him to the back room, pin him to the wall, and rip his clothes off?" Leighton takes a long sip.

"Who doesn't? I'm not into your boyfriend, Iris, but he is fine."

"He's not my boyfriend." The words are quick. An impulse. But they don't feel as true as they should. "We're just having fun."

She nods even though it's clear she doesn't believe me.

"I hope that's true." Dean taps his glass with his pointer finger. "'Cause I don't want to see him turning into some more annoying version of Ryan."

"He won't." Though, given Walker's reaction to everything about his sister, it seems like he'll be miserable and evasive if this ends in flames. Which isn't exactly Ryan, but it's not far off either. "Relationships don't always end like that."

"Mostly," he says.

"You don't think anyone is forever?" I'm not sure if I do either. Not anymore.

"No. Brendon and Kay, that's forever. But most of them—" he motions to Ryan—"end like that. And I don't want to see my friend miserable."

"Is that why you get pissed about his sister coming around?" I ask.

All that joy fades from Dean's expression. His voice gets serious. "Is she?"

I... I don't know. "No."

"Good." He wipes away his frown. "She's bad news."

"Why?" I ask.

"Ask your boyfriend." He pushes away from the counter. "You seem like a cool chick, Iris. Leigh is right—"

"Do not fucking call me that," she says.

"This place can be a sausage fest. Always nice to have a cute chick around. But be careful with this 'we're having fun shit.' He's into you. If you don't want that, then don't fucking lead him on." Dean nods a goodbye then turns and leaves.

Leighton hops down from the counter. "Sorry. He's an idiot."

"No. He's right." I need to be clear about my intentions. How they've changed. I need to tell Walker I want more. To make sure he wants it too.

Chapter Twenty

IRIS

We don't leave until after midnight. I'm exhausted, my stomach is rumbling, and my feet are dying from these heels.

But none of that matters.

Because Walker is wrapping his arms around me. He's leaning in to press his soft lips to mine.

He sucks on my bottom lip.

I dig my fingers into his cotton t-shirt as I pull back with a sigh.

He brushes a hair behind my ear. His eyes stay glued to mine. They promise satisfaction. Affection. Love.

He slides his hand over my ass.

I lean into his touch. This makes sense. This is something I understand. And it's simple. I want him. He wants me. We make each other come.

It's perfect.

He leans in to whisper in my ear. "It's too far to my place."

"Mine is farther."

He rocks his hips, pinning me to the wall outside of Inked Hearts.

Mmm. His body feels so good against mine.

I'm tempted to fuck him right here, on this semi-busy Venice Beach street in the middle of the night.

Really, really tempted.

"Ahem." Someone clears their throat.

Walker turns to the noise. It's Dean.

He motions to the shop. "There's a perfectly good back room."

"Ryan will kill me," Walker says.

"Hey Iris. How you doing?" Dean asks.

"Uh..." Breathless. "Good."

He chuckles. "I bet." He motions to the other side of the street. "I'm gonna get a drink. You're not invited."

Walker laughs. "Wasn't gonna come."

"Damn. That's self-restraint." Dean's earlier *don't break my friend's heart* warning is gone. He's just friendly... ish.

Walker turns back to me. He brings his hand to my hip. Pulls my body into his as he pushes me against the wall.

It's incredibly hot.

I stare back into his dark eyes. "Your place. Now."

His nod is needy. He steps backward, takes my hand, guides me to his parking spot around the corner.

I climb inside. Click my seatbelt. Press my knees together.

It does nothing to stop the heat pooling in my sex.

I need him.

Not just his hands, and his lips, and his cock.

Him.

It's scary how much I need him.

When did this happen? How?

His eyes meet mine as he slides into the car. His smile spreads over his cheeks.

It's a beautiful smile.

It does things to me.

Makes my knees knock together. My stomach flutter. My heart thud against my chest.

"I..." Words form and dissolve on my tongue. How do I say this? *I like you* is too plain. But I don't love him yet. I could. One day. And maybe I will. But not yet.

"You..." He arches a brow. Clicks his seatbelt. Slides his keys into his car and turns them.

"I had a good time." *I want this to be a real thing. More than fun. More than casual. I want to tell you about my past. To explain every single mistake. To show you all my ugly parts.*

"Not too much shit from Dean?"

"Just a little. He's protective of you. It's sweet."

"He's an idiot."

"That too." But I understand. Dean doesn't want Walker getting hurt. I don't either. I... I really, really like him.

He turns back to the window, hits his left blinker, pulls onto the street.

I turn on the radio. Commercial on KROQ. Shitty auto-tuned pop song on KYSR. Even more horrible one on KIIS —the local Top 40 station. "You listen to KIIS?"

"Fuck no. Must have been Emma."

"You give her a lot of rides?"

"She had a phase where she was pissed at Brendon." He points to the aux cable. "You can play some coffee shop shit."

"When you put it that way..."

"Some beautiful, mellow jams that make you want to fall asleep."

I laugh. He's teasing me in that *I like you* way.

We pull onto Ocean. It's only five minutes now. But that's too long.

I dig through my purse, pull out my cell, connect it to the aux cable. I pick my most mellow coffee shop song.

Walker laughs as it flows from the speakers. "This your preferred soundtrack?"

"For studying?"

"For fucking."

Oh. "I've never listened to music before. Have you?"

"Yeah."

"Metallica?"

"No." He laughs. "That breathy, sexy shit."

"You like that?"

"Sometimes."

"You want to put something on when we get home?"

"Dunno. What are we doing at home?"

"Playing Scrabble."

His laugh fills the car. "I concede."

"You go down that easy?"

His voice drops. "Fuck yeah."

My breath catches in my throat. "Do you want to play music after Scrabble?"

"No. I don't. I want to hear every single moan that falls off your lips."

Mmm. Yes. Please. Now.

My limbs get light. Electricity flows through me, from my fingertips all the way to my toes.

I want him so badly.

I like him so much.

I need this to work okay, for him to want me too, for him to accept the Iris who's still struggling to believe she's not her mistakes.

The girl who made all those mistakes.

"I, uh..." I press my lips together. I want to tell him.

My thoughts dissolve as his fingers brush my inner thigh.

"You, uh..." He drags his fingers higher. Under my dress.

Over my panties.

Fuck.

What was I thinking?

Something important.

But it couldn't possibly have been as important as this.

"You okay, sweetness?" He rubs me over my panties.

My response is a groan.

Why am I wearing underwear?

Why do I even wear clothes?

I should live naked in his apartment.

We should be naked in his apartment forever.

Away from all the ugly things in the rest of the world.

He stops at the next light. Montana. "You there?"

I nod. "Can't think."

He chuckles. "Same thing happens to me when all my blood is in my cock."

"How are you so coherent?"

"Practice." He looks back to the street. Strokes me with that thumb. He moves it higher. Higher. "You look fucking amazing, sweetness?"

"Yeah."

"Yeah. I thought about bending you over the counter, rolling that skirt to your waist, and fucking that gorgeous ass."

My cheeks flush. I... uh...

"You want to?"

"Yeah." The words fall off my lips. I... I do? No. I do. A lot. The idea never appealed with Ross, but with Walker... "Tonight?"

"No. I need to feel your cunt around me tonight."

I... uh... "You're doing this on purpose."

His lips curl into a smile. "Yeah." He rubs harder. Harder.

Almost.

The light turns green. He taps the gas. We move forward.

One more street and we turn right. A few more and we turn left. Right. Left. I lean against the seat, arch my back, let a moan fall off my lips.

The car slows to a stop. It turns off.

I stare into Walker's dark eyes. They're filled with desire, yeah, but that's not the most inviting thing about them.

It's the affection.

He undoes his seatbelt. I grab mine and kick the door open. My movements get fast. Reckless.

He clicks the lock. Wraps his arms around me. Pins me against the underground garage wall and kisses me hard.

Fuck, *he's* hard.

And I want that.

"Not here." I bring my hand to his hair to pull his head away. "Need a bed."

He nods and steps backward.

Our path to his front door is messy. Every few steps, we stop to kiss. To tug at clothes. To pant and groan and express everything except our feelings.

Finally, he slides his key into the door and turns the handle.

He whisks me inside and pins me against the door.

But we're not alone.

There's a woman here.

She's tall and thin, with long dark hair and the same dark eyes as Walker.

And she's...

No.

He pulls back to follow my gaze. "Fuck. Bree, what the fuck?"

Bree. His sister.

I... I've seen her at NA.

His sister is a drug addict.

And she knows I'm an addict.

And he...

Fuck.

Chapter Twenty-One

IRIS

She stares at me with recognition in her dark eyes. But it's hazy. She's hazy.

She's high.

Walker is already on the other side of the room. He's calling someone. His parents, I think.

I can't stop staring at his sister.

She keeps asking him to bail her out of messes. That must be an understatement.

But she is trying. I've seen her at a few meetings. The ones in Beverly Hills. One of my friends from rehab talked me into going to sessions that were well-known for celebrity sightings.

We saw a ton of TV actors and musicians, but I still switched to meetings on the Westside. It felt shady trying to see famous people at their weakest.

She was there. Walker's sister.

She tilts her head. "You're Walker's girlfriend?" Her voice is easy. Slow.

"Close enough."

"And he knows you're..." Her brow furrows as she considers her words. Or tries to.

"No."

"Oh."

He tosses his phone on the counter. Runs a hand through his hair.

His eyes go to his sister. "You can't stay here."

"Are you... are you going to let me explain?" She pulls her arm over her chest. Wraps her fingers around the crook of her elbow, covering an injection site.

But it's too late. Too slow. Walker sees it.

His voice drips with frustration "What could you possibly say?"

Her eyes turn down. She looks wounded. Like she really is sorry she's hurting him. Like she has no idea how to stop.

No. It's not like.

She doesn't.

I know. I've been there.

He looks to me and mouths *sorry* then looks back to his sister. "I'll drive you home."

"But." Her eyes go to the floor. "I'm sorry."

He shakes his head *no, you aren't.*

But she is. It's all over her face.

This is way too familiar.

She's here because she trusts him. Because she has nowhere else to go. Because, deep down, she wants help.

Okay, I'm projecting.

But, God, the way he clams up when he mentions her...

There's no way he'll be with a former addict.

There's no way he'll be with me.

He looks to me. "You can stay here or I can drop you off."

I shake my head. "I'll come."

He arches a brow. "You want to?"

"Yeah." I... I have to see this. I have to understand. I have to know if the possibility of us is totally fucked.

~

WALKER'S SISTER SITS IN THE BACKSEAT, HER ARMS FOLDED, her gaze on the window. She doesn't apologize, or try to explain, or comment on the music.

Walker keeps his hand pressed against mine.

He's trusting me with this. With something he doesn't share with anyone. With something that could break his heart.

And I'm holding onto my secret like my life depends on it.

I have to tell him.

But I can't.

The way he looks at his sister—it's like she's tearing his heart out of his chest and stomping it with her heeled boots.

If I tell him, he'll leave.

And he'll never touch me or kiss me or hold me again.

I'll never see his smile, hear his laugh, watch his dark eyes fill up with joy.

My coffee shop music is the only sound in the car. It's soft music, but it's still too loud. Too emotional. Too everything.

I press my lips together.

I stare out the window, watching fancy stores blur together. Then over-sized houses.

We slow.

Park in the driveway of a massive Spanish style house in that neighborhood just north of Santa Monica Boulevard.

Roses line the brick walkway. The lawn is lush. Green. The beige and tan paint is perfect.

Walker turns the car off and slides his keys into his

pocket. His eyes find mine. They beg for understanding, comfort, honesty. "Help me with her."

I nod even though he doesn't need my help. He can carry me, no problem, and his sister is a lot slimmer. Though, she is taller. So it might even out.

He gets out of his car.

I follow suit.

I watch him open the door for his sister, undo her seatbelt, sling her arm over his shoulder.

"I'm okay." She pulls her arm to her side. Stumbles up the walkway.

Walker jogs to meet her. He pulls out his keys, unlocks the front door, steps inside.

She follows.

Then I do.

The inside of the house is just as beautiful. The foyer is a big, airy room with a winding staircase. Skylights let in the glow of the stars. They're dull the way they always are in the city, but they're beautiful all the same.

I follow them up the stairs, to the room at the end of the hallway.

It's a girl's bedroom. And I mean a *girl*. It looks like it belongs to a thirteen-year-old. The sheets and bedspread are pink. The wallpaper is ball gowns and tiaras. The bed is a white four poster thing with sheer lace hanging off the top railing.

It's the perfect place for a princess.

No wonder his sister is this fucked up.

He treats her like a child. Their parents probably do too.

I don't blame him—she's acting like a child, misbehaving for attention—but still.

She needs help. More than this.

He motions to the bed.

She sits. Kicks off her heels. Pulls the covers to her chest.

"What did you take?" I ask.

"Does it matter?" She wraps her fingers around her arm. "Are you going to scold me too?" Her eyes narrow. *We both know you don't have the high ground.*

"Yeah. It's easy to overdose on certain things." I adopt my best *I'm going to be a doctor, well, not that kind of doctor, but trust me, I know this shit* voice. I move closer. "What did you take?"

"She's studying to be a shrink," he says.

"It was only one hit," she says. Like that makes it better.

But it does. To her. I know. I've been there.

"You drink anything?" I ask

She shakes her head.

I look to Walker. "She should be okay."

He nods. Motions to the door. "Go to sleep, Bree."

"Walker, I'm sorry. I want to be better. I do. I just..."

"Call me when you're sober." His words are weary. Like he's tired of repeating them.

He moves to the door, flicks the light off, moves back into the hallway.

I follow him downstairs and back to the car.

He rolls the windows down but doesn't turn the key. The breeze blows over my arms. Crickets chirp. The moonlight bounces off the hood.

He brings one hand to the steering wheel. "I don't want to go home."

"Me either."

"You sure?"

"Yeah."

He nods. "You need to piss or anything?"

"I'm okay."

He nods, turns the key, puts the car in reverse. "I know this is a mess."

It is.

But it's not the mess he thinks it is.

~

I SQUEEZE WALKER'S HAND. I THINK UP A MILLION WAYS to explain this, then a million excuses to keep my lips zipped.

If I tell him, it's over.

But he deserves to know.

He deserves the truth.

I... I don't know what to do here.

Eventually, we find our way onto Pacific Coast Highway.

The deep blue of the ocean bleeds into the sky. We drive far enough into Malibu that the stars start shining.

Walker pulls into a lot on our left. He parks, turns the car off, presses his back against the seat.

"You want to head to the beach?" I don't know what to say. Or how to fix this. I can't. No one can. I know that better than anyone.

He nods *yeah*.

We get out of the car.

He stays a few paces ahead of me as we move toward the water. I step out of my shoes, carry them with two fingers, press my bare feet into the freezing sand.

He stops at the edge of the surf and stares out at the water. "I guess I should explain."

"You don't have to."

"You don't want to hear it?"

"No. I do. I just... I know what addiction is like."

"It's your focus, right?"

"Yeah." My dissertation is on addiction. "But it's not just research. I..." I'm not hijacking his story. He wants to tell me. He wants to share this. I need to support him here. "Go ahead. Start at the beginning."

He nods. "Bree always liked to party. But I thought it was normal. I did too. Well, once I was old enough to get invites to parties. Sometimes I'd go with her. Dean too. We all used sometimes."

"You used heroin?"

"No." He shakes his head. "I had no idea she did for a while. But I tried a lot of other shit. Never quite developed a taste for anything but whiskey."

I nod.

"I thought it was the same for her. She went to college. She kept partying, yeah, but it seemed normal. It's not like I was a paragon of sobriety."

I move closer.

He rubs my arms with his hands. "You're shivering."

I nod.

He slides his leather jacket off his arms and slings it around my shoulders.

It's warm.

Sweet.

Affectionate.

I swallow hard. "What happened?"

"One day, I got this worried call from a party. Asking if I was Sabrina Williams's brother. Telling me she was passed out. That an ambulance was on the way."

"She overdosed?"

"Yeah. A mix of prescription painkillers and alcohol."

"That's a dangerous mix. It's easy to OD."

His nod is weary, like he's been aware of this information for long enough for it to become a thorn in his side. "My parents got really serious. She went to rehab. For a while, she was clean. Then, one day, she wasn't. She graduated to heroin because it was easier to get."

"That happens a lot." It's common. Really common, actually.

"They made due on their threats to stop paying her tuition. She dropped out of school. Lived with some loser boyfriend. Then that went up in flames, and Mom and Dad offered to pay for rehab. She went, did okay for a few months, slipped. It's gone on like that forever. It's gonna stay like this. She doesn't want to get better."

"How do you know?"

"Evidence speaks for itself."

"It isn't like that. Addiction rewires your brain. It's not about willpower."

"Iris—"

"Sorry, I—"

"I'm sure you know a lot more than I do." His voice gets soft. "But I don't need a shrink's help right now."

"You need your friend?"

"Yeah." His eyes meet mine. They're vulnerable. Hurting. "She's gonna die with a needle in her arm and there's nothing I can do."

"I'm sorry."

"Thanks." He pulls me closer.

I can feel every ounce of his warmth. His trust. His need.

He's giving me everything.

And I want everything.

I want to tell him, to explain, but I can't.

Not now. Not here.

"You must think I'm an asshole, wanting to cut her out of my life," he says.

"No." I shake my head. "I understand." God, how I understand. "You can't help someone who won't help themselves."

He brushes a stray hair behind my ear.

The wind blows it in front of my eyes.

His laugh is more happy than sad. "I know there's nothing I can do." He pulls me closer. "But it fucking sucks watching her destroy herself."

"Do you really think you can cut her off?"

"I don't know. I haven't yet."

"I'm sorry."

"I'm used to it."

Tears well up in my eyes. He's hurting so much, and it's exactly the kind of pain I inflicted on everyone in my life.

I did this to Lily. To Mom and Dad. To a dozen other friends who dropped me long before Lily did.

I don't deserve his affection.

I don't deserve his trust.

I don't deserve another chance.

A tear catches on my lashes. Then another.

Walker rests his palm on my cheek. Catches a tear on his thumb. "Hey."

"I'm sorry."

"What for?"

"Everything."

He stares back into my eyes.

But I can't see his. Mine are blurry.

I blink. Bring my hand to my cheek to wipe my tears. "I'm really, really sorry."

"Hey. It's okay." He wraps his arms around me.

I shake my head. It's not. It's really, really not.

"This all for me?"

"No." Yes. Maybe. It's confusing. "I... I like you."

"Like me?"

"A lot." I choke back a sob. "Like I want you to be my boyfriend."

"Damn, I'm charming."

My laugh is anguished. "No, you are. It's not you. I just..." I try to stare back into his eyes, but I can't. I can't hold his gaze. "It's complicated."

"What isn't?"

"Coffee."

He laughs. "Is it your ex?"

Maybe. Ross was the person who introduced me to drugs. He was the last guy I trusted. And that didn't exactly turn out well.

But Walker was right before. Ross barely means anything to me.

How can I explain this without telling him?

How can I stay without telling him?

"I just..." I bury my head in his chest. "I don't want this to end."

"Me either."

"You..."

"Yeah." He runs his fingertips over my cheek. "You sure you want to be part of this train wreck?"

I nod. I'm sure.

But there's no way he wants to be a part of mine.

Chapter Twenty-Two

WALKER

We stay at the beach forever.

The drive home is quiet, but it's not the quiet of earlier. The air isn't heavy or still or stifling.

It's comfortable.

Calm.

It's weird. I've never wanted to lean on someone. To share anything that guts me.

But with Iris...

I trust her.

I want her around.

I want to tell her things. To tell her everything.

After I park, we stumble-kiss our way to my apartment. It isn't the *tear your clothes off* heat of earlier. It isn't that I want to watch her come—I do. Fuck, how I do.

But it's deeper than that.

I lock the apartment door and toss my keys on the dining table.

She pulls my leather jacket tighter as she steps backward.

Her eyes go to the floor. Her expression gets shy. Like this is the first time.

In a way, it is.

This isn't a fuck anymore.

We aren't having fun anymore.

Shit is real now.

Serious.

Intimate.

I motion to the kitchen. "You need anything?"

"Water."

I nod, pour two glasses, bring one to her.

She brings it to her lips and takes a thirsty sip. Her throat quivers as she swallows. Her eyes stay on the floor.

She finishes fast, hands the cup back over, and moves toward the bedroom.

I follow suit. Move through the open door.

She's sitting on the bed, her palms pressed against her thighs, my jacket lying behind her.

I give her a long once-over. Something is different. Wrong.

She looks up at me. Her lips part. There's something on the tip of her tongue, but she swallows it down.

"You okay?" I ask.

She stares back at me like it's the most complicated question she's ever heard. "Maybe."

"Maybe?"

Her eyes fix on me. "Maybe."

"Anything I can do?"

Her voice drops to something low and needy. "Fuck me."

It's a weird request.

But I can't exactly complain.

I sit on the bed next to her. "That's really what you want?"

She climbs into my lap, wraps one arm around my waist, slides the other into my hair. "That's everything I want."

Her lips brush mine. It's soft. Then hard.

My tongue slides into her mouth. Dances with hers.

My need pours into her. This is such a fucked-up mess. I'm pathetic and cold-hearted in equal measure.

But she isn't running for the hills. She's here.

She's mine.

Fuck, she's really mine.

I slide my hand into her hair.

She does away with my t-shirt then climbs onto the bed. She falls onto her back and presses her knees together.

Her blue eyes meet mine. They promise the fucking world.

For once, I want that.

I want everything she can give me.

I nod to the bedside table.

She reaches for it, pulls the drawer open, pulls out a condom. She stares back into my eyes as she pulls her dress over her head.

My fingertips skim her ankles. The inside of her knees. Her inner thighs.

They curl into the straps of her panties.

Her eyelids flutter closed. Her breath catches in her throat. "Please."

Slowly, I roll her panties to her ankles.

I drag my lips up the inside of her calf. The inside of her thigh.

Her fingers curl into my hair. Her hips lift to meet me.

I pin her thighs to the bed and bring my lips to her. No teasing today. I need all of her. Her pleasure, her satisfaction, her trust.

She bucks against my lips as I lick her up and down.

She tastes so fucking good.

I focus on the spot where she needs me most and I flick my tongue against her.

She groans. "Walker." Her voice is needy. Breathless. Like she'll never get enough.

Fuck knows I won't.

I hold her in place as I lick her.

Her thighs shake.

Her groans fill the room.

Her nails dig into my shoulder, a desperate plea for more, for me, for everything.

I want everything.

I want to give her everything.

It's fucking weird.

But fucking amazing too.

I look up at her, watch pleasure spill over her expression, then I turn every bit on my attention to tasting her.

A few more flicks of my tongue and she's shuddering.

Shaking.

Tugging at my hair.

There.

She groans my name as she comes.

I lick her through her orgasm then I drag my lips up her pelvis, stomach, chest, neck.

She looks up at me with every bit of trust in the world.

I bring my lips to hers.

Her tongue slides into my mouth.

She tears the wrapper and slides the condom over my cock.

I lower my body onto hers.

She wraps her legs around my waist.

There.

My tip strains against her.

Then it's one inch at a time.

Fuck. She feels good. Mine.

It's the only thing in my head.

Iris is mine.

She trusts me. Needs me. Wants me.

Not the carefree guy I convince everyone else I am.

Me.

I kiss her harder.

She holds my head against hers, rocks her hips to meet me.

We move together, groan together, breathe together.

We stay locked like that for ages.

Until she's there, groaning against my lips as she comes.

Then I'm there, digging my fingers into her skin, pulling her closer, pumping deeper.

I groan her name as I come.

My cock pulses. Pleasure floods my body. But it's more than satisfaction.

It's everything.

She's everything.

And this is everything.

Chapter Twenty-Three

WALKER

I wake up with Iris in my arms.

The world is brighter. The air is sweeter. The coffee tastes better.

She doesn't even blink when I remind her we have a surfing date.

This is perfect. It's what I need.

She's what I need.

"How am I already melting?" Iris bends her elbow to reach her wetsuit's zipper. "Ah." She grabs it, pulls it down two inches, rolls the Lycra off her shoulders.

"'Cause it works." I move behind her. Roll it back up her shoulders.

"You're evil."

"I know." I slide my hand over her ass. Fuck, this was an amazing idea. She looks good enough to eat. My head already feels clear. Last night—well, the first half—already feels like a bad dream. "I'll make it up to you."

"Oh." She arches her back, pressing her ass against my crotch. "Carry on."

"What are we doing again?"

"What does anyone do at eight a.m.?"

I laugh. We're way past eight a.m. Iris didn't want to get out of bed and... well, I didn't either. "Drink coffee."

"Hmm. This is sounding reasonable."

"No more coffee until you catch three waves."

"Three? Three?"

I nod. Three.

She shakes her head. "I'll never have coffee again."

I nod to the board. "On your stomach."

"Yes, sir." She winks as she drops to her hands and knees on the surfboard. Slowly, she lowers herself onto her stomach.

It's a rental, one of those obnoxious ones covered in foam—my board is way too long for her.

I drop to the sand next to her. It's already warm. Comforting. Like a hug from an old friend.

She turns her head to her side to look me in the eyes. "I could get used to this."

"You'll be begging for more soon."

"Hmm." She lets out a wistful *yes, once we get home* sigh.

I laugh. "You do push-ups?"

"Why would I do push-ups?"

"To improve your surfing game."

"I've done a push-up."

"When?"

"No comment."

My smile spreads over my cheeks. "This is easy—"

"I bet it's not."

"Simple. It's like a push-up, but you jump to your feet at the same time." I put my hands in position and demonstrate a pop-up. I push myself up as I jump to my side. "Land with your knees bent." I lean into the position, modeling catching my balance.

"That's easy?"

I nod.

"You need to work on your definition."

"Trust me. You can do it."

She shoots me some serious side-eye, but, still, she places her hands outside her shoulders.

"On three."

She nods.

"One, two, three."

She pushes herself up and jumps to one side. She lands for a hot second then stumbles off the board, onto the sand.

I catch her. "Great first attempt."

"How do you do this?"

"Practice."

"It's horrible."

"Suits me."

She laughs. "I guess that's true." She wipes sweat from her brow. "It's so hot like this."

"We'll be in the ocean soon."

"You have water?"

"Yeah." I dig it out from my bag and hand it to her.

She pops the lid and takes a greedy sip. She hands it over. Pulls her arm over her chest.

It's funny. That's the same gesture as Bree.

But that's about where their similarities stop and end. Iris is nothing like Bree. She's honest. Smart. Together.

Iris would never pull the kind of shit my sister does.

Her gaze turns toward the sky. "It's beautiful here, huh?"

"Yeah."

"Makes you think. You know, all that stuff about the ocean going on forever? How it never changes?"

"The ocean always wins."

"Yeah." She gnaws on her bottom lip.

It's like last night.

She's thinking something.

Hurting over something.

"You okay?" I ask.

"Maybe."

"Is that your go-to response?"

"No." Slowly, she meets my gaze. Her expression gets soft. Vulnerable. "I should tell you something."

"I know you're freaked about sharks."

"No. Well, I am. But that's not it." She takes a deep breath. "It's about... about the past, I guess."

"Is it important?"

"Yeah."

Fuck, she looks terrified.

I want to be someone Iris can lean on. I want her to be comfortable telling me anything.

But is now really the time?

She went from joyous to miserable like *that*.

Last night was heavy. We need something light. Fun. Easy.

"Will telling me make you feel better?" I ask.

Her brow furrows as she turns over the question. "No, it won't. But this is... you deserve to know."

"That doesn't matter."

"Walker, you—"

"No. Whatever it is, it doesn't matter."

"This will matter to you."

"It won't."

"It will."

My voice gets sure. "No. It won't. The past is the past." I slide my arms around her waist. Pull her closer. "Tell me if you want. That's your call. But if it's something that happened before we met, I don't need to know."

She looks up at me. "But you have no idea what it is."

"I don't care what it is. It doesn't matter. It's not gonna change how I feel about you. I want you exactly as you are."

She blinks, dumbfounded. "Really?"

"Yeah." There's nothing Iris could tell me that would change how I see her.

"Okay. I..." She presses her lips together. "I guess we should get to it then."

"We should."

She motions to the board. "Do I have to do the push-up thing, again?"

"It's easier on land. We need to practice. Get the muscle memory."

"You just like watching me jump in a wet suit." There's still something heavy in her voice.

"It doesn't hurt." I motion to the board.

She rolls onto her stomach, does another pop-up. Sticks the landing.

We go through another dozen. Then a dozen more. She gets flushed and breathless. Fuck, she looks like she's melting.

I know I am. Wetsuits are fucking warm on the sand.

I pick up the board and point to the beach. It's quiet here. Only a few other surfers and a couple having a picnic. We're well into Malibu. Farther than we were last night. But...

I'm not going there right now. The beach is my happy place or some cheesy shit like that. It always clears my head. Helps me make sense of the world.

I lead Iris into the water. Get deep enough to drop the board, watch her climb onto, bring it past the break point.

The ocean is freezing against my hands and toes, but it feels good. Soothing. Invigorating.

I tread water with one hand on her board.

She turns her head to look me in the eyes. Uses her arm as a pillow. "This is relaxing." All that heaviness fades from her voice.

Fuck, that makes me warm all over.

I want this. I want to see that smile every fucking day.

The waves rock the surfboard back and forth. "Can I hang out like this forever?"

"Yeah."

"Really? You'll hang there all day?"

"You underestimate how much I love it here."

"That much?"

I nod. "The ocean is constant. Steady. It can kick your ass a million ways, but it's always there, wearing rocks into sand."

"When did you learn to surf?"

"A friend's birthday party. I was eleven or twelve. I lived at the pool in the summer. Begged my parents to take us to the beach every weekend."

"Did they?"

"Yeah. But they weren't into it. They'd argue over who's turn it was then sit there, under an umbrella, working."

"Working at the beach?"

"You ever see a guy scribbling on a legal pad in board shorts?"

She shakes her head.

"Then you've never seen my dad at the beach."

"What's he do?"

"Business consulting. I'm not sure, exactly. I tune it out."

"And your mom?"

"Same kinda thing. Finance. The details always escape me."

"They worked a lot when you were a kid?"

"Yeah. We had a nanny when I was young, but she didn't really hang out with me. It was always me and Bree. She'd help me with my homework, make me dinner, let me tag along with her friends."

"You were close?"

"Yeah. Best friends. Until she went to college. She was

always there to make shit better. Our parents are the type to sweep shit under the rug. They'd always pretend like everything was fine, try to hide their fights. But they didn't. I always heard them. It freaked me out. Bree would calm me down. Distract me."

Iris's lips press together. Her eyes go to her nails. They're lilac.

"I... um, I guess I should try to actually catch one of these." She motions to the waves breaking toward the beach.

Yeah. I'm here to teach her. Conversation can come later. The beach isn't the place to zone out. The ocean is merciless. It's easy to lose control. Get pulled into the depths or smacked into the sand.

I don't mind taking that risk every time I step on my board.

But I'm not asking that of Iris.

I'm here to protect her as much as I'm here to teach her.

Still. "These are shit waves. After the next set."

"I have no idea what that means."

"Parents didn't make you do Jr. Lifeguards?"

"No. Swim team. Our neighborhood had one."

"Whose didn't?"

"True."

"What was your stroke?"

"Breaststroke. You?"

"Freestyle."

"Of course."

"Of course?" I raise a brow.

"You just seem like the type." She scrunches her brow. Thinking.

About this?

Or about what she wanted to tell me?

It doesn't matter. Either way, I need to guide her through this. To get her focusing on her immediate surroundings.

I nod *uh huh*, even though she's full of it, then I motion to the waves. There's one rolling toward the beach. "Waves come in a set. Three or four, then there's a calm, then another set. The waves in the same set tend to be about the same size. But all the waves here are small. That's why I came here."

"Bunny slopes?"

"Basically." I turn her board in the right direction. "Think freestyle for this. You want to paddle with the wave until you feel it catch you, then do a pop-up. I'll tell when you've caught it. Yell 'Iris, now.' But the ocean's loud. You might not hear me. If you feel like you've got it, go for it."

"Uh..." She stares back at me in horror.

"You can do it. Trust me."

"That's my line."

"I'm stealing it." I press my palms against her board, push myself enough to plant a kiss on her lips.

She tastes good. Like salt and sunscreen and Iris.

A wave breaks and crashes into the sand. "You ready?"

"Yeah."

"I'll tell you when." The next wave isn't big enough. I watch it crest, break, pound the sand. There. The next. Almost. "Now." I push her in the right direction.

She starts paddling.

And just keeps paddling.

She rides the wave all the way to the sand, but she's on her stomach the whole time.

Reasonable for a first attempt. Fuck knows it took me forever to actually get on my feet.

I swim out to meet her, help her bring the board back.

She climbs on. Shoots me a sheepish expression. "I chickened out."

"It takes time to get comfortable."

"Yeah. A long time."

A long fucking time. "Go for it when you're ready."

"No. I want to be ready. Now."

"There's no secret. You just have to do it."

She nods with understanding. Presses herself into sphinx position. Looks me in the eyes. "What do you think you're going to do about your sister?"

"I don't know."

"It's tough."

"You can still walk, you know."

"I know. I don't want to."

"You don't think I'm pathetic?"

"No."

"Merciless?"

"No. I get it. You do cut her off, she dies. You try to help, she might take you with her. And if your parents aren't following through on their threats..." Her voice gets low. Soft. "How can anyone choose between those options?"

"What would you do?"

"Honestly?"

"Yeah."

She presses her index finger into her thumb. Stares at her purple nails. "I'd give her one chance then cut her off."

"Forever?"

"Let her know you'll be there if she gets sober. That the door is always open. But if she's not..." She looks up at the bright blue sky. Then toward the horizon. "It's too calm, huh?"

"You know a lot about this."

"Yeah."

"Anyone you know—"

"No one I loved. I, um... I guess you should talk to your parents."

"They wanted to do dinner tonight. But that was before—"

"I can talk to them if you want. Scare them with research."

"Nothing scares them."

"I can still go. Hold your hand." She presses her lips together. "Or... I don't want to intrude."

"No. I want you there."

She nods. "Good." She turns back to the ocean. "Oh. That's one, a set, right?" Her voice gets bright. "I'm going to catch this one."

"Yeah?"

"Yeah. You'll see. I'm going to have a Roxy contract in no time flat." She looks to me with a smile.

The first waves crashes into the beach.

The next rolls toward us.

"Go." I push her board in the right direction.

She paddles. Catches the waves. Pops up with one messy step. She rides the wave for a second and a half, then she falls/jumps into the water.

It's a smooth fall. Like she's been surfing for years.

She pushes the board back to me.

And she wraps her arms around me and she kisses me like she needs everything I have to give.

Chapter Twenty-Four

IRIS

"Mmmm." I fall onto the bench seat as I take a long sip of my sugary cold brew. Sweet, sweet caffeine. "Thank you, surf gods."

"You're welcome." Walker slides onto the bench next to me. He taps the outside of my knee with the outside of his.

We're both in shorts and t-shirts. We both towel changed at the beach. After about a gallon of water, I'm finally hydrated enough to caffeinate properly.

"Don't you want to eat?" He arches a brow as he takes a long sip of his black cold brew.

"Eventually. This first." I lean back in my seat. Sip. Sigh with pleasure.

He wraps his arms around my waist and pulls me onto his lap. "You make me so fucking jealous, Iris."

"Yeah?" I lean back so my neck brushes against his cheek. It feels warm. It feels better than it has any right to.

"You don't fool me, sweetness. You do it on purpose." He places his palm on my quad and rubs my inner thigh with his thumb. "You sure you're good to do dinner at seven tonight?"

I nod.

"Fuck, we're jumping into relationship fast."

I laugh. "True."

"Too much?"

"No." Not even a little too much.

He brushes my hair behind my ear. "Tell me the truth."

I thought you'd ask. There's no way you're okay with the past being the past. I really, really want to believe that, but I can't. "Yeah?"

"You love surfing."

Oh. "I do." It makes me feel alive and vibrant. A natural high. It makes sense now, why so many former addicts drive motorcycles or jump out of planes. The rush is everything. "Walker, I—"

"Don't tell me you're already backing out."

"No. Of course not. This is, um, part of being a girlfriend. Or whatever we're calling this."

"I like girlfriend."

"Yeah?"

He nods. "I've never been a boyfriend before."

"You're a virgin?"

He nods.

"Not even once in high school?"

"Not even once."

"Wow. I'm not sure I've ever popped a cherry before." I turn so I can look into his eyes. They're dark and beautiful and filled with trust.

Is it really okay keeping this secret?

Is he really okay with the past being the past?

WE SPEND THE AFTERNOON JUMPING FROM COFFEE SHOP TO lunch to coffee shop. We swing by his place to pick up clothes, then we go to mine. We fuck, shower, change.

I spend forever fixing my hair and makeup. It needs to be perfect. So his parents don't see the cracks in my story. So his sister believes I'm honest. So I see Iris the future psychologist and not Iris the fuck-up when I look in the mirror.

He slides his arms around my waist. Brushes his lips against my neck. He's in jeans and a button-up shirt. It suits him more than it should.

It's unfair how good he looks in everything.

"You ready to go?" He slides his hand over my hip.

"Not if you keep doing that."

He chuckles as he steps backward. "I can't help it. You're too fucking tempting."

My cheeks flush. I smooth my dress. Sway my hips as I spin on my heels to face him. "I'm wearing a thong."

"You're evil."

"I learned from the best."

MY CONFIDENCE PLUMMETS AS I STEP ONTO THE hardwood floor. This place is even more beautiful with the sunset flowing through the sheer curtains. It reeks of money, taste, class.

Walker pulls me a little closer. His fingers tense. Then his arms. His shoulders. His jaw.

It's subtle. Almost imperceptible—he keeps a perfect poker face—but it's there. I'm getting good at reading him. At seeing past the carefree smile.

A woman in her fifties in a black shift dress, a royal blue cardigan, and expensive all-business heels crosses the foyer. She's taller than I am, with dark eyes and highlighted dark hair.

Her red lips—a subtle, work appropriate red—press into a

smile. "Walker, sweetie. It's been too long." She turns to me. "You must be Walker's girlfriend."

"Iris," he says.

"Jen." His mom places her hand over her heart. "You can call me Mom, though I'm sure that's a bit premature."

I look into Walker's eyes for some sign on how I should react. Is she really suggesting we're going to get married? I guess it isn't unusual for the mom of a twenty-something guy who's never had a girlfriend before. But still...

"It's nice to meet you." I offer a hand.

She takes mine with both of hers. Shakes. "You too." She releases me then turns to Walker. "I miss you so much, baby." She wraps her arms around him. "I know you have issues with your sister—"

"Let's wait until we sit down," he says.

Her lips curl into a frown as she pulls away. "We worry about her too." She motions *after me* then turns and leads us through the main room and the sparkling, stainless steel kitchen, past the sliding door that leads out to the backyard.

The pool glows against the darkening sky.

It's inviting.

"Iris." Walker takes my hand. Motions to the dining room through the open doorway.

Oh. I'm staring at the pool. Stalling, maybe. What can I really say to his sister? To his parents? *Trust me, I know how hard this is for your daughter. Why? Uh, I just do. No reason. It's not like I'm a recovering addict. You really think I'd keep that from your son? Of course not. I'm not a liar.*

Ahem.

I'm not here to angst about my baggage.

I'm here to support him. To help him confront his parents.

I'm focusing on that.

I follow him into the dining room, to the massive oak table.

He pulls out my seat for me, a perfect gentleman.

I take it, cross my legs, smooth my skirt, hang my jacket off the back.

Walker takes a seat next to me. He nods to his mom. Then to his dad, sitting next to her. "Dad, this is Iris."

His dad nods. "Robert. It's lovely to meet you. I'd offer you a drink, but we're keeping the house dry."

The frown falls off Walker's face. It's news. Good news.

"Oh, that's fine. I don't drink." I press my lips into a smile. "It smells wonderful." Like lemon and cardamom. Which is weird, given the spotless kitchen.

"I wish I could take credit." Walker's mom presses her lips into a smile. "But it's takeout."

"You want me to bring it out?" Walker asks.

"Thanks, baby." His mom smiles.

Walker shoots me a hopeful look as he pushes himself out of his chair. He moves into the kitchen.

His parents' attention turns to me.

His mom takes a long sip from her water glass. She looks at it wistfully, like she wishes it was wine. "How did you two meet?"

Uh... I can't exactly say I brought him back to my place to nail him. "A friend's party."

"I'm always telling my younger coworkers that socializing is the best way to meet someone. I know all the kids are on Tinder and OkCupid these days, but it's not the same as an actual conversation." She takes another sip.

"It's not. I, uh..." Thought he was hot and likely good in bed. "Your son is incredibly charming."

"He takes after his mother." His father nods.

She beams.

It must be true. His dad seems more behind the scenes.

His mom is quiet, but there's something magnetic about her eyes. The same eyes as Walker. And as his sister.

"What do you do, sweetheart?" she asks.

"I'm a PhD candidate." I fold my hands in my lap. "In psychology."

"Oh." She turns to the door, right as Walker enters with a set of plates. "You didn't tell me you were dating a smart woman."

"You didn't ask. You only asked if she was pretty." He sets plates in front of each of us, moves back into the kitchen, returns with silverware.

"She is." She looks to me. "He gushed about how gorgeous you are."

My cheeks flush. "Thank you."

Walker's eyes meet his mother's. "Bree isn't here?"

"She's at a meeting." There's a tone to her voice. An *I don't want to hear your opinion about that*. She turns to me. "I hate to talk shop at dinner, but, sweetheart, what are your thoughts about the twelve-step program?"

She's asking because of the PhD thing.

Not because she knows I've been through rehab. Because I go to meetings. Because I have a tenuous relationship with said meetings.

She has no idea I'm on shaky ground.

That I've ever been on shaky ground.

I muster all the confidence I have. I need to do this for him. I need to help him convince his parents. "It's hard to find accurate statistics, but most suggest that rehab in combination with a twelve-step program works best. Addiction is always difficult. Most people try to quite a few times before it sticks. But having a support network helps."

Walker moves into the room with two trays of food. One of chicken curry. One of rice.

His mom smiles. "Walker mentioned you love Indian

food. We're excited to have him over. And to meet you. Walker has never introduced us to anyone. We thought, maybe..."

"Jen." His dad rubs her hand. "Go easy on the poor girl. Were you thinking about marriage in grad school?"

She nods *true*.

Walker sets the trays down, returns to the kitchen for more.

I try to pick up where I left off. "It's important having people who support you. Friends. Family. And other people who understand what you're going through."

His parents nod along, hanging on every word.

"Will she be back tonight?" I ask.

His mom stares at her glass. "She goes out for coffee after meetings sometimes. She knows to text when she's finished at eight."

They seem like they keep her on a short leash.

So how did she end up at Walker's place high last night?

"Does Sabrina work? That can help, having purpose, feeling like you're part of the world." It's what made the difference for me.

Her mom nods. "Yes, she works at a boutique at the Grove. She loves it there."

She must get into trouble after work. Or before. Or when she says she's working but really goes out with old friends.

It's easy to give into temptation.

It's possible last night really was one little slip. It's possible she is doing well.

"You should ask her manager for her schedule." Walker places a glass of water in front of me then takes his seat. He motions to the food *let's eat*.

"We're trying to treat her like an adult," his mom says.

He fights a frown. "You got my message?"

"Of course. But..." His mom picks up the serving spoon

and scoops basmati rice onto her plate. "We're not throwing Bree back in rehab because of one slip."

He presses his lips together.

"I understand you don't approve of the way we handle things, but we're trying to give Bree her space. She has to come to this conclusion on her own." She sets the spoon back then scoops chicken tikka masala onto her plate.

"That is true." I take the serving spoon, focus on filling my plate.

Walker leans back in his chair. Presses his palms into his thighs. He waits until I'm done serving myself then grabs the spoon, fills his plate.

He stabs a piece of chicken with his fork. "You're right." He makes eye contact with his mom. "We need to treat Bree like an adult. She says this is one slip up, fine. But if she does it again, you need to give her an ultimatum—she gets clean or she's out of the house."

"Sweetie, we have done that." His mother cuts a tiny piece of chicken, brings it to her mouth, chews, swallows.

"No, you've threatened. But you always bail her out. You need to stop. To pull away her safety net." His voice wavers for a second then it's back to confident. "It sucks. I get that. I don't want Bree to die either. But you're not helping her like this. That money is just going to more needles in her arm. She needs to know you mean it, that she can't live here in exchange for a rehab stint a year."

"Walker, sweetie. You don't understand how hard it is for her. She's trying. She goes to meetings every week, sometimes twice a week. She goes to therapy. She wants to get better." His mom takes another tiny bite.

I mix my chicken with rice, scoop a bite. It's amazing, rich, tender, fresh. The tomato sauce is creamy and tangy in equal measures. But it still doesn't taste good.

I can feel every bit of Walker's hurt. His frustration. Like it's mine.

Is this how relationships are supposed to go?

It was never like this with Ross. Not even close.

Walker's voice is low. Hurt. "I know she's trying."

"You do?" I sound more surprised than I mean to.

"Yeah." He runs his hand through his hair. "Part of her wants to get better. But that's not enough. It's not working. I need you guys on my side. I'll be the bad cop. But I still need you to back me up."

His mom turns to his dad. They share a knowing look.

She turns back to him. "And what if she says no and she leaves? Where are we then?"

"Where are we now?" he asks.

"She's with us. She's safe," his mom says.

"Not from herself." His hand curls into a fist.

I reach for him. Place my palm on his wrist.

His fist unfurls. He looks to me like I'm his lifeline, the only person who understands him.

"She checked out of rehab early. How long do you really think it will be until she's using everyday again?" he asks.

His mom frowns.

Hurt seeps into his voice. "This is it for me. I can't keep rescuing Bree. If she doesn't get clean this time, I'm walking."

I take a deep breath and exhale slowly. That's the right decision. The mature, healthy decision.

But it's not easy.

I squeeze his hand.

He squeezes back.

"She's your sister," his mom says.

"I know." He stares at his plate. Mixes chicken and rice. "But I'd rather be an asshole than an enabler."

His mom looks to me like I have all the answers. "What do you think, Iris?"

Okay, this is it. I need to nail it.

"I don't know Sabrina, but Walker filled me in on her history." Under the table, I squeeze harder. "There isn't one answer with addiction, but whatever you've been doing hasn't been working. You need to draw that line. You need to make sure she knows that staying high isn't an option. That it means she's out of the house and out of your lives."

His mom swallows hard. "And if she chooses staying high?"

"She has to hit rock bottom on her own." And we have to hope that's enough.

His mom looks to Walker. "You're sure about this?"

"Yeah. I already called the center. They have a spot for her next month," he says.

She looks to her husband.

He nods.

"We need to think about this, sweetie." Mrs. Williams presses her lips together. "I know that isn't what you want to hear. I know you want all or nothing. But if Bree is destined to use forever, I'd rather she do it here than somewhere else."

Walker's lips turn downward. He stabs a piece of chicken. Stares at his food like it's poisonous. "I'm not gonna wait forever."

She nods. "I know."

Chapter Twenty-Five

IRIS

"You're my good luck charm." Walker brushes a stray hair behind my ear. He stares into my eyes like I'm the source of all the beauty and wonder in the universe.

It's right there on his cell phone. A text from his mom.

You're right. We need to push her. Let's set something up in a few weeks.

His parents are going to throw down an ultimatum.

They're going to push his sister into rehab.

It's fucking weird they're telling him in a text.

But it's good.

My shoulders relax. My chest warms. It's like it's my sister who's finally getting help.

His relief is my relief.

I want this for him so badly. "You would have gotten through that without me."

"Maybe. But I wouldn't take that bet." He plants a soft, sweet kiss on my lips. "Pretty sure that was eighty percent you convincing them."

"It's the PhD thing."

He nods. "Yeah. It would annoy me that they think I'm an idiot because I'm not in school, but I'm too happy to care."

Light bounces off our sleek white table. We're at a trendy ice cream place in Beverly Hills for dessert and... well, I guess it's a celebration now.

My coffee ice cream with chocolate chips on top is rich, creamy perfection.

And he's here. And this is going to be okay.

And we...

Well, if he really does mean the past is the past, then we'll be okay too.

Does he mean that?

I'm trying to believe it.

I want to believe it.

"What about last night?" I suck ice cream off my plastic spoon. "When I stumbled into your place to find your sister high on your couch?"

"She'd have been there either way."

Probably true. "She always goes to you?"

"Yeah." He licks chocolate chip ice cream from his spoon.

"And you're the only person who really lays down the law?"

"As far as I know."

"She wants you to help. Deep down."

"Incredibly deep." He sets his spoon down, slides his arms around me, and pulls me onto his lap.

There's all this trust in his eyes. I want all of it. I want to deserve all of it.

"I feel greedy as fuck."

"Are you about to steal my ice cream?"

He shakes his head. "Taking all your help. Monopolizing the conversation."

"I'm glad to help. And listen."

"Still." He stares up at me. "You're thinking something."

"Always."

"What?"

Something I'm not ready to say. I reach for something else. "About those summer internships."

Walker brushes my hair behind my ear. "Which way are you leaning?"

"I don't know. Do you want me to stay?"

"I want you to live in my bed."

"I'll get chaffed."

"It will be worth it."

My smile spreads over my cheeks. God, he does something to me. Makes me feel like the world is going to be okay. "I can stay."

"You don't have to."

"I know." I want to. "I have time to decide."

He nods. "You're still thinking something?"

"This is good. I'm happy for you. Really."

"Me too." He plants a soft kiss on my lips. "But there's something else."

"Maybe."

"Your sister?"

"Always." It's always the same. But I'm starting to think it's salvageable.

"Anything I can do?"

"No." I take another spoonful of ice cream into my mouth. It tastes sweeter. I'm starting to believe him. "I think I'm going to call her."

"Yeah?"

"Apologize for everything. Ask to see her. To buy her coffee. She works in Santa Monica. I could do it anytime. I just..."

"Scared she'll say no?"

"Basically." I sink into his body, resting my head against his.

"You want me to hold your hand?"

"No. That won't help. My ex... Ross. He was a friend of hers. She wasn't happy about that."

"Oh."

"Oh?"

"You stole her boyfriend."

"No. Maybe. She had a boyfriend at the time." Maybe Lily did have a thing for Ross. She made him sound so great when she described him. I thought it was because she wanted to set us up. But she might have wanted him for herself. "It was more than that. I leaned on her more than she could handle."

He pulls me closer. "Tell me about it."

"Don't you want to celebrate?"

"I want to hear this."

Okay. I want to tell him. But I'm not about to bring down the mood with my ugly past. Not if it doesn't matter to him.

I run my fingers over his neck. "It's a long story."

"I've got all night."

I motion to the door. "This place closes in an hour."

"Damn. I forgot that this ice cream shop is the only place in the world where we can have a conversation. Fuck. We better hurry up."

"Asshole."

"You can come over."

Maybe. I want to. But—"I have an early class."

"We can go to your place. Sleep."

"Can we?"

He laughs. "Fair enough." He turns me so we're face-to-face. "You don't have to say shit. I meant it, Iris. The past is the past. But I want to be someone you can lean on. If you want to talk—"

"I do. I just... I haven't really talked about this with anyone."

His eyes stay soft. Understanding.

"Lily was always the pretty, athletic one. She still is. She's in a volleyball league. She's good. I was more—"

"The *Star Wars* geek?"

"Yeah. I looked up to her. I thought she was the coolest person in the world. She was smart too, but she didn't apply herself. If she wasn't into a subject, she'd half ass it, whereas I'd study even harder, bring home straight As."

"You seem like the type."

"I always got the grades. I did well in college. But then I graduated and I hit a wall. I was lucky. I got a job pretty fast. I was excited about the future. Then... then I got my GRE scores back. They were terrible. I'd bombed. It was the first time I really failed at something."

"That must have sucked."

"Yeah. But I wasn't ready to face the possibility of failure. I couldn't stand how badly I wanted to go to grad school. It hurt. So I told myself I didn't want it. I told myself I didn't need the GRE. I tried to convince myself that my boring administrative job was what I wanted."

"Did it work?"

"Not really. I was miserable. I didn't use my brain at work. I felt so dull and listless. For a while, I tried to fill the gaps with other stuff. Work out plans. Reading three books a week. Drinking too much. Perfecting my winged eyeliner."

"That's why I can't stop staring into your eyes?"

"Of course." I press my palm against his chest. His shirt is stiff, but I can feel the heat of him underneath it. "I was sure I was stuck. That nothing would ever change."

He brushes my hair behind my ear.

"And I felt bad for feeling bad. I had a job even though I had a psych degree. I made enough to afford my own apartment. To get takeout for dinner and buy a membership at the nice gym. I was lucky."

"Most people need more than an apartment to be happy."

"Yeah. I know. I knew. I knew how complicated people were, how much a fulfilling job affects your satisfaction with your life."

"Does school fulfill you?"

"Yeah. I love it. I think, deep down, I knew I wouldn't be happy unless I was pursuing grad school. But I was too scared to face it. It was easier to close myself off to that possibility. But it made me desperate for any sort of approval or excitement. That was when I started seeing Ross. He was a good guy in certain ways. But not others."

"He hurt you?"

"No." Not the way he means. "He always convinced me to do stupid things." Like swallow a handful of prescription pain killers to numb my feelings. "Drink too much. Then get in a car with him even though he'd had a few. Go to a stranger's place. Skip a condom. I was stupid. But I... I am clean, if you were wondering. I got tested a few months ago. We hadn't for a while."

He nods. "I am too."

"Yeah. We, um, I'm on the shot. So, we could not use a condom sometime."

"Fuck, Iris, I'm trying to concentrate here."

"Oh. You want to?"

His nod is heavy.

"I, uh... I should get back to the topic."

"Right away."

God, he looks cute all needy and horny. And sex makes sense. Sex doesn't poke or prod at my secrets. Sex doesn't beg me to spill my guts.

We should go back to my place. Fuck like rabbits. Use our mouths for something much better than conversation.

But he's still staring into my eyes with all the trust in the world.

Like I'm his salvation.

Is it possible he meant it?

That the past really is the past?

That he won't leave when he knows the truth?

Please, please, please let it be possible.

Walker runs his fingertips along my chin.

I force myself to keep talking. "But Ross, he didn't make me happy. So I turned to Lily." Then to drugs. And when that didn't fulfill me, I'd blame her too. "I'd get mad at her. Blame her for my dissatisfaction. I got her fired once."

"Fuck, really?"

"Yeah. I kept calling and showing up at her office. She wouldn't pay attention to me. And I needed... I guess I needed to face reality. But I thought that if only she'd talk to me, she could fix it. She used to fix everything. When we were kids."

"I get that. And the dissatisfaction."

"Really?"

"Yeah. Last few years of high school until I started doing ink. I felt like my life would never go anywhere. Like I was doomed to turn into my parents. I fucked around a lot. It was a good distraction, but it never really satisfied me."

"And now?"

"I love what I do. But I want more out of life too."

"Your friends?"

He nods.

"Your sister clean?"

"Yeah. That's the main thing now. Everything else—surfing, working out, reading—feels like a distraction. I love that shit. But it's not what I really want."

"And what do you really want?"

"To help the people I love." He looks up at me. "Find the

people I love." He brushes my hair behind my ear. "What do you want?"

"I'm still not sure. Not beyond school."

"You'll get there."

I nod.

Right now, I believe him.

Right now, I believe it's possible there will be an us.

Chapter Twenty-Six

IRIS

The past is the past.

I let myself believe it.

I let myself fall harder.

All week, I text Walker about nothing. I go to his place for dinner and a movie and a fuck. I spend the night in his arms. I chain drink coffee. I pour myself into studying and perfecting my research.

It gnaws at my gut.

What if the past isn't the past?

How can he really promise that when he doesn't know what it is?

With the way he looks at his sister, is there really any chance he'll be okay loving a former addict?

I push it aside.

I hold onto his words like they're my lifeline.

They are.

They make me feel strong, safe, confident.

They convince me I can do this.

It's late on a weekday when I pick up the phone and stare at Lily's number.

I press *Call*.

I can do this.

I have to do this.

Even if it means giving up the possibility for a hard no.

Even if it means a whole lot of hurt.

RING, RING, RING.

My fingers dig into the table. I'm alone in my apartment, studying. Well, I'm supposed to be studying.

Ring, ring—

Voicemail.

Hello, you've reached Lily Avery. Please leave a message and I'll call you back.

She sounds happy. Normal. Healthy.

I take a deep breath and exhale slowly. "Hey Lily. It's Iris. Can we talk? I want to apologize. I... I want us to be okay."

I end the call.

My fingers move over the keyboard.

Iris: Can we talk?

I stare at my cell.

For ages, I stare at my cell.

My eyes get dry. My fingers go numb. My heart beats so hard it nearly bursts out of my chest.

Finally, my phone buzzes with a reply.

Lily: I'm sorry, Iris. But I'm not ready to talk to you yet.

Fuck.

I let my cell fall into my lap, I lay back on the couch, pull my knees into my chest.

And I fall apart.

Chapter Twenty-Seven

IRIS

My phone buzzes against my chest. Not in a sexy, fun way—would that even feel good?

In a neutral, *here's a text message* kind of way.

I take forever reaching for it.

It's not from Lily. Of course it's not. She isn't ready to talk. Which is totally understandable. Really. Lying here for an hour, staring at the ceiling, poring over every one of my past mistakes...

I understand.

It's an unfortunate reality, one of those things I can't change, like traffic or taxes or weather.

The sun is going to shine tomorrow. UCLA is going to be a clusterfuck. And I have to wait until my sister is ready to trust me.

Walker: What are you up to?

It's pure booty call. But then it's not. He always starts his texts like this.

Iris: Giving up on studying.

Walker: To?

Cry in the dark by myself.

Iris: I haven't decided.

Walker: You want some company?

Iris: That's a complicated question.

Walker: You say that a lot.

Iris: They all are. There are too many factors. Company is nice, especially yours. But it means giving up the peace of solitude.

Walker: Are you okay?

Iris: No.

Walker: Have you been drinking?

Iris: Do I sound drunk?

Walker: A little.

Iris: No. Just thinking.

Walker: You're being weird.

Iris: How can you tell in a text?

Walker: I can.

Iris: I guess I'm a little worn out.

Walker: What happened, sweetness?

Iris: I called Lily.

Walker: Oh.

Iris: Yeah.

Walker: You want to talk about it?

Iris: Not right now.

Walker: You staying up?

Iris: I'm not sure I have a choice. Why?

Walker: No reason.

~

TWENTY MINUTES LATER, THERE'S A KNOCK ON MY DOOR.

I push myself to my feet. Check my makeup in the mirror. It's a travesty and my wrinkled shirt isn't any better. At least my underwear is cute. And it's not like my boyfriend is going to complain I'm skipping pants.

"Just a minute." I move to the bathroom. Wipe away my

eye makeup, wash my face, pull a hoodie over my tank top. Then I move back to the door.

"Hey." Walker's voice flows through the wood. "I have something for you."

I pull the door open.

He's standing there in jeans, a t-shirt, and a leather jacket. He looks normal. Well, normal hot.

Not like he's here to take all my pain away, to erase my past, to love me despite the devastation I've wrecked.

He holds up the paper bag in his hand. "I'll leave if you want to be alone."

I shake my head and motion *come in*.

"Fuck, Iris. I like that look."

My cheeks flush. "Thanks."

He steps inside. Presses the door closed behind him. His dark eyes find mine. They're soft. Understanding. "You don't have to talk."

I nod.

He wraps his arms around me. The paper bag brushes my back. It's cold. Hard.

Walker runs his fingers through my hair. "I'm sorry."

"I'll be okay." Eventually.

"You say that a lot."

"It's true."

"Yeah, but—fuck, I know this is weird coming from me—but you don't have to convince me you're strong."

"I'm not."

He pulls back, sets the bag on the counter, pulls out a pint of coffee ice cream. "How do you figure?"

"I give in to temptation too easily."

He motions to the ice cream. "Does that mean you don't want any of this?"

"No, I do."

His lips curl into a smile. God, his smile does things to me. It's the silver lining on a cloudy day.

He grabs two mugs from the cabinet, divides the ice cream sixty/forty, hands me the fuller mug.

"Spoons." I nod to the drawer below the microwave.

He grabs two, slides one into his mug, hands the other to me.

I settle onto the couch and wrap a blanket around my shoulders.

I bring a spoonful of ice cream to my lips. Sugar and coffee. Everything I love. Everything that makes me happy.

"You can say anything you want, Iris." He moves closer. "But I'm not here to talk."

I arch a brow.

"Not for that. Wouldn't turn it down, but that's not my intention." He presses his lips to my forehead. "I'm just here."

"You're just here?"

He nods.

"You're sure you've never been a boyfriend before?"

"Yeah."

"You're good at it."

"I'm a fast learner." He brings a spoonful of ice cream to his lips. "You look like you're gonna break, sweetness."

I nod. "I... Lily isn't ready to talk to me. And I get that. Really, I do. I'm not sure if she's still hurting. Or if she thinks I'll be the way I was. What if I do go back to how I was? What if school stops satisfying me? What if I get desperate for anything to make it better?"

"What if? What would you do?"

"I don't know. Talk to my therapist. To you. Work out more. Read. But what if—"

"What did you do before?"

Get high. "Not that."

"Sounds like you've got it figured out."

"Maybe." I'm in a better place than I was. I don't want to self-medicate anymore. Even if it's tempting sometimes.

He leans in to press his lips to mine.

He tastes good, like coffee and sugar and Walker.

"Everybody does shit they regret. What matters is how you pick up the pieces." He moves closer.

"But your sister—"

"She crushes the pieces under her heel. You're nothing like Bree. Trust me."

"What if I am?"

"You're not."

"How can you say that when you don't know?"

"I know you. That's what matters."

I stare back into his eyes. "You promise?" Please promise. Please mean it. Please make today okay.

If the past doesn't matter, then I can tell him when I'm ready to confront it. When I'm sure he won't go from seeing me as Iris the person to Iris the recovering addict.

Seeing myself through his eyes is everything.

I can't lose that.

I don't know how to see myself as more than a recovering addict.

But he does.

He brushes my hair behind my ear. "Of course."

"What if I used to drink all the time?"

"I did too."

I take a deep breath and exhale slowly. I need to feel him out. To see if it's possible he means it. "Or get high?"

"Ditto."

"Really?"

"Yeah."

"But your sister—"

"Refuses to stop."

"Still."

"No still. I know the person you are now. That's what matters to me. If you need a shoulder to cry on, I'm here. If you want to talk, I'm here. But you don't have to tell me anything. Fuck knows there's plenty of shit I'd rather forget."

"You're sure about this?"

He nods. "Maybe you did awful shit. Maybe you killed someone. I don't care. I'll say it as many times as I have to, Iris. The past is the past. Whatever you did doesn't matter. I still like you."

"What if I killed one of your friends?"

"You've met all my friends. They're still alive."

"What if I go out and kill Dean?"

He chuckles. "I've wanted to plenty of times."

"But you'd be okay with that?"

"No, killing my best friend is a deal breaker."

"Damn. There go my plans for the weekend."

"No offense, Iris, but he'd crush you like that—" He snaps his fingers.

"In hand-to-hand fight, yeah, but not if I sneak up on him with a gun."

"This plan is too coherent."

"I'm a nerd, remember?"

"Yeah, you are." He slides his arms around me, blanket and all, and pulls me onto his lap. His eyes go to the TV. "You have a favorite movie?"

"That's a complicated question."

He chuckles. "Is it?"

"Yes." I take a deep breath and exhale slowly. It's lighter. Less of a struggle. I believe him. I believe the past is the past. I believe he's okay leaving it behind.

"How about a comfort food movie?"

"You'll laugh."

"There's no way I'll laugh."

"Wanna bet?"

He nods. "Name your terms."

"Loser makes coffee in the morning."

He chuckles. "There's no way you get up before me to make coffee."

"I have class at nine."

"I have an appointment at ten."

"Ten is after nine."

"I have to prep." He presses his forehead to mine. "But, sure, I'll take that bet."

"*Star Wars*."

He laughs. "Fuck, you got me."

"I told you."

"I'm only laughing 'cause you're so insecure about it." He looks up at me with a smile.

"I'm not a built sex god. I was an awkward kid. It took a long time for me to grow into my nose."

"I love your nose."

"It's a little long."

"It suits you."

"Like the Wicked Witch of the West?"

"Like Jennifer Grey. Pre nose job."

Now, I'm the one laughing. "How old are you again?"

"*Dirty Dancing* is a classic. Bree's favorite."

"What's yours?"

"Of eighties romances?"

I nod.

"*Say Anything*."

"You wanted to be the sensitive artist holding a boom box outside some woman's window?"

Walker laughs. "No. And you're misrepresenting the film."

"Am I?"

He nods. "She hates the boom box thing. It doesn't help win her back."

That's true, actually. "It's hard to believe you ever enjoyed a romance."

"'Cause I'm a guy?"

"No. Because you were very... anti-commitment."

He chuckles. "That's a nice euphemism for slut."

"I try."

"I was different when I was a kid. Love seemed like a good thing. Something that would make you warm, not stab you in the back."

"And now?"

"Fuck. I don't know." His eyes meet mine. "Probably shouldn't tell my girlfriend I'm not sure how I feel about love."

"Still no game."

He pulls me closer. "I'm pathetic."

"You really are."

"You're convincing me."

I press my lips together. "I'm convincing you?"

"That trusting someone isn't the stupidest thing in the world."

"And if it is?"

"Then I'm about where I started." He reaches for the remote and turns on the TV. "This is really fucking tragic, sweetness, but I'm gonna have to ask you to move."

"Oh." I slide off his lap.

He leans in to brush his lips against mine then he gets up, goes to my bookshelf, pulls out my *Star Wars* DVD set. "You want to start with *Episode Four*?"

"Of course." I watch him bend to slide the disc into the DVD player. He really has a fantastic ass. A fantastic everything.

I'm making him believe in trust.

In love.

I...

He's said it a lot now. The past doesn't matter.

I have to believe him. I can't stomach believing anything else.

He turns back to me with that million-dollar smile. "Why's *Star Wars* comfort food?"

"My dad loves it." I take a deep breath and exhale slowly. I had a good childhood, but it's all bittersweet with the distance between me and Lily. "They re-released *Star Wars* theatrically when I was a kid. A tiny kid. Three or four. My dad took me and Lily."

"Your mom wasn't into it?"

"No. She's not a movie person. She's more into books. Nonfiction."

"What's she do?"

"She teaches middle school science."

"And your dad makes bank doing special effects?"

"Yeah. Usually. It's not the most stable industry. But we were never lacking growing up. I guess we have that in common. Running from privilege."

"To Brentwood and Santa Monica."

I laugh. He has a point. We're in two of the most expensive cities in Los Angeles. We aren't exactly slumming it. "Lily fell in love with the movies right away. I always wanted to be like my big sister. So, I said I loved them too. We'd watch them every weekend. And we'd play *Star Wars*. She'd be Luke and I'd be Leia and my dad would be Han, which I guess is kind of weird now that I think about it."

He laughs. "Freudian."

"He's widely discredited. But his work was the basis for huge chunks of psychology. So..."

"That why he's your Instagram handle?"

I nod. "It was going to be Freudian Nip Slip, but I didn't think anyone would get it."

He laughs. "It suits you."

"Thanks."

He slides onto the couch next to me.

I swallow hard. "We had so much fun pretending to go on adventures. And just watching the movies. Once I got older, I started to see more in them. It's like your tattoo, Luke on Tatooine, looking at the moons, wanting more. *Star Wars* has always felt like the promise of more. Of friendship and adventure and purpose. When I watch it, I feel like I can have all that. Even when I can't."

"You think you can't now?"

"Sometimes. But not the way I used to. More like... I'm growing up and I realize I have to make compromises."

He nods.

Warmth fills my chest. Possibilities scared me after the first time I bombed the GRE. That's why I started using. To erase those thoughts.

And now that I'm sober, they're scary in a different way. It's overwhelming, being a blank slate.

But I'm coming around.

Surfing, hiking, sleeping with a dirty talking sex god...

There's a lot of wonder in the world. I'm ready to find it. To open myself up to wanting things as badly as I wanted to get into grad school. To the disappointment that comes when things don't' work out.

I slide onto his lap. "Thank you."

"For?"

"Being here."

"Always."

"I'll hold you to that."

"Good." He unwraps the blanket and pulls me closer.

My hands go to his hair. My eyes fix on his. They're still beautiful, dark, filled with trust and affection.

I believe him.

That he'll be here.

That he'll be mine.

That he'll accept all of me.

He runs his fingertips over my cheeks and chin. Then he's cupping the back of my head with his hand.

He pulls me into a deep, slow kiss.

His tongue slides into my mouth.

Bit by bit, my body wakes up. The heaviness of the day fades away until I'm floating on a wave of desire.

Walker pulls my hoodie over my head.

I push his leather jacket off his shoulders.

He pulls me closer. Sucks on my bottom lip. Softly. Then harder.

It's so fucking good, but it's not enough.

I need every ounce of him. Every bit of his flesh against mine. Every hint of intimacy I can get.

I pull his t-shirt over his head. Then my tank top. My bra. My hands roam his shoulders, chest, stomach.

He feels so good against my palm. Warm. Hard. Alive.

But I need more.

I need all of him.

My lips find his. My kiss gets harder. Deeper. Needier.

All that affection pours from him to me.

And from me to him.

There's trust in his touch. Trust I don't deserve. Trust I desperately need.

His palm plants between my shoulder blades. Slowly, he drags his lips over my cheek and chin, down my neck, along my collarbone.

He takes my nipple into his mouth.

Fuck. That feels good.

My hands go to his hair.

My hips rock of their own accord.

He's hard under me. And I want that. I want every layer

of clothes between us gone. I want every wall between us gone.

I can't have the latter. Not yet.

So I need this.

My hand knots in his hair.

He sucks softly. It sends pleasure straight to my core.

I grind against him.

"Walker." I squeeze my thighs against his hips. "Fuck me. Please."

He pulls me closer. Sucks a little harder. Then it's short flicks of his tongue. Long ones. Soft. Hard. He swirls his tongue around my tender bud. Scrapes his teeth against it.

He toys with me until I'm shaking then he moves to my other nipple and does it again.

I can't take the ache between my legs.

I need him.

I need him more than I've ever needed anything.

I grind against him. "Walker. Please."

He drags his fingertips down my spine, to the top of my panties, then all the way up to the base of my skull.

The softness of his touch sets me on fire.

My entire body is buzzing. Every nerve is awake and alive and screaming for more of him.

I shift my hips. Bring my hands to his jeans. Undo his button. Then the zipper.

I cup him over his boxers. He feels good in my hand, but it's not enough.

I kiss him hard and deep. Then my lips are on his cheek. His chin. His neck.

He groans as I suck on his skin.

His hands knot in my hair.

God, that sound is music. Poetry. Everything.

I do it again.

He groans a little louder.

I push his jeans off his hips as I suck on his neck. Then his boxers.

I wrap my hand around his cock. Pump him as I suck on his skin.

"Iris." His breath gets heavy. Needy.

Yes. That.

Slowly, I work my way down his torso. I drag my lips over his chest and stomach then I lower myself onto my knees.

I look up at him as I brush my lips against his cock.

He shudders.

I do it again.

A groan falls off his lips.

Again.

His palm presses against the back of my head, nudging me forward.

I torture him instead.

I flick my tongue against his tip.

His groan gets low, heavy.

I do it again.

Again.

I do it until he's shaking.

He sighs with pleasure as I take him into my mouth.

He tastes good, like salt and soap and Walker.

His skin is soft but he's so fucking hard.

I look up at him as I take him deeper.

His eyes go hazy with pleasure. His brow softens. His lips part with a groan.

I'm the one driving him out of his mind.

Right now, I'm the only thing he needs.

And that's exactly what *I* need.

I bring my hand to his hip, pull him closer to take him deeper.

Deeper.

It's too much. I nearly gag. But then that's not enough.

I swallow to relax my throat. My fingers dig into his skin. Again, I pull him closer.

Take him deeper.

Suck a little harder.

He presses his palm against my head, nudging me forward, commanding me.

I shouldn't like it.

But I do.

I let him guide me as I work him.

His touch gets harder.

His groans get louder.

He rocks his hips, thrusting into my mouth.

I press my tongue against the base of his tip. Relax my throat.

He rocks into me again.

Again.

There.

His hand knots in my hair.

His cock pulses.

My name falls off his lips as he fills my mouth. He's salty. Sweet.

I swallow hard.

He looks down at me like I'm heaven sent.

I push myself up. Climb into his lap.

He wraps his arms around me and holds me like he's never going to let me go.

Chapter Twenty-Eight

WALKER

I stretch my arms over my head as a yawn escapes my lips. I can't remember the last time I was tired from staying up talking.

There's something intoxicating about Iris. I want to wipe away every hint of pain in those gorgeous blue eyes. I want to destroy whoever or whatever caused that ache.

She deserves a life without hurt.

She deserves the entire fucking world.

I finish checking out my customer, give him the usual aftercare speech, head straight to the single cup coffee maker in the back. It's mediocre, but I need the caffeine.

"Oooh, make me one please," Leighton calls out from her spot at the counter. She presses her hands together—well, her Kindle is between them, but close enough—and shoots me puppy dog eyes.

"You ever get tired of begging?"

Her lips curl into a half smile. "You read my journal too?"

"You don't have a journal."

"That's what you think." She winks. "French Roast. Please. I'll love you forever."

"You won't now?"

She laughs. "Who knows?"

"You're lucky I'm in a good mood."

"You're always in a good mood."

No, I always seem like I'm in a good mood. But the distinction doesn't matter to me at the moment. Everything feels light. Mom's going to put her foot down with Bree. My schedule is filled with badass tattoos. And Iris is... fuck, Iris is everything.

This must be why Brendon is so fucking obnoxious all the time.

I finish my cup then make one for Leighton. I even fix it the way she likes—one packet of half and half and one of raw sugar.

She sighs with anticipation as I hand it over. Slowly, she brings it to her lips—she isn't wearing lipstick today, which is weird—and takes a sip.

Her sigh is heavy, needy. "Mmm. Better than sex."

"It's been too long since you've had sex."

She shoots me a cutting look. "You think I'm not aware of that?"

"I'm not the one comparing shitty coffee to sex."

"It's decent coffee."

"Been too long since you've had good coffee."

"Cocky now that you have a girlfriend."

"'Cause I was hurting for sex before?"

"Please. You're different about it lately."

"I am not." No, I am.

"You didn't deny the girlfriend thing."

"You asking for details about last night?"

"Are you offering?"

Maybe. It feels weird. Wrong. I take a long sip. "You made the abstinence rule. You can pull it anytime."

She shakes her head.

"You have an end date in mind?"

She tilts her head to one side. "Uh... I'll know when it's time."

"Uh-huh."

"I will. It needs to be the right guy. Someone I actually like. And trust."

"Or when you're dripping wet, panting and needy from Kay's kinky book?" Dean slides onto the counter.

"I'm not reading Kaylee's dirty book." Leighton takes another sip. "And it's not that dirty."

"How do you know if you don't read it?" he asks.

"I skim over her shoulder." Her cheeks flush. "Like you wouldn't."

"Invading a young woman's privacy." Dean shakes his head. "Fucked-up shit." He looks to me *right?*

I nod. "Not as fucked-up as deflowering her in an alley."

"I do not need to hear this story again," Leighton says.

"You wanted details," I say.

"About you and Iris. Not about Kay. She's too innocent and cute—"

"You're into chicks now?" Dean's eyes perk. "Can I watch?"

"No. And hell no. But I'm not afraid to admit a woman is attractive," she says.

He shoots her a cutting look. "You think I'm afraid to point out a hot guy?"

"Maybe." She looks from him to me then back to him. "I don't hear you discussing it."

"When's it come up?" He presses his lips to one side, thinking. "Walker's hot."

"Yeah? You two ever experiment?" She presses her hands together. "Can I watch?"

"No. But you can watch me with anyone, Leigh." He winks at her.

"No, thank you," she says.

"How come you're always begging my boy for details?" Dean asks.

"I do not beg." She folds her arms. "And he gives good detail."

"And I don't?" Dean mocks poignant.

"No. You say shit like—" She drops her voice to imitate Dean. "*Oh, her tits were so nice. It was awesome when she sucked me off.*"

He arches a brow. "I don't see the problem."

"Exactly." She looks to me. "You want to explain this to him?"

"Not even a little," I say.

He motions to his empty suite—the client is halfway to the bathroom. "This is going long."

"It's fine. I'm beat. I'm gonna head home." I take a long sip. It's only okay coffee, but it tastes fucking amazing. Everything feels brighter. Crisper. Better.

"Fuck that. It's biceps and back." He winks at Leighton as he flexes. "You can touch. It won't bite."

She rolls her eyes as she fake laughs. But she still ends in a smile. She enjoys Dean's stupidity.

"Next time." I take another sip. "I was up late."

"Fucking Iris?" he asks.

"We were talking."

He tilts his head to one side. "Talking?"

"Yeah. When you like a girl for more than what's between her legs—you know what? I don't want to ruin the surprise," I tease.

"I know what talking is." His eyes narrow. "So it's serious?"

"I guess."

"You gonna go see her?"

"Maybe. She was upset last night." I take another sip. I'm

not dense. I get that Dean is concerned shit's going to change. But it's not. "I'm gonna call. Make sure she's okay."

Dean looks to Leighton. Raises a brow.

She shrugs *don't look at me*.

"You know I'm right here," I say.

"Just find it fucking interesting you'll wait around for her, but you bail on our plans." Dean slides off the counter.

"She has great tits," I say.

"If I thought that was it, I wouldn't fucking care," Dean says.

Leighton clears her throat. Motions to Ryan working on a pretty girl's wrist tattoo—not that he's noticing the way she's looking at him.

He folds his arms over his chest. "This is a fucking inside voice."

"We have different definitions of inside voice." She plops on her stool. Taps her Converse together. "Your shop. Alienate your customers if you want."

"Thanks, I will," he says.

"If Ryan lectures me, I will fucking ruin you," she says.

"He'll lecture me," Dean says.

"He'll lecture all of us." She shakes her head. "You can admit you have feelings."

He looks to me. "She your girlfriend now or some shit?"

"Yeah. And?" I stare back at him.

"Would have been nice to know that."

"Now you do."

"You gonna tell me why the fuck she was asking about Sabrina?"

"She was?" I bite my tongue. "When?"

Dean scoffs. "Guess you don't know everything about her."

Irritation seeps into my voice. "Never said I did."

Leighton looks to me. "At Ryan's party. She seemed really concerned."

Dean's voice gets low. "Why the fuck is there anything to say about Sabrina? Your sister is supposed to be in rehab."

"She checked out early." I try to make my voice even, but it refuses. I'm still pissed. I'm still worried she's going to die with a needle in her arm no matter what I do.

"When?" he asks.

"A few weeks ago."

He shakes his head. "And you didn't fucking tell me?"

"I didn't tell her either. Bree was there. At my place. High. Iris was with me."

"Were you gonna fucking tell me?" Dean asks.

"I can handle Bree on my own." I have for a long time.

All the *I'm gonna fuck with you* falls off his face. His eyes turn down. His lips curl into a frown. "But you don't have to."

"I want to."

"Why? You don't trust me?"

"You know I do."

"How the fuck do I know that?" He shakes his head. "You've been M.I.A., Walker. You like this girl. I get it. I like her too."

"You do?" Leighton's face screws with confusion. She shoots me a *really* look.

I shrug.

He flips her off.

"Seriously, Dean, you've been a total dick to her," she says.

"I'm working on it." He looks to me. "And I am fucking sorry I've been an asshole to your... whatever she is. But you need to work on this shit too. You forget I've known you forever. That smile you plaster on every day is bullshit. I've known it's bullshit. Just not why."

I press my heel into the ground. "It's not bull—"

"Yeah. It is. If Bree showed up at your place high..." He

shakes his head. "You're freaking the fuck out. Imagining the cops notifying you they've found her dead in a fucking alley."

I suck a breath between my teeth. "Sometimes. So what?"

"So, you tell your fucking friends shit is messed up." He takes a step backward. "We can help. I can help."

"How?"

"It was barely a month ago you dragged her to rehab. You think I've forgotten? You were a fucking mess."

Maybe.

"I'm not an idiot. I get that we're not fifteen anymore. I get that you're gonna meet someone one day and it's gonna change shit. But you're better than this."

"Than what?"

"Than ditching your friends for a girl." He nods to his customer, now moving back to his suite. "You barely know her. How do you know she's worth it?"

"I do."

"And if you're wrong?"

"Guess I'm not telling you about it." I fold my arms.

"Fuck, you're stupid." He shakes his head. "Go home. Go to her. Whatever. Gym's off today. Gym's off for the immediate future."

"Dean, come on."

"Dean, what? You're gonna throw me some scraps? No thanks." He turns, shakes his head, saunters back to his suite.

Leighton presses her palms against the counter.

"You think he's right?" I ask.

She stares at her coffee cup. "You really found your sister high in your apartment?"

"Yeah."

She presses her lips together. "Why didn't you tell him?"

"I never tell anyone shit." And I don't fucking enjoy the way Leighton is staring at me right now. With all that pity in her eyes.

"I get it, Walker. I've been infatuated before. You can't get enough of them. You think it's never going to end."

"You saying it is?"

"The honeymoon ends, yeah. She might be the one. You might be forever. I hope so. She's cool and smart, and you deserve someone like that. But the infatuation... it's normal for you to forget your friends for a while. To get all wrapped up in them. But Dean—I'm pretty sure you and Ryan are the only people he trusts."

"Maybe."

"And it's not like Ryan is pouring his heart out over drinks."

"Yeah." Ryan is about as tight-lipped as it gets.

"The last few weeks, you've been different. In the clouds. Ignoring everybody here."

"Maybe."

"No. Definitely." She slides off her stool. "You don't have to apologize to me. I understand. Fuck, how I understand. But a girl's never come between you and Dean. And with Ryan... you can see why he's worried."

"Maybe."

"Your life. Do what you want."

"Doesn't always feel like it."

She tosses her empty cup in the trash can under the counter. "Your sister really check out of rehab early?"

"Yeah." I'm not sure how much of that story Leighton knows. I'd like to keep it to a minimum.

"That sucks. I'm sorry."

"Thanks."

"You want to talk about it?"

"I'll give you one guess."

~

I CALL IRIS AS SOON AS I GET HOME.

Her voice is enough to push the clouds in my head away. But it's temporary. I need more. I need my head clear.

I know just the place.

I text her.

Walker: Meet me somewhere Saturday.

Iris: What's in it for me?

Walker: My beautiful face.

Iris: That's it?

Walker: Yeah.

Iris: I'm in.

Chapter Twenty-Nine

WALKER

"You're evil." Iris throws her hand over her eyes.

"I know."

"Possibly even the devil." She steps into the shade. Her eyes find mine. "Look how empty it is?" She nods to the parking lot. Three out of two dozen spaces are full. "And that." She nods to the white sky. "It's a sign from God that we're supposed to be inside."

"There are places where the sky looks like that all winter."

"Sounds awful. Let's never go there."

I laugh. "What if they have great coffee?"

"Sounds wonderful. Let's drive there right now." She moves closer. Slides her hand into my front pocket. "You look good."

"You too."

She shakes her head. "I look tired."

"Yeah." I slide my arm around her waist. Pull her body into mine. "But still gorgeous."

She looks up at me with those blue eyes.

I press my forehead to hers. I want to breathe in every ounce of her. I want to erase every other thought in my head.

Her eyelids flutter together.

She rises to her tiptoes, slides her arm around my neck, presses her lips to mine.

She tastes good, like coffee and sugar.

She always tastes like coffee and sugar.

She pulls back with a sigh. "I guess we should do this thing."

"You can admit you want to."

"I want to finish and get coffee."

"You want to ride—"

"You."

I laugh. "My board."

"Your cock." Her cheeks flush. "Did I really say that?"

"Yeah."

"It's early. My brain isn't working yet."

"I'm gonna get you up early again."

"Not worth it."

Incredibly worth it. She's adorable tired. "The water will wake you up."

She groans with agony. But her lips still curl into a smile.

I offer my hand.

She takes it, follows me onto the sand, strips to her swimsuit—fuck does she look good in that deep purple bikini—and pulls her wetsuit over it.

I change, grab a rental board, meet her on the sand. The sky is white, cloudy. It casts a soft glow over the deep blue-green water. It makes the world feel still. Peaceful. Calm.

The ocean is the same blue as Iris's eyes.

It's beautiful.

Perfect.

She looks from the board to me. "You're going to make me do more push-up things."

"Can anyone make you do anything?"

A laugh escapes her lips. "You have your ways."

"Do I?"

Her gaze settles on my crotch. "Yeah."

"You think I'd stoop to sexual bribes?"

"You wouldn't?"

"Never thought about it." I might. I nod to the board. "Do five."

"Do me."

"Sure. Strip naked and grab that towel. I don't mind witnesses."

Her cheeks flush. "Later."

"Here? Really?"

"Maybe."

"You're full of shit."

She laughs. "I'm still working up to public sex." She drops to her knees, winks, spreads onto her stomach.

She does her pop-ups seamlessly.

"You've been practicing," I say.

"I'm supposed to exercise, remember?"

"Just supposed to?"

"Okay. I love exercise. I'm now one of the people I used to mock. I blame you."

"You should involve me. Invite me over to watch your tits bounce."

"Hmm. I'll consider that." She does one last pop-up. Smiles as she sticks the landing. "Are you okay?"

"Huh?"

"You were weird the other night. Insistent. Like you were frustrated."

I was. I am.

Dean and I haven't talked since our fight. Last night, we closed out the shop without a single word. It's weird. I hate it.

"Let's get in the water," I say.

She tilts her head to one side, assessing my words. Slowly, she nods.

She follows me. Groans in agony as the water hits her toes.

Water rushes into my wetsuit. It's freezing for a second, then it's warm. Comfortable.

The chill against my hands and toes feels good.

Exhilarating.

She takes the board, slides onto it, paddles over a cresting wave.

Fuck, is there any view of Iris that doesn't make me desperate to tear her clothes off?

I swim out to meet her.

She pushes herself up to a seated position, legs spread over the board, calves in the water.

"You look like you've done this a million times," I say.

Her smile spreads over her cheeks. "Who says I haven't?"

"You secretly know how to surf?"

She nods.

"Prove it."

"Uh..." She looks down at me. Lowers herself onto her stomach so we're eye to eye. "Why were you all freaked?"

I place my arms on the board. Stare back into her eyes. "Wasn't important."

"It was. Or I wouldn't be here at seven thirty." She shifts onto her back and stares up at the white sky. "Your sister okay?"

"Last time I checked."

"Something is up."

"Just a fight with Dean."

"Oh. Because of me?"

"Because of me. I don't want to think about it right now, sweetness."

"Okay." She runs her fingers over the back of my hand. "Does that mean we can go have sex?"

"Yeah. After this."

"Really? After this? You wouldn't leave right now?"

Of course I would. "If you want to know, ask."

"No. We're here. I should—"

"You like surfing."

"Maybe."

"You love it."

"I admit nothing."

"You love hanging out with me."

She turns toward me. Her lips press into a smile. "Possibly. You're cocky."

"You're adorable."

She presses herself onto her elbow. The water rocks her back and forth. "What did I do?"

"Just your smile."

"That's all it takes?"

"Yeah." I've got it bad. It's like a sickness, but I don't want the cure.

She stares into my eyes. She's seeing something, working something out.

But I have no idea what it is.

"You feeling better?" I tread water. It's what I've been doing the last few years. Staying in place.

It's been good. Comfortable.

But I'm done with that phase.

I want to move forward. To her. With her.

"I'll get there eventually." She rolls onto her stomach. "You look cute contemplative."

"Right back at you."

"You know, we still haven't gone bareback."

It's a good thing this water is so fucking cold or I'd already be hard. "You derailed that last time."

She smiles. "You complaining?"

"Fuck no."

"'Cause I can never—"

"Fuck no."

She smiles, victorious.

"I thought you were here to surf."

"I can't decide." She presses herself onto her elbows. "You sure you don't want to talk about Dean?"

"I'll work it out eventually." A wave rolls under us, crests, falls. It's too small, too close to shore. This set is shit. "You want to talk about your sister?"

"No." She follows my gaze to the horizon. "We're awfully evasive for a couple, huh?"

"At least we know."

"We can put it in our wedding vows." Her cheeks flush. "Not that we... I mean, this could be a while, and it could even be that one day, but I'm not shopping for a dress yet."

"Good. We'll elope."

The water rocks her board back and forth. "Will we?"

"Yeah. In Vegas. At that drive through chapel."

She laughs. "No drive through."

"But it's my dream."

"Guess we can't get married."

"What about Elvis?"

"I can do an Elvis theme."

"I'm gonna wear a studded leather jumpsuit."

"Of course."

I adopt my best Elvis voice. "TCB, baby. Taking care of business."

She laughs. "That was awful."

"You do better."

She shakes her head.

"You really can't do a drive through?"

She nods.

"Fuck, is this why they say marriage is compromise?"

"I think so."

"All right, sweetness. I'll give that up for you."

"I'm not sure if I can ask you to make that kind of sacrifice."

"You're worth it."

She is.

I...

I'm falling in love with her.

THE WATER WASHES EVERYTHING AWAY.

We make lunch, watch sci-fi on the couch, drink way too much coffee.

She packs her stuff after dinner. "I have class early."

"I know."

Her eyes find mine. Her cheeks flush. She wraps her arms around her chest. "We still haven't *ahem*."

"Aren't you leaving?"

"Yeah."

"So you're just cruel?"

She laughs. "I guess I like thinking about you desperate and wanting."

"I'll get you back for that."

"I know."

"I think I figured out this shit with Dean."

"Yeah?"

"Meet me at the shop tomorrow at six."

She raises a brow. "To..."

"You trust me?"

"Of course."

"Then I'll see you at six."

Chapter Thirty

IRIS

I take a deep breath as I step into Inked Hearts.

The bell rings.

Eyes turn in my direction. Leighton. Brendon. Walker.

His dark eyes light up as his smile spreads over his cheeks. He's always so happy to see me. Like I'm the sun on a cloudy day.

Leighton smiles. "Hey, Iris. How's it going?"

"Good." I tug at the zipper of my hoodie. My thighs rub together as I walk. These shorts are too short. And too tight.

"Hey, sweetness." Walker moves out from his suite. Wraps his arms around my waist. "You look good enough to eat."

My cheeks flush.

He motions to the bathroom in the corner.

I shake my head. Lean in to whisper. "Are you sure about this?"

"Yeah." He steps back. Moves to Dean's suite.

The blue-eyed tattoo artist is sitting in his chair, scribbling in a sketchbook. He looks up at us with a disaffected expression. "Yeah?"

"It's back and biceps day," Walker says.

Dean looks from Walker to me then back to Walker. "And?"

"You and Iris are coming with me," Walker says.

"Told you. I don't do threesomes anymore," Dean deadpans.

"Cute." Walker shakes his head. "You're right. I've been M.I.A. Not anymore."

Dean taps his pen against his sketchbook.

"From now on, our routine is my fucking religion." Walker runs his hand through his hair. "And I'm gonna keep you in the loop about Bree." Walker looks from me to his best friend. "I want you to know Iris. 'Cause she's gonna be around."

I swallow hard.

Dean looks up at me. "Is this gonna be a regular thing now?"

"No. I hate lifting weights." I press my lips together. "Just... well, you've been an asshole."

He nods *fair enough*.

"But I do want us to be friendly." I tug on my zipper. "I don't want to steal your best friend."

Dean shrugs *you're ridiculous*, but there's relief in his blue eyes.

Walker nods to the door. "Come on. Get dressed. We'll see who can do the bigger curl."

Dean pushes himself to his feet. He motions to the sidewalk.

Walker shakes his head *really?*

Dean nods really.

"At the gym," Walker says.

Dean chuckles. "Done."

~

THIS IS A RICH PEOPLE GYM.

It's ridiculous. The sunset streams through the wide windows, falling over rows of pristine ellipticals, treadmills, and stationary bikes.

The weight section occupies the other half of the room. It's all mirrors and adjustable benches and guys grunting through sets.

It's way beyond my level.

Walker nods to the guy at the counter. "My girlfriend wants to try the place out."

The guy waves me through *cool.*

We move into the gym. Dean motions to the empty mats in the weight section.

Walker nods.

They're saying something.

I have no idea what the something is. Only that it's some friend/guy/tattoo artist code I'll never understand.

Walker tosses his cell and keys on the floor. Kicks off his shoes. Peels off his socks.

Dean does the same.

They stare.

Walker holds up three fingers. Then two. Then one.

They lunge at each other. Grapple into a wrestling headlock. Then they're knocking each other to the ground.

Dean's pinning Walker.

Then Walker's pinning Dean.

They grunt through a dozen positions.

It would be hot as hell if it wasn't so weird.

No... it's still hot.

But weird.

What the hell?

They're a tangle of limbs, jeans, cotton t-shirts.

Then Dean is pinning Walker. And Walker is tapping the ground for mercy.

Dean jumps—actually jumps—to his feet. He nods *okay* and offers his hand.

Walker pushes himself up and shakes.

I stare at my boyfriend. "What was that?"

"How we settle shit," Walker says.

I look to Dean.

He cocks a brow. "You got a problem with that?"

I guess not. "You're good now?" Guys are so weird.

They trade a look. *How is that not obvious?*

Walker moves to me. He leans in to whisper. "I let him win."

"You fucking wish you let me win." Dean shakes his head *please*. He motions to the locker room. "Flirt with your girlfriend. I'm gonna change." He winks at me. "I won't tell if you picture me naked."

And he leaves.

What the...

"That's really it?" I ask.

"Yeah."

I tilt my head to one side. "Really?"

Walker's laugh lights up his dark eyes. "Yeah. Really." He leans in to press his lips to mine.

"I can't believe he beat you."

"I let him win."

"Did you though?"

"That's cold, sweetness."

My lips curl into a smile. This is okay. And, as much as Walker likes to pretend like nothing affects him, his friendship with Dean clearly means a lot.

"I better change," he says.

I nod. "I can't be the only one in shorts."

He gives me a long once-over. "Any way I can convince you to wear these forever?"

"I'm sure you can think of something."

~

DEAN HOPS ONTO THE TREADMILL TO MY RIGHT. "Whatever you imagined, it's bigger."

Walker jumps onto the treadmill to my left. He makes a point of rolling his eyes. "Nobody is interested in your dick."

"Nobody? You want to put money on that?" Dean asks.

Walker laughs. "Sure. How much?"

"Nah, I can't stand to see you lose in front of your girl again. It's pitiful." He looks to Walker. "You casual with that information now?"

"Yeah." Walker turns up the speed on his treadmill until it's matching mine. "I'm not in high school. It's not a big deal."

Dean shrugs *fair enough*. He looks to me as he amps up his speed until it's just a little faster. "You agree?"

"No, actually." I slide my hoodie off my shoulders, hang it on the railing. This is beyond weird. They went from frosty to friendly in two minutes flat.

"Damn. Your girl's already contradicting you. So much for the honeymoon." Dean chuckles. "Good game, though, getting you here in those tiny shorts."

"You looking at my girl's shorts?" Walker's voice gets faux threatening.

"Yeah. What are you gonna do about it?" Dean raises a brow, faux threatening back.

"Fuck her in the next room." Walker winks. His voice is easy. Effortless.

Dean isn't even a little out of breath either.

Damn tattoo artists and their pristine fitness.

My cheeks flush.

"He talks about you a lot. It's fucking obnoxious," Dean says. "As bad as Brendon."

"Is that really possible?" I ask.

"I didn't think so. But, yeah. You better not break his heart. Pretty sure he'll be worse than Ryan," Dean says.

"Don't let Ryan hear you say that," Walker says.

"What's his deal?" I struggle to get the words out. This is fast. But I want to keep up.

Dean's eyes turn down. It's a second then he shakes it off. Back to the troublemaker. "His high school sweetheart cheated on him."

"Oh. That sucks."

"Yeah. He was looking at rings. Ready to make it official. Fuck, he loved that girl more than he loved anything," Dean says.

"How long were they together?" I ask.

"Eight years. Maybe nine. I lost track," Dean says.

Damn. That's a long time.

"It's been a while, but he can't even look at another woman. I'm not sure he's ever gonna be cured," Dean says.

"He's not sleeping around?" Walker asks.

"Not as far as I know." Dean looks to me. "Leigh might have better info. He talks to her. Kinda."

"I'm gonna tell her you called her Leigh," Walker says.

"Good. She's cute when she wants to kill me," Dean says.

"You two flirt a lot." A ton actually.

Dean laughs. "Me and Leigh? Nah, we're just sparring. She's got her heart set on someone else."

"Since when?" Walker asks.

"I'm sworn to secrecy." Dean motions zipping his lips.

"When have you ever kept a fucking secret?"

"She was drunk and miserable. I offered to let her ride Prince Albert—"

Walker scrunches his nose in disgust. "You did not fucking say that."

Dean laughs. "No. I didn't. But I did offer to fuck her. And she started crying about how she wasn't gonna be with anyone until she was with someone she loved. And it slipped out."

Walker shakes his head. "You're full of shit."

"Not this time. Fucking sucks for Leigh, 'cause she doesn't have a chance."

"She's a babe."

"You're saying that in front of your girl?"

I laugh. Sorta. It's more a laugh gasp for air combo. "No, she's a babe."

"I've said too much already." Dean holds his hands up *my work here is done*.

Walker shakes his head. "You're so full of shit." He hits pause on his treadmill, hops off, motions to the water fountain in the back.

I nod *go ahead* then look to Dean.

"He's really into you," Dean says.

"I'm really into him."

"Yeah." His gaze goes to the street. "I'm glad."

"You are?"

"Yeah. Leighton will hang more if you're around. And she's so fucking fun to tease."

"You're really not into her?"

"I'd fuck her, yeah. But I'm not into anyone."

"Ever?"

"Nobody since I was into that chick from *The OC*. Damn, that was back in middle school. Or was it high school?"

"Which one?"

"Fuck if I remember her name." The teasing tone drops from his voice. "Is shit okay with Bree?"

"I don't know. I think it will be. He tell you anything?"

"Not yet."

"His parents agreed to put their foot down about rehab."

Dean's eyes turn down. "Not the first time."

"Oh."

"I know you think I'm a dick. I am. But I don't want to see her tear his heart to shreds again. If something happens, let me know."

"I will."

"It guts him every time she slips."

My lips press together. "He talks about it?"

"Nah. But I can tell."

"Do you think he'll ever forgive her?"

"Eventually. But he shouldn't. She doesn't fucking deserve it."

"You think he'd ever love an addict?"

Dean turns to me. Shoots me a cutting look. "No. If it was a friend. Or a girlfriend... No, I don't think he'd stick around."

"Oh."

"Why do you ask?"

Uh... "It's genetic."

He shakes his head. "Sounds like bullshit."

"No—"

"I hope it's not. But it really fucking sounds like it."

Chapter Thirty-One

IRIS

The entire ride home, I turn over Dean's words.

Does he know better?

Or should I take my boyfriend at his word?

I try to hold onto the question, but my thoughts dissolve as soon as Walker pins me to the closed front door.

His fingers trail up my inner thigh.

His eyes lock on mine.

They fill with every ounce of desire in the world.

He presses his palm against me. "You wore these to torture me, didn't you, sweetness?"

"What if I did?"

"You get off on teasing me."

"Maybe."

"I should torture you for that."

My nod is heavy.

"I will."

My tongue slides over my lips.

He rubs me over my shorts. "You want my fingers in your cunt?"

"Yes." I want all this doubt gone. I want to believe that

he's mine forever. That nothing outside this moment matters. That I'm more than my ugly past.

"You want to come on my cock?" He presses his palm against my hip, holding me in place as he rubs me over my shorts.

My breath catches in my throat. "Yes."

"You want me to split you in half, sweetness?"

"Yes."

"Good. Take off your clothes."

I unzip my hoodie and slide it off my shoulders.

Walker presses his lips to mine. Then it's his hips against mine.

He pins me to the door.

Fuck, he's hard. I want every inch. I want every drop him.

I pull my tank top over my head. Reach behind my back to unhook my sports bra. I'm messy about sliding it off my shoulders.

I can't wait.

I need him.

I need every layer between us gone.

His pupils dilate as he takes me in. He rocks his hips half an inch. Enough to remind me I'm pinned.

Enough to drive me out of my fucking mind.

He brings both hands to my hips, lifts me, pins me to the door with his body.

I wrap my legs around his waist. My arms around his chest. It's like I'm a million miles off the ground. Like I'm in free fall.

I guess I am.

There's no coming back from falling in love with him.

He looks up at me. His eyes are different than normal. Needier and more commanding at once.

His fingers curl into my thighs, keeping me in place.

Slowly, he rocks against me, pressing his cock against my clit.

There's all this fabric in the way, but I can feel his warmth, his hardness.

And—

Fuck.

He does it again. Again. Again.

My eyelids flutter together.

One hand knots in his hair.

The other claws at his muscle-tank. I grab at the cotton thing and hold on tightly.

He tortures me with those tiny movements.

"Walker," I breathe. "Please."

"Please what?"

"Fuck me."

"Not yet."

I tug at his hair. "Please."

"You're not even close to that, sweetness." He digs his fingers into my hip.

Pins me harder.

Rocks a little softer.

I can barely feel him, but, fuck, the way my panties rub against me—

It's like I'm in high school again, dry humping on the couch because it's all I can get.

This can't be it.

I need more.

I need everything.

I claw at his back. His skin is slick. I can't get a grip. Fuck, I lost my grip a long, long time ago.

He looks up at me like he's going to give me the world.

And like he's never going to relent.

Heat pools in my sex. Desire races to my fingers and toes.

"Walker." My hips shift. It gets me more of him. Harder.

It's not enough. It's closer, but it's not enough, and it's even worse being that much closer. "Please."

"Please what, sweetness?"

"Make me come."

"How?"

I murmur something incomprehensible.

He rocks into me again.

Again.

Again.

"Please," I breathe. "Fuck me." I don't give him a chance to respond. I press my palm into the back of his head to bring his lips to mine.

I kiss him with everything I have to give.

His tongue slides into my mouth. His hips rock against mine.

I pull back to suck in a deep breath, then my lips are on his again.

He claims my mouth with his tongue.

Slowly, he unwraps my legs and sets me on the ground. His fingers trail the waistband of my shorts.

Then he's tracing their hem.

The seam that runs between my legs.

"Fuck." I groan against his mouth. I press my palm against his stomach, reaching for him.

He wraps his hand around my wrist and pins my arm to the wall.

Fuck. I love it when he's in control.

How do I love it this much?

My sex clenches as he pins my other arm to the door.

He's going to fuck me against the front door when there's a couch ten feet away. A bed in the other room. A shower.

That's how badly he needs me.

How little he can wait.

"Walker." I fight his grip.

He pins me harder. "Hands at your sides, sweetness."

"Or?"

"Or I stop."

I shake my head. No. Anything but that.

He brings one hand to my stomach. Traces the seam of my shorts back and forth.

And back.

And forth.

God, his soft touch...

My sex is aching.

I've never been this empty. This needy. This desperate to be full.

He does it again.

Again.

Again.

"Please." The word is a plea and a curse in equal measure.

I hate him. I need him. I love him.

No... I don't love him yet.

Or maybe I do.

It's been too long since I've cared about someone. Since I felt every drop of it, rather than the ones that made it through my high induced haze.

He brings his lips to mine as he slides my shorts off my hips. My panties go with them.

I kick them to my feet. Spread my legs. Arch my back in a desperate plea for more. For him. For everything.

His fingers trail up my thigh with that feather-light touch.

Closer.

Closer.

Almost.

There.

He teases me with his index finger.

He adds his middle finger.

He teases and teases and teases.

"Fuck, Iris." He nips at my bottom lip. "You're wet."

"You're hard."

"Turn around." He steps back.

"Strip."

"Turn around first."

I swallow hard as I spin on my heels.

"Hands on the wall."

I plant my palms against the front door.

Clothes hit the floor.

He moves closer. His cock nudges against the flesh of my ass.

Desire pools between my legs. I arch my back. Rise onto my tiptoes. "Please."

"Not yet." He keeps one hand on my hip. Brings the other to my sex.

He teases with one finger.

Two.

Three.

There.

He slides all three fingers inside me. It's hard. Intense. But it's not enough.

"Fuck me." I rock my hips to push him deeper.

"You're not ready yet, sweetness." He drives deeper. Deeper.

Too deep. It hurts.

But then that fades and it only feels good.

"You have no fucking idea how hard I can go." He drives deeper.

"Walker."

"You want it hard?"

"Yes?"

"Rough?"

"Yes."

"You want me to come in that pretty pink cunt?"

"Please."

"Fuck, Iris." He pulls his fingers almost all the way out then slams them into me again.

Maybe he's right. Maybe I can't handle it this hard and rough.

But that's how I want it.

I want it to own every one of my senses.

To push every other thought away.

I need to forget everything but his body against mine.

He drives his fingers into me again and again.

My heels fall onto the floor. My fingers slip.

He brings his hands to my wrists to reposition me.

Then his hands are on my hips and his lips are on my neck.

He sucks on my skin. Then it's his teeth against my tender flesh. A soft bite.

A harder one.

My sex clenches. "Fuck, Walker." I lean my head to one side, offering my neck to him. "More."

He bites me harder this time. Pain melts into pleasure. My limbs get light. Desire spreads down my torso.

"Fuck me. Please."

"Beg me."

"Walker, please." I rock my hips. "Fuck me. I want to come on your cock. I want you inside me."

He scrapes his teeth against my neck.

"I want to feel you come." I suck in a shallow breath. "Please."

He tugs at my hips, pulling me into position.

His tip strains against me.

Then it's one inch at a time.

Fuck. My world goes white as he slides inside me. Walker. It's the only thing in my brain. The only thing anywhere.

That's his flesh against mine.

Nothing in the way.

All that trust flowing between us.

Trust I desperately need.

He rocks his hips, slamming into me.

My hands slip. I catch myself just before my face hits the wall. The door. Whatever that is.

He takes my hands, places them as high as they'll go. Presses his hips against mine, his chest against my back, his chin against my ear.

He pins me to the wall until I'm nearly flat. Until there's barely any space between us.

He drives into me. It's hard. Deep.

Fuck. That feels good. Intense. A little painful. But so fucking good.

He does it again.

Again.

My cheek hits the door. Then my forehead. I cushion the impact with my right arm.

I rise to my tiptoes, arch my back as he's driving into me.

His fingers dig into my hip as he groans.

His lips go to my neck. He plants a sucking kiss on my skin. Then it's the scrape of his teeth.

He bites me as he drives into me.

He does it again. Again. Again.

My eyelids flutter together. My hips rock to meet him. My tongue slides over my lips.

"More." I can't believe I'm asking for more. I can't believe how much I need more.

He bites me harder. My flesh stings. Fuck. That hurts. But I need it. I need him marking me.

His nails dig into my skin.

He drives into me with a hard, steady thrust. "Say my name."

It rolls off my lips as a groan.

"Again." He drives harder.

I groan his name again.

Deeper.

Again.

Deeper.

My words are messy mumbles. The world is a messy mumble. Pleasure and pain and need and desire and satisfaction and secrets and honesty all rolled into one.

"Fuck, Iris." He pulls back. Untangles our bodies. Nips at my neck and shoulders.

"Please." I'm achy without him. Empty. "Come inside me. Please."

"You first." He brings his hand between my legs. His thumb brushes my clit.

Fuck, that feels good. But I need *him* inside me. I shake my head. "Please, Walker. Please." My voice breaks into a whine. "I need you inside me. Please."

His teeth sink into my shoulder.

I take his wrist and place his hand on my hip.

He brings the other to my waist, pins me to the wall, and drives into me with one steady thrust.

He does it again.

Again.

I close my eyes. I soak in every ounce of him.

A few more thrusts and he loses control of his breath.

He groans. Shakes. Pants.

He goes harder. Too hard. I'm smacking into the wall. It hurts. But then it's still not hard enough.

I rock my hips to meet him. "Come for me, baby." The words fall off my lips seamlessly. That's what he does to me.

He lets out a low, heavy groan.

He drives into me again. Again. Again.

He tugs at my hair.

With his next thrust, he comes. His teeth sink into my neck. His hips rock against mine. His cock pulses inside me.

He spills every drop.

"Fuck." He drags his lips over my neck and shoulders. His breath stays heavy. Needy.

He brings his hand to my chin, turns my head.

My lips find his.

His tongue slides into my mouth. Dances with mine.

His fingers find their way down my stomach. My pelvis. There.

He rubs me with his index finger.

He brings his hand to my breast and toys with my nipple with his thumb.

Fuck. That feels good.

I kiss him harder.

Deeper.

I push every other thought away.

Tension builds between my legs. I'm already so close. So desperate for release.

His tongue slides around mine.

His fingers brush my clit.

His thumb makes circles around my nipple.

There.

All that tension in my sex builds to a fever pitch. It knots tighter and tighter and tighter.

Everything releases.

I groan against his lips as I come.

Pleasure spills through my pelvis, stomach, thighs.

I bring my hands to his hair.

Kiss him harder.

Pull him closer.

Soak up every drop of him.

Chapter Thirty-Two

IRIS

Our takeout and sci-fi marathon is too perfect.

As is Walker's attempt at teaching me how to stir fry.

And the second lesson, where I actually get it.

And our third time out surfing. And the fourth. I actually know what I'm doing. It's fun. It's thrilling. And he's there, with me, on his board, showing off in that Walker kind of way.

And the next week, fucking and cooking and eating and binging on TV at my place

And the one after, hiking and surfing and coffee drinking and fucking everywhere.

And the week after.

And the week after...

We make each other laugh and smile and moan and it's perfect.

Then Dean texts—how the hell did Dean get my number?—to get me in on a surprise party for Walker's birthday next week.

And I make up a plan to tell him.

Not because he needs to know.

Because I believe the past is the past.

Because I believe he'll stay.

Because I can finally look at myself in the mirror and see a whole person.

Not at his birthday. Not at a party.

After finals. When we celebrate. When we go out to the beach to take in a beautiful day.

That's when I'm going to tell him.

It's a few weeks away. And maybe I shouldn't wait.

But I need it to be right. I need it to be perfect.

THE BELL RINGS.

Sun streams through the sliver in the door frame. It's the middle of the afternoon. Walker is supposed to come in for his shift. That was the only way to make this plausible.

Dean and I decided a blindfold and an *I'm surprising you, baby, just follow me* would be too obvious.

Well, Dean complained that it would be too disappointing. That any *follow me* surprise should lead to dirty sex, that no matter how fucking awesome this party could be, it could never compare to fucking in some shady bar.

And... well, I agree.

A Converse clad foot plants on the mat. Walker's sneakers. And that's his leg. I think. It's hard to tell his calf from any other muscular, skinny jean clad calf.

Someone nudges me.

Someone else whispers.

My heart thuds against my chest. Did I drop too many hints? Is this way too obvious? Effort is more important than surprise. What matters is that we care enough about Walker to plan this. What—

The light flicks on.

Walker blinks hard—that light really is bright.

"Surprise." Someone yells it. Then everyone is yelling it. I'm yelling it.

The door swings shut behind him.

He looks around slowly. "Fuck, can't believe I didn't see that coming." His eyes lock with mine. "The blinds are never down in June."

I mouth *do you like it?*

His lips curl into a smile. His eyes light up with something dirty and devious. An *I'd like you naked in my bed a hell of a lot better*.

"Dean, you're so good at planning shit." Dean mimes offense. "I'm so fucking lucky you're my friend."

Leighton laughs. "No one has ever said that."

He looks to her with faux offense. "That hurts, Leigh. That cuts me deep."

"Uh-huh." She taps her heeled sandals together—she's sitting on the counter.

Dean is leaning against it, next to her. Ryan is on her other side, with his usual glum look. Well, he looks a bit less glum than usual. I'm pretty sure this is happy by Ryan standards.

"Thanks." Walker smiles. "You're the best." Walker offers a high five.

Dean takes it, pulls him into a hug, pats him on the back. It's not one of those guy hugs where they seem afraid to get too close.

They're comfortable. Like brothers.

Walker steps back. Looks to me.

I motion to the room. *Go ahead*.

He nods and moves on to thanking/accepting Happy Birthday's from everyone else. Brendon and Kaylee are here. As is Emma and a male date. Or maybe a friend. It's not clear from the way they're standing. He's cute, but he seems a little uptight for her.

There are another half a dozen people I don't know—plus Sandy and John. Dean really went all out. He *is* a good friend. A great friend even.

Dean nudges Leighton with his shoulder. "You want a drink?"

"You have anything good?"

"You think I'd skimp for Walker's birthday?" He folds his arms. "I only have good shit."

"Should I measure your love by how much you spent on booze?" She looks to Ryan. "What if he loves Walker more?"

Ryan shrugs. "Never doubted that."

"Really?" She tilts her head to one side. "You're okay with your brother loving his BFF more than he loves you?"

Again, Ryan shrugs.

She shoots me a look. *You buying this?*

Dean laughs. "He's just playing hard to get." He reaches out and musses Ryan's hair. Despite being the younger brother, he's about two inches taller than Ryan.

"Hey." Ryan fixes his hair. "I know you're desperate for any edge you can get, but don't fuck with the hair."

"An edge?" Dean cocks a brow. "Really?"

"Yeah. We both know all the women here are looking at me," Ryan says.

"Say they are? What's it matter? You haven't looked twice at a girl since... it's a party. I'm not gonna bring her up." He turns to Leighton. "Usual?"

She nods. "Yes, please." But there's something in her voice. A frustration. Her gaze shifts to Ryan. She studies him like her life depends on it.

He takes a long sip of his drink and lets out a soft sigh.

Her teeth sink into her lip.

She's into a guy she'll never have.

And Ryan is still heartbroken over his ex.

That must be it.

Dean turns to me. "What's your poison?"

"Just orange juice, thanks." I force a smile.

Dean shoots me a curious look, but he still turns and moves to the bar.

Leighton makes a point of pulling her gaze away from Ryan. "How long has it been now? You and Walker?"

"A few months." I do a quick check of the math in my head.

Her eyes get dreamy. "Damn. I never thought I'd see the day. You two look good together."

"Everyone knows that." Walker steps toward us. He goes straight to me. Slides his arms around my waist. Brings his lips to my ear. "Tell me you're not wearing anything under that dress." He drags his fingertips over my hips, feeling for panties.

"Would you really want to know that?" My skin buzzes from his touch. "You have to wait."

He shakes his head and motions to the back room.

Dean clears his throat. He hands a drink to me, hands another to Leighton, sips the third.

Walker shoots him a *really?* Look.

Dean nods. "Yeah. Make it really fucking loud. You know I only watch amateur porn."

Leighton laughs. "Everyone in California knows that."

Dean looks to me. "Did you know that, Iris?"

"I got it the tenth time you mentioned it." A lot of the last month of awesomeness has involved hanging out with Walker's friends. Even talking to them one-on-one. It feels good, being accepted by the group, communicating with people who aren't obsessed with grad school or sobriety.

Walker presses his lips to my neck as his fingers skim the

hem of my dress. "Not sure if I can bring myself to torture Leighton like that."

She's making a point of not sleeping with anyone.

She says it's because she makes bad choices with guys.

But, really, it must be because she's into Ryan. Though, being into Ryan does suggest she makes bad choices with guys. He's the dictionary definition of emotionally unavailable.

Ahem. I'm not shrinking her. Or him. No matter how fascinating it is. From a psychology perspective. It's not that it's juicy gossip. Not at all.

"Nah, the audio porn is good for her. Gives her something to spank it to when she gets home," Dean says.

Her cheeks flush. "Shut the fuck up."

"Girls don't spank it," Ryan says.

"That's true." I lean into Walker's touch. Mmm. Contemplating sex in the back room. It *is* his birthday.

"Girls masturbate," Dean says. "Let me ask Emma." He waves in her direction. "Em. Do you touch yourself?"

She rolls her eyes and waves him off.

He laughs. "That's a yes."

"Of course girls masturbate," Leighton says. "But we don't 'spank it.'"

"Jill off?" he asks.

"Ew." Her nose scrunches in distaste. "You're twenty-five. Why can't you say 'masturbate'?"

Ryan shakes his head *kids these days*.

"I don't care what you call it sweetness. As long as I can watch sometime." Walker slides his hand under my dress. Presses his palm against my bare ass. His fingers curl into the back of my thong. "Mmm. Bad girl."

I clear my throat.

"You gonna finger her right there?" Dean asks. "'Cause I'm very happy to watch that." He nudges Leighton. "You?"

"Uh..." She takes a long sip of her drink. "I'm interested to see when they stop."

"That's good. Real coy shit, Leigh." Dean laughs.

"Call me Leigh again and I'm dumping your Belvedere on your head," she says.

"You'd waste good vodka?" He feigns offense.

"I can't think of a more satisfying use," she says.

Walker drags his fingertips over my skin.

He laughs. "They're still going at it."

She laughs too. "Amateur porn, huh?"

Even Ryan nods. "Maybe that's his birthday present."

Dean nods. "Shit. Never took you for an exhibitionist, Williams. Guess it's true what they say. You never really know someone." His eyes meet mine.

I swear, he's talking about me. About my secret.

But how can he know?

How can he be sure?

I swallow hard as I turn back to my boyfriend. "You have something to tell me?"

He nods. "I'm gonna take you to that back room and fuck you so loudly everybody here fucks themselves to us tonight."

Well...

Uh...

My blush spreads over my cheeks, down my chest. Every part of me gets hot at once. I... uh...

He presses his palm into my lower back. "You want everyone to hear you come, sweetness?"

I barely manage to nod.

He smiles as he pulls my body into his.

~

WE EXIT TO A SLOW CLAP.

It's just Dean slow clapping, but still.

Leighton laughs. "We barely heard anything."

Dean shakes his head. "We heard every second."

Sandy looks to me. "We heard... well, Iris, you're really loud."

Oh God.

Kaylee adjusts her cream cardigan. "It wasn't *that* loud. You weren't any louder than Walker."

Ryan plops on the counter next to Leighton. "You're both loud."

"Sorry." I smooth my dress. Fix my hair.

Walker beams, proud.

God, this is embarrassing. Hot. But also embarrassing.

I bury myself in my boyfriend's chest.

He wraps his arms around me. Leans in to whisper. "You keep doing that, I'm gonna have you again."

"You're unusually insatiable."

"Existential dread."

I laugh. "Really?"

"I can't think insightful shit?"

"No, you can—"

"Sounds like I can't."

"It's just not the type of thing you usually say." I stare into his dark eyes. "You look good for your age."

"Do I?"

"You're thirty-five, right?" I tease

He shakes his head. "Eighty."

"Really?"

He laughs. "Maybe."

"You have to tell me your skin care routine. You look amazing."

"Not a day over forty?"

"Yeah." I reach up to run my fingers through his hair. "You look twenty-five."

"That a good thing?"

"It suits you." I rise to my tiptoes and press my lips to his. "I should get your present."

He nods to the back room. "It wasn't that?"

My smile spreads over my lips. "Better."

"Unless it's a tape of you fucking yourself, it's not."

"A tape?"

"Any format."

"Okay. It's almost as good." I squeeze his hand as I step backward. This gift really is perfect.

The bell rings. Heeled footsteps move through the door.

Conversations drop to a murmur.

The room gets quiet.

Too quiet.

No...

Walker's sister is here.

She spots me and folds her arms. Her eyes fill with something. Regret or threat or offense. I don't know. But I don't like it.

I swallow hard.

Walker looks to me. "Give me a minute."

“Of course.” I nod, but the steadiness in my voice is bullshit.

Chapter Thirty-Three

WALKER

Sunset streaks the sky orange.

Waves crash half a dozen blocks to the east.

The beach breeze blows over my arms.

But that isn't why I'm cold.

It's the serious look in my sister's dark eyes. The one that usually precedes *I'm sorry I slipped again. Please rescue me. Please justify my bad decisions*.

"Hey." My sister pulls her arms over her chest. She plays with her black tank top. "I, uh, Dean mentioned the party. I wasn't sure if you'd want me here."

Fuck, that's a difficult question. "You okay?"

"Same old, same old." She stares at her dark nails. "Mom keeps dropping hints that I should go back to rehab."

Sounds like Mom. She's yet to set a date for Bree's not exactly an intervention. According to Mom, Bree hasn't slipped up again, so she's not in need of an intervention.

I don't know what to believe.

I never do.

"It's for the best," I say.

Bree shakes her head. She presses her red lips together.

She always looks put together. Even when she's high. "I... I'm not here about that." She pulls a small envelope from her pocket. "Can we have one day of normal?"

"That's up to you."

She offers me the envelope. "No, Walker. It doesn't matter what I do. You look at me as a pathetic screwup. I don't blame you. I know I've made your life hard. I know you don't believe I care about getting better. But I do." Her eyes turn down. "Just take it, okay?"

I do. "Thanks."

"You can open it. Or do it later. It's up to you."

"You want me to open it now?"

Her nod is sad.

Am I this much of an asshole?

I can't deny any of her claims. Bree is a pathetic screwup. It's a dick thing to say, but it's the truth.

She grinds my heart to dust every chance she gets.

Maybe she isn't doing it on purpose.

But she certainly isn't doing anything to stop herself.

The envelope is royal blue. Like my room at home—our parents never really let our rooms grow with us. Hers is all princesses and ballerinas. Mine is baseball and surfboards.

"I do care, Walker. I love you. I want you to be proud of me." She twirls a dark strand around her finger. "I just..." Her voice cracks. It's heavy. Like she's about to burst into tears. "Open it, okay?"

It's like we're kids again. Like we're the only two people who have a fucking clue our parents aren't perfect. Like we're gearing up to watch a marathon of 80s movies—half sci-fi, half romance, all with enough candy to make us sick.

Bree never was good with moderation.

I unpeel the envelope and pull out the card. There's a cartoon picture of two bears hugging—one is wearing a baseball cap, the other is wearing a tutu.

I know you're my brother...

But sometimes you're unBEARable.

Happy Birthday

Her neat handwriting is all over the bottom half of the card.

Happy Birthday, Walker. I know it's been a long time since I've been the older sister you deserve. I'm sorry I've been so "unBEARable." And sorry for the silly pun. It made me think of that trip we took to Big Bear, the one where Mom and Dad locked themselves in the cabin.

Love,

Bree

"There's something else." She unfurls her palms to show off a small, round token. "I know you think I'm not trying. But you're wrong." She holds out her hands.

It's her two-month chip.

"I'm going to meetings. And therapy. I want to be better. I want to feel like a real adult, and not some screwup who's still living with her parents when she's pushing thirty. I know I had those slip ups... I know I let you down. But I really am trying." She blinks back a tear. "I'm sorry. I didn't come here to—"

"No, it's okay." I pull my sister into a hug. Two months sober. Fuck, I can't believe it.

My shoulders feel lighter. My chest feels looser. Everything feels warmer. Brighter.

Maybe she's telling the truth.

Maybe this is going to be okay.

Maybe there's no dramatic left turn in Bree's story. Maybe rehab stint five was enough.

I stare back at my sister. "What changed?"

"Well." She bites her fingernail. "I guess I realized that you might forgive me one day."

Huh? "You thought I wouldn't?"

"Of course... And I'd understand. I deserved it. But when I saw you with Iris."

What the fuck? "What's she have to do with it?"

Bree's eyes fill with surprise. "She hasn't told you?"

"Hasn't told me what?"

"Oh. I... forget I said anything." She presses her lips together. "Please. Forget it."

"Forget what?"

She shakes her head. "I can tell I'm getting glares from your friends. I owe a lot of them apologies, but I'm not going to hijack your birthday—"

"Bree, what the fuck are you talking about?"

"Iris."

"What about Iris?"

She swallows hard. "Never mind."

What the hell could Bree possibly know about Iris? My fingers curl into fists. "Tell me."

She presses her lips together. Something fills her eyes, something I haven't seen from her in a long, long time.

Pity.

I blink. It's still there.

My sister pities me?

What the fuck?

This doesn't make any sense.

She's met Iris once. What could she possibly know?

"Bree. What the fuck?"

"I shouldn't say anything."

"What the hell does that mean?" I stare back into her eyes.

"Iris..." Her dark eyes streak with regret. "I've seen her at NA."

No. There's no fucking way that's true. "Bullshit."

"She got up. Told her story. It had a lot of ugly parts. It was brave and I... I shouldn't have said this." Bree presses her lips together. "Even if you're my brother. She... I... shit." She takes a step backward. "I love you."

"Yeah."

"Walker?" Her voice is sincere. "Are you okay?"

Every single molecule of her expression is sincere.

"You saw my girlfriend at NA?"

She nods. "I wish I was lying. Really. You deserve a good thing. But, whatever you want to believe, your girlfriend is an addict."

No.

There's no way.

She's full of shit.

Even if she sounds really fucking honest.

Chapter Thirty-Four

WALKER

The party is quiet. Thank fuck Dean pulled the curtains down, because everyone is staring at me. Even the people who don't know Bree. And the ones who have no idea she's an addict.

Dean shoots me a look. *You okay?*

I nod even though I'm not.

This is fucking bullshit.

There's no way Iris would keep that a secret.

There's no fucking way.

I slide the card into my back pocket. I go straight to the bar. Fill a plastic cup with ice and whiskey.

It's good shit. Goes down smooth. Sands the edges off my thoughts.

There are soft steps behind me. The click-clop of women's shoes. Iris's steps. She's wearing those wedges she can't walk in.

Fuck, it's adorable, the way she stumbles. And those things make her the perfect height to pin her to the wall.

But she...

I...

This doesn't make sense.

I finish my glass. It's too much, too fast. But I don't care. I need the buzz pushing my thoughts away.

Her fingers skim my shoulder. "Is your sister okay?"

"Yeah." I refill my glass. Take another swig.

"Are you?" Her voice gets soft.

Is that bullshit too?

Did she mean anything she told me?

My stomach twists as I take another sip. The whiskey fails to help. I can't even taste it.

"Walker..."

"Yeah?"

"What happened?" She moves closer. "Is she using again?"

"No." I take another sip. Turn to face Iris.

Her blue eyes fix on mine.

They're sweet. Sincere.

But are they?

Has she been lying to me all this time?

"She's good. Two months sober." My throat burns, but I take another swig anyway.

Confusion fills Iris's eyes. "Something about that upset you?"

"Yeah."

"Yeah?" She smooths her dress. Stares at her purple nails.

"She said some fucked-up shit."

Her lips press together. Her eyes fill with dread.

She knows what I'm going to say.

She knows she's found out.

How the fuck does she know?

How the fuck does everyone else know everything?

A deep breath does nothing to break up the tension in my shoulders. "Bree said she saw you at NA."

"Oh."

"I told her that's bullshit." Please, Iris, please tell me it's bullshit. "You'd have told me if you were an addict."

Her eyes turn down. "I..."

"What the fuck, Iris?"

"I'm sorry." She moves closer. Reaches for my wrist.

I pull my arm to my side.

"It was casual. It was none of your business."

Maybe. It feels hollow. It feels like more bullshit.

"You said the past was the past. You said it didn't matter. That I couldn't tell you anything that would change things." Energy drains from her voice with every word. "Did you mean it?"

I did.

But I...

This...

Fuck, this doesn't make any sense.

She wipes a tear from her eye. "I should have told you. I know that. But you'd have left."

"No." My voice rises. It's too fucking loud. I'm causing a scene.

But it's my birthday.

I can cause a fucking scene if I want.

"Yeah, you would have. That doesn't make it right, but... I... I guess I wanted to believe you." She struggles through her words. "To believe it was possible you might love me anyway."

My eyes find hers.

Those same beautiful blue eyes.

Filled with that same hurt. Usually, I'm desperate to destroy it.

But now?

Fuck, my head hurts.

Iris takes a step backward. "I'm sorry. I should have told you."

I try to find words, but they're too ugly. Too raw.

What the fuck can I say?

I did mean it, that the past didn't matter.

It didn't.

But it does.

I'm a fucking liar.

As bad as she is.

No, worse.

But that doesn't change shit.

I still can't stomach this.

I still—

I swallow the last drop of my drink. It still fails to offer clarity.

I don't know much. But I do know this. "You should go."

Her heart breaks. Fuck, I can see it all over her face.

I still hate her pain.

But I still can't do this.

This still doesn't make any sense.

Her eyes go to the floor.

Without a word, she turns, and moves to the door.

It swings shut behind her.

Everyone looks at me.

Fuck that. I refill my drink.

Dean steps forward. He tries to grab the cup. Knocks it over instead. "You're not going after her?"

I shake my head.

I don't see how it can be anything else.

I don't...

This doesn't make any sense.

"What the fuck, Walker? You're crazy about her." He scratches his head. "What the hell is wrong with you?"

"You heard everything. You know the answer."

"She's an addict. So what?" Something fills his eyes. Guilt.

"You knew?"

"Suspected."

"So that lecture about friends helping each other. That was bullshit?"

"You're being a fucking idiot."

"Fuck you." Fuck the entire world. Is there anyone I can trust not to keep shit from me?

"You're gonna regret this tomorrow."

"No. I'm gonna regret being sober tomorrow."

Someone steps forward. "I'll talk to her." That's Leighton. She sounds worried.

But it's a blur.

It's all a blur.

It's all bullshit.

It's all a fucked-up mess.

Chapter Thirty-Five

IRIS

A tattoo shop in Venice Beach is a terrible idea.

There's nowhere to park.

I keep taking the bus here. Because Walker keeps driving me home. But now...

Where the hell is the bus stop anyway?

I pull my cell from my purse. Unlock the screen. A drop falls on it.

A tear.

I blink and another catches on my lashes.

Fuck.

This is bad.

This is so bad.

No... it's worse than bad.

It's over.

That look in his eyes...

He hates me.

He hates me and there's nothing I can do about it.

"Hey." Heels click on the pavement. "Shit." They stumble. "These stupid shoes are too loose." Leighton catches herself.

She takes a shaky step forward. Forces her raspberry lips into a smile.

"I appreciate whatever this is, but—"

"You *want* to take the bus?"

"How did you..."

She motions to the bus stop to my left.

Oh. Duh. I'm way too out of it. "I'll be fine."

She pulls her keys from her purse. "I'm leaving. This is my last offer."

"I..." I press my lips together. "Did you hear everything?"

"Enough."

"You think I'm a liar too?"

"It's none of my business."

"You really believe that?"

She presses her lips to one side. "Depends on the day." She motions to the street to our right and nods *follow me*.

I don't want to take the bus.

And she isn't looking at me like I'm the scum of the Earth.

I follow her down the side street. We walk in silence for a few blocks.

She hits her key fob and an old silver sedan's lights turn on. "Go ahead." She motions to the passenger side door.

"Thanks." I open it. Slide into the car. Click my seatbelt.

She gets in, slides the key into the ignition, looks to me. "You, um... You live in Brentwood, right?"

"Yeah. It's easiest to take eleventh to Wilshire."

She nods *sure*, turns the key, puts the car in drive.

Music flows through the speakers. Something familiar. It was popular when I was in high school. Well, Leighton looks about my age, maybe a little younger, so I guess it was popular when *we* were in high school.

I lean back in my seat. Smooth my dress. Press my heels together.

She's quiet as she pulls onto eleventh.

I watch the sun sink into the horizon. The pink sky is beautiful. But it doesn't stick.

"Can I ask you something?" My voice is soft. Unsteady.

She nods. "Shoot."

"Do you think Walker will forgive me?"

"Honestly?"

"Yeah."

"No."

My stomach drops. She's right. I *know* that. But hearing another person say it...

Fuck.

She turns onto Wilshire.

"You think I'm an asshole?" I ask.

"Did he really lay on that 'the past doesn't matter' shit?"

"Yeah."

"Then no. You're not an asshole. You made a mistake. Everyone does."

"Will he ever see it that way?"

"I hope so." Her fingers tap the dash. "But I really don't know."

Chapter Thirty-Six

WALKER

"Either you're an idiot or you have a deep appreciation for irony." Brendon hoists my arm onto his shoulder.

"He's an idiot." Dean grabs the other.

Fucking assholes.

I don't need their help.

I can get wasted and stumble home on my own just fine.

Dean drags me up the steps to my apartment.

"Fuck you." I try to pull my arms to my sides, but there's two of them and one of me. It isn't happening.

Fuck this.

Fuck the entire universe.

"Didn't work the first time." Dean motions to the door. "Hand me your keys or I'm digging through your pocket."

"You're holding my arm." I grit my teeth.

"You're being a child." He shoots Brendon a look and releases my right arm.

"Thanks." I flip him off, dig into my pockets, take out my keys. The pewter Millennium Falcon, the one Iris bought me, mocks me.

I can see her soft lips pressing into a smile. I can hear her nervous giggle. *Do you like it? Tell me you like it.*

Was she high?

Thinking about getting high?

Did she mean a single fucking thing she said?

Dean grabs the key. Slides it into the lock and kicks the door open.

"I can walk." I plant both feet on the ground.

They share a look. *Can he?*

I use their distraction to pull my arm free. Stomp into my apartment.

All right, I stumble.

I'm drunk, yeah, but not drunk enough.

I won't be drunk enough until the entire fucking world is a blur.

I can't think about this. I need it far away. I need to forget every time Iris ever smiled.

I need to forget how badly I want her.

How much I meant it when I said *the past is the past.*

I did. I really fucking did. I was sure there was nothing ugly in her past. I was sure there was nothing like this.

I...

My head pounds.

My heart aches.

Brendon fills a glass of water and hands it to me.

I drink. Even though they're both assholes.

There. I set the glass on the counter. The damn thing only makes me think of her.

Her lips on mine.

Her thighs wrapped around me.

Her groans in my ears.

She's all over this room.

And my bedroom.

And the shop.

Even the fucking ocean—the one place where shit always makes sense—makes me think of her.

"We should hide his wallet," Dean says. "So he can't go out again."

Brendon shakes his head. "He won't."

"Go fuck yourself." I press my hand against the wall. The room is spinning. But it's not from too much whiskey. It's my world tilting on its axis.

I know all the signs.

They were there.

It was obvious. How cagey Iris got about Bree. How she kept alluding to some secret I'd never forgive. How she looked at me when I tore her clothes off—like it might be the last time.

But I didn't see it.

I didn't have a fucking clue.

Chapter Thirty-Seven

IRIS

I wake up with a familiar headache. An *I've been crying all night, my body is deprived of sleep, salt, and water* headache.

Coffee and sugar only make it worse.

I'm a zombie at school. I absorb nothing in my classes. I fumble over walking undergrads through experiments. I stare at the results without a clue as to what they mean.

Work is the only thing that makes sense to me.

And even that is fuzzy.

A LONG WALK HELPS. THE POUNDING FADES TO A DULL ache. My thoughts settle. The world comes into focus.

I manage to sleep. To get up on time. Shower. Eat breakfast. Drink coffee. Pretend to pay attention at school.

I even make it to the gym. And manage to read a little.

But, all day, I think of him.

He might hate me.

He might never want to see me again.

But then he might not.

He might forgive me.

He might still care about me.

I wait until I'm home. Until I'm fed and showered and ready for bed.

And I text him.

Iris: I'm sorry.

Chapter Thirty-Eight

WALKER

My phone buzzes against the end table.

Fuck. I thought I turned that off.

Who the hell is texting at this hour?

I squeeze my eyes shut. Rub my temples. My head is still aching. It's been aching nonstop for days. Ever since I saw Iris's heartbreak written all over her face.

I did that.

But she—

Fuck.

This still doesn't make any sense.

I pull my arms over my head. Let out a heavy exhale.

That must be her.

Whatever it is, I'm not ready to hear it.

I'm not ready to piece this together.

My cell's notification light blinks. It mocks me with its brightness.

I turn over. Pull the blanket over my head. Block out every bit of light in the room.

It doesn't help.

My head keeps pounding.

My thoughts stay on her.

All the sincerity in her blue eyes.

How much of it was real? Was she high when she was with me? Did she sneak off to the bathroom to swallow a handful of pills?

I don't know what to believe.

I toss and turn forever. Eventually, my thoughts slow. I drift into an uneasy sleep.

I dream about her.

I wake up wishing she was here.

Fuck, this isn't how it's supposed to go.

I'm supposed to hate her more than I want her.

It should be like one of those angry breakup songs. *How could you do this? How could you lie to me? I don't need shit from you anymore.*

It is...

But there's this other verse.

Come back. Explain. I miss you. I need you. I'm pretty sure I love you.

I get up. Piss. Brush my teeth. Wash my face. Make coffee. It's good shit. French roast.

But it makes me think of her.

Everything I do as I get ready makes me think of her.

I check the time on my cell. It's early enough for this.

And there's her text.

Two words.

I'm sorry.

I don't want to believe it.

But I do.

~

THE COLD WATER NUMBS MY HANDS AND FEET.

It wakes up my tired brain.

It sends all my thoughts right back to Iris.

I paddle past the break point. Watch waves form and crash on the sand. Wait for the right set.

Turn my board. Catch a wave. Hop to my feet.

It's an amazing ride.

But I barely feel it.

I barely manage to balance.

My head isn't in the game.

It's on Iris.

The way she smiled as she propped herself up on her surfboard.

The way she looked at me like I could take all her pain away.

All that shaking in her shoulders as she tried to tell me.

The way it stopped when I promised it didn't matter.

I spend the entire morning at the beach. I catch wave after wave. I manage to clear my head enough to balance.

But I still drive home thinking of her.

I still shower thinking of her.

I still get dressed wanting to wrap my arms around her.

I MUSTER UP THE ENTHUSIASM TO HIGH-FIVE MY CUSTOMER on his way out the door. He sat through a huge piece of ink. It's a badass design. The kind of thing that usually excites me. That usually demands every bit of my attention.

It helped. It did.

Iris stayed in the back of my mind.

But now that my distraction is gone, my brain is flashing a neon sign. *Iris* in capital letters.

I force a smile as the guy walks away. It fades as soon as I turn into the shop. We're past our usual closing time. Except for Ryan and Leighton whispering over something at the counter, the place is empty.

They look cozy. Strangely cozy given Ryan's usual attitude toward conversation.

His misery finally makes sense to me.

It's like I'm missing a limb.

But it's worse. Because it's like the limb told me to go fuck myself and removed itself from my body.

All right, that doesn't make any sense.

I'm not an idiot. I get that this is my doing as much as hers. But that knowledge doesn't help with the ache in my gut or the pounding in my head.

I need a drink.

Or twelve.

How can I be pissed at her for using when I'm willing to let whiskey wash all this away?

The logic does nothing to soothe me. Or warm the ice around my heart. Or get the *I hate her* and the *I need her* halves of my brain to make up.

She should have told me. We both know that.

But then it shouldn't have mattered. Not this much. I meant it. I did want her exactly as she is. I did believe the past was the past.

But what if it wasn't the past?

What if she's still using? Or thinking about using?

Fuck. She could be high right now.

She could be as desperate to get out of her head as I am.

Ryan turns to me and nods. He motions to his suite. *Let's talk*.

Uh...

I'm not sure Ryan has ever wanted to *talk* to me.

Lecture me, yeah.

Deliver news, sure.

Go over some business shit, of course.

But conversation about something other than work?

No. I'm getting ahead of myself. It might be about work. Maybe he's finally going to stop vetoing all potential new hires as *not serious enough*.

He moves to his suite. Shoots me a *get the fuck over here now* look.

All right. I take the bait. It can't be worse than the thoughts going around my head.

I join him.

He shakes his head, sending his wavy hair all over the place. "You're an asshole."

"That it?"

"You flung your girl's dirty laundry all over the room."

"She's not my girl anymore." I lean against the divider wall. "What's it to you?"

He shrugs.

"That's it?" Seriously, what the fuck?

"Yeah."

"What? Am I stealing your thing?"

"Fuck no. You don't wear misery like I do."

Fair enough. It's natural on Ryan. Like he was born with a frown. Hell, I barely remember him with a smile. He was never the happiest guy in the world, but when he was around Penny...

"You love her, huh?"

"Why do you care?"

"Fuck, Dean was right. You're stupid."

"How the fuck do you know about that?"

"He's my brother." He taps his head in the *duh* motion. "You do realize you're my friend?"

"Yeah. And?" We're not exactly buddy-buddy. We rarely speak. Don't get me wrong. I like Ryan. I want the best for him. But I'm not expecting an invite to be his groomsman... in some parallel universe where he's interested in love.

"Believe it or not, I don't want to see the entire world miserable."

"You've been sulking over your ex cheating for a year."

"And?"

"It's been a few days."

"You like being miserable?"

"Do you?"

"That's not the point."

"Yeah, it is." I'm done with this conversation. I can be a miserable asshole if I want. If anyone understands that, it should be Ryan. "What? You get free rein to hate the world but I don't?"

"I don't sulk."

"Yeah, you do."

He shakes his head *stupid kids*. "It's not that she cheated."

"What is it?"

"She's gone. Yeah, I hate her for sleeping with that asshole. But, no matter how much I hate her, there's a gaping hole in my chest the size of her."

"You'd take her back?"

"I don't know. Doesn't matter. She's still with him."

"You really keep tabs?" The pounding in my head lessons. Fuck, it's nice thinking about someone else's problems. About anything that isn't how much I hate Iris. And how much I want her.

"People talk."

"You don't look at other women."

"I'm not doing it again."

"But you could fuck half the girls you ink."

"If I was an asshole who preyed on my customers, yeah."

"Please. I only fuck women who beg me for it."

"Whatever you want to believe."

"Don't make me go into detail."

"Doesn't bother me."

"I will."

He shrugs *and?*

I shoot him my best side-eye. "You could find girls easy."

"I don't want to fuck some chick I won't remember."

"Why?"

He shakes his head. "It would take too long to explain it to you."

"So you've gone a year?"

"So what?"

"A year? How the fuck do you live?"

"I have a hand."

"Still."

He rolls his eyes. "I have standards."

"You don't ever want to love someone again?"

"Do you?"

Fair enough. But I don't want to talk about me. I don't want to think about how fucked this is. "You and Leighton—"

"Are friends."

"You sure?"

"Yeah. She thinks I'm a miserable bastard."

"You are."

He flips me off.

"You do hang a lot."

"So do the two of you."

True. But she doesn't smile at me the way she smiles at him. And Ryan only smiles around her. "Would you fuck her?"

"She's not interested."

"If she asked?"

"Fuck off." His cheeks flush. He shakes his head. Actually stammers over his words. "I'm lecturing you here."

"This topic is better."

"For you."

"Yeah." I take a deep breath and exhale slowly. That pounding deepens. Heaviness spreads over my body. It's like a switch. *Thinking about Iris, pain. Thinking about anything else, relief.* "Does that gaping hole in your chest ever go away?"

"No. But it gets better." His expression gets intense. Well, more intense. Ryan is always intense. "Did you really tell her the past is the past?"

"Yeah."

"That makes you the asshole."

"I know."

"She didn't do anything wrong."

"She should have told me."

"Is that really why you're miserable?"

"Yeah." What the hell else could it be?

"Bullshit. It's something else. I don't know what. But it's not that she didn't tell you."

"It is."

He shakes his head. "You should fix this."

"I can't."

"You can."

"All right, I can. But I don't want to."

"'Cause you convinced her to keep a secret?"

No. "Fuck off." Asshole is right.

But it's more than that.

I did convince her to keep this a secret.

But now I don't know what to believe.

If any of it was real.

I know addicts. And they're full of shit.

"You care about her?" he asks.

"Yeah."

"You still want to make her happy?"

"Part of me does."

"Tell the other part to get lost. She made you happy, Walker. That's fucking rare. Get over yourself and get her back."

"What if I don't?"

"You probably won't. You've been a fucking idiot about it. No reason to believe you'll change."

"Then why this talk?"

He shrugs.

"You want to help."

"No shit."

"You want to believe in love."

He shakes his head *you're crazy.* But there's something in his eyes. He does.

"You want to get a drink?"

"Not if I'm gonna have to cart your plastered ass home."

I chuckle. "You're more fun than you let on."

"Don't tell anyone."

"I won't."

"You know I'm gonna keep lecturing you."

"I know." Part of me hopes he gets through to me.

Chapter Thirty-Nine

IRIS

It feels like a million years pass.

I stare at my cell during boring lectures. Between classes. At lunch. During coffee breaks. When I get home. When I finish yoga. When I sit down to study.

When I'm in bed not really trying to sleep.

All week, nothing.

All weekend, nothing.

I try to convince myself to give him time. To give him space.

But I can't.

I need to explain this.

I need to look him in the eyes.

I only hope it's enough to convince him to forgive me.

Chapter Forty

WALKER

My cell burns a hole in my pocket.

It's still there.

I'm sorry.

The two words feel like a dedication.

Like everything.

My stomach is in knots. Half of me is screaming *call her.* The other half is screaming *never speak to her again.*

I check the time. Fifteen minutes until my next appointment. Fifteen minutes in my head, turning over my options.

Leighton is sitting at the counter, reading something on her Kindle. Her eyes meet mine. She raises a brow. The same thing she's done every day since my birthday.

Are you really going to sulk when you could call Iris?

You're making yourself miserable. And you're annoying miserable. Not like Ryan or Brendon. They know how to do miserable. You don't.

We've had that conversation way too many times.

Maybe I don't wear miserable as well as Ryan does.

But Ryan is the king of miserable.

Those are big shoes to fill.

I stare back.

She shrugs. "What?"

"You know what."

"I'm reading."

"You gave me a look."

"You're pissy today."

"Go fuck yourself."

"I will. Later." She slides off her stool. "I'm making coffee. You want one?"

"Yeah. Thanks."

"You're welcome." She takes a step toward the Keurig. "You could call her."

"I'm aware."

"You'd be less annoying."

"Where's the fun in that?"

She shrugs *suit yourself*, but there's concern in her blue-green eyes.

She still wears her eyeliner the same way Iris does. That long line. Hers is purple. Iris's is a dark brown.

It makes me think of her.

The entire shop makes me think of her.

The whole fucking world makes me think of her.

She's right.

Ryan is right.

But it's not enough to convince that other part of me, the part that doesn't trust Iris.

That hates Iris.

That hates how badly I still want to wipe her pain away.

IRIS IS SITTING ON MY DOORSTEP.

She's in that black dress, the one that's tight on her tits and loose around her hips.

I know every inch of that dress. Exactly how it feels against my hands. The smell of it—cotton mixed with her shampoo. The way it hugs her curves.

My body wakes up at the sight of her. It wants hers. That's something I understand.

My heart beats harder. My blood pumps faster. My limbs get light.

My body is a traitor.

But, fuck, it's good to see her.

She presses her palms into her thighs as she looks up at me. Her knees knock together. Then her toes. Her inner feet. Her heels. "I... I know this is crazy ex-girlfriend stuff."

"Yeah."

"I'll leave if you ask me to." She pushes herself up.

I offer my hand.

She takes it.

My body threatens to take over. To push every *how can I trust her* thought to the back of my head.

"I want to talk to you." Her fingers brush my palm as she pulls her hand to her side. "I want to explain."

The need in her eyes guts me.

I still want to wipe all her pain away.

And I still can't trust her.

"Can I do that?" She presses her lips together. "If you don't let me explain, I'll have to keep 'accidentally' running into you at Blue Bottle. And what if you're with some other woman? It will be awkward." She gnaws on her bottom lip. "I'll start yelling something like *how could you move on so quickly? Did you ever care about me? Does she even know you're using her?* Cause a big scene. Get all three of us banned from every shop on Abbot Kinney."

She still does something to me.

I hate that she does something to me.

This would be easier if I hated her. If that was the end of it. "That does sound awkward."

"And wrong, being deprived the best coffee near the shop." Her lips curl into a half smile. "Can I come in? Please? I'm running low on dignity at the moment, so I will stoop to begging."

"Yeah." I unlock the door and open it for her.

She bends to grab something from the concrete—a tiny silver gift bag—then she steps into the apartment.

I follow, closing and locking the door behind us.

The place is sparse. Empty. Not a speck of dust in sight. Cleaning is somewhere between *reading* and *filing taxes* on the list of things that might help me forget her.

It didn't work.

Nothing works.

She still owns my thoughts.

She still keeps me up all night.

I have no idea how to make it stop. Maybe this is it. Maybe I need one last taste so I can forget her.

She turns to me. Holds up the gift bag. "This, um, this was for your birthday. If you don't want it—"

"Thanks."

Her smile is sad. Weary. She looks as tired as I feel.

I take the bag, set it on the counter, move into the kitchen. "You want something to drink?"

"Water."

"Sure."

"You still keep the place dry?"

I grab two glasses from the cabinet and fill them with water. "Yeah. I can't imagine having booze here."

"For Bree?"

I nod.

She smooths her dress. Rocks from one foot to another. Plays with her short hair.

I move to her. Offer her a glass.

She nods *thanks* and drinks with greedy sips. "Thanks. I was only waiting for an hour or two. But I didn't know how long it would be so I didn't want to hydrate."

I motion to the bathroom.

She shakes her head. "No, I walked over to a coffee shop halfway through that. I, uh..." She moves forward. Sets her glass on the counter. Keeps her back to me. "Walker, I... I get it if you hate me, if you never want to see me again. But wait until I explain to judge." She lets out a heavy exhale and pulls her arms over her chest. "If you still hate me, I'll leave. And I won't contact you again."

I move toward her. Set my glass next to hers.

She takes a deep breath. "I really am sorry."

My fingers skim her shoulders. "I know." I know she's sorry. I know I convinced her to stay quiet. I know she hurts as much as I do.

But that doesn't help clarify any of this.

I hate her and *I need her* are still tearing my heart in half.

It shouldn't matter.

If I can't trust her, that's it.

But it doesn't feel like it.

It feels like this is fixable. It has to be. I need her to fill that Iris shaped hole in my gut. Or I need to erase her from my mind.

One of them.

I don't know which.

"Oh." Her voice is soft. "Do you not... I... Uh..."

"Were you high?"

"What?"

"With me?"

"No. Never. That fight with Ross, it was about me going to rehab. I haven't touched anything since that. Since January."

"Look at me."

"I can't."

"'Cause you're full of shit?"

"No." Her exhale is heavy. "Because if you still hate me, I'm going to burst into tears, and I'd like to save that one scrap of dignity I have."

"Iris. I need you to look me in the eyes when you say it." I drag my fingertips down her arm. "Please." I want to believe her. I want to be able to believe her.

My fingers skim her shoulders.

Her hips shift. She presses her back into my chest. "Walker, I... I... Uh... What is this?"

"Look at me. Please."

Slowly, she turns to face me. Her blue eyes fill with vulnerability. She's hurting, yeah, but she's not lying.

"Tell me again."

"I haven't touched anything since before rehab."

"What did you use?"

"Heroin."

Fuck. I knew she'd say that. Deep down, I knew it. The place she got that tattoo—that's where Bree always had track marks.

But still, hearing it on her lips...

She takes a deep breath. "Do you want me to leave?"

"No."

"You want me to stay?"

"Yeah." I do. But then I don't.

I need her to be *my* Iris again.

But that Iris doesn't exist. She was some idea I had of her.

And that was on me, yeah.

But that doesn't make this any easier.

I need to turn my thoughts off.

I need the world to make sense.

I need her under me.

I slide my arm around her waist. Pull her closer. I shouldn't do this. She's not here to fuck me.

But I have to.

Her eyes bore into mine. They ask for everything and promise more. "Walker, I—"

I bring my hand to the back of her head and pull her into a slow kiss.

She groans against my lips. Her fingers dig into my t-shirt, pressing the cotton into my skin.

She's eager. Hungry. Needy.

Mine.

No. I need to erase that thought from my head.

Somehow.

"Walker." She slides her hand under my t-shirt. "I can't do this unless I know what it means."

"I need you."

"But—"

"I don't want to need you. I don't want to think about you. It aches. Like a part of me is missing. I want it back. Tell me how to get it back."

"I don't know."

"You're burnt into my brain."

She stares into my eyes. "Walker—"

"You're all I think about." I press my forehead to hers. "I need it to stop, Iris. I need my thoughts back."

She swallows hard. "But you want to fuck me?"

I want every ounce of her. And I want to destroy every memory of her. "I hate being away from you."

She presses her palm against my torso. Her eyes get soft. Hazy. "Tell me this won't be the last time."

"I can't."

Her eyelids flutter together. She rises to her tiptoes. Presses her lips to mine.

All her need pours into me.

All my need pours into her.

I don't know how to explain this. I wish I did. I wish it made sense.

I need her.

And I need her gone.

My fingers dig into her skin. "I don't want to hurt you. But I don't know what else to do. I need you so badly right now."

She presses her forehead to my chin. "Say it again."

"I need you."

Her nails dig into my skin. "Has there been anyone else?"

"No. You're all I think about."

"Me either. I mean me too. I mean—" She presses her lips to mine. Tugs my t-shirt up my torso.

I help her get it over my head.

My hands go to her hips. Then under her thighs. I lift her into my arms.

She wraps her legs around my waist.

I carry her into my bedroom. Set her on the bed.

She looks up at me.

We've been here a few dozen times. But it's different. It's never been all of her and all of me.

It's never been this desperate. This needy.

She kicks off her flats.

I unbutton and unzip my jeans. Push them to my knees.

She shimmies out of her panties. Motions *come here*.

I strip out of everything and climb onto the bed.

She wraps her hand around my cock. Kisses me as she strokes me.

Fuck.

I roll her dress up her thighs, her pelvis, her stomach, her chest. She breaks our kiss to toss it over her head.

I do away with her bra.

She drags her hands up my torso.

Her eyes lock with mine as I climb on top of her, nudge her knees apart.

She nods *yes, now, please.*

But she isn't ready.

I drag my fingertips up her inner thigh.

Her breath hitches as I stroke her. "Walker." Her hand knots in my hair. "Please."

Please forgive me. Please listen. Please love me.

I rub her harder. I want to give her all that. But I don't know how.

I only know how to give her this.

Her eyelids flutter together. She turns her head to one side. Groans my name.

Fuck, she's beautiful like this.

I stroke her with slow circles.

She tugs at my hair.

I watch pleasure spill over her expression as she inches toward the edge. Her brow softens. Her lips part. Her head tilts back.

There.

She groans my name as she comes on my fingers.

She's lost in it for a second. Then she blinks her eyes open. Stares back at me. Nods *yes, now, please* as she spreads her legs.

I plant my hands at her shoulders.

Slowly, I bring my body onto hers.

One inch at a time, I thrust into her.

Fuck. She feels good.

Mine.

It's like every time before. It sticks in my head. She sticks in my head.

She's—

Fuck.

I wrap my arms around her.

Sink into her as I thrust into her.

She lifts her hips to meet me. Brings her hand to the back of my head. Pulls me into a deep, slow kiss.

We stay locked together, moving together, groaning together.

She's mine and I'm hers.

And there isn't a single layer between us.

No deception. No baggage. No hurt.

Just her need pouring into me.

And my need pouring into her.

Until she's there, groaning against my lips, clawing at my back as she pulses around me.

It pushes me over the edge.

Pleasure spills through my body as I come.

She holds me as I fill her.

We stay locked together. We stay a sweaty, breathy mess.

I stay hers.

And she stays mine.

Chapter Forty-One

WALKER

I wake up empty.

She's still burnt into my brain.

No, it's worse. My sheets smell like her. I can still taste her on my lips, feel her under me, hear her groaning my name.

I still want to wipe away every bit of pain in her eyes.

I still need her like I need oxygen.

My morning routine does nothing to wipe Iris from my brain. There's coffee in the carafe, my favorite French Roast.

The present is there, on the counter.

There's a note under it.

The ball's in your court. Call me if you want to talk. Or "not talk."

I don't know how to sign this,

Iris.

It's rambling, nervous, perfect.

I stare at the shiny silver bag for a long time. Eventually, I pick out the tissue paper.

It's a signed copy of *Saga*.

I hate that it's perfect.

I hate that I want to call her and beg her to come over.

Stay in my bed all day. Let's forget the world. Let's forget everything.

Just be here.

Just be mine.

THERE.

Almost.

I finish the last line. "You're done."

The girl in the chair sighs with relief.

I turn the gun off. Set it down. Wipe my brow. This is where I say something encouraging. Congratulate her on making it though her first tattoo. Congratulate her on how awesome it looks.

It looks fucking amazing.

But that does nothing to convince me to smile.

"Here." I turn her toward the mirror.

Her eyes go wide as she takes in the words on her ribs. They're lyrics to her favorite song. She's been humming it for the last twenty minutes.

I've never heard it before.

But they're solid lyrics.

The kind of shit that makes you think about love. And losing it. And how far you'll go to get it back.

They might as well scream *you miss Iris*.

"Oh my God." Her eyes go wide. She looks up at me with a hazy smile. "This is so cool, Walker. Thank you." She throws her arms around me and squeezes tightly.

It's normal. Even if she's only wearing gauze and tape over her tits.

I pat her back. Hug her the way I usually do. It feels

weird. Wrong. I don't want intimacy. I don't want gratitude. I don't want anything but Iris.

And Iris eradicated from my thoughts.

"You did great." I clear my throat. "You'll be back to add the chorus in no time."

Her giggle is nervous. She pulls back. Grabs her t-shirt from the chair.

"We have a back room—"

"It's fine." She pulls her shirt over her head.

I take her to the counter. Give her my usual after care speech. Accept a generous tip. Ignore Leighton's glare.

The customer's smile gets wider. Her eyes fix on mine. "I know you're probably sick of this song, but my friends and I are doing this karaoke thing, and I'm gonna sing it, and probably flash the entire room." Her cheeks flush. "You could come. If you want."

Leighton glares.

"Send me the details on Instagram." I walk the customer to the door. Yeah, her name eludes me at the moment. Now that I'm out of the chair, every bit of sense in the world eludes me.

"You smell like pussy." Dean pushes himself onto the counter. Offers Leighton an *ain't I cute* smile.

She shakes her head *no, you're not.*

I stare back at Dean. "I don't." I showered last night. And again this morning. I scrubbed myself raw trying to erase the scent of Iris.

It didn't work.

I can still smell her shampoo.

I have no fucking idea how the smell of her shampoo found its way onto every item of clothing in my closet, but it did.

My entire apartment is mocking me.

The entire world is mocking me.

"No. But you look just fucked." Dean nudges Leighton. "Doesn't he?"

She pushes her lips to one side. "Kinda, yeah. A lot." Her lips curl into a frown. "Does that mean it's over?"

"No."

She arches a brow.

"It was her."

She claps her hands together. "Really? You're back together? That's great, Walker. I knew you'd come to your senses."

"No." I run my fingers through my hair. I don't know how to explain this. Even to myself.

"Was it breakup sex?" Her voice gets soft. "Don't do breakup sex. Trust me. It's so much worse after."

"You tell me now?" I don't sell it as a joke.

"She wants to be with you." Leighton slides off her stool. She moves around the counter. "She's sorry. You're crazy about her."

"And?"

"What's stopping you?"

"Why do you care?"

"You're my friend, you idiot."

"Thanks for the concern."

"You are being an idiot," Dean says.

"See. That means a lot coming from him." Leighton slides her hand into the pocket of her denim skirt. "Why do you want to be miserable?"

"Why do you care?"

"I told you—"

"Why do you really care?"

"I TOLD YOU!"

"That can't be it."

"It's not a conspiracy. I like you. I like Iris. I like you and Iris together. I like hanging out with her. You have good taste in girlfriends."

"Then call her."

"You're okay with that?" she asks.

No. I'm not okay with anything. I'm not okay with the sun shining or the world turning. But—"We're not together. She can do what she wants."

"I'm going to."

"Good."

"Really, Walker. This isn't a dare. I'm going to call and take her out."

"Are you asking permission?"

"Kinda."

"Are you going to fuck her?"

"No. I'm not into chicks. What if I was?"

I shrug, but I don't sell it.

"You know she's going to fuck someone else one day," she says.

"You have a point?" Irritation seeps into my voice.

Dean and Leighton exchange a look. Something about me. About how pathetic I am.

But I can't muster up any concern about that either.

They're right. I'm pathetic. I'm sulking instead of figuring this out. I'm giving into every ugly impulse in my head.

I need this to make sense.

How the hell do I do that?

"You know she's an addict," I say.

"Yeah, everyone at that party knows thanks to you. Which was a dick move, by the way. You know there are ways to have fun that don't involve drinking yourself stupid?"

"Enjoy it," I say.

"I will." She folds her arms. Stares back at me. "This isn't a bluff. I want to be her friend. And I want to take someone to eighties night."

"You know I'll always go with you, Leigh," Dean says.

"Someone who won't scare off every guy nearby," she says.

"You're breaking your dry spell?" He raises a brow. "You promised you'd put me at the top of the rotation."

She laughs. "I did not. And you don't even want to sleep with me."

"Babe, how could you say that?"

"You don't."

"You overestimate me."

"Not possible." She looks to me. "I am going to invite her."

"Good." But I don't sell that either.

Chapter Forty-Two

IRIS

Why is it so purple in here? At least it suits Leighton's hair. It's this amazing silver-lavender color. It's so cool. She's so cool. Even right now, in this sweaty, all-ages club, she has this effortless air about her.

The same as Walker's.

Only with a lot more *tough chick* and a lot less *surfer boy*.

She throws back her glass. "That really doesn't work with diet coke."

"Or orange juice." I finish my last sip. Drop it on the counter. Tap my toes together. The stool at the bar is perfect. Especially since there's no booze tonight. This is one of those clubs that does all-ages once a week.

Tonight is the night.

Eighties night.

Thank God for that.

Ice clinks as Leighton tilts her glass from one side to the other. She looks at me. Presses her plum lips together. Tries to think up something to say besides *Walker is an idiot, huh—*

we covered every ugly detail on the drive here. And the walk to the club. And for our first round of mocktails.

He is.

But I'm tired of thinking about that.

Of waiting for him.

Of staring at my blank cell phone screen, wondering when he's going to finally call.

I have to life my life. Even if there's a gaping hole in my heart.

"You're thinking about him again," she says.

My nod is reluctant.

"What about?"

"Everything."

"Hmm."

"Is he as miserable as I am?"

"Worse. No. You're pretty bad." She slides off her stool. "But it's less sympathetic on him."

"I'm the one who fucked up."

"No. I've heard this from both of you. Well, more from you, because he's all sulking *I don't talk about my feelings, that's for girls* about it. But I know enough. This is on him too." She offers her hand. "Come on. Let's dance. You'll feel better."

"I'll feel better if he forgives me."

"True. But I can't help with that."

I laugh. "Don't make me repeat the serenity prayer."

"You don't like that stuff?"

I shake my head. "Feels like I'm reciting from a poster."

"'Cause you are." She motions *come on*.

But I stay on my stool. "The other night, I asked him to tell me it wasn't the last time."

"And?"

"He said he couldn't." I draw circles on my glass. Orange juice isn't enough. I need to obliterate my thoughts. To chase away all this agony. Just for tonight. Just one time. Just a little—

"That's fucked up."

"I know."

"Was it good?"

"It was everything."

"Okay. That's enough moping. Get up. We're dancing."

"But I—"

"Too bad." She takes my hand, pulls me off my stool, pulls me into the throng.

This is a small club. It's dark. Dirty. Crowded.

An unfamiliar song fades into *Like a Virgin*.

Leighton laughs. "Who was yours?"

"College boyfriend."

"Good?"

"Give you one guess."

She laughs. "His first time too?"

"No. He thought he was incredibly skilled because he'd lost it in high school."

She spins on her toes. Laughs as she catches herself. "And he didn't know how to blow your mind?"

"Not quite." I catch the beat, but I can't find the joy of it. Or the thrill. This is a ridiculous, fun, over the top song. But it's falling flat. "What about you?"

"The coolest guy at my high school. He was a senior. I was a freshman. We were at a party. I thought the way he kissed me meant we were in love. Stop me if you've heard this one before."

"He sounds like an asshole."

"Yeah. But he was loaded." She laughs.

"That's something."

"It really is." She offers her hand.

I take it.

She helps me spin.

I throw my arms over my head. Finally, the music hits me. The tension in my shoulders melts bit by bit.

I let my eyelids flutter together.

I let my hips move of their own accord.

The song fades into *Every Little Thing She Does is Magic*.

I try to block out the lyrics. To forget the thrill of being with someone who sets you on fire.

Leighton must notice I'm slipping. She taps me. "You're gonna be a shrink, right?"

"A research psychologist, yeah. What about you?"

"Oh. I guess I don't know. I've thought about apprenticing."

"Why don't you?"

"I'm not sure I want to spend my life in a tattoo parlor."

"You don't love it?"

"I do, but..."

"It doesn't grab onto your heart and refuse to let go?"

"It might. I'm not sure. I asked Ryan to show me how to do some stuff, but then... it got weird."

"Weird how?"

"I was touching him. And he was so close. And, ugh, how obvious is it that I'm crazy about him?"

"Only a little."

"Does Walker know?"

"I don't think so."

"Don't say anything."

I motion *my lips are sealed*. "You think he sees you that way?"

"God no." Her movements slow. "Ryan has tunnel vision with his ex. And he... I'm not sure he even knows I'm a woman."

I'm not sure about that. But I'm not exactly in the mood to argue. "Is it that hopeless?"

"Yeah. It's awful. We're friends and I love being his friend, but it hurts being that close. It's agony."

I nod.

"You know how it goes. It hurts. But it would be worse if we weren't friends. Sometimes, I let myself believe it will happen. But it's been a year, and he's still miserable."

"That sucks. I'm sorry."

"Thanks. Didn't I say something about dancing instead of talking?"

"You did."

"Let's do that." She motions to two guys behind us. Raises a brow. *Want to?*

They're dressed in bright pink and bright orange t-shirts, both wearing electric blue pants and fire-engine red sneakers. They look like the type who want to share a girl.

Which could be fun, I guess.

If it was possible to want someone who isn't Walker.

It will be one day. Maybe. In theory.

Leighton takes my staring as a yes. Motions *come here* to the guys.

The one in the orange shirt nods to me. "I like your wrist warmers."

I'm in my best eighties Madonna getup—fishnet wrist warmers, heeled boots, a tight pink dress. It's not exactly 80s, but it's close. "Thanks."

"You want to dance?"

"Sure."

He slides his arms around my waist.

I let him lead. I let my eyelids fall together. I let my thoughts drift around the room. Then out of it. Then all the way over to the Westside, to Walker's apartment, and the way he looked at me like he wasn't sure if he loved me or hated me.

The song shifts to *Take My Breath Away*.

Eighties guy's hands slide over my hips. He pulls me closer. Like we're high schoolers at a dance.

I try to find the joy in it. He's a good dancer, this is an awesome song, a cute guy wants my body against his.

He's warm and tall and breathing.

A distraction.

Something that will erase Walker from my thoughts for a solid three minutes. Or maybe even ten. I shouldn't underestimate Eighties Guy.

I look up at him. He's plenty cute. And he's decked in that silly outfit. He must be game for anything.

But it wouldn't matter if he was Kit Harrington.

He's not Walker.

So he's not interesting.

I finish the song, excuse myself, dance in the corner by myself. Leighton is somewhere. I think that's her lilac hair. I think she's still with Eighties Guy's friend.

Hazel eyes catch mine. A broad guy looks me up and down. He offers his hand.

I nod. Find the beat of *Sweet Dreams* as his hands find my hips.

My eyelids flutter together.

I soak in the sad song. It's perfect. Miserable. Like everything in my head.

The guy—I don't know anything about him besides that he's not Walker—pulls me closer.

He leans in to whisper in my ear. "What's your name, baby?"

"It doesn't matter."

He laughs. Moves his hand to my lower back. Just over the top of my ass.

I close my eyes.

Move my hips in time with the music.

With his.

But he's too close.

His hands are too much. They're going too low.

Then they're not.

"What the fuck, bro?" Not-Walker scoffs. "I'm dancing here."

"You're done."

What?

I blink a few times.

That's... he's here.

God, he looks good. As miserable as I feel, but good. Same dark hair. Same dark eyes. Same strong shoulders.

He slides his arm around my waist.

I stare up at him. "What are you doing?"

"You want him touching you?"

No. But that isn't relevant. "I have a phone."

"I called three times."

That's possible. I can't exactly hear with eighties jams overpowering every thought in my head.

His fingers dig into my skin.

I struggle to inhale. "What is this?"

"You want me to stop?"

No. "What the hell do you think you're doing throwing guys off me?"

He holds my body against his. "I don't want anyone else touching you."

"You don't get a say in that."

"I know." He pulls me closer anyway.

Fuck, it feels good.

I let my eyelids flutter together. I soak up all the warmth of his touch. It feels right. For the first time since I climbed out of his bed, I feel whole.

His voice is soft. Sincere. "I can't stop thinking about you."

"You want me or you don't, Walker. You can't have it both ways."

"I know." He steps backward. Takes my hand and motions to the edge of the dance floor.

What the hell does this mean?

I should demand an explanation.

But I don't. I follow him off the dance floor. All the way to the back entrance.

To a dark alley.

The door swings shut.

Music pours through its cracks.

Walker brings one hand to my hip and the other to my cheek. "Why'd you leave the other morning?"

"You hate me."

He shakes his head. "No. I want to hate you. But I can't."

"What the hell is this?"

"You were supposed to give it back, Iris. You were supposed to make it stop."

I swallow hard.

"Nothing makes sense to me anymore."

"Then let me explain."

He nods. "After."

"After?" Oh. *After*.

He presses his forehead to mine. "*This* is the only thing that makes sense." His fingers dig into my hip. "Tell me you need me."

"I do."

"That you want this." His voice drops to something equal parts demanding and desperate. "Tell me you want to come on my cock in this dirty alley."

"Tell me it isn't the last time."

"I can't." His fingers dig into my skin. "I want to listen." He drags his lips over my chin, neck, earlobe. "After that, I don't know."

That's fair.

Or maybe that's my libido talking.

At the moment, I don't really care.

He smells so good. Like the soap in his shower. Like Walker.

I reach for the reasonable part of my brain. "Someone will see."

He traces the hem of my dress. "Do you care?"

"No."

"Did you go out looking for someone to take home?"

"No."

"Why not?"

"No one is you." I brush my cheek against his.

His fingers skim my inner thighs. "Tell me you want this, sweetness."

I nod.

"Tell me you want to come on my cock."

"I do. Please."

His fingers curl into my panties. Slowly, he pushes them off my hips.

He bends to pull them to my ankles. Then off my feet, one at a time.

He drags his fingertips up my body as he rises. Higher, higher, there.

He teases me with one finger. "Fuck, you're wet."

I reach for him. Get his waistband. Slide my palm over his crotch. "You're hard."

He nods as he drives two fingers into me.

I fumble over his button. His zipper.

There. I push his jeans off his hips. The boxers.

Mmm.

That's Walker, hard and ready for me.

About to be mine.

I pull my dress to my waist.

He brings his hands to my hips, lifts me and pins me to the wall in one swift motion.

I wrap my legs around his waist, my arms around his shoulders.

He stares down at me.

I dig my fingers into his skin. Nod *yes, please, everything*.

Slowly, his tip strains against me.

Then it's one inch at a time.

Fuck.

It's like coming home.

This is where I belong. With him. His.

No secrets, no lies, no bullshit.

Nothing but our bodies.

Nothing but—

His lips find mine. His kiss is hard. Hungry. Desperate.

Mine is the same.

Nothing else makes sense.

Nothing but this.

Nothing but him.

I bring one hand to his hair. I rock my hips to meet him.

He rocks back, driving deeper, pinning me to the wall.

It's hard and dirty and rough and perfect.

His tongue slides around mine.

His fingers dig into my flesh.

He fucks me with steady thrusts, winding me up, giving me everything he has.

My clit rubs against his pubic bone.

My hand knots in his hair.

My sex clenches.

Fuck.

Each thrust tightens the knot inside me. Pleasure pools between my legs. It aches, being this close to release.

He winds me tighter.

Tighter.

There.

I groan against his lips as I come. My sex pulses around him, pulling him closer, pushing him over the edge.

I can feel it in the way his nails dig into my skin, in the way he nips at my lip, in the way he shakes.

A few more thrusts and he's pulsing, groaning my name as he comes inside me.

Fuck, that feels good.

He feels good.

I let my muscles go slack.

He pulls me closer. Sets me on the ground. Looks down at me like I'm everything he wants.

Maybe I am.

Maybe this is going to be okay.

Maybe he really will be mine.

Chapter Forty-Three

IRIS

Walker's car hugs the curve of the Malibu mountains.

Tegan and Sara flows from the speakers. The song is soft, remorseful, a text alert?

Huh?

Oh. My phone flashes.

Leighton: You fucked him, didn't you?

I grab my cell and shoot her a reply.

Iris: Maybe.

Leighton: Girl, if he pulls any more "I don't know" shit, I will kick his ass.

Iris: You, personally?

Leighton: I might ask Brendon, Ryan, or Dean to do it for me. But I'll make sure it gets done.

Iris: Thanks.

Leighton: Anytime.

"That Leighton?" he asks.

"Yeah. Just telling her I left."

"She want to kill me yet?"

"Yeah, but that seems normal for her."

"It is."

I set my phone in the cup holder, lean back in my seat. Watch the ocean whiz by. "Where are we going?"

"Someplace where we can see the stars."

That sounds perfect. Though it also means heading way into Malibu. Which means we're stuck together for a long drive back to my place if that doesn't go well.

It's a bold play.

But that's Walker.

He wants something, he takes it.

I just hope he wants me.

THE SKY IS DOTTED WITH STARS. THEY'RE EVERYWHERE. Brighter than I've ever seen them.

Walker pulls his leather jacket from the backseat, slings it over my shoulders, one at a time, then he grabs a blanket from the trunk.

"You keep that in your car?"

He nods.

"For impromptu picnics?"

"You never know when you'll need the perfect scenery for a heartfelt conversation."

My lips press together. "Really?"

His laugh lights up his dark eyes. "No. It's for after I surf."

"Oh." That makes more sense.

He leads me onto the sand, lays the blanket down, motions *after you*.

I lie back. Stare at the stars. They're beautiful. Bright. Perfect.

He lies next to me.

Two dozen feet away, waves crash into the beach with a soft roar.

The back of his hand brushes my wrist.

I take a shallow breath. Try my best to exhale slowly. "I don't know where to start."

His fingertips brush my palm. "At the beginning."

"I'm not sure where that is." I take a deep breath. Exhale slowly. Wrack my brain for the best place to start. Okay. That works. "I was miserable after college. That was true. I hated my job. I hated my friends. I hated how much I hated them. And I did try hobbies for a while. Working out. Reading. Even knitting."

He nods.

"It was a little after New Year's. I was determined to revamp my life, to find fulfillment no matter what. That was when I started seeing Ross."

"The guy you left for rehab?"

"Yeah. He was a clean-cut programmer type. But he also liked to party. I thought it was just booze and pot. But it wasn't. He didn't do it around me at first. Don't get me wrong. We'd get drunk as all hell. But that was it. I knew it wasn't healthy. But it felt normal. Especially with Lily's friends. You know the bro-grammer stereotype?"

"Yeah."

"They were like that. Always getting plastered. So I started getting drunk too. It was an easy way to forget."

"I've been there."

"You have?"

"Of course. The last few weeks... I want to do whatever it takes to make this ache go away." His fingertips brush the back of my hand.

"I'm sorry, Walker. Really. I never wanted to hurt you."

"I know."

"I was terrified to tell you. But it was more that I wanted to believe the past didn't matter. I wanted to believe I was more than a bunch of mistakes. You looked at me like I was this fascinating mix of passions and ideas and quirks. Whereas, whenever I looked in the mirror, I saw a recovering addict, period. And I wasn't ready to let go of the way you saw me. I needed to believe I was more than sobriety."

"I did mean it."

"But you..."

"I can't explain it either. I still don't understand it."

"Oh. Well... Where was I?"

"Your ex drank a lot."

"Yeah. He did. That was normal for a while. One day, we were at his friend's birthday part. It was a little after I got my second round of terrible GRE scores. It was all I was thinking about. And I was so tired of thinking about it. I wanted to do anything to make it stop. Or I thought I did. Because when I saw his friend using—"

"Using?"

"Shooting up. Heroin. I thought it was ridiculous. Like something out of a movie. Who did heroin? Didn't they know about blood communicable diseases? Hadn't they seen *Requiem for a Dream*? We got into this huge fight about it. I told him I was never going to hang out with those people again. He called me uptight. I called him an asshole. We both apologized, agreed not to talk about it."

He moves closer.

"But his friend was at the next party. He looked so calm, so at peace. Like nothing could be wrong. And everything felt so wrong. And I thought... well, I thought that maybe Ross was right. Maybe I only judged because I didn't know how good it could be."

He drags his fingertips up my arm.

"I hadn't been drinking. I knew better than to mix opiates and alcohol. Well, back then, I cared enough not to do it. And it wasn't like the guy was doing heroin. He was just swallowing some prescription stuff. Stuff I could get from a doctor. I convinced myself it couldn't be too bad. After all, I'd taken Vicodin when I got my wisdom teeth out. It didn't make me feel much besides tired. So when he offered me one, I took it."

"Was that the first time?"

"Besides after my wisdom teeth, yeah."

"How did it feel?"

"Like nothing would ever hurt me again."

"You hated your life that much?"

"Yeah." I stare at the bright stars. "I wasn't ready to confront it. I wanted to feel anything else. Anything good. But I wasn't going to start using drugs like one of the people I'd read about. Like some pathetic addict. I convinced myself it was like drinking. It is. Just stronger. More addictive. Dangerously addictive."

His exhale is heavy.

"For a while, I'd get high on the weekends. Then it was all weekend. Then most nights. I... I made a lot of bad decisions. But I held it together pretty well. Until I didn't. I'd get to work late. Skip meetings. I got reprimanded. I told myself I'd stop. And I did, for a while. I tried, I really did. But I couldn't take the withdrawal. I caved."

"How many times?"

"Half a dozen."

"For how long?"

"Two and a half years. More or less. I tried, hard, to stop after my sister found my stash. We were getting ready for a wedding. She saw it in my makeup bag and freaked out. Threatened to tell our parents. I promised I'd stop."

"Did you mean it?" He stares into my eyes, demanding an explanation.

I wish I had a better one. I wish the truth was less ugly.

But it is ugly.

And I'm done running from it. "I wanted to stop. The

look on her face—it was awful. I never wanted to see that again. I tried. But... you know what it's like when you try to kick caffeine?"

"I never have."

"When you go too long without a coffee? Get a headache? Get irritable? Want caffeine like you've never wanted anything?"

"Yeah."

"Multiply that by a thousand. I wanted to make her proud, but it was easier being high. More comfortable. She caught me again. Asked me to choose. I told her I chose her, but—"

"You stayed high?"

Is that judgment in his voice? Or is it understanding?

I don't know.

I need to tell him all of this.

And I need him to accept it.

I can't do anything about the latter. So I guess I have to focus on the former. "I wasn't ready to stop yet. I wasn't ready to let go of my comfortable numb, to feel everything. It got to be this cycle. I felt awful lying to her. Then pathetic for being so weak. Then I'd be more desperate to get out of my head. So I'd do whatever I could get my hands on."

He stares up at the stars.

"There was still a part of me that wanted more. I studied a lot. Managed to pass the GRE. Kept applying to grad schools. Then I got into UCLA. And I was sure that was it. That I'd stop."

"Did you?"

"For a while. Long enough to start classes. Settle into my routine. But Ross was still using. There was always something around. I slipped."

His dark eyes fix on mine. "Why'd you stop?"

"My mom walked in on me shooting up. She started

crying. She was worried I was going to die. It was like with Lily, but a million times worse. I knew, no matter what, I couldn't do that to her. So I agreed to go to rehab. And I took off winter quarter. And that was that."

"When did you get out?"

"February."

"Fuck, that's nothing."

"Four months." It feels like it's been an eternity.

"You ever want to use?"

"Sometimes. But it's a passing impulse. The ugly consequences are too fresh." I take a deep breath and exhale slowly. "This, you leaving, whatever we should call it. This has hurt more than anything has in a long time. But I haven't even looked at a bottle. I don't want to be numb anymore. I get it if you don't believe me, if you can't trust me, but I really, really don't want that."

He stares into my eyes.

"Do you believe me?"

"I want to."

"Do you think... I, uh, I wanted to tell you, Walker. I did. But the only person I'd told dropped me as soon as she found out. And being with you, feeling normal, it was everything."

"Yeah, it was."

"After I saw your sister high... you hate her, don't you?"

"Part of me does."

"Is she really sober?"

"Seems that way."

"That's great. Really." I stare back at him. "Would you have left if I told you that night we found your sister?"

"Probably."

"Now?"

"I don't know."

"Oh." I let my eyelids flutter together. I lean into his touch. "I... I think I'm in love with you."

"Iris."

"You don't have to say anything. Actually, don't. Not until you're sure you want to do this. Because I don't want to know you love me. Not if you're going to leave."

"Okay." He presses his palm into my lower back and pulls my body into his.

"Do you hate me?"

His lips brush my ear. "No."

"Think I'm pathetic?"

"You're strong, overcoming all that."

"Yeah?" I blink back a tear. I need his words and his touch and his understanding.

But this might be it.

This might be the last time we're this close.

"Yeah." He presses his lips to my cheek.

"Do you want to be with me?"

"I need more time to figure that out."

"Okay. How much?"

His laugh is sad. "I don't know."

That's fair. But—"I haven't decided on my internship."

"Still?"

"Yeah. I know. I'd rather be here. But if there isn't an us, if you don't want to be with me, then I can't be here. Not for a while."

He nods.

"So, uh, I have finals. And then I have to answer."

He brushes a hair behind my ear. "You're nervous."

"You're deciding if you want to be with me."

"True."

"Which way are you leaning?"

"I don't know, sweetness. My head is a fucking mess."

Chapter Forty-Four

WALKER

I step into the cozy meeting room. Nod a *sorry* to the guy at the podium. Take a seat on one of the scratchy folding chairs in the back.

This is an open meeting. Mom assured me that friends and family are welcome. She offered to come with me. She came close to insisting.

But I have to do this alone.

Whatever happens with me and Iris, I need to make things right with my sister.

All right, I'm hoping that fixing this will fix my head. That it will reconcile those two halves of me—the *I want Iris more than I want anything* and the *how will I ever trust her again?*

It's worth a shot.

The guy keeps spinning his story of hitting rock bottom. How he missed an important meeting because he was too high. How it led to this ugly spiral. There's hurt in his voice. But that's not what has my attention.

It's the strange pride. He's glad shit got that bad. He's glad he almost lost everything.

It was the only way.

He steps down. Someone else steps up. A meeting leader. Something like that. I went to a few of these with Bree the first time she got sober. After her first relapse, I did everything I could to stop giving a shit.

Not that any of it worked.

He steps down. Points to someone in the crowd.

To Bree.

She stands and moves to the podium. Turns to face the room. Her eyes catch mine. They fill with concern.

I smile.

She smiles back. Mouths *thank you*.

I mouth *don't mention it.*

She looks to the room. "Hi. I'm Sabrina. And I'm an addict. Most of you know me. I'm here every week. It's been a tough two and a half months. I've been tempted. The other night, I went to the movies with a few friends. There was a bar at the theater. They didn't know I was sober, and I wasn't in the mood to talk about it. I kept looking at the Patron, thinking of how smooth it would taste, how easy it would be to forget that I'd totally fucked-up my brother's life. But I sat with the urge. I felt it. Then I felt it pass. It... It was okay. I wanted it, but I didn't need it." She nods to the room. "Thank you."

She moves back to her seat.

That same guy moves up to the podium, thanks her for speaking, invites someone else.

It goes like that for a while. Everyone spills their guts. Sometimes it's something happy. Pride over hitting a milestone. Sometimes it's a tragic tale of rock bottom. Sometimes it's something small. A slip or an almost slip.

Sometimes it's huge. The forgiveness of a loved one.

A life pieced back together.

The sense everything is going to be okay.

~

When the meeting clears out, I wait for Bree in the back of the room. She's different here. There's no heavy burden on her shoulders. It's like when we were kids.

She's happy. She's wise. She's looking forward to her future.

She finishes talking to a girl about her age then makes her way to me.

Her steps slow. She presses her lips together. "I never thought I'd see you here again."

"Me either."

Her voice is sincere. "Is everything okay with Iris?"

"Maybe. That's not why I'm here. At least not the main reason." I run my hand through my hair. This is not my strong suit. But I need to do it. "I'm sorry, Bree. I've been an ass to you."

"I deserved it."

"Maybe. But you were right. I wasn't gonna forgive you. Or myself. I was sure you'd keep fucking up. That can't have helped."

"I... I don't know what to say."

"I'm glad you're doing well. It means the fucking world to me."

Any nervousness falls from her expression. Her lips press into a smile. Her eyes fill with relief. "Really?"

"Yeah." I pull my sister into a hug.

She squeezes back. "Does this mean you're coming to Thanksgiving?"

"I think so."

"And Sunday dinners?"

I laugh as I step backward. "Maybe."

"Mom will be over the moon."

"I only said maybe."

Her smile spreads over her cheeks. "You said it like a yes."

I smile too. I want that. I want things to be okay with us. With my parents.

She takes in my expression. "No offense, but you look miserable."

"I am."

"We have coffee. Good coffee. Most people here drink a ton of it. Or smoke. Or both." She moves closer to the table. Grabs a paper cup and fills it with java. "You still take it black?"

"Yeah, thanks."

She hands me the first cup, turns back to the table to pour a second. "What happened with Iris?"

"It's a long story."

She fixes her coffee with half-and-half and sugar. "What's the short version?"

"I thought I didn't care about anything that had happened before. That the past was the past. I told her as much every time she tried to confess. I stopped her."

She nods *understandable*.

"But I did care."

"Of course."

"Why?" I need to understand this. I need to know how I could have meant those words when they feel like such bull-shit now.

"Walker. You saw me almost die. Twice." She takes a long sip. "Of course you're going to be nervous your girlfriend could be in the same place."

"It's more than that."

"What?"

I'm not sure. My coffee doesn't have any answers. But it is good. "I thought I knew her."

"Do you?"

"Yeah." I know the way she giggles when she falls off my

surfboard. And how she squeals when I pick her up. And that shy smile when I tease her about *Star Wars*. But I didn't know this. I didn't have a clue.

Bree leans against the table. "How long were you dating?"

"A few months. But it feels like more. I... I'm pretty sure I'm in love with her."

She makes an *aww* sound and presses her hand to her heart. "Really?"

"Yeah."

"Oh my God. This is my big sister moment. You've never loved a girl."

"Never."

"You haven't even liked a girl since high school."

I nod. I haven't. I haven't considered it since Bree started using.

"But you're... it's bad. Or you wouldn't have that look on your face."

"Was it me not knowing she was an addict that tipped you off?"

She plays with her coffee cup. "I really shouldn't have said that. If she'd told you a few weeks later on her own time..." Bree shakes her head. "That was so fucked-up of me. Unforgivable. The anonymous thing is serious. It's the only way people can really share. And I violated that. I... would it bug you if I apologized to her?"

"No, but I—"

"Shit. Maybe I shouldn't. Maybe that would only make it worse." She takes another sip. "Sorry. You, well... what happened?"

"I freaked. She left. We've talked a little since, but... I don't know how I feel."

"Yeah, you do. You just said you love her. Oh my God. This is so romantic. I'm going to have to watch *Dirty Dancing* when I get home."

I cringe.

"Huh?"

"Don't you think she looks like Jenifer Grey?"

"No. Maybe the nose. But her complexion is all off." She refills her cup. "Don't get me wrong. She's pretty. But I know you care about more than that. Do you care about more than that?"

"Hey."

"Hey what? You're still a guy."

"She's smart. Funny. She's embarrassed by how nerdy she is. Even when she's full of nervous energy, she barrels into shit. She goes for it."

Bree's smile widens.

"What?"

"You totally love her."

"I do."

"So? What the hell is the problem?"

"I don't know if I can trust her. I want to..."

"But you told her the past was the past. She didn't betray your trust."

"Yeah." That makes sense. It does. But it doesn't *feel* right.

"Okay. She should have told you. But this isn't about her. It's about you. Well, and about me. Sorry. I kinda fucked this up for you on both sides." Her laugh is nervous.

"Yeah. But it's still on me."

"Well... can you forgive her?"

"I do."

"Can you trust her one day?"

"I hope so."

She grabs my arm. "No *I hope so*. You can. I know you can. So stop with the bullshit. If I can get sober, you can trust this girl you're madly in love with."

"Yeah..."

"Oh my God. What's with this sudden mellowness? I

know that's your thing, Walker. But don't be an idiot. You love her. You can get to trusting her again. You really think you're going to meet another girl who makes you feel like this?"

I can't help but smile. "You're back to your old self."

"Not quite. But I'm getting there." She takes another sip. "Are you gonna fix this?"

"I don't know."

"You should."

I chuckle. "Have you always been this wise?"

"Only about certain topics." She plays with a strand of dark hair. "I... I really am sorry, Walker. If it wasn't for me, you wouldn't be such a mess."

"Am I that bad?"

"Depends on the scale." Her voice gets soft. "You're a good brother. And a good guy. I hope you figure it out."

"Me too."

Chapter Forty-Five

IRIS

Somehow, I manage to fall asleep.

I manage to get up, eat my breakfast, drink my coffee, go to school, study, work out, read.

Then I do it again.

Every day, it's a little easier to focus. To push Walker from my head.

He's still there, in the corners of my mind, waiting to pounce, to take over, to promise to either tear my heart in half or tape it back together.

I manage to spend most of Saturday studying.

And all of Sunday.

And then routine takes over, and I lose myself in the one thing I know I want.

Well, the thing that isn't him.

Chapter Forty-Six

IRIS

I nearly jump into the hallway.

That's it. Research done. Projects done. Last final, done.

I stretch my arms over my head. Force my feet toward the door.

It's a gorgeous June day. The sun is high in the bright, cloudless sky. It bounces off the beige pavement and the silver signs. It bounces off the whites of my sneakers.

He knows today is my last day.

He knows I have to decide.

He knows this is his chance. Our chance.

I... uh... God. I plant on a concrete bench, press my knees together, suck the last drop of water from my bottle.

My cell fails to offer insights. My only text is from my Mom. My only emails are SPAM. My voicemail is empty.

The ball really is in his court this time.

All I can do is wait.

~

EVERY PART OF ME GOES WARM AT ONCE.

He's sitting on the front steps. Holding two iced coffees.

He wouldn't bring iced coffees to dump me. Or maybe he would. Maybe those are consolation iced coffees. Maybe he's just that considerate.

My steps are shaky. Are my feet even on the ground? I'm not sure.

Walker pushes himself to his feet. He holds up the plastic glass on his right. "Two percent and extra sugar."

"Thanks." My fingers brush his as I take it. It's like the first time. It wakes up all my nerves. Sends a buzz all the way to my toes. "And the other one?"

"You want both?"

"I'm just asking."

His lips curl into a half smile. "You're greedy."

"You're... handsome."

His laugh lights up his dark eyes. "Good one."

"You try flinging good comebacks after staying up till four a.m. studying." I move closer. Close enough to touch him, kiss him, hold him. "I, uh... you want to come in?"

"Yeah."

"Follow me." I take a long sip of my iced coffee. It's perfect. Exactly as sweet and creamy as I like it. But it's not helping pull me back to Earth.

I grab onto the railing to climb the stairs. Okay. This is easy. Just a dozen steps to my apartment. I place one foot in front of the other. I do it again. Again.

It takes every bit of my focus, but I get to my apartment, dig my keys from my backpack, and unlock the door.

Walker presses it open. "After you."

"Thanks." I step inside.

He follows. Closes the door.

He lets out a chuckle as he looks around the room. "I can see where your priorities lie."

I keep my back to him. Pull my arm over my chest. "Cleaning isn't my thing."

"It looks good. Lived in."

"Lived in, maybe. But not good."

He laughs. "Not good." His fingers brush the back of my hand. "You're shaking."

"Yeah."

"Because of me?"

"Yeah." I suck coffee though the straw. "I, uh, can I get you anything?"

"You could turn around."

I shake my head. "I'm not sure about that."

"No?"

"What if I know it's over from the look on your face? I can't deal with that."

He laughs. "You sound sleep-deprived."

"I am."

"I'll promise to smile."

"You could tell me."

"I will. But I need you to look at me first."

I shake my head.

His fingers curl around my wrist. "I can come around."

"I can turn."

"I can run faster."

"Don't be so sure. I've been working out."

"Running?"

"No. But, I, uh... tell me. Please." I suck more iced coffee from my straw.

His voice gets soft. "I will." He tugs on my wrist gently. "After you look at me."

Slowly, I turn to face him.

He really is a sight for sore eyes. His dark hair is hanging in loose waves. His brow is soft. His dark eyes are full of joy.

This is good news. It has to be.

His sets his coffee on my counter then brings his hands to mine. Slowly, he unfurls my fingers, and sets my cup on the counter.

"That's especially cruel." I try to make my words teasing, but they don't land. It is cruel, taking away my one comfort. My one distraction. Staring at me with all that affection in his dark eyes if this is...

I swallow hard. I can't think that. Not yet.

His hands go to his jeans. He undoes the button.

My brow furrows. "What the—"

He laughs. "Give me a second." He turns and pulls his jeans down his hip. Then his boxers.

There's a flash of something on his hip. Purple, green, black. But his shirt is in the way.

Slowly, he lifts his shirt.

My eyes go wide.

My jaw hits the floor.

That's... he... I...

"I've never seen you speechless." His voice is confident. Cocky even. But there's more to it. Pride. Affection. Everything.

"I, you, uh... Can I?"

"Yeah."

I trace the black lines. They're beautiful. Perfect. The flower is in full bloom, unfurling, inviting everyone.

A purple iris.

"I... I..." I trace the outline again. His skin is soft and he's so warm. So close. So mine.

He's really mine.

This means he's mine.

I trace it again and again. "You..."

He nods. "I..."

"But..."

"I told you, when I want something, I take it."

"But you didn't have to." I stare into his dark eyes. "You already have me."

He slides his arms around my waist. "Can't be too careful."

"But, I, uh... I thought you... you didn't trust me."

"I didn't know if I could."

"But you... I thought you didn't want to be with an addict."

"I didn't." He brushes my hair behind my ear. "I kept trying to find a way to convince myself to hate you. But I couldn't. I kept thinking of that sad, scared girl desperate for comfort. I kept thinking of the way you looked at me that day we went surfing."

"I wanted to tell you."

"I know. And I stopped you. I knew it was something big, and I stopped you."

I nod.

"I wanted to believe there was nothing ugly in your past. That you didn't have any baggage or ugly parts or secrets. I wanted to believe it didn't matter. That I was over everything with Bree. But I wasn't. I'm not. I'm not gonna lie to you, Iris. It's gonna be hard for me at first. I'm gonna be terrified you'll slip."

"I worry too."

"I'm gonna go out of my fucking mind every time I'm not sure what you're thinking or where you are. But I'm going to get over it. It's gonna take a long time, but I am going to get over it."

"Okay." I press my palm against his chest. "I have to figure it out too. How to be honest with someone. How to share the ugly things."

"I want to be there to help you."

"I want you to be there."

His fingers dig into my hair. "I love you, Iris Avery."

"I love you too."
He pulls me closer.
And he kisses me like he's sure I'm his.
I am.
And he's mine.
And it really is perfect.

Epilogue

WALKER

Iris scoops sugar into her coffee. One spoonful. Two. Three.

Four.

This is getting ridiculous. "You're gonna get a cavity."

"We're celebrating." She fills the last quarter of her mug with milk then looks to Mom. "Thanks for making coffee."

Mom laughs. "Is it still coffee like that?"

"It's perfect." Iris offers me the mug. "Taste it."

I shake my head.

"Afraid it will blow your mind?" Her voice lifts to a teasing tone.

"You can bait me better than that." I stare back into her blue eyes. I still get lost in them. I still want to swim in them.

She lowers her voice to a whisper. "I can. But you can't handle it." She spreads her legs and pulls her skirt up her thighs.

She's wrong—I can handle it. I can get her panting, begging me to fuck her. I should torture her to prove it.

I would. If we were anywhere else. My parents have been through enough of their children horrifying them.

We've been coming to Sunday night dinners for months now. We're usually polite at the dinner table, but before and after...

Mom clears her throat.

Dad chuckles. "They're young and in love. We were worse."

Mom nods *true*. "Have you discussed marriage?"

"Mom!" Fuck, I know Mom adores Iris, but this is getting ridiculous. She drops hints about marriage nearly every Sunday.

Half of me wants to demand she stop. The other half is too enamored with the way the questions make Iris's cheeks flush and her eyes get dreamy. She thinks about it, about us being forever.

I think about it too. I can see it. The two of us on the beach, under an altar decked with purple flowers, proclaiming our love to the entire world.

Yeah, I think a lot about stripping her out of a tight, low-cut dress (hey, it's *my* fantasy), pinning her to the wall, and having my way with her.

But I think about the rest of it too. Calling her my wife. Seeing my ring on her finger every morning. Waking up and falling asleep next to her.

We're not ready for that—she's made it very clear she's waiting until she's done with school—but we'll be there. One day.

And after tonight...

"Baby?" Iris runs her fingers over my chin.

"You look gorgeous today. I say that yet?" I ask.

"A thousand times," Bree says. "But it's cute." She turns to Mom. "Aren't they adorable?"

Mom makes the *hmmm* noise. "Yes. But we're having dessert. Not *dessert*."

Dad chuckles.

Bree giggles through her words. "Oh my God, Mom. Did you just make a sex joke?"

Mom smiles *maybe I did, maybe I didn't*, then she's back to her usual all business poker face. "Your generation didn't discover sex."

Bree laughs.

I laugh too. "Feels like it sometimes."

Iris blushes. "I'm sorry, Jen."

Mom beams at Iris calling her by her first name. "It is sweet. But not at the dinner table."

Iris mouths *sorry*.

Dad chuckles. "Remember that weekend at your parents' place."

Mom turns to him. Her cheeks flush. She leans in to whisper.

Gross. My parents are talking about sex.

She regains her composure. "This is excellent coffee, Walker. Thanks for bringing it over."

"Sure thing," I say.

"Try it the *right* way." Iris offers her mug again. She raises a brow *you okay?*

I nod as I accept the cup. My plan for tonight is perfect. But it's getting closer. It's right after we leave. And, fuck, I'm not used to being this nervous.

I sip Iris's coffee. "This is sweeter than the pie." I hand it back.

Her smile spreads over her cheeks. "That's the point."

"Is it?" I ask.

She nods. "Dessert—" she nods to her slice of pumpkin pie, then to her mug—" then more dessert."

Bree laughs. "She's making a lot of sense."

"You always think she's making sense," I say.

"What can I say? Your girlfriend is a smart woman," Bree says.

Iris nods *uh-uh*. She isn't paying attention to our conversation. Her gaze is on her cell.

That look can only mean one thing.

Lily replied.

Iris tries to pretend like she's okay waiting until her sister is ready to make up. I guess she is *okay* waiting. It's not like she has a choice.

But I can tell it wears on her.

She ceded the holiday to her sister, because she didn't trust her parents to be honest about whether or not she'd be at dinner.

She spent an hour composing a *Happy Thanksgiving* text this morning. She's been checking her phone, waiting for a response, all day.

I squeeze her hand. Lean in to whisper. "You okay?"

She nods. "I just need some air." She pulls back. Looks to my family. "Excuse me. Thank you so much for dinner. It was lovely." She grabs her purse and moves to the kitchen, then toward the back door.

Mom, Dad, and Bree shoot me the same look. *Are you going to leave her alone with that?*

They adore Iris. After everything with Bree, I thought Mom would freak about Iris's past, but she didn't. She only loves her more for it. She's always going on about how proud of Iris she is. About how lucky I am to have such a strong girlfriend.

And, yeah, about how lucky I'd be if Iris was my wife.

I agree.

And I will marry her. One day.

But this, just being with her, is amazing. I want more—I always want more of her—but I can wait until she's ready.

"Thanks for dinner." I push myself up. "I love you."

Everyone says it back.

I move into the kitchen, through the sliding glass door, to the backyard.

Iris is sitting on the edge of the pool, shoes next to her, feet in the water. She turns toward me. Wipes a tear from her eyes.

Fuck. It's bad.

I move closer. "You want me here or you want to be alone?"

She looks up at me. "No. Walker. It's... It's okay."

"Yeah?" I drop to my knees next to her.

She nods as she shows off the display.

Lily: Happy Thanksgiving to you too. See you at Christmas?

Every bit of tension in my body melts. I forget about what I'm doing after this. I forget about every awful thing that's ever happened.

"She forgives me." A tear rolls down her cheek. "Well. Maybe not yet. But enough to talk to me."

I wrap my arms around her.

She leans into my touch. "I never thought she'd forgive me."

"I know."

"I never thought you'd forgive me."

"Me either."

"But you did." She presses her forehead to mine. "And you... You're here."

"Always."

Her fingers dig into my t-shirt, pressing the cotton into my skin. "You promise?"

"Yeah."

"What if I start using again?"

"You won't."

"But what if I do?"

"Sweetness, you know I hate thinking about this."

"I know..." *But you have to. It could happen. We have to be realistic.*

"I'll make sure you get help." I brush her hair behind her ear.

Iris slipping is my worst nightmare.

At first, it was a plague on my thoughts, this constant fear she'd start getting high again. That I'd be the one to push her into using with some stupid fight.

I still wake up terrified some days. I still have moments where my head goes to dark places because she's too quiet. Or home late. Or evasive. Or moody.

I'll never get over it. Not completely.

But it gets easier every day.

The fear fades quickly now. I trust her.

I know it takes more than that. I know there are going to be times where it's harder or easier.

But, whatever happens, I want to be there to hold her up.

To ease her burden.

To watch her dreams come true.

"You want to talk about it, sweetness?"

"Later." She presses her lips to mine.

She tastes good, like sugar and coffee.

Like she's everything I want.

She pulls back with a sigh. "Can we go home? I need... I need things to make sense."

"Yeah." That is a brilliant idea. But—"I have a stop planned."

"Something good?"

"Yeah."

"What?"

"You trust me?"

"Yeah, but—"

"You trust me or not?"

"Of course."

"Then let me surprise you."

She stares into my eyes. Slowly, she nods.

I offer her my hand.

She takes it and I pull her to her feet. I pick up her shoes, then scoop her into my arms and carry her into the kitchen.

She laughs. "Show off."

But she still slides her arms around my neck.

She still sighs as she rests her head on my chest.

I FIND A SPOT ON THE STREET, IN BETWEEN A TESLA AND A Prius. It's so Santa Monica it hurts.

All right, being sandwiched by an electric car and a hybrid isn't all that entertaining. It's more my desperate need for a distraction.

I turn the car off, pull my keys from the ignition, force my voice to an easy tone. "After you."

Iris stares into my eyes. "After me?"

"All right. After me." I undo my seatbelt, step outside, close the door. The cold air wakes me up. Even after twenty-five years in Southern California, I forget how much the temperature drops at night.

I'm freezing. But there's no way I'm reaching for my leather jacket in the backseat.

If I look Iris in the eyes again...

I take a deep breath. Exhale slowly. Slide my hands into my front pockets. This is the logical next step.

But, fuck, what if she says no?

What if I'm reading her all wrong?

I let nerves settle in my gut. I'm doing this tonight. No matter what.

Iris steps out of the car. Hugs her purse to her shoulder. "You're shivering." She holds up my jacket.

"You are too."

She shakes her head, despite the obvious goose bumps on her arms.

I nod *you are* then move around the car and pull her closer.

She nestles into my chest. "Not anymore."

"Me either."

She slides a hand under my t-shirt, presses her palm against my stomach. "Walker, what is this?"

"A surprise."

"But you..." She looks to the apartment building to our right. It's two stories, ten units, with a pool in the center. "Okay."

"Put on the jacket."

"You put it on."

"I'm more stubborn than you are."

"Want to bet?"

"Yeah. If I win, I get to make you come."

"If you lose?"

"I don't really care. I'm gonna make you come either way."

She looks up at me as she intertwines her fingers with mine. "This sounds win-win."

"What the fuck are we talking about?"

Her smile spreads over her cheeks. "I don't remember."

"Me either." I lead her to the complex's gate, punch in the code, open the door for her.

She folds the jacket over her arm as she steps inside.

The pool glows against the dark sky. It casts wavy lines over the planters of succulents and the white wrought iron gate.

It's suburban paradise.

In the middle of Santa Monica.

Yeah, it's a little farther from the beach. But it's a hell of a lot bigger. And it's not *that* much more expensive than my place.

It's not cheap—not by a long shot—but it's well within our budget. If she wants it to be *our* budget.

If she wants it to be our place.

I have to hold onto the railing as I climb the stairs. It's like my soles aren't making contact with the ground. I'm floating. Or maybe I'm spinning. One of the two. Or both.

It's only a dozen steps to the door. I kneel, punch the code into the lockbox, pull out the key.

"Walker..." Iris taps her heels together. "Is this—"

"Still a surprise." Nerves creep into my voice. It isn't like me. But then the last six months haven't been like me either. I never thought I'd let anyone this close. I never thought I'd fall in love. I sure as hell never thought I'd ever be desperate to live with a woman.

But it's the only thing missing from my life.

I rise, unlock the door, push it open. "After you, sweetness."

"Walker..." Her eyes meet mine. "Is this... Are you... Do you..."

"Yeah."

"Yeah?"

I nod.

Her tongue slides over her lips. "Really?"

"I'm trying to do this a certain way."

"What way is that?"

"The way that gets a yes." I press the door wider. "After you."

"Okay." She steps onto the hardwood.

I follow. The main room is about the size of mine. There's space for the TV and a couch in the nook on the right. The kitchen is on the left. It's tiny, the way all Southern California kitchens are, but it's ours.

Well, almost.

"It's more expensive than my place. But a lot cheaper than both of us paying rent for our own apartments." I take her hand and lead her to the bedroom. Right now it's an empty room with a mirrored closet, an attached bathroom, and a window that looks out on the ocean. But it will be our bedroom.

Iris's eyes go wide as she stares out the window. "Is that really the view?"

"Yeah."

"It's beautiful."

"The other room is too." I squeeze her hand as I lead her across the hallway. "I figured it could be our office. Mostly yours. Or all yours. If that's what you need."

"All mine?"

"Yeah."

"I've never had my own office."

My eyes stay glued to her. "I'm more than happy to share my tiny apartment with you. But I figured you need space to do work."

"I do."

"It's ridiculous. You should live in my bed."

"You mean our bed?"

Every part of me goes warm at once. "Yeah. Our bed."

She turns to me. "Can we really afford it?"

"Yeah." *We* is my new favorite word. Or maybe *our*. Or maybe *Iris*. No, that's been my favorite word forever now. "I know you're busy with school until the quarter ends. I'll take care of everything. All you need to do is say yes."

"But we have to apply—"

"Done."

"And my lease. It's not up until July—"

"Done."

"But how?"

"Does it matter?"

She wraps her arms around my waist. "No. I just... I want to be sure."

"I'll text the landlord now. We can move in December first."

"Yeah?"

"Yeah." I brush her hair behind her ear. "It's ours. All you have to do is say yes."

"Yes. Of course." She rises to her tiptoes.

I lean down. Our kiss starts soft. Then it's harder. Her lips part to make way for my tongue. Her moans vibrate down my throat. Her fingers dig into my t-shirt.

"We need to christen it."

"It's not ours yet."

I pull out my cell, find the landlords number, shoot him a *we want it* text. "Now it is."

"But what if someone else offers more?"

"They won't. Trust me. It's ours."

"But—"

"I'll clean up after." I set my cell on the windowsill. "Unless you don't want me to pin you to that wall."

She shakes her head.

"You *don't* want to come on my cock?"

"Don't even—" She tugs at my t-shirt.

I move forward.

She steps backward.

We dance like that until her ass hits the wall.

She looks up at me, her smile spreads over her cheeks, her eyes hazy with desire. "Okay."

"Okay?"

She nods. "We should christen it."

I push her skirt up her thighs. "Sweetness, I need a lot more than *okay*." My fingertips brush her skin. Just above her knee. Then higher. Higher.

"Walker..."

"Better."

"Don't tease. Please. I..." She rocks her hips as she looks up at me. "I need you. I need this."

"I need you too." I press my palm against her, over her panties. "I need you so fucking badly."

Her response is a groan.

I rub her over her panties.

"Walker..." She tugs at my t-shirt. Pulls my body into hers.

I pin her with my hips. I grind against her until she's groaning into my mouth.

She pulls my t-shirt over my head.

I suck on her bottom lip. Drag my hand up her thigh. Tug her panties to her knees.

She kicks them off her feet. Breaks our kiss to stare into my eyes. "Fuck me."

My fingers brush her cunt. "Not yet."

"Now."

My cock whines to be inside her. But not yet. Not until she's ready.

I tease her with one finger.

She digs her hands into my hair.

Two.

She pulls me into a long, deep kiss. Her tongue slides around mine. Soft. Then harder.

I push my fingers deeper.

She rocks her hips to meet me.

Deeper.

Her nails dig into my shoulder. "Walker. Please." She nips at my neck. "Please."

Fuck, that sound is music.

That sound is the best thing I've ever heard.

No. Iris coming is the best thing I've ever heard. But this is a close second.

She reaches for my jeans. Undoes the button. The zipper.

I push them—and my boxers—off my hips.

She wraps her hand around my cock. Pumps me with a steady rhythm. "Mmm. Please." Her eyelids press together. "I need you inside me."

My balls tighten. Fuck, the way those words fall off her lips...

"Legs around me." I sling my arms under her thighs, and pin her to the wall.

She stares up at me with every ounce of desire in the world.

My tip strains against her.

Then it's one delicious inch at a time.

"Fuck." My nails dig into her flesh.

Her hands knot in my hair.

She squeezes me tighter.

I pin her harder.

Kiss her deeper.

She holds my head against hers. She kisses me like she's claiming my mouth. She rocks her hips like she's claiming my body.

She doesn't have to. I'm already hers.

And she's already mine.

And now I'm going to wake up next to her every fucking day.

That's fucking everything.

With my next thrust, my last conscious thought slips away.

We stay locked like that, tongues dancing, limbs tangled, hips rocking together, until she's there.

She breaks our kiss to groan my name. She tugs at my hair as she pulses around me.

Fuck, that feels good.

A few more thrusts and I'm there. I groan her name into

her neck. I pin her to the wall, thrusting through my orgasm, letting pleasure spill to every finger and toe.

I feel it everywhere. I feel *her* everywhere.

She sighs as her muscles go slack. "Fuck." She presses her lips to my neck. "I love you."

"I love you too."

Slowly, I untangle our bodies and set her on the ground.

She pulls on her panties.

I don my t-shirt. Return my jeans to their rightful place.

Well, I'd rather never wear these things. I'd rather live naked in *our* bed.

But there's too much shit I want to do. Too many places I want to see. Too many things I want to teach Iris.

I want the entire world for her.

I want to be by her side, for every single thing life throws at us.

Author's Note

Authors will often tell you we love our books equally, and it's true. But we love some of them more equally than others. Those that come easily, that seem to spring straight from our fingers, are a little easier to love. Playing was one of those books.

Right away, I knew Walker and Iris intimately. I knew exactly what brought them together and what kept them apart. That the reason why they'd work so well together was the same reason he'd run a million miles away. Only addicts, and those in their orbit, truly understand addiction and they way it wrecks everything in its paths.

This isn't the first time I've written about addiction. It isn't the second either. I find myself drawn to characters with troubled pasts, but usually it's the heroes who are struggling more than the heroines. There's something compelling about hanging out in a broken hero's head, about diving into his thoughts, and feeling every inch of his pain. (Or maybe that's my adolescence spent falling in love with broken lyricists talking). In romance, so many heroes are a fucked up mess.

But we—both readers and authors—rarely allow our heroines the same latitude.

Will readers love a heroine struggling with addiction? I don't know. I'm still nervous about the reception. But I try not to let fear stop me from what I want to do. And I love writing about men and women who need a little help figuring it out.

When I was younger, I wanted to write about how fragile and ephemeral relationships were. I want to make people feel the kinds of things my favorite songs made me feel. I had no idea romance existed, much less that I'd be writing it full-time in a decade. But this—writing these coming of age romances, full of sex and laughter and pain and joy and messy, complicated feelings—is what I'm meant to do. And being able to share it with readers means the world to me. With this book, I felt I hit my goal a little better than I usually do. I guess you could stay I stuck the landing.

I'm so glad you've joined me on this journey.

As always, thank you for reading.

I hope I'll see you for *Pretending*, a fun, sexy, angsty pretend to be my girlfriend romance featuring tortured tattoo artist Ryan. (Talk about hanging out in a broken hero's head!)

If you'd like to stay up to date on the latest Inked Hearts or Crystal Kaswell news, please join my mailing list, join my Facebook group, like my page on Facebook, or friend me on Facebook.

Acknowledgements

My first thanks goes to my husband, for his support when I'm lost in bookland and for generally being the sun in my sky. Sweetheart, you're better than all the broken bad boys in the world.

The second goes to my father, for insisting I go to the best film school in the country, everything else be damned. I wouldn't love movies, writing, or storytelling half as much if not for all our afternoon trips to the bookstore and weekends at the movies. You've always been supportive of my goals, and that means the world to me.

A big shout out to all my beta readers. You helped give me the confidence to put out a book a little more heartbreaking than usual. And also to my ARC readers for helping spread the word to everyone else in the world.

A special thanks to my fellow pop-punk addict, Molle, for fangirling over music with me, for talking me through my business decisions, and for reminding me that loving my work matters as much as all the marketing money in the world.

Athena Wright, you are the best author BFF a girl could ask for. Thank you for your feedback, for being my chat buddy, and for always being there to give me the perspective I need. And thank you for mocking me when I deserve it and telling me no when I need to hear it.

To my cover designer Letita, thank you for your work in making my rock star series perfect. And thank you so much to Wander and Jacob Cooley for the perfect image. To my editor Marla, thank you for whipping the story and the prose into shape. And thanks to all the other book bloggers who helped get the word out.

As always, my biggest thanks goes to my readers. Thank you for picking up *Playing*. I hope you'll be back for *Pretending*.

Also by Crystal Kaswell

Dangerous Noise

Dangerous Kiss - Ethan

Dangerous Crush – Kit

Dangerous Rock – Joel

Dangerous Fling – Mal

Dangerous Encore - series sequel

Sinful Serenade

Sing Your Heart Out - Miles

Strum Your Heart Out - Drew

Rock Your Heart Out - Tom

Play Your Heart Out - Pete

Sinful Ever After – series sequel

Inked Hearts

Tempting - Brendon

Playing - Walker

Pretending - Ryan - Coming March 2018

32194687R00241

Printed in Great Britain
by Amazon